190/13

D0394174

THE MASTERHARPER
OF PERN

THE MASTERHARPER OF PERN

ANNE McCAFFREY

THE BALLANTINE PUBLISHING GROUP • NEW YORK

A Del Rey ® Book
Published by The Ballantine Publishing Group

Copyright © 1998 by Anne McCaffrey

http://www.randomhouse.com

Library of Congress Cataloging-in-Publication Data
McCaffrey, Anne.
The masterharper of Pern / Anne McCaffrey.—1st ed.
p.   cm.
"A Del Rey book"—T.p. verso.
ISBN 0-345-38823-2 (alk. paper)
1. Pern (Imaginary place)—Fiction.   2. Dragons—Fiction.   I. Title.
PS3563.A255M35   1998   97-30896
813'.54—dc21

Manufactured in the United States of America

First Edition: January 1998

10 9 8 7 6 5 4 3 2 1

Because she is always gracious and supportive,
this book is most affectionately dedicated to
Shelly Shapiro
and to her husband, Tom Hitchins, and their
daughter, Adrianna

ACKNOWLEDGMENTS

As usual, I am indebted to a variety of people for their help and input in writing this volume. Not the least of whom is Master Robinton (aka Frederic H. Robinson), who was quite upset that I had ended his life so abruptly. I would suspect it of a tenor, but for a baritone to insist on another encore is almost unheard of. But I have recently been asked—via the impressive Del Rey Website—to *explain* certain facts which had not previously been brought to light anent Pern pre-*Dragonflight* history. As Robinton had a fine Pernese hand in most of it, it behooves me to tell the story from his viewpoint.

I would like to thank Dr. Will Chlosta of St. Mary's Hospital (New Haven) for reading over the medical, and sartorial, inclusions.

This time, my gratitude to Marilyn and Harry Alm as first readers is immense since they saved me from several time discrepancies and inconsistencies. Their knowledge of Pern is extensive and better remembered than mine at times. I am also grateful to my daughter, Georgeanne Kennedy, for reading two sets of proofs within four days: a true labor of love.

Most of all let me thank Tania Opland and Michael Freeman for their invaluable contribution on the musical side. When I asked them if they could possibly supply some of Robinton's early compositions, I didn't realize that Tania had always wanted to be Robinton, from the days when we first met in Fairbanks, Alaska. Mike has already made up a tune for me, the Dragonlady, so his inclusion was natural.

Finally, let me thank the numerous folk online in January and February whose id's helped me find character names.

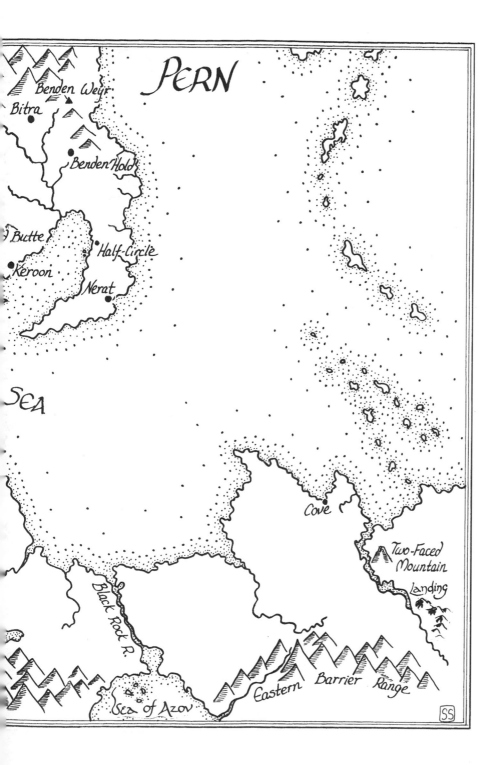

THE MASTERHARPER
OF PERN

Chapter 1

▼▼▼▼▼▼▼▼▼▼▼▼▼▼▼▼▼▼▼▼▼▼▼▼▼▼▼▼▼▼▼▼▼▼▼▼

"One thing sure," Betrice said wryly as she wrapped the squalling, wriggling baby tightly into the fine cotton sheet his mother had woven for just this moment, "he's got your lungs, Petiron. Here! I've got to make Merelan more comfortable now."

The howling baby, his face brick-red with his exertions, tiny fists clenched, was deposited into his alarmed father's arms.

Jiggling the babe as he had seen other fathers do, Petiron carried him to the window to get a good look at his firstborn.

He didn't see the looks passing between the midwife and her assistant, nor did he see the younger woman leave quietly to summon a healer. Merelan's bleeding was not tapering off. The midwife suspected that something had been torn; the baby had been breech, and was large-headed, as well. She packed ice in towels around Merelan's slim hips. It had been a long labor. Merelan lay limp in the bed, exhausted, her face white and lined. She seemed bloodless, and that worried Betrice more. There was such a risk in a transfusion: despite the similarity in color, blood differed from person to person. Once, long ago, healers had known how to tell the difference and match the blood. Or so she'd heard.

Betrice had suspected that Merelan would have trouble delivering, for she could feel the size of the child in the womb, and so she had asked the Healer Hall to stand by. There was a solution of special salts that in extreme cases could help a patient overcome the loss of blood.

Betrice glanced over to the window and managed a little grin at the father's inexperienced handling. Harper Petiron might be, and play for hours at a Gather, but he'd a lot to learn about fathering. For that matter, he was lucky enough to have a son at all, considering Merelan had lost three in the early stages of pregnancy. Some women were born to bear many, but Merelan was not one of them.

Merelan's eyes flickered open and then widened with joy as she heard the lusty cries of her newborn.

"There now, he's here and all the parts in the right place, so you may rest easy, Singer," Betrice said, stroking Merelan's cheek.

"My son . . ." Merelan whispered, her usually magical voice raspy with exhaustion. Her head turned in the direction of the noise her baby was making, and her fingers twitched on the stained sheet.

"Soon, Singer. Let me clean you up . . ."

"I must hold him." Merelan's voice was feeble, but her need was fierce.

"Now, you'll have plenty of time to hold him, Merelan," Betrice said, a hint of sternness in her soothing tone. "I promise you that." And hope I'm not lying in my teeth, she added to herself.

Just then Sirrie and the healer arrived. Betrice breathed in relief when she saw Ginia and the bottle of clear liquid she carried that might mean the difference between life and death for the new mother.

"Petiron, go take that yowling child of yours and show him off," Ginia said in a peremptory tone, scowling at the nervously jiggling father. "They've all been waiting in the Hall to see him in person, not that anyone doubts he's here with that set of lungs. Off with you!"

Petiron was only too willing to go. He'd been as much help as he could be, rubbing Merelan's back and sponging her sweaty forehead during the long labor, and he desperately needed a drink to soothe his nerves. He'd been so afraid for Merelan toward the end, especially right after the birth when she seemed to shrink into nothing in the bloodied bed. They wouldn't have told him to leave if it weren't all right, he was sure of that! He was also sure that he'd never put Merelan in such danger again. He hadn't known just how difficult child-birth was.

"The lungs on him!" Ginia said with a mirthless smile. She bent to examine Merelan. "She's torn all right. You can give her some fellis, now, Betrice. Sirrie, strap her arm to that splint board. She needs fluid. How I wish we understood more about whole blood transferences. That's what she really needs, with all she seems to have lost. You know how to find a vein with the needle thorn, Sirrie, but if you've trouble, let me know."

Sirrie nodded and began her ministration, while Ginia did what she could to mend the torn flesh. The baby's protests were still audible despite the distance between this room and the main Hall.

"She's fighting the fellis, Ginia," Betrice said anxiously.

"What's she saying?"

"She wants her baby." Then Betrice mouthed words that Ginia could easily read: "She thinks she's dying."

"Not while I'm here, she isn't," Ginia said vehemently. "Get the babe back. It won't hurt her to have it suckling, and that would help contract the womb. Either way, it'll calm her, and I want her as calm as possible right now."

Betrice went herself and brought the now outraged infant back, grinning broadly at his ferocity and grip on life.

"He'll put fight back into her with his own, so he will," she said, smiling as she laid the baby beside Merelan, whose right arm instinctively curled about her child. He found her breast with no help from anyone. And Merelan sighed with relief.

"I swear he's doing the trick," Betrice said, amazed at the sudden flush of color in the singer's cheeks.

"I've seen stranger things happen," Ginia replied, glancing up. "There. That's all I can do . . . except caution Petiron that she's not to get pregnant again. I doubt she can, but he'll have to restrain himself."

The three women grinned at each other, for the entire Hold knew how devoted the couple were to each other: enough so that thinly disguised love ballads about their adoration circulated Pern.

"With all the talent available on this continent, it isn't as if Petiron had to breed a choir," Ginia said, rising.

Briskly the women changed the bedding for fresh, Merelan barely stirring as they did so, the baby clinging tightly to her. When Ginia and Betrice felt they could leave her safely in Sirrie's care, she was asleep, but looking far less pallid.

"Tell you one thing," Betrice confided in the healer, "she won't be all that pleased having just one baby."

"Then we'll see that she fosters others. It's far better for a child to have siblings than not, especially the way Merelan's going to dote on that boy. Keep that in mind next year. That is, if she continues to pick up strength."

Betrice gave a snort. "She'd better. I've a reputation to keep."

"Don't we all!"

It was Petiron who objected to his spouse fostering the children of others. He found it hard enough to share her with their son, and he didn't believe other fathers and mothers when they informed him that young Robinton, for that was what they named him, in memory of Merelan's father Roblyn, was a good child and very undemanding.

"I always thought Petiron a generous man," Betrice told her spouse, MasterHarper Gennell.

"Why have you changed your mind?" Gennell asked with mild surprise.

She paused, pursing her lips—she was not much of a tattler.

"I'd say he was jealous of the time Merelan spends with Robie."

"Really?"

"Not that it's much, for I think she's aware of his resentment and does her best to ease it all. But young Mardy's had another child for all I warned her not to, with her third not yet a full Turn old—" Betrice sighed with exasperation. "—and Merelan could help . . . if Petiron weren't so set against it."

"Young Robinton's what?"

"A full Turn next Third Day and already walking, stout as you please. Tending one in a cradle during the day to give Mardy a hand wouldn't be troublesome. Robie's no trouble and as sweet as his mother." Betrice beamed with an almost maternal pride.

"Leave it for now, Betrice," Gennell said. "There's all this excitement over Petiron's new Moreta Cantata at Turnover with Merelan as the major soloist."

"I can't say I like her working so hard at it, though, Gen, and that's the truth, for she isn't fully recovered from such a difficult birth . . ."

Gennell patted his spouse's capable hand. "Petiron wrote the music for her, and there isn't another soprano with her range in all Pern. I can quite understand how he'd be jealous of anyone taking up too much of her time."

"Unless it's himself doing it, you mean."

"There's more than one way to accomplish the same purpose, you know." He caught and held her eyes and smiled.

"At it again, are you?" Betrice said with no heat and some affection. Gennell was not MasterHarper of Pern just for his expertise on every instrument in the Hall.

"No," he replied cheerfully, "but I'll get *at* it on this matter now that you've been good enough to point it out to me. Petiron's a good sort, you know. And he really does love the boy."

Betrice firmed her lips together. "Loves him, does he?"

"You doubt it?"

She regarded her spouse critically. "I do." She curled her hand around his arm. "But then I have you as an example. You were as eager to tend the first of our five as the last, and they have certainly turned out well. Oh, Petiron *looks* in the cot now and then, or at the child when he's toddling in the yard, but only if you remind him that he's fathered a son."

Gennell picked at his lower lip and began to nod. "Yes, I believe I see what you mean. But I don't think loading Merelan with Mardy's latest is going to remedy a fatherly absentmindedness—especially as Petiron's so involved in the Turnover rehearsals."

"Them! Well, let's hope he doesn't wear Merelan out beforehand."

"That I can oversee," Gennell said briskly, "and will. Now, off with you." As she turned away, he managed an affectionate slap on her backside as he resumed his task of assigning newly promoted journeymen to the many holds and halls which required such services.

Merelan sang the difficult role of Moreta in the Turnover cantata that her spouse had written for her, dealing with the cadenzas as easily as if they had been mere vocalizes. The warmth of her voice and the effortlessness of her performance held the audience—and Petiron—enthralled. Even those resident in the Hall who had heard her practicing and were well aware of her vocal abilities were on their feet, awed by her skill. Merelan not only had the superb breath control to support her coloratura voice, she could also imbue such emotion in her tone that there were many with tears in their eyes when her voice trailed off as Moreta and her dragon jumped *between* on their last, fatal transfer. Fort's Lord and Lady Holder were so enthusiastic that they started the rush up to the stage, to be sure she heard their compliments.

Petiron beamed as she modestly accepted praise, subtly reminding people that the music her spouse had written was a joy to perform. He didn't seem to notice how pale she was. But Betrice did, and she gave the singer a potent restorative drink in the brief interval during which those in the chorus not required for the next part of the program filed out of the stands. Merelan would be singing—less demandingly—in the second part of the evening's entertainment, but she was off-stage during the male chorus that came next.

Betrice watched the singer all through that and saw her color gradually return. And when she rose to sing a descant to the final selection, she did not appear as faint as she had earlier.

When the evening's program was over and the Hall cleared for the dancing, Fort's Lady, Winalla, sought out Betrice.

"Is MasterSinger Merelan all right, Betrice? She was trembling so much when Grogellan and I were speaking to her that I feared to let go of her hand."

"I had a restorative drink ready for her," Betrice said at her most noncommittal. It was kind of Lady Winalla to be concerned, but this was a Harper Hall affair, not the business of the Hold. "She puts so much into her singing, doesn't she?"

"Hmmm, yes, she certainly does," Winalla said, tacitly accepting the rebuff and moving on to speak to other guests.

If it surprised Petiron when Merelan caught a chill and developed a feverish cough, he was the only one.

"Sometimes I think that man is only interested in her for her voice," Betrice said waspishly to Gennell as she returned to their apartment after a shift of nursing the singer.

"That may well be a good deal of her importance to our resident composer," Gennell said. "No one else could manage either the range or the difficulty of the vocal scores he creates, but that isn't all he sees in her." He cleared his throat. "He was besotted with her beauty from the moment she came to us from South Boll for training. In fact, well before we realized what a superb natural voice she had." He looked off into the darkness beyond the glowbasket by the bed, remembering the first time he had heard her effortless scales. The entire Hall had stopped all work just to listen.

Betrice chuckled as she slid under the new furs, a gift from all the journeymen of the Hall this Turnover. The pelts had been sewn together in the most beautiful pattern. She let her hand linger on the soft fur of the edging. "Never seen a man more smitten in my life. He just stared. And she couldn't take her eyes off him. Mind you, he's attractive enough even if he isn't often a merry person. Just as well Agust was her vocal teacher, or she'd never have progressed past vocalizes."

"So remember how Petiron would hang about in the courtyard just listening to them as if he'd nothing better to do with his time," Gennell said, reaching out to close over the glow-basket. Absently he patted Betrice's shoulder and then punched the pillow for a spot to lay his head.

Just when Gennell thought he'd settled the question of which journeyman should take which assignment, more holders applied for trained personnel he did not have. With a hard winter, it was impossible to ask journeymen to tour from one hold to another, spreading their services by spending four sevendays in one place and then moving on. Every family had the right to learning, to be instructed in the Teaching Ballads so there was no misunderstanding about what was due whom and when.

He thought longingly of the times, now several hundred Turns back, when the six Weyrs of Pern had assisted the major Halls with dragon transport. Those on the east coast still had Benden Weyr, so Lord Maidir could boast of dragon rides to distant Holds and Gathers whenever he needed them. But Fort Weyr had been empty over four centuries, and no one really knew why.

Gennell had once looked at the Records kept in the Archives of both the Harper Hall and Fort Hold and there was only the one entry, shortly after the end of the last Pass.

"The MasterHarper was asked to Fort Weyr this fifth day of the seventh month, first Turn after Pass End."

That was it: short and cryptic. In other similar instances when the MasterHarper was called to the Weyr, a fuller explanation was given.

The next entry was by the then-MasterHarper, Creline, dated a full two months later when Fort Hold's tithe train duly arrived with supplies and found the Weyr abandoned, and nothing but broken pottery on the top of the midden heap. Other Holders had noticed that their flags requesting dragon assistance had gone unanswered and, while annoyed by the discourtesy, people were far too involved in relaxing after fifty Turns of ground-crew duty to wonder much about the absence of dragons from the skies. It was enough that Thread was gone.

A Conclave had been convened when it became all too apparent that five of the six Weyrs were empty. Benden's two Weyrleaders were mystified as well, truly surprised by the abandonment, and by Benden's being the only remaining Weyr.

Many theories had been put forth. A favorite claimed that a mysterious disease had spread through the five Weyrs, killing both dragons and riders. But that didn't account for the missing weyrfolk or the absence of every stick and stitch belonging to them. Benden Weyr had even sent a wing, with reliable Hold and Hall passengers, to scan the Southern Continent in case all five Weyrs had—for some unknown reason—decided to resettle south, despite the hazards of that country.

The matter was under discussion, often heated, for Turns afterwards and no one the wiser for all the talk.

Then Creline performed a new work, which he called the Question Song, and which was to be included in the compulsory Teaching Ballads. Gennell had made a mental note to return the song to that category since someone—he wouldn't like to point a finger—had let it drop out some time before he became MasterHarper. Such things happened: but they shouldn't, considering the importance with which Creline had treated the work. Odd song. Haunting melody. Yes, worth reviving.

Another fifty-five Turns remained before Threadfall was due again. That is, Gennell amended to himself, if it *was* going to Fall again. Many believed Thread was gone forever. A common theory claimed that the Weyrs had been bound by some bizarre suicide pact, leaving only Benden to carry on the draconic traditions. That made no sense whatever to a thinking man. But at least he was unlikely to have to contend with *that* in his term as MasterHarper. With a sigh of relief, he firmly turned his mind toward sleep.

Merelan's cough developed into a chest cold shortly after Turnover. Sniffles and coughs were prevalent during the beginning of any new Turn when the weather remained cold and snowy, and young Robinton and Petiron both suffered from colds, but they threw off the worst of the infection quickly. But Merelan's cough seemed determined to linger, and she could rarely get through a vocal exercise without having to break off in a spasm. For the first time, Petiron became seriously worried about her health.

So did Betrice and Ginia, for the singer had quickly lost what weight she had gained after the baby's birth—and more.

"You've really nothing big coming up in the way of rehearsals, have you?" Ginia asked Petiron privately after delivering another bottle of cough mixture for Merelan. With a certain degree of reluctance, he shook his head; had he not been sick, he most assuredly would have started composing something extravagant for the Spring Gathers.

"Well, then," Ginia continued, "I happen to know the MasterHarper is looking for someone to provide basic instruction at a hold in South Boll. Not far from where Merelan was born. So why don't you ask him to allow you to take the post? I believe the accommodations would be adequate for a small family like yours. The Ritecamp traders just arrived here, and their route takes you close by Pierie Hold."

Before Petiron could produce a good reason why he couldn't leave the Harper Hall at that time, he and his small family were on their way south, their baggage loaded on pack animals that Master Gennell ordered. He sent along two good Ruathan-bred mounts, as well. Master Sev Ritecamp was only too happy to oblige the Harper Hall and had agreed to take them to the very door of Pierie Hold.

"If Master Petiron wouldn't mind taking some time of an evening to learn some of our youngsters their Teaching Ballads. They're in dire need of some educating," Sev had suggested very politely. "And maybe give us a new song or two in the evening around our fire."

"That would be only fair," Merelan said when Petiron was not as prompt as he could have been in agreeing. Then she winked at her spouse, knowing very well that he hated doing "basics" with beginners, while she enjoyed teaching the very young. So long as the children were taught, it really didn't matter who did the teaching. As MasterSinger, she knew her Teaching Ballads and Songs as well as Petiron did.

The young daughter of the Ritecamps' leader had a toddler the same age as Robie, though not, Merelan privately thought, as sturdy as her lad, but she doubted that Dalma would mind watching two who could amuse each other while Merelan taught.

MasterHarper Gennell was delighted to have a master to assign for however short a term. Betrice had a word with the Ritecamp healer about Merelan's condition and waved farewell with the rest of the Hall.

Although the Ruathan runnerbeasts provided were well trained and easy riding, Merelan at first rode in Dalma's efficient housewagon, since she knew herself incapable of managing the antics of a mount right then. Petiron, less familiar with riding beasts, was more often on the lead wagon seat, talking to Sev Ritecamp or his father or his uncle or whoever was the day's guide. Despite his forebodings and initial dismay, Petiron soon began to relax and enjoy the trip. Having overheard the favorable comments about the Ruathan breed, he offered Sev's eldest son the chance to ride his mount, and consequently he found all the Ritecamp men more genial toward him. He even enjoyed the nightly music sessions, for almost everyone in the thirty wagons of the train played some instrument and could carry intricate parts. Many had good voices, and he found himself conducting four- and five-part harmonies to some of their favorite ballads and airs, as well as teaching them the newer songs.

"They're nearly as good as fourth-year apprentices," he said with some surprise to Merelan at the end of the third evening's session.

"They do it for fun," she said gently.

"There's no reason they cannot do it better and have fun, too," he said, not at all pleased at her subtle rebuke over his attempt to improve the harmonies.

"Now, hold still, while I put the salve on your face," she went on, holding his chin firmly while she pasted his cheeks and nose with the remedy for the windburn he'd acquired.

With her that close to him, he could see she had more color in her pale cheeks, though she still coughed so hard it made him wince to think what damage she might be doing her vocal cords. But she didn't seem quite as strained about the eyes and mouth as she had been.

"Are you all right, Mere?" he asked, holding her by the arms.

"Of course, I'm all right. Why, it's an answer to one of my childhood dreams: going adventuring in a trader's van."

She favored him with the wide smile that put dimples in both cheeks, and she was more *his* Merelan than she had been since before her pregnancy. He folded her into his arms, hugging her—remembering to be gentle, as he felt how thin she still was in his embrace. That reminded him what he might not have, and he was about to put her firmly away from him when she clung tightly.

"It's safe enough," she murmured and he clasped her with a passion that he had been aching to express but had sternly repressed. He didn't even have to worry about an inopportune interruption from the baby sleeping in the spare crib in Dalma's wagon. So he loved Merelan with a single-minded urgency that had been denied him far too long. Nor was there any reluctance in her response to him.

The slow trip south was really a very good idea.

At some point during that ambling three-week journey to the southern tip of South Boll, Petiron realized that he had been nearly as strung out, emotionally and physically, as Merelan. Being in the Harper Hall, with music, musicians, and instruments constantly heard, caused one to think only of music to write for instruments and voices to perform. On the road, he was not compelled by the tacit competition rampant in the Harper Hall to produce yet more complex and glorious sounds. He had an opportunity for the first time since he had started his apprentice years to realize the richness—as well as the simplicity—of life all around him.

He'd come from Telgar Hold, one of the largest, so he had never really been short of the necessities of day-to-day existence. Living in the Harper Hall had been a continuation of his childhood's conditions. He took so many things for granted that it was a lesson to him to be denied easy access to, say, the well-tanned hides for musical compositions that he was accustomed to covering with quick, large notations. Now he learned to write economically, using small marks that allowed him to fit more than one work on a single hide.

Eating was another thing he had never given much thought to. Food arrived in the Hall with no indication to those who dined of its acquisition or preparation. Now he learned to hunt and fish with the other men of the caravan, even as the women gathered firewood and nuts and, as they continued to the warmer areas, early greens, fruits, and berries.

Petiron could stride along with the other traders all day long now, and Merelan, too, put on weight and became weather-tanned, and fit. She walked part of each day with Dalma and the other young mothers, at a pace slow enough for the youngest toddler to keep up. Her cough disappeared and she was once again vivid with the beauty that had stopped Petiron's heart five Turns earlier. And he began to realize just how restrictive he had been in the Harper Hall; so immersed had he become in composition and practice that he had forgotten that other things existed in life: a normal life.

The caravan camped for three days by one of the Runner Stations, and, as usual, the Station Master sent his runners out in all directions to alert those who lived far off the southern road.

"Some of these people are very shy," the Station Master told his guests. "You might even find them . . . well, a bit . . . odd."

"You mean, from living off in the hills?" Merelan asked.

Sev scratched his head. "They got odd notions, you might say."

Merelan knew there was something that he was not saying, and she couldn't understand his sudden reticence.

"Ah, d'you have something that isn't Harper blue?" he blurted.

"I do," Merelan said, "but I don't think Petiron does. You mean, he might aggravate someone?" She smiled to show that she perfectly understood.

"Ah, yes, that's about the size of it."

"I'll see what I can do about keeping him occupied," she said, smiling sympathetically.

Everything went very well the first two days. The morning of the third, Merelan was entertaining all the children with game songs and teaching them the gestures that went with them, when a very tattered girl, eyes wide with delight, moved with surreptitious stealth closer and closer. When she was near enough, Merelan smiled at her.

"Do you want to join us?" she asked in a carefully soft voice.

The girl shook her head, her eyes wide now with a mixture of longing and fear.

"Oh, please, everyone else is here," Merelan said, doing her best to reassure the timid child. "Rob, open the circle and let her in, will you, dear?"

The child took another step and then suddenly squealed when she saw a man charging from the trader's wagon, right at Merelan's circle.

"You there . . . you stop that, you harlot. You evil creature, luring children away from their parents . . ."

Merelan didn't realize at first that he meant her. The child raced into the shelter of the heavy plantation just beyond the clearing, but that didn't seem to cool the man's fury, for he charged right up to Merelan, his arm raised to strike her.

Robinton ran to clutch his mother's skirts, frightened by the wild threats and crazed behavior. Sev, the Station Master, two of the male runners, and three other traders charged to her rescue, Sev just in time to push the attacker off balance and away from Merelan. The children were by then all weeping and running away.

"Easy, Rochers, she's a mother, singing baby songs," Sev said, holding the man away.

"She's singing, ent she? Singing comes first, don't it? Singing to lure kids away! She's evil. Just like all harperfolk. Teachin' things no one needs to know to live proper."

"Rochers, leave be," the Station Master said, exercising considerable force to pull the man away, shooting embarrassed and apologetic glances at Merelan.

"Come, Rochers, we need to finish dealing," said one of the traders. "Come on, we'd nearly shook hands . . ."

"Harper harlot!" Rochers shouted, trying to free a fist to wave at Merelan, who was clinging to Robinton as much as he was clinging to her.

"She's *not* a harper, Rochers. She's a mother, amusing the kids," the Station Master said, loudly enough to try to drown out what the man was saying.

"She had 'em dancing!" Spittle was beginning to form in the corners of his mouth as the men pulled him back to the wagons.

"Get into Dalma's wagon, Merelan," Sev said quickly. "We'll clear him out."

Merelan complied, picking Robie up in her arms and trying to calm his frightened sobs. She slipped behind a tree and through the wooded verge until she could duck into Dalma's wagon, one of the last in the Station clearing. She was shaking when she got inside it, and she nearly shrieked with fear when someone pushed open the little door. But it was only Dalma, her face white with anxiety. She embraced Merelan and tried to soothe Robinton all at the same time.

"Crazy, woods crazy," she murmured reassuringly. "Who'd've thought he'd even notice you over there, playing so nicely."

"What did he mean?" Merelan said, trying to control her sobs. She'd never been so frightened in all her life. Especially since she had joined the Harper Hall, which was held with respect everywhere she'd gone as a MasterSinger. "What *could* he mean? He called me a harper harlot. And how can singing be bad? Evil?"

"Now, now." Dalma held Merelan tightly against her, stroking her hair and patting her shoulder, or patting Robie, though he had recovered within the safety of the wagon and Dalma's comforting presence. "We run into some real odd folk now and then. Some of 'em have never met a harper, and some don't hold with singing or dancing or drinking. Sev says it's because they can't make wine or beer, so it has to be evil. They don't want their children to know more than they did or you'd better believe it—" And Dalma gave a sour little laugh. "—they couldn't keep them from leaving those awful jungles."

"But it was the way he said 'harper'. . ." Merelan swallowed at the tone of hatred in which the word had been uttered.

"Now, now, it's all over with. Sev and the others'll see those woodsie ones leave."

"And that dear little girl . . ."

"Merelan, forget her. Please."

Although she nodded in compliance, Merelan wondered if she would ever forget the wistful hunger in that child's face: a hunger for music, or maybe just other children playing. But she stayed in the wagon until Sev came to say that the woodsie ones had left and to apologize for exposing her to such a distressing incident.

There were no further upsets, although she did learn that not every hold the traders stopped at had the benefit of harper education. It was true that there were really not enough harpers to do more than stop in once or twice a year, but Merelan was still shocked at the realization that there was a significant number of cots and small holdings where no one could read or count above twenty.

She didn't dare discuss that observation with Petiron, but she knew she would discuss it with Gennell when she got back. Though it was all too likely he was well aware of the lack.

Usually the trade caravan made a special occasion for those they visited, and Petiron was no longer merely resigned to performing in the evenings; he *enjoyed* it. So many good voices, so many instrumentalists—not as expert as those he was accustomed to playing with, but good enough, and, more importantly, willing enough to add to the evening's entertainment. He also acquired variants of ballads and airs that were traditional with the smaller holders but unknown to him. He jotted those down. Some of them were quite sophisticated and he wondered which was original: the Harper Hall's versions or those that had been passed down through generations in the holds.

One of the most nostalgic ballads—about the Crossing— could indeed be turned into an instrumental piece, starting with the basic melody, haunting enough, and then embellishments added. To transcribe this, Petiron acquired enough of some of the reed-based writing material that was a local product. It had a tendency to absorb so much ink that his scores were a bit blotchy, but he could amend that when he got back to the Harper Hall. He had always prided himself on his musical memory.

They reached Pierie Hold halfway through the morning of the twenty-first day of travel, even with a full two-day halt at Merelan's home hold. She had a chance to see her family, to exchange news and see all the new babies and congratulate the recent pairings—and to show off Robinton.

Petiron was warmly received by the aunt and uncle who had reared Merelan when her own parents had died in one of the fierce autumnal storms that battered the western coastline. He was truly amazed at the number of really fine, if untrained, voices that her hold had produced.

"Not one of them but can't carry a tune," he told her after the first evening. "Which aunt did you say gave you your first training?"

"Segoina," she said, smiling at his astonishment.

"That contralto?"

She nodded.

He whistled appreciatively.

"She insisted that I be sent to the Harper Hall," Merelan said with considerable humility. "She ought to have gone, but she'd already espoused Dugall and wouldn't leave him."

"And wasted that glorious voice on a hold . . ." Petiron rather contemptuously indicated the sprawling redstone dwellings that comprised the hold.

"Segoina has never wasted her talent," Merelan said a bit stiffly.

"I didn't mean it that way, Mere, and you know it," Petiron replied hastily. He had seen the genuine respect and love that existed between the two women. "But she'd have been a MasterSinger . . ."

"Not everyone would find that as productive as we do, Petiron," she said gently but so firmly that Petiron saw he would offend her with further comment. Indeed, she thought wryly, remembering Rochers, the woodsie, not every Pernese approved of harpers.

When they were settling into Pierie Hold, his misgivings about this assignment returned. There were only three rooms for their quarters: the baby would have to sleep in with them, at the foot of the bed that took up nearly all the room, though there were storage compartments cut into the rear wall of the cliff. The larger room was clearly for daily affairs, including kitchen work, with an outer wall hearth. The third was more of a cubicle than a room and served the purpose of toilet and bath, though Merelan said gaily that most everyone bathed in the sea. Petiron gazed askance at the flight of steps that led down to a sandy crescent of a beach where some of the hold's fishing sloops were moored.

He was soon to learn that people here were more accustomed to doing everything outside, either in the wide open patio where various workstations were situated, or under the shade of a vine-covered arbor larger than all the individual accommodations put together. There were even two sections fenced off for toddlers and the slightly older children, complete with a little pond where they could safely wade, sand to play in, and a rather extensive collection of toys. Already, Robinton was tottering about carrying one of the stuffed toys.

"That can't be a dragon he's been playing with, is it?" Petiron asked Merelan. Dragons were never toys; it would have been blasphemy to play with one.

"No, silly. It's supposed,"—Merelan grinned reassuringly up at her astonished spouse—"to be a fire-lizard."

"A fire-lizard? But they died out centuries ago."

"No, not entirely. My father saw one, and Uncle Patry said he'd seen one this past year."

"He's sure?" Petiron had a pragmatic streak that required proof.

"Indeed he is. And we've empty shells gathered from flotsam to prove that they exist, even if they aren't much in evidence."

"Well, if they've shells . . ." And Petiron was mollified. Merelan turned her head away so that he wouldn't see her smile.

She was quite aware of Petiron's opinions about everything here in Pierie Hold, but there was no sense in arguing with him about his misconceptions. In general he was a fair man, and she was sure he'd come round. He might even get to like living here, away from all the bustle and overstimulation of the Harper Hall. She had been so pleased with his thanks to Sev, Dalma, and the other traders. He'd meant every word he'd said to them, about learning so much on the route and that he had enjoyed the evenings, and the teaching. He'd learned to feel comfortable on a runnerbeast, so she knew she could talk him into taking trips to the other nearby holds where her brothers and sisters lived. Especially as she would have to leave Robinton behind so as not to irritate Petiron by his son's constant presence. Not only was he weaned now, but Segoina was almost panting to have a chance to tend him. If only Petiron could learn to like his son a little for his own sake, and Robinton's, rather than see him as a rival for her attention.

Teaching came first, and Petiron divided up the forty-two prospective students into five groups. The beginners, novices, middle, and advanced were of mixed ages, since some had had a little more training from a parent than others; the final group was made up of the five who were much too old to be included in the regular classes. Those he'd teach in the evenings by themselves—not that anyone was embarrassed.

"Living up in the mountings, never had the chance to learn nothing," Rantou said, unabashed. The stocky timberman had glanced over at his young spouse who was visibly pregnant. "That is, until I met Carral, here." Then he blushed. "Really like music, even if I doan know much. But I gotta learn so the baby won't have no stupid for a father."

Despite having had no formal training at all, Rantou could produce the most amazing sounds out of a multiple reed-pipe, although he waved aside Petiron's earnest desire to teach him to read music.

"You just play it all out for me once, and that'll do me."

When Petiron paced about that evening in the privacy of their little home, terribly upset that an innate musician of considerable talent was risking talented fingers with saw, ax, and adze on a daily basis, Merelan had to calm him.

"Not everyone sees the Harper Hall as the most preferential occupation, love."

"But he's—"

"He's doing very well for a young man with a family on the way," she said, "and he'll always *love* music, even if it is not his life the way it has always been yours."

"But he's a natural. You know how hard I had to work at theory and composition, to get complicated tempi—and he manages cadenzas after one hearing that it would take you, good as you are, days to command. And Segoina told me he makes . . . *makes* the gitars, the flutes, the drums, all the instruments in use here . . ." He raised both hands high in exasperation and frustration. "When I think how hard I had to work to walk the tables for journeyman for what he just picked up listening to me, I—I'm speechless."

"Rantou doesn't *want* to be a musician, love. He wants to do what he does do, manage forestry. Even the instruments he makes are just a hobby with him."

"That may be very true, Mere, but what you fail to realize is that the Harper Hall *needs* more young folk to train up than come to us. Pierie needs a full-time journeyman, not a vacationing one." Petiron was pacing and rubbing his hands together, a sure sign to his spouse of his rising agitation. "Everyone has the right to learning—that is the traditional duty of the Harper Hall. We are desperately short of harpers."

"But people do learn the Teaching Ballads and Songs, as they have here," Merelan said. "As I did."

"Only the usual ones, but not *all* the important ones," Petiron said sternly with a scowl. When he frowned like that, his heavy eyebrows nearly met over the bridge of his aquiline nose. Though she'd never tell him, Merelan adored his eyebrows. "They don't know the Dragon Duty Ballads, for instance."

Merelan suppressed a sigh. Was it only people brought up in strict Harper Hall tradition who believed that Thread *would*, not just *might*, return in the next fifty or so Turns? Or was their belief merely an extension of the traditions of the Hall?

"You are teaching those as I am. And I don't think anyone here, now that they've met you and seen me again, would take it amiss if you did suggest that one of the more talented youngsters looked toward the Harper Hall as a life's work."

Petiron gave her a strange look. "You don't?"

She pursed her lips. That tone was his driest and most repressive: the one he reserved for apprentices who had not studied hard enough to suit his exacting standard.

"There was plague, you know, as well as that storm that took many lives from this hold," she said as casually as she could. "This may be a small hold, but to do all that is required properly also takes a fair-sized population. Sometimes there are none to be spared."

"Yet they spared two lads to the Weyr," Petiron said begrudgingly.

Merelan tried to hide her laugh behind her hand but couldn't, the look of him was so jealous.

"And I suppose *you* wouldn't have accepted being Searched for the Weyr?"

"I wasn't."

"I know, but if you had been Searched by Benden Weyr, would you not have gone?"

"Well," he said, hedging, "I certainly don't dispute the honor of being Searched . . . but not everyone Searched Impresses a dragon."

"They Impressed greens," Merelan replied.

"Then they were lucky indeed."

"Neither of them would have been good as harpers," she added, with a twinkle in her eye.

"Now that's not fair, Mere," Petiron replied stiffly.

"Think on it a bit, my darling," she said and continued to neatly fold the clothes that she had laundered that afternoon.

It was Petiron who was almost apoplectic with fear when he heard that Merelan was teaching Robinton to swim.

"But he's only just started walking," he protested. "How can he swim?"

"All our children learn to swim in their first year," Segoina told him. "Preferably before they learn to walk, because they remember swimming from their womb days."

"They *what*?"

Merelan put a warning hand on Petiron's arm, for his body was rigid with shock at the dangers *his* son had just been exposed to.

"It's true," Segoina went on. "Ask at the Healer Hall when you return." Petiron recoiled slightly, but Segoina continued affably. "It is the best time to remind a child of what it knew in the womb. And then we don't have to worry so constantly, with us so near the sea as we are." She pointed down the steps to where a gentle surf made white scallops on the equally white sand. "There is a rite of passage that requires a lad to dive from that height," and she pointed to the headland that jutted out a fair distance into the sea, "to prove he is a man."

Petiron visibly swallowed and blinked furiously.

"Do you swim?" Segoina asked blandly.

"Yes, actually I do. We had the Telgar river to learn in."

"It's much easier to swim in the sea than in a river. More buoyancy." Segoina turned away before she could catch the apprehensive expression on Petiron's face.

Merelan controlled her amusement. If he hadn't been able to answer positively, it was obvious he feared that she would have immediately appointed herself his instructor. He swam well enough, and the midsummer races were months away. By then they would be safely back at Harper Hall. She sighed, for she would have liked to stay for the Full Summer Gather when the entire Peninsula gathered for races, both in and on the water as everyone tested his or her skills at swimming and sailing.

It was as well, Merelan thought as they continued on to their quarters, that he was over the age when he would have been required to make the high dive. That was also a feature of the Full Summer Gather. Maybe she could talk him into it . . .

He'd learned so much about himself, as well as how the ordinary people lived. As a lad at Telgar, he had been more inclined to scholarship, which was why he had been sponsored to go to the Harper Hall in the first place. So he had had little chance, as an adult, to expand his horizons—until now. And he'd never looked fitter, or more handsome. Hair down to his shoulders, skin tanned, he was more secure on the back of a runner, could walk a good day's journey, and had done more harpering than his duties at the Hall had ever required of him. If only he could be more in harmony with his own child . . .

When Robinton began to talk, she told herself, when he needed to learn things a father should teach his son, *then* the affection and pride would develop. At least Petiron had shown himself nervous about his child's safety with the swimming business.

That much was obvious when Petiron accompanied spouse and son to the cove beach the next First Day. By then, Robinton was paddling happily, not the least bit concerned if he fell under the water, though a white-faced Petiron snatched the sun-browned little body up into his arms, startling Robinton. Wide-eyed with surprise, the boy struggled to be released back into the water that was such fun, the waves lapping bubblingly around his ankles and pushing treasures of flotsam for him to examine. He even gave the next smooth pebble, a very pretty red one with white intrusions making a pattern, to his father to be admired. And Petiron did, without any prompting from Merelan.

When it was handed back to him, Robinton toddled off to place it with the growing pile of unusual objects he had retrieved. Then he was off in another direction, running as fast as his legs would take him to see what his cousins had discovered among the seaweed they had just hauled up onto the beach.

"Sit, love," Merelan said softly, patting the woven reed mat beside her, where the sunshade cast a shadow. "He isn't far from help, should it be needed."

"Isn't he younger than the lad of Naylor's?" he asked with the first bit of paternal comparison he had ever exhibited.

"By two months," Merelan said nonchalantly.

"He's a full hand taller," Petiron said, his tone almost smug.

"He'll be a tall man when he gets his growth," she said. "You're not short, nor were my parents. How were you in height against those brothers of yours?"

"I suspect Forist will be taller, but the other three won't make his height," said Petiron, who had never liked his brothers at all.

"Nor yours." Idly she brushed sand out of his heavy dark brown hair, flicking it off his shoulder and giving herself the excuse to touch his warm smooth skin. She liked his back. He had muscled up a great deal. Not that he would ever carry much flesh; he was too intense to put on weight. But he looked better than he ever had and she loved him more than ever.

He glanced up at her, saw her look, and responded to it. Catching up her hand to his lips, he nibbled at her fingers, never breaking eye contact.

"When Robie takes his afternoon nap, can we find shade somewhere?" he asked, his breath coming a trace faster.

"We can indeed," she murmured, feeling her own ardor rising to meet his. "Segoina has given me a potion that will make it safe all the time for us."

When they did return to the Harper Hall, everyone remarked on the tremendous improvement in Merelan's health, on how big Robinton had grown in six months, and how much the change had improved Petiron's temperament.

Chapter 2

▼▼▼▼▼▼▼▼▼▼▼▼▼▼▼▼▼▼▼▼▼▼▼▼▼▼▼▼▼▼▼▼▼▼▼▼

Petiron was working on his latest score when a soft noise distracted him. Listening, he could hear it coming from the other room. Merelan had stepped out on an errand; Robinton was having his nap.

The faint noise was an echo of the theme he was hastily inscribing before he lost it—he didn't realize that he had been humming it as he worked. Irritated, he looked around for the source of the mimicry.

And found his son awake in the trundle bed and humming.

"Don't *do* that, Robinton," he said in exasperation.

His son pulled the light blanket up to his chin. "You were," he said.

"I was what?"

"You hummmmmdded."

"I may, you may not!" And Petiron shook his finger right in the boy's face so that Robinton pulled the blanket over his head. Petiron pulled it down and leaned over the little bed. "Don't you ever mimic me like that. Don't you ever interrupt me when I'm working. D'you hear that?"

"Whatever did he do, Petiron?" Merelan exclaimed, rushing

into the room and hovering protectively at the head of the cot. "He was sound asleep when I left. What's been going on?"

Robinton, who rarely cried, was weeping, stuffing the end of the blanket into his mouth as the tears crept down his cheeks. The tears were more than Merelan could endure, and she picked up her sobbing son and cradled him, reassuring him.

Petiron glared at her. "He was humming while I was writing."

"You do; why shouldn't he?"

"But I was writing! How can I work when he does that? He *knows* he's not to interrupt me."

"He's a child, Petiron. He picks up on anything he hears and repeats it."

"Well, I'm not having him humming along with me," Petiron said, not the least bit mollified.

"Why shouldn't he if you wake him up?"

"How can I possibly work if you're both interrupting me all the time?" He flung his arms up and stalked out of the bedroom. "Do take him somewhere else. I can't have him singing in the background."

Merelan was already halfway across the sitting room, her crying son in her arms. "Then you won't have him in the background at all," she said in a parting shot.

"I don't know when I've been more annoyed with him," she told Betrice, who was fortunately in her apartment when Merelan tapped at her door.

"I don't suppose he noticed that the child hums on key," Betrice said in her droll fashion, clearing the mending from the padded rocker so that Merelan could calm her child.

Merelan blinked at Betrice and then began to chuckle. "I'm certain he would have mentioned it if Robie were off-key. That would have been injury added to insult." Then she paused. "You know, Robie hums along with me when I do my vocalizes. I hadn't realized it before. There now, little love." And she dried Robie's eyes with an edge of the blanket he was still clutching to his mouth. "Your father didn't really mean to yell at you . . ."

"Ha!" was Betrice's soft response.

"But we do have to be quiet when your father's working at home."

"He has his own studio . . ." Betrice put in.

"Washell borrowed it to speak to those parents who wandered in unannounced."

"Only Washell could get away with that."

"So, my little love, we'll just have to learn to keep our hummings to just you and me from now on. And let Father get on with his important work."

"Ha! More of his incomprehensible, meaningful, and significant musical conundrums. Ooops, sorry!" Betrice covered her lips with an unrepentant hand. "I *know* he's the most important composer in the last two centuries, Merelan, but could he not once contrive a simple tune that *anyone*—besides his own son—could sing?" She rose and walked to the wall cupboard, where she opened one door.

Merelan regarded Betrice without rancor. "He does rather complicated scores, doesn't he?" Then she smiled mischievously. "He just likes to embellish."

"Oh, is that what it's called? Give me a simple tune that I can't get out of my mind!" Betrice said. Having found what she wanted, she returned to Merelan. "But we both know I'm a musical idiot for all the MasterHarper and I have been espoused now thirty Turns. Here you are, my fine lad. Much more appetizing than blanket to chew on." And she handed Robinton a sweet stick. "I believe you prefer peppermint."

The tears were nearly dry, but the gift brought the winsome smile back and a clear "t'ank you" from the recipient. He pushed himself straighter on his mother's lap, accepted the offering, and leaned back against his mother's comforting body as he sucked happily on the sweet.

"I'm not criticizing Petiron, Merelan," Betrice said earnestly.

Merelan smiled gently. "You say nothing that isn't the truth, but he's much easier to deal with, generally speaking, when he's composing."

ANNE McCAFFREY

"Which seems to be often . . ."

Merelan laughed. "Petiron naturally complicates things. It's a knack he has," she said indulgently.

"Humph. He's a very lucky man to have such an understanding mate," Betrice said emphatically, "as well as one who can sing what he writes as easily as she breathes."

"Ssssh." Merelan put a finger to her lips. "Sometimes I have to work very hard to keep up with him."

"Never!" Betrice pretended disbelief, then grinned broadly at the MasterSinger.

"It's true, nevertheless, but," and Merelan's expression softened with pride, "it's wonderful to have such challenging music to sing."

Betrice pointed to Robie, happily sticky-ing up fingers, face, and blanket. "What are you going to do about him?"

"Well, first off, I shall see that Master Washell never has need of Petiron's studio again," Merelan replied, her usually serene expression resolute, "and I shan't leave the pair of them together unless I'm positive Robie's fast asleep."

"That sort of limits you, doesn't it?" Betrice said with a snort.

Merelan shrugged. "In a Turn or so, Robie will be in with the other Hall children during the day. It's a small enough sacrifice to make for him. Isn't it, love?"

"It's all too true," Betrice said with a wistful sigh. "They're young such a short time—even if it feels like an age while they're growing up and away from you." She sighed again.

Merelan felt something sticky and, looking down at her son, saw that the sweet had fallen from his hand to hers.

"Will you look at this?" she said softly, peering with a loving smile at the thick lashes closed on his cheek.

"Here, put him on the daybed."

"I don't mind holding him," Merelan protested. "You've work to do."

"Nothing I can't do while minding a sleeping child. Go on off and do something by yourself for a change. If you aren't tending him—" She pointed to Robinton. "—you're minding him." Her finger jerked in the direction of Merelan's quarters.

"If you don't mind . . ."

"Not at all. Unless you want to help with *my* mending?"

Betrice chuckled over the alacrity with which Merelan rose.

When Robie was well into his third Turn, he picked up a small pipe that had been left on the table. It wasn't his father's, because Robie knew his father did not actually play a pipe or a flute. And since this wasn't his father's belonging, he could touch it—and experiment with it. He blew in it, masking the holes with his fingers as he had seen others do. When the tones that came out were not similar to the ones so effortlessly made by the other players, Robie tried different ways until he did make the proper sounds. As quietly as he could.

He did not know, of course, that his mother's well-attuned ear heard his initial attempts. Since they improved as he continued, she was inordinately pleased. Sometimes, despite a strong musical tradition in a family, there was one born who was tone-deaf or totally disinclined to do much about an innate ability. She had wondered how she would be able to placate Petiron if his son turned out to be musically incompetent. Because one way or another, Petiron would be determined to impart suitable musical training to his only child. Now she did not have to worry about that. Her son was not only inclined to musical experimentation, he also had a good ear and, it would seem, perfect pitch.

When Petiron was busy with students, Merelan would often whistle simple tunes within her son's hearing. Petiron did not like her whistling—possibly because he couldn't, but more likely because he felt that girls shouldn't. Despite how much she loved him, she privately admitted that some of his attitudes, including this one, made no sense to her.

Robie picked up the tunes she whistled as effortlessly as he had learned the scales on the pipe. When he started doing variations on the airs, she had to restrain herself. She wanted desperately to tell Petiron that his son was musical, but she did not want her three-Turn-old son suddenly rushed into training. It could turn the boy off music entirely. Petiron was marvelous with the older lads, but far too strict for the youngest apprentices. She worried about the zeal with which he would train Robinton.

So one afternoon, she asked Washell, the Master who taught the youngest, to help her with the dynamics in a quartet they were both rehearsing for Turnover. A jovial, easygoing man in his sixth decade with a rich deep bass voice, he arrived with some cakes just out of the Hall ovens and a fresh pot of klah.

"So why is it that you really want to see me, Merelan?" he asked after she had profusely thanked him for the refreshments and served them. "The day you can't carry your own part in anything Petiron writes, I'll resign my Mastery."

"Oh, but I do need help, Wash," she said airily. "Robie, come see what Master Washell has brought us!"

She hadn't needed to call him. The delectable aroma of warm pastry had wafted into the next room, where he had been flat on his stomach, making doodles in a sand-tray that had been a recent gift from his mother—a preparation to teaching him his letters and, possibly, the scales.

"I 'mell 'em," he said, still not quite able to pronounce the sibilants with the gap in his front baby teeth. "I 'mell 'em. T'ank you, Master Wa'ell."

"My pleasure, young'un."

Merelan's stage setting was complete. "Here!" she said briskly. "This measure where the tempo changes so rapidly—I'm not sure I've the beat correctly. Robie, give me an A, please."

Washell's gray brows went up his balding head and his eyes glittered as Robie produced the tiny pipe from his trouser waistband and played the required note.

Then Merelan sang the troublesome measures, deliberately shorting the full quality of one whole note. Robie shook his head and with his fingers beat out the appropriate time.

"If you've got it right, m'lad, you play it the way I should sing it," Merelan said casually.

Young Robinton played the entire measure and Washell, who looked first at Merelan and then at her son, folded his hands across his stomach and caught her eyes, nodding with comprehension.

"Thank you, dear. That was well done," Merelan said, and she allowed Robinton to have a second cake. He stuffed his pipe away under his trousers' waistband and sat on the little stool to eat the cake.

"Indeed and I couldn't have done better myself, young Robinton," Washell said solemnly. "You played that perfectly, young man. I'm glad that your mother has you here to keep her strictly in tempo. Do you know any other tunes on that pipe?"

Robie glanced at his mother for permission. She nodded, and he licked his lips free of crumbs, pulled out the pipe and lifted it to his mouth, and began to play one of his own favorites. When he had finished, he gave his mother a second look.

"Yes, go on," she said with a little flick of her fingers.

He looked for a moment at Washell, who knew enough to keep his expression polite, and then the boy closed his eyes and started the round of variations he liked to wind about that tune.

Washell bent his head down, over his heavy chest, until he was peering directly at Robinton, who was now oblivious, wrapped up in his piping, fingers dancing, stopping, busy over the little pipe's holes. The instrument was small and could have produced an unpleasantly shrill sound, but the way the youngster handled his breathing and instinctive dynamics sweetened it to a delightful lilt.

As one variation followed another, Washell cocked his head in amazement and gradually turned his eyes to Merelan, who was totally relaxed, as if this performance were a daily marvel. Suddenly the muted sounds of the choristers ended. Immediately Merelan leaned forward and tapped Robinton out of his concentration. He looked almost rebellious.

"That was a very good one," his mother said, casually appreciative. "New, isn't it?"

"I t'ought it up a' I wa' playing," he said and then glanced coyly up at Washell. "It fitted in."

"Yes, dear, it did," Merelan replied agreeably. "The trills were very well done."

"Nice to have a pipe just the right size for you, isn't it?" Washell began, extending his hand for the instrument. Robinton, with a touch of reluctance, handed it over. Washell tried to put his large fingers over the stops and ran out of pipe, looking so surprised that Robinton giggled, covering his mouth and glancing quickly at his mother to be sure this was acceptable behavior. "Maybe you'd like to see some of the other instruments I have that might also be the right size for a lad like you to play on. This one is much too small for me. Isn't it?" And Washell handed it back with a little flourish. Robinton grinned up at the big man and tucked his pipe back under the waistband, out of sight under his loose shirt.

"I think you could manage to get the pitcher and the cake plate back down to the kitchen, couldn't you, Robie dear?" Merelan asked, rising to open the door as she spoke.

"Can. Will. Bye." And he walked quite sedately down the hallway with his burden. Merelan closed the door.

"Yes, my dear Merelan, you do have a problem growing up here. May I extend you my compliments as well as my assistance? If we move patiently, what is an astonishing natural talent can be nurtured. I admire Petiron in many matters, Singer, but . . ." Washell sighed with a rueful smile. "He can be single-minded to the point of irrationality. He will, of course, be *delighted* to discover his son's musicality, but quite frankly, my dear, I would be sorry to be that son when he does. Which is obviously why you have sent for me, and I take that as the highest compliment you could pay me."

"Petiron will push him too far and too fast . . ."

"Therefore we will lay the groundwork carefully, so that his father's tuition will not be the sudden shock it could be."

"I feel so . . . treacherous, going behind Petiron's back like this," Merelan said, "but I know what he's like and Robie *loves* to make music. I don't want that to be taken from him."

Washell reached across and patted her nervously drumming fingers. "My dear, we can put Petiron's single-mindedness to our advantage. I gather he has no idea that the boy has learned to pipe?"

Merelan shook her head.

"Right now, of course," he went on, "he's up to his inky fingers with Turnover music to write and the rehearsals and then the Spring Gathers, and I shall have a word with Gennell myself about this. If you permit?"

She nodded.

"Why, I do believe the entire Hall could be in on the secret education of our burgeoning young genius . . ."

"Genius?" Merelan's hand went to her throat.

"Of course, Robinton's a musical genius. Though I've never encountered one before in my decades here, I can certainly recognize one when I get the chance. Petiron's *good*, but he is not quite in the same class as his son."

"Oh!" The little exclamation she let slip before she guarded her mouth with her hand was far more eloquent than she intended.

"A child who can tootle that ridiculous little pipe into the sweetest tone and then produce rather sophisticated variations on a simple theme at three Turns *is*, unquestionably, a genius. And we must all protect him."

"Oh! Protect him? Petiron's not a monster, Washell . . ." She shook her head vigorously.

"No, of course, he isn't, but he does have rather strong views about his competence and achievements. On the other hand, what else could he expect of a child from such a fine musical background, who is being raised in the Harper Hall with music all around him."

"Not all the Hall children are musical by virtue of their environment," Merelan said in a droll tone.

"But when one is, as your Robinton, there couldn't be a better environment, and we shall see that the matter is handled as diplomatically and . . . kindly as possible. I give you my hand on that, MasterSinger Merelan." He held it out and she took it gladly, the relief—and even her guilt at the promised subterfuge—easily read by Master Washell. "We'll do no more than what the lad is able, and willing, to absorb. Ease him gently"—his thick fingers rippled descriptively—"into the discipline so that when"—and he clapped his hands together—"we suddenly discover that this five . . . maybe six-Turn-old lad is so musically inclined, why we can be as surprised and delighted as Petiron will be."

"But won't Petiron be at all suspicious when he discovers how much Robie already knows?"

Washell raised his arm in a broad gesture. "Why, the boy absorbed it from his parents, of course. Why would he not, with two such talented musicians?"

"Oh, come now, Washell. Petiron is scarcely stupid . . ."

"With musical scores and instruments all around . . . you'll doubtless mention that you've heard him humming tunes now and then . . . on key. That you gave him the little pipe, and a drum, since he begged for them. Bosler will say he only thought to amuse the lad one afternoon while you were busy with rehearsing and taught him how to place his fingers on the gitar strings . . . It won't be hard to get our Master Archivist to connive to teach the boy more than his letters . . . And we'll all be so amazed that Petiron will have such a student to bring on. He's always better with the quicker students, you know. They don't try his patience the way the younger or slower ones do." Thoroughly pleased with the plot he was spinning, Washell once more patted Merelan's hands reassuringly. Then abruptly, he pulled the quartet sheet between them. "Beat it out one more time, Merelan, as I sing the bass line. You should—"

The door opened, and there were Petiron and Robinton.

"I really do think, Petiron, that you write some passages just to tease me," she said. "And did you get the plate and pitcher safely down to Lorra, dear?"

"I did, Mother."

"Well, then, off with you, Rob," his father said, giving his son a slight push toward the other room. "That you should have any trouble with the tempi surprises me, Merri."

"Because your scribbling is almost unreadable, Petiron," Washell said firmly, his bass voice rumbling in mock rebuke. "See here?" His thick index finger pounded the culprit measure. "One can barely see the dot. No wonder Merelan was having difficulty with the beat when she couldn't even see the dot after the half note. It's clearly marked on my copy, but not on this."

Petiron peered down at the offending score. "It is a little faint at that. Sing it for me." And he gave her the upbeat.

Washell could not resist singing the bass line as Merelan faultlessly sang hers.

"You did help, Wash, thank you so much," she said. "And thanks for bringing along the cake and klah."

"My pleasure, MasterSinger." Washell bowed, smiling benignly at both before he turned and left the room.

"Really, Merelan," Petiron said, peering at the offending measure, "are you having headaches again?"

"No, love, but it was faint and I wasn't expecting a hold just there. How did the rehearsals go? They sounded fine at this distance."

He flumped himself down in the stuffed chair and hauled his feet up on the stool, heaving a sigh. "The usual problems. They seem to feel that a glance at the score when they hear me coming up the stairs is sufficient study, but toward the end, they were beginning to grasp the dynamics. Nice of Washell to rehearse with you."

"Yes, he's such a sweet person."

"Washell?" Petiron regarded his spouse with some astonishment. "You know what the apprentices call him . . ."

"I know, but you have no need to repeat such a scurrilous title," she said with a severe scowl. Petiron frowned. "A glass of wine?" she offered, going to the cabinet. "You look tired."

"I am. Thank you, love."

She poured two glasses. She needed one herself.

"I'll join you." Handing a full glass to him, she slipped to the arm of the seat and pulled his head to her shoulder. Really, in spite of his faults, she did love him most profoundly, especially for his devotion to and composition of music. Until Robie was born, their life together had been idyllic!

The one aspect that neither Washell nor Robie's mother had considered was the child's enthusiasm for things musical. They did not expect quite how swiftly and eagerly, over the next few months, he absorbed his lessons and learned how to play the various instruments. No sooner had Master Ogolly taught him musical notations and the value of the notes on the staff, signatures, clef, and measure, than young Robie jotted down the variations he had created on his first simple tunes.

Merelan had the hard job of suppressing such enthusiasm within their quarters, especially since Robie wanted to show his father what he was doing because he hoped his father might approve of him then.

"But Father lik'th muthic. He writ'th it, too," Robie said plaintively. He still had trouble with his "s" sounds though he had extended his working vocabulary, as well as his musical aptitudes.

"That's just it, my love." Merelan hated herself for such hypocrisy. "He hears it all day long, has to cope with such stupid students and—"

"Am I thupid, Momma?"

"No, love, you are not the least bit stupid, but your father does need quiet and a rest from music when he's here with us . . ."

"I gueth . . ." Robie said sadly.

"The Big Spring Gather is so important, and you know how hard your father is working on the new score . . ."

"Yeth, he ith." Robie sighed.

"Can you smell the sweet cakes, dear?" she asked, grateful for that diversion.

Robie dutifully sniffed and a smile broke over his sad little face. "Do you think . . ." he began hopefully, brightening.

"You'll never know until you ask Lorra, will you?" Merelan said, turning him toward the door. "And be sure to ask for enough for me and your father, love."

Kubisa, who taught the youngsters from Fort Hold as well as the Harper and Healer Halls, allowed young Robie into her classes before his fourth Turn began.

"He's well advanced as far as *wanting* to learn, Merelan," the woman said. "I could wish half my class were at the same level, but I'll give him little extra musical type things to do while the others are catching up."

Then there was a morning when Kubisa brought a bloody-nosed, sobbing Robinton back to his mother for aid and comfort.

"Oh, Robie," Merelan said, folding her weeping child in her arms while Kubisa busied herself getting a wet cloth to clean his face.

"They wuz hurtin' him," Robie sobbed.

"Hurting who?" Merelan asked, more of Kubisa than her son.

"I'll say this for Robie, he may be young and small, but he knows who needs his protection."

"Who needs it?" his mother asked, carefully mopping away the blood.

"The watch-wher," Kubisa said.

Merelan paused, surprised and beginning to feel more pride than concern. The apprentices were not above sticking bright glows into the Harper Hall watch-wher's lair to make the light-sensitive creature cry. Or throwing him noxious things, know-ing the creature would eat just about anything that came within the range of its chain. Rob would always run and tell an adult if he saw such antics.

"Were they being mean to the poor beast again?"

Sniffling, he nodded his head up and down. "I made 'em stop, but one of 'em busted me one."

"So I see," his mother murmured.

"Some of the beastholder children who really ought to know better," Kubisa said. "I'll have a word with their parents, now that I've delivered Rob to you." She patted his head. "I'd pick on someone my size, next time. Or better still, have your father teach you how to duck."

Grinning, she left the apartment.

"I can teach you how to duck, my brave lad," Merelan said, hugging him again, knowing that such training did not fall in Petiron's scope of paternal duties. "I used to be able to beat some of my big brothers and cousins when I got going."

"You?" Robie's eyes widened at the very notion of his mother beating anything, much less big brothers and cousins.

So she gave him his first lesson in hand-to-hand combat, and showed him how best to head-butt an assailant. "It keeps you from having bloody noses, too, if you use your head in a fight."

That daily respite of his hours with Kubisa gave Merelan a rest from constantly being alert to intervene between her son and his father. The subterfuge she had to practice was wearing on her nerves. However, she—and Kubisa—could at least honestly report Robie's excellent conduct and progress in school.

"And you're learning all the Teaching Ballads?" Petiron asked absently.

"Yes, and I can prove it." Robinton wanted so desperately to please his father, but he never seemed able to, despite how hard he tried to be good, obedient, courteous, and, most of all, quiet.

Somewhat surprised at his son's tone of voice, Petiron leaned back in his chair. With an indolent and supercilious wave of his hand, he indicated that Robie should perform.

Merelan held her breath, unable to think of a single thing to say to postpone Petiron's discovery of his son's talent.

Robie took a breath—properly, not gasping air into his lungs as so many novices did—and then launched into a note-perfect rendition of the Duty Song. Petiron did look a trifle surprised at the firmness of tone the boy projected in his treble voice. Petiron beat the time with one finger on the armrest but he listened with a much less disdainful expression on his face.

"That was well done, Robinton," he said. "Now don't think that learning one song is all you have to do. There's a significant number, even for children, to be learned, word- and note-perfect. Continue as you have begun."

Robinton beamed with pleasure, turning to his mother to see if she also agreed.

Merelan could barely keep from sobbing with relief as she came forward and tousled his hair. "You have done very well indeed, my love. I'm proud of you, too. Just as your father is." She turned to Petiron for his reassurance, but he had already turned back to the apprentice scores he was correcting, oblivious to son and spouse.

Merelan had to clench her hands to her sides to keep from roaring at him for such a curt dismissal. There was so much more Petiron could have said. He could have mentioned that the boy was on pitch throughout, with good breath support and that his voice was actually very good. But she controlled her anger and took Robie, who couldn't quite understand why he hadn't pleased his father more, by the hand.

"We'll just see," she said in a firm, loud voice, "what Lorra might have as a reward for knowing *all* the verses and the tempi perfectly!"

When she slammed the door behind her, Petiron glanced over his shoulder, then went back to marking a very poorly executed apprentice lesson.

"**R**eally, I wanted to . . ." Merelan's fists were clenched as she paced about the small floor space in Lorra's little office-sitting room off the main Hall kitchens. "I wanted to *kick* him."

"Really?" Lorra recoiled a bit from her friend's vehemence. She had taken one look at Merelan's expression when she stalked into the kitchen and immediately assigned the two scullery girls to feed Robinton some of the freshly baked bubbly pies while she took the MasterSinger into her office. Lorra knew that Betrice was away from the Hall on a confinement, and she was rather complimented that Merelan would turn to her at all.

"I mean, I've heard third-year apprentices who couldn't sing the Duty Song as well," Merelan said, venting both anger and frustration as she pounded around the room. "Not a note wrong, not even a poorly timed breath. Why, the performance was excellent."

"Petiron said that much, didn't he?" Lorra asked, hoping to soothe the Singer.

"Yes, but there was so much more he *could* have said. Robie sang splendidly, better than a lad of fourteen, and he's barely four Turns! And Petiron acted as if it was no more than he expected of his son."

"Ah!" Lorra pointed a finger at her distraught visitor. "You've said it. He *expected* such excellence from his own son! If Robie hadn't been as accurate and correct as Petiron expected, *then* you'd've heard all about it, now wouldn't you?"

Merelan paused in her pacing and stared at the headwoman. Then, with a rueful laugh, her anger dissipating, she sat herself down in the other comfortable chair, chuckling.

"You're right, of course. If Robie hadn't been note-perfect, he would have had to repeat the Duty Song until he was. Oh, by the First Egg, what am I to do? The boy so much needs, and wants, his father's approval. He's never, never going to get it."

"Shouldn't wonder, since Petiron's shyer about giving credit where it's due than any other Harper in the Hall. But," Lorra pointed out, "now you don't have to fret so much about when Petiron finds out his own son is lengths ahead of him musically."

Merelan shot Lorra a stunned look.

"Oh, c'mon, Merelan," Lorra returned, "you know it yourself. The boy's already more of a musician than apprentices three times his age. I shouldn't wonder but that he makes journeyman by the time he's sixteen."

"A journeyman has to be eighteen . . ." Merelan began in a feeble denial.

"Well, by the time he's sixteen, we'll see. Meanwhile, I'd say that after today, you won't have to watch Robie around his father so carefully. It'll be easier for Rob, too. It's obvious to me that Petiron won't notice much until Robie's voice breaks and he realizes his 'infant' son is nearly a man."

"Really?" Merelan asked pensively, considering Lorra's facetious words seriously.

"Wouldn't surprise me in the least," Lorra replied with a flick of her fingers. "Now you stop fretting so much. The strain's coming out in your voice—I'm sorry to mention that to you, but I don't think anyone else would. Except Petiron, and it's as well he hasn't noticed. Or am I overstepping the line?"

"No, you're not, Lorra. Never." Merelan hastily laid her hand on Lorra's plump forearm. "I just didn't think anyone would notice. I've just been vocalizing and tried to go easy on my voice . . ."

"Not easy when you're in between a rock and a hard place with those two men in your life." Lorra leaned forward and patted Merelan's nervously drumming fingers. "I'm not a healer, but a glass of wine would not go amiss right now. For both of us." She rose and went to the cabinet, taking down a wineskin and two glasses. Merelan waved away the courtesy but Lorra insisted. "There're a lot of things Petiron won't notice, including wine on your breath, if that's what you're worried about. And right now you need to relax, which is what my herbal cordial will help you do."

Merelan glanced out of the office at Robie, who was making the girls giggle, his round, happy face smeared with deep purplish berry juice. She settled back, accepting the glass.

"Has Master Gennell told you about the new girl yet?" Lorra asked.

"Halanna?" When Lorra nodded, Merelan went on. "Yes, I'd a letter from the Hold's Harper, Maxilant. He's done as much as he can with her vocal training and says she's too good to be messed up by an amateur like himself." She smiled over Maxilant's modesty.

"Petiron would be happy to have a good contralto on hand, too," Lorra said. She sang in that range, though never as a soloist. "Odd, isn't life? You never really know how things'll turn out until they do, do you?"

"No, you don't." As Merelan sipped, she could feel the cordial seeping down her veins and the knot of tension in her belly beginning to ease.

"She's of an age with the Hold daughters here, so I've placed her with them in the cottage," Lorra said. "They may be here only until Turnover, but they'll help her ease into the routine here. It can take a bit of getting used to, can't it?"

ANNE MCCAFFREY

Merelan couldn't help smiling at Lorra's use of the word "routine" in connection with the Harper Hall. No two days were ever alike in the fascinating, and sometimes frantic, atmosphere within this rectangle. She did very vividly remember her own first days there and would help young Halanna as much as she could, to become accustomed to the requisite study and practice. In fact, if Lorra was correct about Petiron, and she rather suspected the headwoman was, Merelan herself would welcome having a female student to bring on. She'd have less time to fret herself into stress over all the confrontations she imagined between son and spouse.

Chapter 3

▼▼▼▼▼▼▼▼▼▼▼▼▼▼▼▼▼▼▼▼▼▼▼▼▼▼▼▼▼▼▼▼▼▼

Halanna arrived, and created an instant impression on all who met her of an overly self-confident seventeen-Turn-old young woman who found fault with everything at the Harper Hall, and especially the cottage where she was lodged. She was accustomed to a room of her own, she informed Isla, who acted as foster mother to her charges; she'd never be able to sleep, sharing a room. Why was there so little fresh food to be had when she was used to plenty of fruit? The weather was dreadful and she hadn't the right clothing, though the three large bundles laboriously taken up by carrier beast from the ship that had delivered her at Fort Hold Harbor contained an immense quantity of clothing. Nor had she sufficient space to arrange half her things in the dinky room she had to *share*! And where could she practice in peace and quiet with all the instruments and voices blaring constant cacophony into the rectangle.

The only one who found her at all bearable was Petiron. Once he heard her sing, he dismissed Merelan's remarks about her lack of discipline and a lack of general information about music that was close to illiteracy. He was jubilant over having a contralto with such a rich timbre and wide range with no "break" whatever. He immediately began to write contralto solos into the Turnover music he was currently composing. He discounted Merelan's suggestions that the girl would not be able to "read" the contralto line, much less manage the tempi changes or the cadenzas.

Unfortunately, Petiron's approval merely increased Halanna's already overbearing manner. Merelan needed all her tact, and the weight of her position as MasterSinger, to get the girl to do the vocalizes that would strengthen her breath control, sustain her range, and prepare her for the rigors of singing Petiron's sort of vocally extravagant music. That Petiron had also envisaged a soprano/contralto duet did nothing to help Merelan, for it automatically put the girl on a par with a MasterSinger, which Halanna clearly was not, despite an amazing natural voice.

Merelan hadn't a jealous bone in her body and was quite willing to prepare the girl or remedy the gaps in her education—if Halanna had been the least bit amenable. But the younger singer decided that, if she was good enough to sing a duet with the leading MasterSinger of Pern, she had no need to do such dull exercises and study vocal scores. She sang *loudly,* completely ignoring any dynamic alteration for the appropriate performance of a song or aria, concerned only with showing off the power of her vocal equipment. "Soft" was an unknown quality.

"If she keeps on shrieking like that," Washell said to Merelan when she approached him for advice on how to deal with Halanna, "she won't *have* a voice in a couple of Turns. That'll solve that problem rather neatly, I'd say."

"Washell!" Merelan was shocked by the acid tone of his voice.

He raised his eyebrows, wrinkling his forehead, and gave her a long look.

"Of course, it's a lot harder to sing softly, since it requires considerable breath control. I've had many difficult students in my life as a teacher, m'dear, but that one is unique in my experience. Whatever was Maxilant thinking of to encourage her to think so highly of her ability?"

"Sheer desperation, I'd imagine," Merelan replied with understandable disgust. "And a chance to get her out of his hair."

"You may be right. Though how he could let her get away with so *little* fundamental understanding of note values is really beyond me."

"And quite possibly beyond Halanna," Merelan added. They exchanged understanding grins.

"Let Petiron handle this one, m'dear," Washell said, winking. "He won't like her messing up his music, you know."

"There is that," Merelan mused, and then grimaced. "Only he's likely to find me lacking as an instructor. And I'm not!" she added with a touch of desperate anger in her voice.

"By no means, m'dear, as everyone else in the Hall will vouch." Washell patted her arm. Then he paused, thinking. "There may be another way. We'll contrive. Just you wait and see."

Many of the masters, and even journeymen, at the Harper Hall were eccentric in one fashion or another, traits which were respected or, sometimes, endured as a necessary evil. But they had all put in the essential work to master the basic mechanics of music. Halanna could not be bothered with such slogging. Merelan kept at it, as obstinate in her attempts to instruct Halanna as the girl was to avoid such lessons.

Halanna was an accomplished flirt, and quickly isolated those whom she would favor—because of their rank, either within the Hall, or from prestigious holds. She chose only the attractive journeymen and masters, of whom there were quite a few just then, back at the Hall either for reassignment or to take part in the Turnover rehearsals. Not only did she have a voice, even her worst enemies had to admit that she was a beauty. Blonde hair bleached almost silver by the sun of Ista, a flawless tan that accentuated her light green eyes and white, even teeth, a figure more mature than that of most girls her age—and she knew far more than she ought of how to flaunt her sensuality. She did not obey the cottage keeper's basic rules, deciding they were for children and not the daughter of a holder, though all the other boarders were the same rank, and some more prestigious than hers. She was caught time and again sneaking in late at night.

Then Halanna took a dislike to Robinton.

Merelan conducted her voice lessons in her own quarters, as they were spacious enough and offered some privacy. Right now, preparing for the Turnover celebrations, she was coaching quite a few students and often had to schedule them when Robie was not in the Hall nursery school. He had always played quite happily and quietly in the other room. Halanna said his very presence so close to her was distracting, even with the connecting door closed, and she hated anyone to overhear her lessons.

That was too much for Merelan. Nor was that an excuse to find favor with Petiron, who was busy dreaming of the success of his new composition.

"Since it *is* so important to you, love," Merelan said from behind gritted teeth, "I really think you ought to take over her coaching. As you may have observed," she added, knowing perfectly well that he hadn't, "she will probably do better with a male coach. I've already more than I can handle with the secondary parts."

"But I can't teach her what you can," Petiron protested in surprise. Merelan was, in his estimation, much the better vocal coach, and he couldn't quite understand how she was having difficulties with a voice as fine as Halanna's. "You're not annoyed that I've written in a duet for you to sing with her?"

"Me? No, why should I be? She has a magnificent voice, but she's a little shy on technique and I know she'll respond better to your comments."

Petiron was not at all sure of that, but there was something about Merelan's attitude that made him keep his private views to himself. He anticipated no trouble at all.

"She's a musical *idiot!*" he railed when he returned from her first lesson with him. "Haven't you been able to teach her *any-thing* in the full month she's been here?"

"No," Merelan said quietly, and pointed to the closed door where Robinton was taking a nap.

"But she can't even read notes, even when I beat out the tempo for her. Nor is she able to maintain pitch when I change signatures. She expects me—me—" And Petiron laid an eloquent hand on his chest. "—to teach her the entire score by rote. Could Maxilant have done that with her?" he inquired in a petulant tone.

"I believe Maxilant only raved on about her beautiful voice, love, and said nothing about the lacks in her general musical education." Merelan spoke as levelly as she could, having great difficulty masking her inner jubilation.

"She wouldn't vocalize to warm her voice and told me"— Petiron swung on his spouse—"that you didn't bother . . ."

"I didn't 'bother' because I could never get her to see the necessity, Petiron," she replied with considerable vehemence. "Washell is of the opinion that if she continues to sing *in alt* for another few years, she won't be able to squeak."

Petiron recoiled in surprise at his gentle spouse's critical remark.

"No wonder you were so eager for me to coach her," he said almost sullenly.

"If you can't, no one in this Hall will be able to," she said, looking him squarely in the eye. "She might believe you, where she's certain I'm jealous of your interest in her."

Petiron scowled. "Aren't you?"

Merelan laughed. "My love, I wouldn't be that child for all the diamonds on Ista's beaches. Washell's right, you know. She won't have a voice left if she keeps on this way."

"He is right," Petiron admitted and scowled more deeply. "Well, she is *not*—" He paused dramatically. "—ruining either the duet or the aria. I shall make some changes in both that will put the music at a level she should be able to sing."

Merelan merely nodded.

When Petiron held his next session with Halanna, she was so

insulted that she tried to walk out on him. The argument that ensued was heard by nearly everyone on the rectangle as the two voices, one baritone and one contralto, rose in volume and piercing clarity.

"You can't do that!" Halanna began, an astonished screech in her voice.

"Oh, yes I can! You're incapable of singing what I wrote."

"Incapable? How dare you?"

"How dare you address a master in such a tone, young woman! I don't know what Maxilant taught you, but it wasn't manners and it certainly wasn't how to read a simple score."

"Simple score? You're notorious all over Pern for the complexity of your music. I never hear anyone singing what *you* write. No one can!"

"The first-year apprentices have no trouble. But then, they can read music and know the value of the notes they're singing."

"I do, too, know how to read music."

"Then prove it."

"No!"

"You will sing."

"You can't force me!"

Many allowed as how they had heard the crack of flesh hitting flesh. And it was true that the right side of Halanna's face was darker than the left when she was finally allowed to leave the studio. But she did begin to sing in a much muted voice. And she continued to sing the music as written until she did so correctly, sometimes until she was hoarse.

"I hope he didn't push her too far," Merelan murmured to Washell.

"Perhaps it might be better for all of us if he did," he replied uncharitably.

After that session, Halanna hurried out of the studio and disappeared. She was seen a little later on her way across the great Fort Hold courtyard to the cottage, where she slammed and bolted the door of the room she still shared.

What they didn't realize, until the next morning, was that

she had bribed a drum heights apprentice to send an urgent message to her father, Halibran, saying she was being abused. Petiron admitted that he had slapped her, to stop her hysterical ranting—to which everyone in the Hall had been audience. Any master was permitted to chastise a student for inattention or failure to learn assigned lessons.

When MasterHarper Gennell and Journeywoman Healer Betrice interviewed her about the impropriety of her action, not to mention the content of the message, she was defiantly tearful.

"No one understands me in this place. I'm being humiliated at every turn, and I had expected so much from you!" she said. "So much, and you're like everyone else after all!"

Betrice later told Merelan she almost laughed out loud at such a performance.

"No one has humiliated you, young woman," Gennell replied, as stern as Betrice had ever seen him. "You were welcomed, and the very best instructors assigned. You have been paid a high compliment by Master Petiron, who wrote a part especially to show off your voice—scarcely a humiliation, but an honor you seem unable to appreciate. You will apologize to Master Petiron for your unresponsiveness—"

"Apologize?" Halanna rose from the stool in amazement. "I am the daughter of a holder, and I apologize to no one. He's to apologize for slapping me, or—"

"That's enough out of you," Gennell said, and turned to his spouse. "She's to be quartered in an appropriate room and given only basic rations."

That was more easily said than done. It took Gennell, Betrice, and Lorra to get her, screeching and struggling, up to the third story of the Harper Hall to one of the spare rooms used by messengers or overflow guests. She refused to eat the food supplied at mealtimes and actually emptied the first three pitchers of water until her thirst got the better of her histrionics. Since it took nearly six days before her clandestine message brought results, she got hungry enough to devour what she was given, though she refused to apologize or promise to remedy her attitude. Such interviews usually resulted in her hurling threats and promises of just retribution at those trying to talk sense

ANNE MCCAFFREY

into her. Even MasterHealer Ginia had no luck in trying to talk sense into the girl.

The sentry on the Fort Hold eastern tower spotted the ten armed men racing up the harbor road and blew the alarm, alerting both Lord Grogellan and the Harper Hall. Having been informed of the illegal drum message, Grogellan assembled a larger force from his sons, nephews, and armsmen to meet the newcomers just as they turned into the Harper Hall quadrangle. Master Gennell, Betrice, Ginia, Petiron, and Merelan were waiting on the broad steps, and every apprentice, journeyman, and master had found some vantage point from which to view the confrontation.

As Halibran and his troop halted their runners, he had no trouble locating his "abused" daughter, screeching at the top of her lungs from an upper window.

"She's been at it again, Father," one of Halibran's riders said in disgust. "She was the one abusing, I've no doubt." The resemblance to his sister was obvious and he was not the only young blond male in the group with a similar cast of countenance.

Halibran, dismounting, waved the young man to hold his tongue. Not a major holder, though a wealthy one from the produce of his lands and the mines under them, he had none of his daughter's arrogance as he mounted the steps and held out his hand to the MasterHarper.

"Since she is sequestered, I assume that Halanna has not seen fit to apologize. Let me do so in her stead," he said, allowing everyone to heave sighs of relief.

Master Gennell, however, shook his head slowly. "It is her place, not yours, Holder Halibran, to make restitution for her behavior and her refusal to accept the usual necessary disciplines of the Harper Hall. She has much to learn."

The screeching, which the new arrivals were pointedly ignoring, took on a shriller note.

"The fault lies in me," Halibran said with a weary sigh. "Her mother died at her birth, and with six brothers, she has been much cosseted."

The brother who had spoken gave an almost imperceptible shake of his head and then looked away. The other two managed not to grin, but it didn't escape anyone that they had probably tried to get their father to school his daughter's behavior.

"What did happen that made her send such a message?" Halibran asked.

Gennell opened his mouth, but it was Petiron who stepped forward and answered.

"She is musically almost illiterate, Holder Halibran," he said in a flat and firm voice, "although I know Harper Maxilant to be a competent musician."

"Maxilant did suggest that the Hall might succeed where he was failing," Halibran said, raising both gloved hands in helplessness, his answer directed more to Gennell than to Petiron. "I should not have sent you our problem." He turned back to Petiron. "And?"

"When she repeatedly refused to learn a simple score . . ."

No one of the Harper Hall group so much as batted an eye at Petiron's remark.

". . . and started to rant in an hysterical fashion, I slapped her. Once." And Petiron put up one finger in emphasis.

Everyone on the steps nodded.

"We all heard the entire argument," Master Gennell said, and he pointed to the studio windows. "And the single slap."

"She'd need more than one," a brother said.

"We shall take her off your hands," her father said in an almost meek tone, though it was obvious that he was probably not one whit less proud than his daughter.

"Nonsense," Master Gennell said, just as Petiron stepped forward to protest. "With your permission, we shall continue to discipline her—firmly—until she realizes that such behavior gets her nowhere in either her relationships with others or in learning the lessons you asked us to teach her."

Halibran was astonished; the brothers muttered amongst themselves.

"That is too fine a voice to be misused," Master Gennell said, glancing up in the direction of the outraged cries. Strips of clothing flapped out of the window and drifted to the ground. "Or abused. We have disciplined recalcitrant students before now. She may be," and Master Gennell paused significantly, "unusually obdurate, but give me leave to doubt she is beyond redemption."

"I'd say she is," the brother murmured, and received a buffet on his leg from his glaring father.

"Give us until the Spring Solstice, Holder Halibran, and you will be pleased with the change."

"How do you propose to achieve that?" the holder asked, tucking his gloved thumbs into his thick riding belt and regarding not only Gennell but the others on the top step.

"If you would make it . . . exceedingly . . . plain to her," Gennell said, "that such antics cut no ice with you, that you will no longer condone her behavior or rescue her from its consequences, she will soon capitulate."

Halibran considered as he removed his gloves, stowed them in the saddle bag, and flexed his fingers. "If she does, it will be the first time in her life," he said, "but it had better come now." He opened and closed his fists.

The expression of profound satisfaction was mirrored by all three brothers and, indeed, the other six men of the party.

"I'll lead the way," Gennell said affably, and as Betrice and Ginia fell into step with Holder Halibran, they disappeared into the Hall.

"Is that the girl you said had a superb voice, Petiron?" Grogellan asked, moving up to the steps from where he and his men had witnessed the interview.

The oldest brother, recognizing that this was the Lord of Fort Hold, respectfully dismounted and gestured for the others to do so, inclining his upper body politely to one of higher rank. Just then Halanna's voice rasped to an even higher note, almost a wail, and Petiron winced.

"If she keeps on forcing the upper register like that," Washell remarked to no one in particular, "she may end up soprano instead of alto. If she's any voice left at all."

"Hmmm," was Grogellan's reply, as he turned his head up to the window. "She certainly shouldn't be allowed to carry on like that."

"It's a specialty of hers," the oldest brother remarked. "She's developed it into a fine art, and none of us"—he included his brothers—"could do a thing about it."

Grogellan looked at him with such a glare that he grimaced, shrugging his shoulders. Fort's Lord Holder did not approve of sons criticizing their fathers, no matter what the cause.

"Any moment, now," Washell said, grinning in happy expectation.

He was right. Halanna's shriek broke off abruptly. There was a long wait for those on the ground before her voice was heard again, and this time her shout was defiance mixed with astonishment. That tone altered to outraged cries, screams, and finally into penitent sobs which gradually, over the next few minutes, dwindled into silence. Or at least to a level that was not audible to those below.

To give him credit, the oldest brother controlled his expression as he turned to Washell. "Our mounts need to be refreshed before we start back," he said.

"Then follow us," Grogellan said. "You will guest at the Hold, for I know the Harper Hall is presently filled to capacity." He gestured for the Istans to follow him.

The oldest brother, astonished and grateful for Grogellan's hospitality, looked from him to the doorway of the Harper Hall. "I should await my father." He turned back to Grogellan. "I am Brahil, and those two are my brothers, Landon and Brosil," he said by way of introduction. "And Gostol, here, is our good captain who sailed us here."

Grogellan nodded approval of Brahil's manners and, leaving the young man to wait for his father, he swept the others ahead of him toward the Hold. "How was the sea on your way here, Master Gostol?" he asked, assuming the duties of a genial host.

The Istan holders stayed three more days, until Halanna finally capitulated—from sheer physical exhaustion. Ginia had naturally attended the girl after each session with her father and, although she was discreet, she did imply that it was no more than the child required to make her mend her ways.

"For so many children, disapproval is sufficient, or a rap on the knuckles," she said to Merelan, who was genuinely worried when Halanna showed no signs of repentance after the second chastisement. "Then there are some who have to have manners thumped into their heads. Oddly enough, they seem to recover more quickly than the sensitive child who is only verbally rebuked."

"But . . ."

"He uses only his hand, and it's more her pride that's been offended than her butt end," Ginia said. "If the issue is not forced now, she will become far worse in later years and end up disgracing her entire family and hold. That can't be allowed."

"It's just that we've never had a child that difficult," Merelan said.

Isla joined them, breathless from a fast walk across the courtyard. "He's taking most of her clothing back with him and has asked me to provide warmer garments. Just a few, and nothing fancy, though I did talk him into permitting one nice outfit for Gathers and performances." She looked almost regretful, though Halanna had driven her to despair with her snide comments and spiteful ways. "Only she's not to pick it out. I'll let Neilla do so. She has the best taste and the most forgiving heart."

Halanna was required to apologize to the MasterHarper, Journeywoman Healer Betrice, and Master Petiron for her intransigence. Gennell had wanted to include Merelan, but the singer put her foot down. She would have the instructing of the humbled girl, and that was going to be hard enough to handle without the child experiencing further abasement.

"She brought it on herself," Halibran said sternly.

"That does not require me to compound it," Merelan said, lifting her chin to match his attitude.

"You are a gracious lady," he said, relenting and bowing to her.

Halanna was granted a room to herself, the attic one, which had sufficient space for her much reduced wardrobe. Her father had left instructions with Master Gennell to take disciplinary steps if she did not apply herself to her lessons.

"And, if you should decide this regimen doesn't suit you," her father said in so cold a voice that Merelan shivered, "and attempt to run away from the Harper Hall, I will have the drums repudiate you across all Pern. Do you understand? You wanted to sing, you wanted to come here to the Harper Hall so you could improve your voice. Now you will do just that and nothing but that! Do you understand, Halanna?"

Head hanging after the ordeal of apology, she murmured something.

"I didn't hear that. Speak up."

A flash of her old spirit flared in her eyes but vanished when her father lifted his hand. "Yes, Father. I understand." She stood, head up, lips and chin trembling slightly. Satisfied with her demeanor, he strode out of the MasterHarper's office.

"MasterSinger Merelan will be your primary instructor, Halanna," Master Gennell said. "You will review your foundation lessons with the first-year apprentices"—he was almost glad to see the flare of dismay in her eyes. Her punishment had not broken her spirit, even if it had quelled her arrogance—"until you have learned enough to graduate to the more advanced classes. Although classes have begun for the day, Master Washell has given permission for you to arrive late this morning. Now go on to room twenty-six. And you'll need this slate and chalk."

He handed her the items she had refused to carry or use in her first days at the Harper Hall. As she went out the door, he noticed she pulled her shoulders back, steeling herself to go in amongst the lowest of apprentices and face whatever their reaction to her presence might be. The girl had courage. Gennell had, however, made very sure that she would not be the butt of any youthful mischief. He had given a stern lecture to the apprentice contingent that they were to behave properly at all times in her presence and never refer to the incident or they'd have worse of the same.

In fact, the affair had subtly improved the behavior of even the more inventive miscreants among the apprentices. But that didn't keep many of the principals from deeply regretting Halanna's intransigence.

Petiron did not restore the more complex music he had written for contralto voice, but Halanna did sing at Turnover. In the duet with Merelan, she modulated her tone to match the soprano, so that it was technically well sung, though the contralto part did not match the soprano in the joy that the song had been written to express.

Petiron was profoundly disappointed in her performance, having worked so hard with her to produce the dynamics he had "heard" during composition.

"Don't you dare chide her, Petiron," Merelan said, intercepting him after the performance. "She's done well, all things considered. No one can beat joy into music unless it comes from the heart."

"But her voice . . ." Petiron was beside himself with dismay. "She could so easily have risen to the occasion."

"Give her time, love, give her time. She may not be as rebellious or arrogant as she was when she first came here, but give her time to realize how much she has learned and how much her voice has improved. If you can't say anything complimentary, say nothing." She looked over to where Halanna was being surrounded by Fort Hold guests who were complimenting her on her lovely voice and splendid performance. "She was note-perfect, you know, and her breath support was excellent. And her presence couldn't have been improved on. Say that. She'll know where she failed."

Petiron opened his mouth and, while Merelan knew he wanted to complain that his satisfaction had been diminished by her lackluster performance, he observed Halanna accepting the compliments with a genuine modesty.

"Oh, well. *You* were splendid, Mere."

"I'm glad you think so," she said, and if her tone was a little dry, Petiron missed it as he was surrounded by those wishing to congratulate composer and MasterSinger.

Chapter 4

▼▼▼▼▼▼▼▼▼▼▼▼▼▼▼▼▼▼▼▼▼▼▼▼▼▼▼▼▼▼▼▼▼▼▼▼▼▼

Of Halanna's family, only the second brother, Landon, was able to attend the Turnover performance, since Halibran had unavoidable hold obligations. She was glad enough to see her brother, and he seemed more affectionately inclined toward her. Patently impressed by her demeanor as well as her singing, he remarked several times that he didn't recognize his own sister, she'd changed so much for the better.

Merelan took him to one side after his third loud pronouncement.

"I wouldn't make so much of her . . . good behavior, Landon," she said kindly.

"But she *has* changed," he protested.

"Yes, but do you have to rub it in?"

"Oh, yes . . ." He rubbed his tanned chin and gave Merelan a charmingly penitent smile. "I see what you mean. But she's certainly turned inside out, and not before time, if you ask me, though you didn't. When she was a toddler, she was such a sweet thing . . ." His voice trailed off. "Who's that?" he asked, suddenly suspicious as he noticed a young man in elegant Turnover finery leading his sister onto the dance floor.

Merelan recognized one of the younger Ruathan nephews, Donkin, who was currently fostering with Lord Grogellan. As he had a good strong tenor voice, he usually joined the Harper Hall chorus. He'd been no more attentive to Halanna than half a dozen others brought in for the Turnover performance. But, being from Ruathan Bloodlines, he'd be quite acceptable to the most particular of fathers as a possible spouse.

"Ruathan, you say?" Landon echoed, quite able to recognize Donkin's suitability. "Is she showing any preference?"

"Not that we've observed."

"Still keeping your eye on her?"

"No more than we keep our eyes on any of the young women in our care," Merelan replied pointedly.

"She has learned her lesson, then?"

Merelan thought his attitude was a shade arch, but he was himself young and had spoken to and treated his sister kindly since his arrival. "She has learned a good deal more about the mechanics of both producing her voice and music in general. She has proved a good student."

"My father said she may stay on, if you think she should." Now he sounded less self-confident and there was a hint of plea in his tone.

"She has scarcely begun to learn the repertoire suitable for her range," Merelan told him willingly. "And she has learned to play flute and gitar well enough to do ensemble work. We would certainly like to train her as far as she is willing to go."

"She'll be willing, I fancy," Landon said, his eyes watching Halanna going through the steps of the dance with the agile Donkin. The two were obviously enjoying themselves.

Halanna was smiling more tonight than she had done since her father's disciplining. And about time, too, Merelan thought.

"Come, Landon, you can't spend all your time as observer. I'd be happy to introduce you to any number of girls here."

"I'd like to dance with *you*, if you'd permit it, MasterSinger." He managed not only a charming smile but a graceful bow.

Merelan glanced about to check on Robie, playing with some other children his own age at the edge of the dance floor, and

Petiron, who was explaining something, with considerable gesturing, to one of the harpers home for Turnover. Eventually he would remember that she loved to dance and oblige her, but she was quite willing to start with Landon.

"I'd love to dance, Holder Landon," she said and took his offered hand.

One of the features of the Turnover celebrations was that everyone got a chance to play or sing—even those as young as Robinton and the other nursery children. They performed a song on the second day, each of them using a percussion instrument: tambourine, chimes, triangles, tom-toms, cymbals, and the hand bells. Robie had been chosen to beat the tempo on the small drum with the knucklebone, and Merelan glowed with pride at the fine and complex rhythm he managed.

She was disappointed that Petiron was too deep in discussion with Bristol, the Telgar Harper, to notice Robinton's performance. Bristol, like Petiron, was a composer, though his interests lay more in balladic works for the gitar than in full chorus and orchestra. His work was easy to remember and enjoyable to sing—though Merelan grimaced to even think so disloyally.

She was rather surprised, and certainly gratified, to see Bristol speaking to Robie later that afternoon. Robinton, his little face serious, was explaining something to the harper, who paid him the courtesy of attentive listening. If only Petiron would do the same . . .

She reminded herself that this was Turnover and the new Turn was nearly on them. Just one more day of freedom from the usual routine. She was pleased with her hour's recital of the old, traditional airs that had been part of these festivities since Fort Hold was founded. She'd had no trouble holding her audience and the applause had been generously prolonged though she had kept her encores to three. As MasterSinger she knew when enough was enough. There were plenty of other performers to take the Turnover stage.

Halanna had given young Donkin quite a few dances each evening, but she also partnered other lads, and Merelan was glad to see the girl relaxing and enjoying herself. Maybe that would restore the vibrancy that had initially characterized her rich voice.

Merelan had overheard Halanna saying something to her brother that puzzled and alarmed her.

"Petiron's very strict and makes you measure up to his standard," the girl told Landon with a little grimace. Then she added in an entirely different, almost spiteful tone, "I can't wait until he realizes that that kid of his has far more talent in his little finger than he's got in all his fancy notes and difficult tempi."

How had Halanna known of Robie's innate musicality? She'd never paid any attention to him; in fact, she had steadfastly ignored his existence when she knew the child was in the next room during her lessons with Merelan. And what satisfaction would Halanna take when the father discovered his son's talent?

That problem caused Merelan not a few anxious hours, though she kept telling herself that surely Petiron would be delighted to realize his son was musically inclined. "Inclined" was an understatement: Robinton seemed to absorb music as some children absorbed food. She was also aware that the child kept a cache of meticulously written tunes and airs; Washell and Bosler had told her so. They'd said that the music was "delightful." Then there were the glances they had exchanged. She had been so pleased to hear their good opinion of Robie's progress that perhaps she had failed to realize the significance of their exchange. That was when she first saw the drum he had made and used in the percussion orchestra at Turnover.

"Master Gorazde helped," he had informed her when he brought the drum home, "but I painted . . ." He ran a rather dirty finger along the blue and red lines that not too raggedly decorated the rim. "An' I cutted the skin oh so careful." His eyes had rounded as he used a pretend knife in his hand to demonstrate how hard it had been to cut the hide. "An' I nailed it." His mother did note that the brass nails were well aligned.

"Master Gorazde had me make dots where the nails go so they'd look even." He ran a finger along the shiny line. "Hard work." And he grinned up at her.

"Lovie, I don't know when I've seen a better one. I'll bet you could sell it at the Harper Gather stall!"

He clutched the drum to his chest, which took doing because it overlapped his chest. "No, not this one, my first 'stament, and I gotta improve a lot before Master Gorazde'll put a Harper stamp on it for sale."

With a pang to her heart, Merelan said nothing as he put it carefully on the shelf near his father's worktop. Maybe Petiron would notice and comment on it.

Two days later it was no longer in view, and when she looked for the drum, she finally found it hidden in his clothes chest. He never played it again.

"Drum? What drum?" Petiron asked, surprised when she casually mentioned it.

"The one Robie made for the percussion group at Turnover."

Petiron frowned, and she was so distressed by his genuine puzzlement that she wished she hadn't asked. That the little drum, so lovingly constructed, had been so carefully concealed ought to have been warning enough.

"Oh, that one," Petiron said, turning back to checking apprentice papers. "If Robinton really did have a hand in making it, I wouldn't have passed it for a Harper stamp."

Merelan abruptly rose and, murmuring that she must see Lorra, left the room before she either burst into tears or threw something at her insensitive spouse.

As she stormed downstairs and out into the crisp evening air, pausing only to throw a jacket over her shoulders, she knew that she would never, ever, mention Robie's efforts to Petiron again. He didn't deserve to have such a talented child.

"He's far ahead of the other youngsters," Kubisa told Merelan during the teacher's usual spring evaluation. "He's poring over any Record Ogolly lets him see. In fact, Ogolly's having him copy some of the more legible documents from the last Fall. I also don't think it's wise to isolate him from his own age group. He needs their companionship. All children do. But I'll say this for him: he won't stand for any teasing or bullying."

"You don't have any problems with that, do you?"

Merelan knew that the apprentices were often apt to pick on a lad who tried to push himself forward, and occasionally they would taunt a slower boy, but the masters kept a tight rein on any physical violence and chastised culprits for verbal harangue. Some of the final-year apprentices were apt to take grudges against one another, but those were generally settled by a wrestling match overseen by a journeyman. To be a harper conferred sufficient dignity and privilege that few would jeopardize their chance to achieve journeyman status by gross misconduct. Inevitably, there were subtle competitions during the fourth year.

"I have to be truthful, Merelan. Some of them are jealous of his quick mind."

"Well, I can scarcely punish him for that," Merelan said, trying to suppress a spurt of outrage.

Kubisa held up both hands in simulated defense. "Easy, mother, and I won't tell you who, either," she added before Merelan could open her mouth. "That's for me to know and handle. And I have. I ask Rob to take one of the slower ones off to hear their lesson. He's actually very patient—more so than I would be with that rascal, Lexey."

"Lexey? Bosler's youngest?"

"I know you know that Lexey has learning difficulties, but Rob has him repeat his lessons until he knows them by heart." Kubisa sighed. "Sometimes late life babies are a little . . . backward. And Rob made up another tune, one that Lexey can actually remember, to help him with place names." She reached into the folder and brought out a scrap of hide, cleaned so often that it was almost transparent, and handed it to Merelan. "Robie's a caring child and a born teacher."

The MasterSinger had no trouble identifying the writer of the tiny, precisely placed notes and hummed the tune. Simple and very easy, up the C scale and then down by thirds.

Fort was first, South Boll then
Ruatha came and Tillek, too.
Benden next and north Telgar . . .

Easy enough for a child to sing, but effective with the tune itself as an aid to memory.

"That's not bad," Merelan said.

"Not bad?" Kubisa stared at her in disgust. "For a child five Turns old? It's incredible. Washell wants me to use it in class as a Teaching Ballad."

"He does?"

"He does, and we don't intend to tell Petiron, either." Kubisa's tone was almost defensive. "I never ask Rob to do these. He just does them. Should I discourage him, Merelan?" She couldn't quite keep her expression neutral.

"No, don't discourage him, Kubisa. And thank you for your understanding."

The interview troubled Merelan for several days but she could see no way to mention Robie's abilities to Petiron. As usual, he had music he had to compose—this time for an espousal at Nerat. He planned a duet between Merelan and Halanna, and a very ambitious quartet, making use of a fine young tenor who would soon be walking the tables to become a journeyman. Petiron was always bemoaning the loss of any good tenor voice, and Merelan entertained the wry hope that Robie might end up in the tenor range as an adult. At least he sang on key in his childish treble. Even if his father never noticed. These were the times when she was very glad that she wasn't able to bear more children, or foster them.

That spring young Robinton had a revelation that made a tremendous impact on his mind: he met dragons.

He'd always known they existed, and once in a while, a wing would be seen flying in formation high overhead. He knew that Fort Weyr had been empty for several hundred Turns and no one knew why. He knew, from Teaching Songs and Ballads, why there were dragons: that they kept Thread away—though he didn't understand why Thread was so dangerous. People's clothes were made of thread, and they wouldn't wear something that was dangerous to them, would they? When he asked Kubisa about it in class, she said that Thread was a living organism, not spun and woven as was the undangerous thread that went into clothing. This bad Thread fell from the sky and hungrily ate anything living it touched, from grass to runner- and herdbeasts, and even people. Her listeners got very still at that, and no one even squirmed when she went on to explain how dragons kept Thread away from Halls and Holds. However, she ended on a bright and pleasant note: that bad Thread was not likely to bother them and they might live their whole lives without seeing it fall from the skies.

"Then why," the logical Robie asked, "do we keep singing about it?"

"In appreciation of those times when the dragons did keep the danger away," she said at her most reassuring.

Robinton asked his mother about Thread and got much the same answer, which really wasn't sufficient to satisfy his curiosity. If the dragons were so important, and they were still flying the skies of Pern, they were there to keep Thread away. They *were* keeping it away, but there weren't as many as there used to be—not with five Weyrs empty. Would they be enough if Thread came?

Lexey had told him once—Lexey talked a lot to Rob because he would listen to him—that his mother kept telling him that if he didn't behave better, they'd leave him out for Thread to get.

"You know so much, Rob. Would it?" Lexey asked plaintively, scared enough of the threat most times that it achieved the object of making him more obedient—at least for a few days.

"I never heard of it being done to anyone, no matter how bad you are. And 'sides, there isn't any Thread in the skies right now."

"But, if I was bad enough, would it come to get me?"

"Hasn't yet, has it?" was Robinton's logical reply. "You were awful bad yesterday, making a mess with the colors when you were told to clear them up."

"Yes, I was." Lexey grinned in retrospect, thoroughly pleased with himself. "But it was so fun." He'd smeared every surface in the classroom while Kubisa was out on an errand. She'd made him clean it all up—which was almost as much fun for Lexey as doing it—but he'd had a real scolding from her and his mother for the state of his clothes. "Mother was real mad at me last night." But that seemed to give him a satisfaction that Robie couldn't understand. He always tried very hard not to upset either his mother or his father—especially his father.

Lexey's paint smearing occurred the day before the dragons came, so they were sort of on top of Robie's mind when they came circling down into the big Harper Hall courtyard. His parents were busy packing for their trip to Nerat so he'd been told to go outside and play. He always missed his mother, but it would be nice to stay with Kubisa and her daughter Libby, where he could sing and play his pipe or his drum without worrying about annoying his father. It was his turn to hop-it without smudging the chalk lines on the flags, and his attention was utterly focused on the movement of his feet—until Libby made him miss the longest hop by suddenly pointing skyward in astonishment.

"Oh, look, Robie!" she cried.

"That's not fair . . ."

His complaint died as he realized that the dragons soaring above were coming closer to the Harper Hall, rather than the Hold, where they usually landed. Half a wing of dragons—six of them. As they swept closer, backwinging, their hind legs stretched downward to land in the Harper Hall rectangle, Robie, Libby, and Lexey pressed themselves tightly against the wall to stay out of the way. As it was, two of the dragons had to land outside, since the four made the big quadrangle suddenly appear very small.

The ridged tail of a bronze was so close to Robie that he

could reach out and touch it. Which he did, greatly daring, while Lexey regarded him with staring eyes, aghast at his impudence.

"You'll get left out for Thread for sure, Robie," Lexey whispered hoarsely, pressing his sturdy body as close to the stone wall as he could, well away from the dragon's tail.

"He's soft," Robie whispered back, surprised. Runnerbeasts were soft, and the spit canines, but watch-whers had hard hides, sort of oily. At least the Harper Hall's ol' Nick did. Were watch-whers another kind of dragon, the way runnerbeasts were another kind of herdbeast?

No, they most certainly are not, a voice said in his mind. The dragon turned his huge head to see who had touched him, causing Lexey to hiss in alarm and Libby to whimper a bit in terror. *Very different from dragons entirely.*

"I do apologize. I didn't mean to insult you, bronze dragon," Robie said, giving a jerky little bow. "I've never seen one of you up close before."

We do not come as often to the Harper Hall as we used to. It had to be the dragon speaking, Robie decided, because the deep voice couldn't have come from anyone else nearby. The rider had dismounted and was standing on the steps talking to Robie's mother and father.

"Are my mother and father going to ride on you to Nerat?" Robie knew that was why the dragons had come, to take all the harpers to Nerat for the espousal. His mother had told him that. Going a-dragonback meant they didn't have a long land journey to make, so they wouldn't be away long, and besides, it was a great honor.

They are harpers? the dragon asked.

"Yes, my mother's MasterSinger Merelan and my father is Master Petiron. He writes the music they're going to sing."

We look forward to hearing it.

"I didn't know dragons liked music," Robie said, greatly surprised. That had never been mentioned with all the other things he'd learned about dragonkind.

Well, we do. So does my rider, M'ridin. Robie could not miss the affection with which the dragon named his rider. *He asked especially to convey your mother and father. It will be an honor for us to take a MasterSinger to Nerat.*

"*Who* are you talking to?" Libby asked, her eyes still wide with fright for Robie's presumptuous behavior toward the huge and powerful creature.

"The dragon, a 'course," Robie said, having no real sense of doing something unusual. "You'll be careful with them, won't you, dragon?"

Of course!

Robie was certain the dragon was laughing inside. "What's so funny?"

I have a name, you know.

"Oh, I know that all dragons have names, but I've only just met you so I don't know your name." Robie turned his head ever so slightly to be sure his friends were observing how brave he was. And courteous.

Cortath is my name. What is yours, little one?

"Robie . . . that is, Robinton, and you will fly my parents very carefully, won't you?"

Of course I will, young Robinton.

Greatly reassured by that, Robie took advantage of this unparalleled opportunity and asked, "Will you be fighting Thread when it comes back?"

The tail gave such a convulsive twitch that it nearly swept both Lexey and Robinton, who were nearest, off their feet. The dragon swerved his body around so that his great head, with its many-faceted eyes swirling with a variety of colors rapidly turning into orange and red, came closer to Robie.

Dragons always *fly when Thread is in the sky* was the unequivocal answer.

"You know the song then?" Robie asked, delighted.

But, before Cortath could answer, his rider was at his head, turning it back so that he could introduce the bronze to Merelan and Petiron, standing beside him. A nervous apprentice hovered discreetly behind them, carrying their various sacks.

"Robinton, what are you doing back there?" his father

ANNE MCCAFFREY

demanded, noticing him at last and gesturing for him to get out of the way.

"We were just playing hop-it, only Cortath landed in the middle . . ." At the boy's words, the great dragon Cortath courteously moved his feet. "It's all right, Cortath. You smudged the lines a bit with your tail, but we can fix it when you leave."

"Robinton!" His father roared, scowling his amazement. Robinton risked a nervous glance at his mother and saw her slight smile. Why was his father angry with him? He hadn't really been doing anything *wrong*, had he?

"Cortath says he's enjoyed conversing with your son, Master Petiron," M'ridin said with a reassuring chuckle. "There aren't that many children these days who will, you know."

Robinton's sensitive ears caught the plaintive note in the tall, bronze rider's voice. He opened his mouth to say that he'd be happy to talk to Cortath any time, when he saw his mother raise her finger in her signal for him to be silent and noticed the deepening scowl on his father's face. So he looked anywhere but at the adults.

"Out of the way now, boy," his father said, gesturing urgently.

Robinton scooted off toward the Hall, Libby and Lexey well in front of him, all too relieved to be allowed to leave.

"Good-bye, Cortath," Robinton said. Seeing the dragon turn his head to follow him, he waved his fingers in farewell.

We will meet again, young Robinton, Cortath said clearly.

"Shards, Rob, you were lucky," Lexey said enviously.

"And brave," Libby put in, her blue eyes still as wide as saucers in her freckled face.

Robie shrugged. He was probably lucky he hadn't been close enough to his father for a smack at bothering a dragon, but he didn't think he'd been particularly brave. Though he should not, perhaps, have compared a *dragon* to a watch-wher! He'd caught the insulted note in the dragon's voice, and he guessed he was lucky Cortath had deigned to speak with him, instead of just lashing out with his tail at the presumptuous boy.

"Did you hear what Cortath told me?" he asked his friends.

"They're leaving," Lexey said, pointing as the dragons suddenly leaped skyward. As the great wings swirled up dust and grit from the courtyard, the children hastily turned away to protect their faces. When they turned back, rubbing dirt from their eyes, the dragons had already risen above the high, pitched roof of the quadrangle. Robinton waved frantically, recognizing Cortath's bright bronze coat and his passengers, but he didn't think even his mother was looking down just then. The next moment, all had disappeared and the courtyard looked emptier than ever. He felt oddly sad that the dragon had gone—as if he had missed something very important but he didn't know what it was. He realized that he didn't really want to know if his friends had heard the dragon, too. After all, *he* had been the one who had done the talking, so it was *his* special encounter. He was not covetous by nature, but some things you kept to yourself, because they were *yours*, *your* doing, and should be savored quietly.

If, later, Lorra noticed that Robinton wasn't as talkative as he usually was with her, she chalked it up to his parents' absence. At least, his mother's absence. That didn't explain the odd little happy smile on his face as if he were enjoying some secret thought. She liked taking care of young Rob. He was no trouble at all, especially when he would, as he did now, take himself to a corner in the kitchen and play on the pipe that was always tucked into his waistband. The tune he played wasn't familiar to her, but then, he was always making tunes up. She didn't have the time, just then, to find out if he'd made up a new one. But later, as she put him to bed, she asked about it.

"Yes, about dragons," he said sleepily.

"You were in the courtyard when they came? Of course, you were, saying goodbye to your parents," Lorra said. She snugged his bed fur up against his chin. "You must play it for me sometime."

"No, it's all mine," he mumbled, and Lorra wasn't sure if she had heard him right. He usually couldn't wait to play her a new tune . . . because, as she thought with some acidity, *she* listened, even if his father did not. But he was asleep before she could ask him what he meant.

Late in the autumn, when everyone knew that there was a clutch of eggs on the Hatching Ground at Benden Weyr, Robinton met dragons for the second time. They came on Search. He already knew about Search, since it was the subject of a Teaching Ballad, about the duty of Hall and Hold to allow any person the dragons chose to go to the Weyr. Most of those who went to a Weyr became dragonriders, a high honor. If dragons liked music, as Cortath had told him they did, maybe they'd like Robinton's tunes and no one would object to having a dragonrider who had musical training. By the time he was old enough to be Searched, he'd be at least a second-year apprentice.

When the wing landed in Fort Hold's courtyard, he was playing—hop-it again, actually—with Lexey, Libby, Curtos, and Barba. Barba was not his favorite playmate—she was awful bossy—but the moment the dragons landed, she started shrieking and ran into the Hall. Robinton ran, too: right for the dragons.

"Cortath?" he called out, racing across the vast courtyard as fast as he could toward the three bronzes who had landed to one side. He ducked in among the greens and blues, completely unaware that it was actually the greens and blues who were sensitive to those who might make good Impressions.

Cortath is not here today.

Robie stopped short, breathing hard as he realized that, indeed, his good friend was not there. "But I wanted to talk to him," he said, almost in tears with disappointment.

I will tell him a harper boy regretted his absence.

"I'm not a harper . . . yet," Robinton admitted, identifying the not-so-bright bronze as the one who had spoken to him. "Would you mind my talking to you? If you've nothing better to do for a moment? May I ask your name?" And he executed a half bow to show he was being respectful.

You may. I call myself Kilminth and my rider is S'bran. What is your name?

As if you'll remember, said another dragon voice. It was the very dark bronze one. *It is only a child.*

Who hears dragons when they speak, so I will talk to him while our riders are busy. It is nice to talk to a child who hears.

He's not old enough to be Searched.

Don't mind Calanuth, Kilminth told Robie in a somewhat supercilious tone. *He's too young to have much sense.*

Who's talking about having some sense?

Oh, curl up in the sun, and then Kilminth lowered his head down to Robinton.

Robie was a touch nervous at the size of that head, but the eye nearest him—almost bigger than his sturdy little-boy body—was green and circling idly. He could see himself reflected over and over again in the facets closest to him, making him slightly dizzy. The upper facets, however, reflected the sun and the sky. Did seeing all those different things make a dragon dizzy, too?

No, but it helps us to see Thread coming from above us when it falls.

"When is it going to?"

The dragon seemed to consider this question for such a long moment that Robinton wondered if he should have asked it.

The Star Stones tell us that.

"They talk?" Robinton didn't know about Star Stones yet. He knew about the Eye and Finger Rocks, but not Star Stones.

They are the Star Stones.

"Oh."

The dragon swung his head up, staring at a distant mountaintop. The maneuver was a bit frightening to a small boy so close to the ground, but he wouldn't have budged just then for anything. Talking to another dragon was too precious to be scared of. *Have you not seen the Star Stones at Fort Weyr?*

"No one's allowed up at the Weyr," Robinton said, eyes wide. *Ah.*

"Why does that make you sad, Kilminth?" Robie asked.

The dragon lowered his head again, the eye closest to him tinged with darkness; sadness, Robinton thought.

The Weyr has been empty so long.

"Will anyone come back to it?" That's what Robinton thought the dragon wanted to know.

When Thread falls again.

"So, there's one brave lad here at Fort Hold, is there?" A tall rider, skinnier than Cortath's, came up and tousled Robinton's hair.

"I'm from the Harper Hall, bronze rider S'bran," Robie replied.

"Oh, my fine friend here's been chatting with you that you know my name?" S'bran hunkered down, on a level with Robie. His blue eyes were twinkling. "Hall or Hold, you're a right one. Want to be a dragonrider when you grow up?"

"I'd like to, S'bran, but I'm to be a harper."

"Are you now?"

Robinton nodded his head emphatically. "My mother says I'll make the best harper ever. Can one be a harper and be a dragonrider, too?"

S'bran laughed and Kilminth's eyes whirled slightly faster. Robinton's jaw dropped. Was that how dragons laughed?

No, we laugh like this, and the sound that came from Kilminth's throat was just like S'bran's.

Robinton was delighted and giggled. "I didn't know dragons laugh."

The infectiousness of his giggle made both rider and dragon laugh again, the rider's a full third higher than the dragon's. Robinton was charmed by the harmony.

"C'mon, S'bran," another rider yelled. "We've three more stops to make today, you know."

"All right, all right, I'm coming," S'bran said. Unfolding from his crouch, he gave Robinton's hair a second friendly rubbing. Then he leaped to the short forearm Kilminth raised and was lifted high enough to throw his leg over the next-to-last ridge on the dragon's back. "Best stand back, laddie. This big fellow of mine will raise a lot of dust."

Robinton scurried to one side, but swerved the instant he heard the sound of wings beating. Raising his forearm to protect his face from the sand and grit, he lifted his other arm in a farewell salute.

Another time, young harper, he heard Kilminth say, and then they had all spiraled high enough to go *between.* Once again Robinton felt the same sort of odd emptiness that had followed Cortath's departure. He sighed deeply. They hadn't told him if he *could* be a harper and a dragonrider. So that probably meant he couldn't be. Which would please his mother. She had set her heart on his being a harper, and that would take a lot of hard work and many years. He might even be too old the next time there were eggs on the Hatching Ground. There was only the one queen, and she didn't clutch that often.

Scuffing his way through the neat drifts that the dragon wings had made of the dirt on the courtyard, he returned to the Hall but not to the game. He wanted to be by himself and recall every word Kilminth had said to him. And every word Cortath had said to him, as well. Those two incidents were so very, very special to him, and truly his alone.

"Did I see you out in the Fort yard when the dragons were there?" his mother asked when she joined him for supper. She'd been teaching during the Search.

"Yes. The bronze calls himself Kilminth," he said, but that was as much as he intended to say. He filled his mouth with beans so he wouldn't be able to answer another question.

"That's nice," she said, nodding in approval of his eating so well. Sometimes he didn't have much of an appetite, but he did tonight. "Did you know they found two lads on Search? One from here and one from the Hold."

"Who went from here?" The sudden notion that a harper could be Searched startled Robinton so much that he spoke with his mouth full and his father reprimanded him.

"A second-year apprentice, Rulyar, from Nerat," his mother answered.

"He plays gitar and sings tenor," Robie said, secretly delighted. Maybe he *could* be a dragonrider and a harper.

"Fancy Robinton knowing that," Petiron remarked, surprised.

"Oh, Rulyar's minded Rob a time or two during evening rehearsals," Merelan said off-handedly. "Told me that he missed his small brothers," she added, glancing at her son with the look that meant he wasn't to mention that Rulyar had been teaching him gitar fingering for the last few months. Robie would miss Rulyar; he hoped that his mother could find someone else to teach him.

That night, he dreamed of dragons, sad and tired ones who were trying to tell him something, only he couldn't hear them. It was as if his ears were clogged with the sands of the courtyard. And they wanted so very much for him to hear what they were saying—something especially for him to know! Then he saw Rulyar, clear as day, on a brown dragon, and Rulyar waved at him, urgently trying to say something, too, but the distance between them was too great for Robinton to hear.

He was somewhat amazed, a sevenday later, when he heard that Rulyar had Impressed a brown dragon who called himself Garanath. The Fort Hold boy had Impressed a green.

"That was to be expected," he heard his father say, but he didn't dare ask why that was expected.

Chapter 5

▼▼▼▼▼▼▼▼▼▼▼▼▼▼▼▼▼▼▼▼▼▼▼▼▼▼▼▼▼▼▼▼▼▼▼▼▼

R obinton was nine when his father, looking for some musical score, came across those Merelan kept safely in her worktop drawer.

"Whose scribblings are these?" he demanded, pausing to read the top one. Without even noticing that his wife was speechless, he looked at two more before tossing the tight roll back in the drawer. She seemed stuck in the doorway, an open message in one hand, a very odd expression on her face.

"What are you looking for in my desk?" she asked, fighting to keep her voice reasonable. She was furious with him for discarding the—to her—priceless examples of her son's musical genius, let alone going through her things.

"Any blank sheets. I've run out," he said, irritably pawing through the variety of objects, rather disgusted by the clutter. "You really ought to clean this out once in a while, Mere."

"I keep cleaned pieces there, in plain sight," she said, enunciating each word with angry clarity and pointing with a stiff finger to the box on the top of her desk.

"Oh, yes." Lifting several out, he began to examine each one. "Mind if I borrow these?"

"Only if you replace what you take." She was having difficulty remaining calm and had mangled the message into a ball.

"Well, no need to get huffy," he said, suddenly noticing her stiff posture and angry glare. "I'll get more at lunch." He started out of the room and then turned back. "Who did write those tunes? You?" He smiled in an effort to appease her anger. "Not bad."

She was so angry at his condescending smile and tone that she blurted out the truth. "Your son wrote them."

Petiron blinked in astonishment. "Robie wrote those?" He started back to her worktop, but she moved swiftly from the door to stand in front of it. "My son is already writing music? You're helping him, of course," he added, as if that explained much.

"He writes them with no help from anyone."

"But he must have had some help," Petiron said, trying to reach around her for access to the drawer. "The scores were well-written, even if the tunes are a trifle childish." Then his jaw dropped. "How long has he been writing tunes?"

"If you were any sort of a father to him, paid any attention to what he does, ever asked him a single question about his classes," Merelan said, letting rip all her long-bottled-up frustration, "you'd know he's been writing *music*"—she stressed the word—"for several years. You've even heard the apprentices singing some of the melodies."

"I have?" Petiron frowned, unable to understand either of his mate's shortcomings: not telling him about his own son's musicality and not informing him that *apprentices* were learning songs written by his own son. "I have!" he said, thinking back to the tunefulness he'd heard from Washell's classes. Of course, the songs were suitable to the abilities of the age group but . . . He stared at Merelan, coming to grips with a sense of betrayal that he had never expected from her, his own spouse. "But why, Merelan? Why keep his abilities from me? His own father?"

"Oh, so now he's your son, instead of mine," Merelan snapped back. "Now that he shows some prowess, he's all yours."

"Yours, mine, what difference does it make? He's what— seven Turns old?"

"He's *nine* Turns old," she snarled, and stalked out of the room, slamming the door hard behind her.

Petiron stood staring at the closed door, the echo of the definitive slam ringing in his ears, the hand that held the clean sheets held up in entreaty.

"Well, I never . . ." And he sank back against the worktop, struggling to cope with her attitude and this incredible revelation about his—no, *their*—son. He let a full breath escape, trying to assimilate the revelation, as well as his spouse's bewildering accusations. Then he shook himself and returned to his study, anxious to transcribe it from the sandtable. But as he sat down, he found himself unable to pick up where he had left off, not after Merelan's stunning disclosure.

If a nine-Turn-old boy had composed those tunes, youthful and simple as they seemed in his cursory glance at them, then his—their—son already had sufficient musicality to warrant serious training. Their son was *nine*? How *had* the Turns gone by so quickly? Of course, inundated by music as the child had been, he would undoubtedly have absorbed certain facets of basic education. His little tunes might only be variations on themes he had heard, rather than original. But what had upset Mere so much? Why had she taken such offense at his mistaking the boy's age? Well, he would certainly look more closely at that roll of music. Even if they proved only to be variations, that was creditable enough to require some special tutoring to hone a perhaps genuine gift up to a good professional standard. Why, his son could be a journeyman!

The thought unexpectedly pleased Petiron, and he realized that he had never given much thought to Robinton's future. One didn't, did one, until a child approached his teens and an apprenticeship. Although Petiron thought himself well able to be impartial toward his own flesh and blood when it came to giving the boy proper musical education, he might run into some criticism. It might be better if he apprenticed Robinton to one of the better traveling masters—at a good Hold, where the boy would learn to appreciate his own Hall the better by comparison. Yes, that was a good solution, and it would leave both himself and Merelan more time for their important work.

Merelan had been oddly distracted lately. She needed to concentrate on the more important aspects of her general teaching.

Where had she put those tunes? They'd been to the left in the drawer. He began to rummage about. She was usually very precise where music was concerned, but the contents of the drawer were in considerable disarray. There was no sign of the roll. She must have taken it with her when she had been so incensed with him for not knowing Rob's age. But however did a man relate to his son until the boy was old enough to understand his father's precepts and philosophies? Able to appreciate his father's achievements? Able to accept his father's training? No, Petiron decided at that instant, he would keep Robinton under his direction, to be sure that he received the requisite training. Nor would Petiron make a favorite of his son in the Hall simply because of their relationship. The boy would have to measure up to the same standards as every other apprentice . . .

"Robinton!" he called as he strode purposefully to the boy's small room in their quarters. The door was ajar and the room rather neat, considering that a child lived in it. The bed was made, the few toys were neatly stacked on the shelf; and then he noticed the pipes beside the toys, and the small harp case. Someone else was teaching his son how to play the harp!

Now Petiron began to feel a righteous anger. Merelan was behaving in a most peculiar fashion. First by her silence over Robinton's ability and then by letting someone else train *his* son . . .

He strode out of the room and out of his quarters; he was starting down the stairs when Master Gennell came out of his rooms at the top of the steps.

"Ah, Petiron, I need a moment of your time . . ."

Petiron stopped, glancing down the steps, wondering where Merelan had gone in such a huff and where his son might be. The MasterHarper had the right to a moment of his time whenever he so chose. This was not a good moment, however, for any interview, no matter how pressing. For once common sense, rather than professional courtesy, prompted the MasterComposer. He had to find both his spouse and his son.

Now! Before more damage could be done in the matter of Robinton's training.

"Now, Petiron," Master Gennell said, frowning when he saw the hesitation, the conflict of duties.

"With respect, Master . . ." Petiron began, barely keeping his tone civil.

"*Now*, MasterComposer," Gennell said firmly.

"My son . . ." Petiron tried the only viable excuse available.

"It is about your son I wish to speak with you," Gennell said, and his frown so surprised Petiron that he found himself altering his direction toward the MasterHarper's rooms.

"About Robinton?"

Gennell nodded and ushered the MasterComposer into his workroom, shutting the door firmly behind him.

"About Robinton." He waved Petiron to a seat before he sat, opposite, clasping his hands in a way that indicated a matter of grave importance was about to be discussed. "As MasterHarper I have certain duties and responsibilities toward those in my Hall." Petiron nodded and Gennell went on. "I have assigned Merelan to Benden Hold for the next year."

"But you can't—" Petiron half rose from the chair in surprised indignation.

"I can and I have," Gennell said in such a flat tone that Petiron sank back again. "Oh, I know you are already composing new arias only she has the voice to sing, but I think you've been overworking her—" And Gennell held up one finger. "—and have been totally ignoring your son."

"My son . . . I need to discuss my son with you, Gennell. He has written—"

Gennell held up a second finger. "You are apparently the only one in the entire Hall who is unaware of Robinton's genius."

"Genius? A few simple tunes . . ."

"Petiron!" Gennell's voice echoed the impatience in his scowl. "The boy reads music—even music you have written—and plays it on pipe or gitar without hesitation or error. He has made instruments that are good enough to have a Harper stamp."

"That drum he made was not up to standard," Petiron began.

"At that, his first drum was nearly good enough. The others he has made in the past few months have already been sold. So have the multiple pipes and his first flute—"

"The pipes are in his room . . ."

"He is already considered an apprentice by the rest of the Hall's masters, MasterComposer Petiron," Gennell said. "We are careful to take him only at his own pace—and his progress has him ahead of most second-year apprentices."

Petiron's mouth dropped. "But he's *my* son . . ."

"A fact that you only seem to have recognized very recently," Gennell said in much the tone he would take with an erring journeyman. Then his expression softened. "You are the best composer we have had in the Hall in over two hundred Turns, Petiron, and you are honored as such. It is your single-mindedness that can produce such extravagant and complex music, but it has also given you less than perfect vision about other, equally important matters: such as your son and your spouse. Therefore, since I had a request from Benden Hold for a master in the vocal traditions, I have assigned Merelan to the post. At her request. As the Benden Lord Holder has children Robinton's age, he will accompany his mother."

Petiron rose indignantly. "I'm his father—have I no say in this?"

"Until a boy child is twelve, it is traditional for him to be in his mother's care unless fostered to a family."

"This has all been conducted with precipitous and unnecessary haste," Petiron began, clenching and unclenching his fists, trying to control the rage that was boiling up inside him. Not only were his paternal rights being denied, but why was his spouse, usually so understanding, suddenly rejecting him?

"On the contrary, Master Petiron," Gennell replied, shaking his head slowly and sadly, "the decision was neither an easy nor an abrupt one."

"But . . . she was there!" Petiron waved a shaking hand

toward his own quarters on the level above. "She cannot have gone far . . ."

"A Benden dragon arrived this morning with a further entreaty from Lord Maidir for her to accept the posting, especially as his contracted harper, Evarel, has been advised to rest by the Healer. She took the message up to your quarters to discuss it with you. I admit to being surprised that she returned and accepted it. She told me that she felt it was in both her interests and Robinton's that she do so."

"Because I didn't know my son's age?" Petiron heard his voice rise to tenor range in surprise.

Gennell blinked in such an honest reaction that Petiron had to accept that *that* subject had not come up. Still, Merelan's acceptance of any posting away from him, away from the Hall, was so uncharacteristic of her that he could think of no reason at all beyond that rather trite one.

"About that I do not know, Petiron, but she and the boy will already have reached Benden Hold. She asked Betrice to pack up what she and Robinton will need. Doubtless you will hear from her shortly with a private letter."

Petiron stared at his MasterHarper, having great difficulty absorbing what he had just heard.

"If it is a mother's right to have her child until he is twelve, then I shall not interfere with her maternal instincts," he said so harshly that Gennell flinched. "At twelve I shall have him." With that, both promise and threat, he turned on his heel and stalked out of the MasterHarper's workroom.

Chapter 6

▼▼▼▼▼▼▼▼▼▼▼▼▼▼▼▼▼▼▼▼▼▼▼▼▼▼▼▼▼▼▼▼▼▼▼▼▼▼▼

His mother never did explain exactly why she came to his classroom that morning, to speak quietly and briefly to Kubisa, whose face gave away nothing. She just gave him his heavy jacket to put on, while she cleared the contents of his desk into a carisak, adding the roll of things that Kubisa handed her.

There was something about his mother's attitude that warned Robinton not to ask questions. The rest of the children in the classroom were whispering excitedly; two had even left their seats and were peering out the window.

That was when Robinton saw the wing claws of a bronze dragon in the courtyard.

"I don't think you'll mind riding a dragon today, dear," his mother said, as she carefully closed the classroom door behind her. She had the half-full carisak clutched under her arm and took his hand to guide him down the steep steps.

"Ride a dragon?" He stumbled in surprise, and was glad of the tight hold she had on his hand.

"Yes, we're going to Benden Hold. Lord Maidir sent a dragon for us."

"He sent a dragon for *us*?"

Robinton was floored. Yet there were Betrice and Masters Bosler and Washell, handing up carisaks to the bronze rider, who was securing them to the dragon's harness. As his mother briskly rushed him across the court to the dragon, he looked about for his father.

"Your father's not coming with us," his mother said with an odd catch to her voice. Before he could protest, she had swung him off his feet and up to the bronze rider's waiting arms. Then she mounted and sat behind him.

I am Spakinth and my rider is C'rob. Cortath and Kilminth say you hear us.

"I'm going to get to ride you?" Robinton asked, his voice nearly a squeak in his excitement.

"You're certainly getting to ride my dragon," the rider said. Robinton tried to crane his head around and look up at C'rob. "Yes, I am," he said. Then he realized he was holding on to the neck ridge in front of him in a fierce grip, and instantly relaxed. "Oh, I beg your pardon! I didn't hurt you, did I?"

Of course not, the ridge is there to hold on to, Spakinth said in the same instant C'rob laughed and said, "You won't hurt a dragon that way, lad." And then he leaned to one side and regarded Robinton with raised eyebrows. "But then Spakinth is telling you, too, isn't he?" The rider seemed surprised.

Robinton grinned back, flexing his fingers around the ridge just for the feel of it. "Cortath and Kilminth have spoken to me, too."

"Have they . . ." And then C'rob's attention was taken by Merelan's arrival behind him. "Just hang onto my belt there, MasterSinger," the rider said. "I've your son safely tucked forward."

"Then may we leave?"

Robinton thought his mother must be as excited as he was to be mounted on a dragon, because her voice, when she answered, was quavery.

In the next instant, his head was thrown back against C'rob's chest as Spakinth sprang upward. Robinton barely heard himself let out a whoosh of "ohhhhhh" over the noise the wings made . . . like all the sheets in the Harper Hall flapping in the wind on the laundry line.

He squealed again as Spakinth circled eastward, spiraling higher, the tall roofs of the Harper Hall buildings diminishing so fast he hadn't breath for a second cry of amazement as the spiral took them high over Fort Hold's massive precipice. Briefly he saw white faces turned skyward and wondered if they could recognize him perched in front of the dragonrider on bronze Spakinth.

"Don't be afraid, now, Robinton," C'rob said, almost shouting in his ear. "We're going *between* . . ."

And then they were! Robinton held his breath, far more terrified of the awful cold nothingness around him than of the worst of his childish nightmares.

I am here. You ride me with C'rob and the woman. I will keep you safe, young Robinton.

And before a scream of fear could rise in Robinton's throat, they were out of the cold and the black and wheeling above another Hold cliff.

"That's Benden below you, lad." C'rob patted his shoulder. "And not a peep out of you. Nor did you wet your breeches."

Robinton was stunned by such a shocking suggestion and stiffened under C'rob's hand. Very quietly, so not even Spakinth could hear and think badly of him, Robinton knew that, just a moment longer in frigid *between* and he might well have disgraced himself.

Many do, young Robinton, but never you.

And young Robinton sat up straighter and loosened the vise-like grip he found he had taken on the neck ridge. He hoped dragons didn't bruise, and he smoothed the places where his fingers actually had made an imprint. Spakinth said nothing, as he was busy landing, which required powerful backwinging to set himself down just in front of the steps up to the smaller outer court of Benden Hold.

"They're here! Spakinth and C'rob brought them. She's come!" And out of the wide open front door a crowd of children spilled.

Spakinth curved his neck and lowered his head toward those racing down the steps.

Always noisy, always noisy, the dragon said, more to himself than to either his rider or Robinton. Robinton was later to learn that C'rob had fathered five children at Benden Weyr, and consequently his dragon was well able to handle the swarm that converged on him, stroking his hide and his eye ridges when he lowered them enough.

Then Lord Maidir and Lady Hayara, who was carrying one child and obviously pregnant with another, came out to welcome the MasterSinger and her son. As Merelan slid down Spakinth's side, C'rob settled Robinton between the next two ridges up so he could stand on Spakinth's lifted foreleg and assist the boy to the ground. Holder children swarmed up the dragon's side—momentarily stunning Robinton with what seemed like rudeness to him—to untie the carisaks. They weren't the least bit afraid, as Libby and Lexey had been, but then, Robie thought, they'd be used to dragons at Benden Hold, since Benden Weyr was still inhabited. Each grinned at Robinton, identifying themselves politely, but he was so confused by the onslaught of new impressions and their enthusiasm that he couldn't remember who was who. Then his mother took him by the hand and led him to be formally introduced to the Holders.

He bowed before he shook hands, just as he'd been taught, and was rewarded with smiles.

"We want you to be happy here at Benden Hold," Lady Hayara said.

Robinton thought she looked very young, not much older than Halanna, and Lord Maidir looked older than even Master Gennell. Then Lord Maidir gestured for the stocky lad, standing just behind him, to come forward.

"This is Raid, my eldest son, MasterSinger," the Lord Holder said with pride, laying an arm across the boy's shoulders.

A shaft of totally incomprehensible envy swept Robinton. His father had never done that. His father didn't even touch him—that he could remember. And then a girl, not as old as Raid, pushed through to Raid's other side, neatly pushing

Lady Hayara aside. And Robinton caught a quickly hidden flare of dismay on Lady Hayara's face and the indifferent look on the girl's.

"And this is my eldest daughter," Lord Maidir said, "Maizella."

"I'm so glad you've come, MasterSinger," Maizella began in a fervent tone, and stepped forward to grab and cling to Merelan's hand, her eyes round with excitement and her voice coming out breathily.

"Our Maizella has a lovely voice," Maidir said, proudly, "and Raid, if you can overcome his shyness, has an excellent baritone. Falloner there, the one with all the curls, still has a fine clear treble . . ."

As Falloner was just then standing close to Robinton, he gave him a "what can you do with adults" shrug and grin—and that was their first meeting.

"Oh, you," Lady Hayara said, stepping closer to her spouse now that Maizella had moved.

Robinton sighed. He knew by the expression on Maizella's face and her stance that his mother was going to have trouble with this one. He saw by the quirk of his mother's mouth that she realized it, too. But Merelan smiled soothingly and said that she'd be delighted to teach any and all who wanted to learn how to sing properly.

"Actually, she shrieks more than she sings," Falloner said in a low voice to Robinton, and the merriment in his eyes was conspiratorial. "Did you like riding Spakinth? C'rob won the toss. He usually does." Then, when the lad saw that he had confused Robinton with this confidence, he added, "I'm weyr-bred, but my father insisted that I get some teaching here. So here I am."

"You're weyrbred?" Robinton eyed the lad.

"I am, and I don't have a tail or fangs, nor will I, even if I Impress a bronze." The boy's thin face momentarily stiffened with determination before the careless grin replaced it. "And I will. And be Weyrleader and save Pern from Threadfall."

"Really? Cortath said that dragons must fly when Thread is in the sky."

"You better believe it," Falloner said stoutly. Then he blinked in surprise. "Cortath spoke to you?"

"Falloner."

Both boys turned at Lord Maidir's voice.

"You know the quarters made ready for the MasterSinger and young Robinton," Benden's Lord went on. "Why don't you show him the way and take up his things?"

"Of course, Lord Maidir," Falloner said with quick courtesy. He turned to Robinton. "Which are yours?"

Robie looked at the pile on the steps and wasn't quite sure. Their departure had certainly been swift. Mother had packed for him.

"The two with the red straps," Merelan said, pointing and giving his shoulder a reassuring squeeze. "And that small one there." Robinton did recognize that as the one in which she had put the contents of his desk, and while that wasn't very long ago, it seemed to him that a great deal had happened in a very short time.

Falloner threw the school sack at him and then hefted the other two, though Robinton tried to take one from him.

"Nah, let me. This once," Falloner said and added, grinning, "You don't know how many steps there are to your quarters. C'mon."

They started into the Hold then, hearing Maizella and Raid squabble briefly over who was to have the honor of taking the MasterSinger's carisaks. The other youngsters were vying for the chance to show her the schoolroom, and the adults were attempting to contain all the youthful spirits and enthusiasm.

Robinton had been in the Great Hall of Fort Hold often enough to recognize immediately that Benden was not as big. Fort had been the first Hold; Benden had come much later and had had to be made without all the Ancients' equipment that would have made the job so much faster and easier. It faced southeast, so the Hall was quite sunny, and it was as big as the Harper Hall's main one.

"We're not supposed to use those stairs," Falloner said, pointing to an impressive flight that centered at the north end of the Hall, dividing at the first landing and then curving left and right. "Holder's family lives to the right, the outside tier." He led Robinton through a door to a little hallway. "These are what we use, and don't make a mistake and get caught taking the shortcut."

The Hall seemed to go up forever, where a dim rectangle cast some light down it, abetting the glowbaskets that were spaced along the walls. The steps seemed to have been carved out of the solid stone of the Hold and were slightly worn in places from centuries of use.

They seemed to be climbing a long way before Falloner struck to his right at what was actually the third landing. Then they were in a long corridor that stretched in both directions, covered with a thin padding that deadened the noise of their boots. Falloner turned left, and Robinton thought they were traveling parallel to the outer wall of the Hold. There were doors on either side of the corridor, though some of the glowbaskets clearly needed to be changed.

"One of the jobs we get," Falloner said, grinning over his shoulder at Robinton as they passed the third of several dull ones.

"At Harper Hall the apprentices have to do it," Robinton said, panting a bit as he tried to keep up with the longer-legged weyrboy.

"Lord Maidir's fair and so's Lady Hayara, so don't believe anything Maizella says about her," Falloner added. "How old are you?"

"Nine Turns."

"Good," Falloner said with approving relief.

"Why?" Robinton asked, but then they turned into a much broader corridor, its floor carpeted so they moved more quietly. It was just like the masters' level in the Harper Hall.

"We're nearly there," Falloner said, "and we beat the others here." He grinned in triumph and pushed wide the half-opened door, gesturing for Robinton to precede him.

"This is where we'll be living?" Robinton exclaimed, pivoting on one heel to see all around him. There were four high but narrow windows, letting sunlight spill into a room that was much bigger than theirs at the Harper Hall. There was even a standing harp in one corner, which made Robinton decide that this must be a schoolroom, too, which would account for its generous size—except there were no desks or enough tables to seat even half the children who had thronged the courtyard entrance.

"You'll be in here," Falloner told him, striding across the thick rugs to a door on the right. Robinton crossed quickly to join him and looked in at a room much the same size as his had been at home. He was much relieved. Falloner took his school sack from him and lobbed it to the bed and dropped the other two on the floor. Then, tugging Robinton by the arm, he took him across the room toward the two doors set in the left-hand wall. "Even have your own bath," he said, opening the inner-most door and uncovering a glowbasket to show the sanitary amenities. At home, they had a toilet and a wash basin in their quarters, but not a full bath like this, with a tub long enough for his height. His mother would love that.

The outer door opened into another bedroom, as grandly furnished but not as large as the main room, and still bigger than the one his mother and father shared at the Harper Hall.

He whistled in surprise and approval, turning his head this way and that to take in all the furniture and even the paintings hung on the walls.

"Will it do?" Falloner asked, cocking his head, obviously amused by Robinton's goggle-eyed inspection.

"Mother will certainly like it. She loves dark red things."

Then they heard voices in the hall, and the others arrived. Nodding in surprise to see that the two lads had arrived so quickly, Lady Hayara gestured for Merelan to precede her into the room.

"We even have a bathtub, Mother," Robinton exclaimed. "Over my head, at least!"

Merelan laughed at him, but behind her Maizella raised her eyebrows contemptuously. Robinton was about to bristle when Falloner winked at him, reminding him of what he'd said about the girl a few minutes before.

"More high than wide like ours at the Hall," he added defensively.

"We tap into the Weyr's heat source here at the Hold," Lady Hayara said, "which is such a blessing. So many holds have to heat bathing water. I do hope you'll be comfortable, Merelan," she added as she led the way to the larger bedroom. "I think there's enough room for a small bed in here, if you'd rather your son sleeps—"

"Goodness me," Merelan said with a laugh, "Robinton's much too big a lad not to have his own room."

Robinton wanted to put his tongue out at Maizella for the haughty expression on her face, but he knew his mother wouldn't like him to. She reminded him of Halanna, and he really didn't need to have to deal with another Halanna disliking him.

"Well, we'll let you get settled in then. Come on, children, you can make friends at suppertime," Lady Hayara said, resettling the child she carried in her arms as she gestured for the others to clear out. "Ah, I see there's a tray for you since I know you've missed your usual lunchtime coming here. We'll be eating in another two hours, you know, what with the time difference coming east and all."

Merelan smiled her gratitude and escorted her hostess to the door, the rest of the children following. When they were gone, she turned to Robie.

"Well!" she said with a big sigh, and then she smiled—a sad sort of smile—at her son. "Let me see your room, love."

"It's a lot like mine at the Hall, Mother . . ." And Robinton trailed off, the sadness in her smile suggesting he'd better not ask *why* they had left so abruptly and with no warning.

Though he did not follow her, his mother did look into his room in a perfunctory fashion.

"Did you and Falloner make friends on your way up?" she asked, wandering about the living room and touching this and that.

"He's weyrbred," Robinton replied, still somewhat awed.

"Yes, he is. And I hope he's as eager to learn as the others. That's why I'm here." And then she sat down in a chair and burst into tears.

Robinton rushed to her side, patting her arm and stroking her hair. His mother rarely cried. She hugged him to her, her tears soaking his shirt, but he knew only to hold on to her and repeat that they'd be fine, they were together, and Benden Hold seemed nice and the Lord Holders were so friendly and wanted them here.

"Yes, they do want us here, don't they?" she said finally, giving herself a little shake and sitting up straight. "I'm sorry to have sprung this on you so abruptly, Robie, but Lord Maidir's been after me to come and teach music to these very promising youngsters. Suddenly, I thought it might be a good idea for both of us to take a break from the Hall. Master Gennell thought so, too, and urged me to take the posting. And there was the dragon . . ."

"Spakinth is his name," Robinton said when she paused.

She smiled through the last of her tears. "How do you know that?"

"He told me."

"C'rob told you?"

"No, Spakinth."

She tilted her head to one side. "You can hear dragons?"

"Well, when they want me to, I do."

"Oh, Robie!" She embraced him tightly. "Not many do. It might even mean you'd Impress, and *that* would solve everything." She spoke the last over his shoulder as if more to herself than to him.

"But I could still be a harper, couldn't I?" He hadn't had a definitive answer to that question from the dragons. Maybe his mother would know.

"I think that depends on many things," she said, drying her eyes, and suddenly she seemed more like herself. "Like if there's a clutch when you're the right age. Dragons don't have as many eggs during an Interval, you see, and you're only Impressionable until you're twenty, and the weyrbred have preference. At least, you'll get to understand more about the Weyrs, and that's all to the good."

Again her remark was not meant for him, but he didn't mind because he'd like to know more about the Weyrs. The abandoned Fort Weyr was forbidden by order of Lord Grogellan. That might have been one reason why every boy had to go up there alone for a night when he turned twelve, or he'd be considered cowardly.

"Will I be able to visit the Weyr?" Robinton asked eagerly. That way, he'd know what a Weyr was like, and then an empty one wouldn't be as scary.

"I think that's likely. One of the reasons I'm here is to help C'gan, their current Weyrsinger. He desperately wants more training." His mother gave a little laugh. "I'll be so busy I won't—" She broke off and stood up. "Well, let's get ourselves settled in, shall we? Or are you hungry enough to sample what's here?"

Robinton spotted the large selection of sweet biscuits and pointed.

"Well, just two of them, so as not to spoil your appetite. I'll have one, too—they smell so good. Fresh . . . every bit as good as Lorra makes." And she chattered away as she insisted on helping him put his things away. "I didn't want to overload the dragon," she said, "so I didn't bring everything you own, love, but your newest drum and pipes . . . we've my gitar to practice on, and maybe we can get enough wood for you to start your own, because I know Master Bosler said you could start preparing the wood, which takes most of the time it takes to make a gitar, you know. I'm sure we can find gut for strings when it comes time to do that step. And your new Gather clothes, because they entertain quite a bit here at Benden, Lord Maidir and Lady Hayara being so popular on this coast. There's a schoolroom, too, so we'll just leave these in the carisak now, shall we? Now, that's done and you can help me."

As he did, Robinton knew that his mother hadn't brought many of her own clothes. Only one Gather dress and one of the long, fine dresses she'd use when she gave concerts. And while she had lots of new musical scores, mainly the ones she'd teach from, there was nothing in his father's familiar broad script. That was odd. His stomach felt a little queasy suddenly, and it wasn't from eating the sweet biscuits.

"Mother, will Father come visit us?"

She paused, her back to him at that moment, and slowly turned, her expression unusually bleak.

"That will be up to your father, Robinton," she said, and turned back to fuss with the things in the top drawer of the chest. "Likely he'll come to the Spring Gather here at Benden," she added in a totally different tone of voice, as if it made no difference to her at all. "Now, let's wash up, shall we? I think that soon enough it'll be time to eat." She gestured toward the fading light and then pulled the heavy drapes across each of the narrow windows, as if shutting out more than the end of this day.

At dinner that night, Robinton had a place with the Hold children. It was a crowded table for his age-group—he counted twenty-four—but Falloner had held a place for Robinton beside him.

"No, you got to take his things up," one of the Holder boys said, rushing to crowd into the space on Robinton's right. "Mother said we've all got to make him feel at home, and you had your chance."

"Rob and I are buddies," Falloner said loftily, "but you can sit on the other side, Hayon. He's Lady Hayara's oldest son," he added and started naming everyone at their end of the table. "Rasa's beside him, then there's Naprila, Anta, Jonno, and Drevalla on the other side."

Robinton had a moment to glance up at the head table where his mother sat beside Lord Maidir, with Raid on her other side and Maizella by her stepmother.

"They got graduated off the younglings' table last year," Falloner said with a sniff. He took the bread and board from the serving drudge and started cutting neat slices from the loaf, flipping them from the knife point up and down this end of the table until everyone had a piece. "Stew, I betcha," he added. His bet was a fair one, because the next thing to come was a big pot.

"My turn," Anta said, standing up and grabbing the ladle before he could.

"Fair enough, only don't slop," he said, sitting down again and shoving a friendly elbow into Robinton's side as he grinned.

The upper table was not receiving stew, Robinton noted, but bowls of soup first and then slices of what looked like wherry, sauces, dishes of vegetables, and individual loaves of bread. He also noticed that his mother was mushing her food around her plate instead of eating, although she was talking to both father and son and seemed her usual self. Except she didn't smile as much as she usually did at the head table in the Harper Hall. He didn't hear her laugh once. The stew was good, and so was the bread, and he was hungry. And the "afters" served at their table were small cakes and fruit that disappeared with amazing rapidity, though Robinton didn't see them all eaten at the table. Maybe his mother was getting special treatment what with her being MasterSinger, which he felt was only right and proper. Especially as he was getting specials, too.

His mother sang, too, after the head table finished eating. And there were good voices joining in the choruses, so he wondered why Benden Hold would need a MasterSinger of his mother's standing. A good journeyman would have done as well. No, she was also here to teach Maizella. Robinton wrinkled his nose: It was obvious from the loud way the girl was singing that she thought her voice was good. It wasn't bad, he had to admit, but she didn't need to shriek and she hadn't much breath control.

His mother sang only four songs, though, and smiled and nodded encouragingly when instruments appeared and she gestured for the musicians to come forward into a unit closer to the head table. There were two gitarists, a tall, pale older man and a younger one who looked enough like the older to be son or nephew; one violinist who played with his instrument held on his knee instead of under his chin, but his fingering was very good; a woman playing flute; two pipers, both young; and a drummer who had the sense to keep to a mute beat. Of course, when Merelan gestured encouragingly, the rest of the Hold sang the choruses to her first song. The harmonies weren't bad either, Robinton decided, though he didn't sing out as he would have done back in the Hall. Falloner sang lustily in a good strong alto treble, however, as did all the other younglings at the table—showing off to him, probably, but Robinton was used to the way new-come apprentices to the Harper Hall acted, so he pretended not to notice.

"It doesn't cost any marks to be gracious, no matter where you are or what you're doing," his mother was always saying. "No singer of a professional caliber would think of drowning out other singers" was another point she often made. Especially when she had been having all that trouble with Halanna. He hoped Maizella wouldn't be as difficult.

Although he knew all the words, Robinton didn't sing along with her in the new song she presented as her final one of this evening. Then she sweetly begged to be excused for such a short program, but she promised she would be more forthcoming when she'd caught up with Benden time.

She sat down to very enthusiastic applause and shouting.

Falloner then nudged Robinton and rose. "Can you find your way back to your room, Rob?" he asked. "That was the signal for us to get out of the Hall and let the adults have it to themselves."

Lady Hayara had risen, too, and gestured toward the younglings so that they all obediently rose and started to leave the Hall. His mother caught his eye and motioned him to wait for her.

"I'll go up with Mother," Rob said, though he would have liked more time to ask Falloner questions.

"You're lucky," Falloner said under his breath. "A room of your own. I have to sleep in with a half a dozen. Oh, well, I did at the Weyr, too," he added in a philosophical tone. "I'll see you tomorrow, I 'spect."

"Thanks, Falloner," Robinton said, a little shy but meaning his thanks. Falloner grinned a response as he started herding some of the younger ones ahead of him toward the inner staircase.

Robinton never did find out from his mother the real reason for their precipitous departure from the Harper Hall, but he did learn that no one at Benden Hold had ever expected the famous MasterSinger to come there. And because she curbed the loudness of Maizella's rather good basic voice, she was very welcome indeed, not just by the girl's disenchanted half brothers and sisters, but by many of the adults who resided in the Hold. Lord Maidir was a good man, and generally fair, but he adored his daughter, Maizella, who at sixteen hadn't the wisdom or common sense that characterized her brother, Raid. Robie found him a bit stuffy and prim, but Raid had inherited his father's sense of fair play and would take criticism from any of the more senior members of the large group of people who managed the big Holding. Unlike his sister, he was popular. And there was a discreet understanding that Hayon, Rasa, and Naprila, the older of Lady Hayara's children, were to be protected from Maizella, who either teased them outrageously or ignored them as the fancy took her.

Inured to such tactics as Robinton was, having survived Halanna's antics, he learned to smile and keep his tongue in his mouth. He had a sort of revenge a little later when his mother required Maizella to sing duets with him. He knew he had a good treble voice and had been more than adequately trained by Washell as well as his mother. In fact, he would have stepped into Londik's place as senior boy soprano when Londik's voice changed, but he'd also observed what happened to apprentices who flaunted their prowess. Besides which, his mother wouldn't have stood for such behavior from him for one moment longer than it took to twist his ear to remind him to keep his place.

Dealing with Halanna had also taught Merelan a trick or two about overdeveloped conceits.

"Sing with a child?" The girl's tone was insulting.

"Singing with a well-trained treble voice, which my son—"

Merelan paused briefly. "—has, will prove how much more he already knows about singing than you do. Shall we begin at 'Now is the time' . . . ?"

Merelan lowered her left eyelid just slightly at Robinton as she raised her arms to beat out the measure, and he was ready. He knew she meant that he should sing out now, something he had not done before, since he knew better than to dominate in group singing. Maizella almost missed her entrance, she was gawking so hard at him. Robinton enjoyed this moment of ascendancy and, from the susurrus of whispering from the rest of the class, so did the others.

Maizella, naturally, tried to drown him out, and his mother canceled the beat and called her to order.

"In duet singing, the voices must balance for the best effect. We know you can sing the crawlers out of their webs, Maizella, but there are none in this room." Merelan regarded those tittering with a stern eye. "From 'Now is the time'—and sing *with* the treble, not against him."

This time Maizella modulated the volume and even she could sense the effective difference—though she didn't, from the scowl on her face, appreciate it.

"That was much better, Maizella, much better. Let's see if we can blend in the third voice." And when the soprano line began, it was Merelan who sang it and showed, by her example, exactly what she had meant by balancing voices.

The rest of the children in the class clapped as the song ended.

"You didn't tell me you could sing like that," Falloner accused Robinton as they trotted out to the courtyard where they had a half hour's respite from lessons.

"You didn't ask," Robinton said, grinning.

"You been waiting to show Maizella up?"

"Not waiting," Robinton said, bouncing the large goal ball. There was a hoop set on a pole, and the aim was to see how often one could get the ball through the hoop each go. Rob was pretty good at goal ball but, just as he was aiming, he saw the dragons flying in a distant formation and missed the hoop entirely.

Falloner intercepted the ball from Hayon's hopeful hand and lobbed it neatly through the hoop, catching it deftly and returning to the white line to toss again.

Robinton ignored all that, keeping his eyes on the rapidly disappearing V of dragons.

"Better get used to seeing 'em in the sky, or you'll never get a turn at goal ball," Falloner said on their way back to the classroom after their recess.

"I suppose you're used to it," Robinton said, "but to see them like that, the way the music says, well, that was special to me."

Falloner gave his friend an odd look. "Yes, I guess it would be. Just like you singing as good as any harper I've ever heard is a surprise for me. Say, let's scare the watch-wher!" He grinned from ear to ear.

Robinton stared at him. "But you're weyrbred."

"So what? They're not dragons, and it's good fun to see how loud you can make it so—" Falloner never finished that sentence, because Robinton head-butted him to the dirt, then flopped down on his chest, holding a fist in readiness.

"I don't let watch-whers get teased, not at Fort, or the Hall, or here!" he said in a loud and forceful voice. "Say you won't?" And he cocked his arm further, ready to strike.

"But it's not hurting them . . ."

"If they scream, they hurt. Promise?"

"Sure, whatever you say, Rob."

"You mean it?"

"On my hope of riding a dragon!" Falloner said fervently. "Now let me up. I've a stone digging in my ribs."

Robinton gave his friend a hand up and then brushed him off. "Just don't let me catch you breaking your word."

"I gave it to you!" Falloner said in a surly tone. "Don't know what's got into you."

"I just don't like to hear them scream." Robinton gave a convulsive shake. "Goes right through my ears and down to my heel-bones. Like chalk on a slate."

"It does?" Now Falloner gave himself a shake at the thought of that sound. "Doesn't me, but . . ." He held his hands up defensively as Robinton made a fist again. "I'll keep my word." He shook his head, though. Robinton's unexpected behavior was beyond his comprehension.

There were, of course, other teachers at the Hold, to cope with the basic reading, writing, and figuring that all children were obliged to learn before their twelfth year. After that, they would take up apprenticeships to whatever Hall their inclination suited them, or go on in their family Hold's work. With a large Hold like Benden, there were enough pupils to be divided by age and ability. But all had their hour of daily musical training with the MasterSinger.

Without ever calling attention to the assignment, Merelan had her son teaching some of the younger children their scales and how to read music, since he was actually well ahead of whatever Falloner and Hayon had learned from the Hold's previous harper. Robinton never minded such duties. He liked seeing the little ones learn more quickly because he knew exactly how to get them to learn it—the way he had with Lexey. In the privacy of their own quarters, his mother tutored him at his own pace, and encouraged him to use one of the instruments when he was composing. For he still wrote music. He couldn't *not* write. Tunes just pushed against his temples until he had to put them down, especially when he saw dragons in the sky. And, accustomed as he had become to not mentioning this activity, no one, not even Falloner, knew that the songs Merelan was teaching them had been composed by Robinton.

"This isn't like the Harper Hall, Robie," she explained carefully the day before she introduced the first of his melodies. "Where everyone knows you. I don't want to put you at a disadvantage. Do you understand what I mean?"

Robinton thought a moment. "Yeah, Maizella would go all tissy about having to sing something I wrote." And he made his grin as understanding as he could. "Can we tell her someday, though, Mother?" he added wistfully.

She ruffled his hair. "I can promise you that, my love. When it seems auspicious?"

"That means 'favorable,' doesn't it?"

She chuckled. "It does . . ."

"Harpers use that word a lot."

"Harpering is not just knowing the words and melody to a lot of songs . . ."

"And not just knowing when to sing them, either." He finished the saying for her.

She tilted his face up to her and regarded him with a very pensive expression on her face. "I think, my darling son, that you are going to make a splendid harper."

"I plan to," he said, grinning impishly at her.

She gave him a quick hug and then asked to see the lessons she had set him in contrapuntal theory.

A few evenings later, Merelan asked Maizella to sing a new song after dinner. At first, the conversations didn't abate, but gradually a respectful silence rewarded the noticeable improvement in both tone and volume. Maizella sat down flushed with achievement and didn't notice that the applause was more from relief than approval. Then Merelan had her and Robinton sing the duet they had practiced in class.

By now, Merelan had identified other good voices in the Hold, and gradually the evenings featured four-part harmonies and the addition of several more instruments, as well as more new songs and a far larger chorus.

Then about six sevendays after their arrival at Benden, Falloner told Robinton that the Weyrleaders were coming to the Hold with some of the wingleaders and their women.

"They come often?" Robinton asked, awed. Would his mother ask him to sing for the dragonriders? There would surely be music after dinner.

Falloner shrugged. "Often enough. S'loner and Lord Maidir

get along real well because Benden believes in the dragon-riders and Carola, who's Weyrwoman, is the daughter of Hayara's oldest sister. So they're kin."

"S'loner?" Robinton couldn't help gawking at his friend. He knew how weyrfolk named children—generally using some part of the father's as well as the mother's name. "*Your* father's the Weyrleader?"

"Yeah." Falloner gave an indifferent shrug. Then he grinned at Robinton's startled expression. "That's one reason why I'm sure to Impress a bronze and why I'll get the chance to stand on the Hatching Ground as long as there're eggs clutched. There've been a lot of Weyrleaders in my lineage." He straightened up proudly. "And why I'm here because I'm supposed to learn more than I'd get taught at the Weyr since we don't have a Hall-trained harper. If I'm going to lead the Weyr in the next Fall, I've got to know more than the average bronze rider, don't I?"

"I guess you do," Robinton murmured, still trying to cope with the status of his friend.

"Ah, don't go looking at me like that, will ya, Robie?" And Falloner gave his shoulder a friendly buffet.

When they were in their own quarters, Robinton had to tell his mother.

"I knew that, dear, and it's one reason I encourage your friendship with him. Falloner's a good-hearted lad and intelligent enough to want to learn. I feel that it's very important for you to have this chance to get to know something about how the Weyr operates. Especially as we only have the one now." She looked off into the middle distance for a long moment.

"Isn't that what the Question Song is about?"

"I didn't know you knew about that one," she said almost sharply, staring at him. "How did you come across it?"

"Oh, when I was copying out some of the worm-eaten music in the Archives. Master Ogolly says I write with a good, neat hand, you know." He preened a bit.

"Yes, I do know, love." She finger-stroked a part into his thick dark hair. "Do you know the music?"

"Of course, I do, Mother," he said, mildly indignant. She, of all people, should know that he memorized music after one hearing or one reading.

"Yes, you would, wouldn't you, dear." She gave a final pat to his hair. "Well, run over it in your mind. It might be suitable for tonight. And a treble voice would make it more poignant, I think. Yes, rehearse it, dear."

Falloner was not at the head table as Robinton thought he might be, since S'loner was his father. Carola was not his mother and, as Falloner took his usual place next to Robinton, he muttered something about her disliking S'loner's weyrlings.

"Aren't weyrlings small dragons?"

"Yes," Falloner said with a little snort. "Applied to us," he explained, sticking his thumb into his chest, "it's not a compliment. All she can get is girls. When she has anything."

Robinton nodded and decided maybe now wasn't the time to ask more questions about the Weyr. Besides, the special dinner was being served, special even for those at the lower table, since Nerat had sent up fresh redfruits and other delicacies, transported a-dragonback.

Robinton had watched with awe as the great beasts, having deposited riders and burdens in the courtyard, rose to the top of Benden's cliff, spacing themselves along the fire heights. The golden queen, Feyrith, settled in the exact center; the other ten dragons, including her weyrmate, settled on either side of her, like guardians. Which was silly, because there wasn't anything on the entire planet that would attack a queen, much less eleven dragons. Robinton thought they were the most beautiful creatures he had ever seen as they peered down at the courtyard, their beautiful faceted eyes gleaming in the late spring evening. He hadn't thought "bronze" could come in so many different shadings.

"Cortath? Kilminth? Spakinth?" he thought daringly.

No one answered his tentative query. Well, maybe none of the bronzes he had spoken to before were on the heights. He could scarcely pick out the individual features from this distance. Or maybe because they were guarding the queen, they couldn't talk to a little boy.

The evening entertainment was nearly more splendid than the meal that had preceded it. Not only were there acrobats, but a man who could make things disappear—and reappear from behind Raid's ear or Maizella's sleeve—or produce the world's smallest canine from his cloak or a tiny tunnel snake from under the cap on his head.

When everyone had settled down again after that diversion, Merelan signaled for the group of singers and players she had been practicing with to take their places. Robinton hurried to join them. The Duty Song, which was one of the first Teaching Ballads taught by any harper to a class, should be sung in honor of any dragonrider guests: Robinton had heard it practiced prior to every Gather. From the quick look he shot at the Weyrleaders, they were expecting it, but they hadn't foreseen a proper instrumental accompaniment. Nor the quality of the soloists. Robinton waited for his mother's signal and sang the first verse, noting the surprise on S'loner's face. So Robinton sang the words with all his heart for this special audience.

S'loner kept right on smiling and tapped out the rhythm as the chorus came to "From those dangers dragons-braved." The applause was suitably enthusiastic, his loud clapping leading the others.

Then Maizella stepped forward from her place in the chorus. Robinton heard the rustle: dismay or annoyance. They were in for a surprise, too, now that his mother had taken the girl in hand. Instead of planting herself in a defiant way, as if to indicate that she was going to sing and everyone had better listen to her, she came to the front in a quiet and professional manner and then looked to Merelan, who was accompanying her on the gitar.

Robinton couldn't miss Weyrleader Carola's expression—total dismay—until Maizella started singing. Even S'loner regarded the girl with a pleased look and murmured something to Maidir, who nodded and smiled back.

Merelan sang harmony to the chorus of the song, which had four verses. The hearty applause was certainly as much an improvement as her performance, and there was a nice rumble of remarks as she stepped back.

Merelan beckoned for the rest of the chorus to attend her signal, and they sang a ballad that was new in the Harper Hall and had such a beat to it that, before long, everyone was stamping or clapping to the rhythm.

The band played new music, and although Robinton caught a few sour notes, he knew how hard they'd worked. A few more rehearsals and performances and they'd be as good as any Gather band. But he was glad he'd be singing with just his mother to accompany him. And he was next. At her gesture he came to her side. Flute in one hand, she put her other arm around his shoulders as she made her introductory remarks.

"This song is very old, and although it's supposed to be in every harper's repertoire, it has lately been sadly neglected. I don't even find it in the very comprehensive Benden library, so it's about time I reintroduced it to you all." She smiled at the audience. "You children will be learning it next week, so listen closely." With that she put the mouthpiece to her lips and nodded to her son.

Gone away, gone ahead,
Echoes roll unansweréd.
Empty, open, dusty, dead,
Why have all the Weyrfolk fled?

Where have dragons gone together?
Leaving Weyrs to wind and weather?
Setting herdbeasts free of tether?
Gone, our safeguards, gone but whither?

Have they flown to some new Weyr
When cruel Threads some others fear?
Are they worlds away from here?
Why, oh, why, the empty Weyr?

There was a stunned silence when Robinton let the last note die away and his mother lowered the flute. Almost an embarrassing silence, and yet he knew he had sung it well. Everyone looked at the pair of them, as if they couldn't believe their ears.

Then there was the noise of chair scraping, and S'loner rose to his feet, his expression almost severe.

"I thank you, MasterSinger, for that beautiful rendition of the classic Question." And he inclined his body to them both with the greatest respect. "It has haunted every Benden Weyrleader for generations. I learned it as a weyrling, but I haven't heard it in . . . oh, decades now. I think it needs to be heard more often. Maybe someone will find its answer."

"Then, S'loner, do you believe that Thread will return?" asked a man, rising from the far end of the head table. Robinton hadn't seen him before, but he must be a Benden holder of some prosperity to judge by his clothing and where he was seated.

Robinton was close enough to see Carola tug at S'loner's sleeve, her brows drawn together in a scowl. Rob glanced over to where Falloner still sat and saw an eager expression on his friend's face. The entire audience seemed to hold their breaths.

"We've another fifty Turns to go before the Star Stones will tell us yea or nay, my friend. But the dragons are here and Benden keeps up its strength. That is the pledge we made to Hold and Hall when the first dragon cracked its shell. It is one that I, and every Weyrleader after me, will keep!" Then he bowed again to Merelan, caught Robinton's eyes briefly, and sat down.

Quickly then, Merelan gestured for the instrumentalists to strike up a merry tune. That was also the signal for the drudges to come and clear the tables, to make space for dancing in the center of the Hall. There was a lot more talking while the tables were cleared, dismantled, and stored to one side, chairs rearranged, and the younger children taken off to their beds.

Robinton was playing hand drum for the early sessions of the dancing, so he didn't get a chance to speak to Falloner that evening. But the next morning in music class, the moment he and his mother entered the room, Falloner leaped on him, hauling him by his shirt to one side.

"Who told you to sing that?" he demanded in a harsh whisper, his expression intense, almost accusing.

"Mother," Robinton said, having hoped to hear something else from his best friend, maybe "You sang that well."

"Shards but it had Carola going!" Falloner grinned. "S'loner must've been over the moons with delight. Our old harper didn't know it and couldn't find it even when S'loner made him hunt through the Records for it. He only knew that he'd learned it. It's possible G'ranad, the Weyrleader before him, struck it out of our Teaching."

"It's in Harper Hall Records," Robinton said. "I had to copy it out several times for harpers going off on assignment."

"Well, one thing sure, you made my father very happy."

"Why?"

"Because he *knows*—" Falloner paused significantly, his expression oddly intense. "—that Thread will come again. And he's fighting to get others to believe it. That song *is* a warning, as well as a riddle." He clapped Robinton on the back. "And I'll be following him, on a fighting bronze. Just you see if I'm not."

"But, even if Thread comes, it's not due for another fifty Turns or more, and you and I will be *old*."

"Fifty isn't old when most dragonriders live to their tenth decade and better. Old M'odon's nearly one hundred and ten, and there's nothing decrepit about his brown Nigarth."

"Does he remember Threadfall?"

"Naw, he's too young for that, but his great-grandfather flew it."

Just then Merelan called the class to order. "We're going to learn the new song, today, the Question Song. Weyrleader S'loner particularly asked me to teach it. Robinton, if you'll sing it again for us so we can start learning the melody, we will honor that request, as we should honor all dragons and their riders."

Five days later a green rider came with an invitation for the MasterSinger and her son to dine at the Weyr and, if she would be so kind, to bring some of the new music that had been heard in Benden Hold.

Robinton was never sure if it was because he had sung the Question Song or because the Weyrleaders wanted his mother to sing more for them.

"Of course it means I'm to sing, love," she said, grinning at her son, "so we'll take instruments with us. But I'm glad that you've been invited, too. I've wanted you to see Benden Weyr." She paused and then winked conspiratorially at him. "Then, when you have to spend that night up at Fort Weyr, you won't be the least bit scared."

"How did you know about that?" The apprentices did not tell anyone, certainly not the girls.

Merelan chuckled. "There's a lot that goes on in the Hall that is known but not talked about, lovey. Not that, for a single moment, I would think *you'd* be frightened of just an empty place."

Robinton puffed his chest out. "But aren't all the Weyrs different?"

Merelan considered this. "Yes, and in fact there are maps of the interiors lodged in the Archives . . . or should be. Another thing that I must check on when we get back."

"When are we going back, Mother?" Not that he really wanted to, if he was being honest with himself. He really, truly liked it here at Benden, and especially Falloner. He had never had a best friend before.

He felt his mother smoothing his hair.

"Do you miss the Hall?"

"Not when I get my lessons from you," he said, grinning up at her. "You're harder on me than Master Washell or Kubisa."

"I am, am I?"

"And it's great to have you to myself," he added and felt her hand hesitate.

"But you don't, Robie," she said, and her voice sounded so funny that he looked up at her to see why. He caught the hint of her frown. "You share me with Benden Hold and all its students."

He thought that over for a moment. "Yes, but it's not the same."

"No, it isn't," she said very slowly. "However, you and I must do some practicing so we'll show them our mettle."

Later, Robinton told Falloner about the invitation. "Will you be coming up, too?" he asked, practically dancing in his delight.

"Me? No, why should I be?"

"But . . . but . . . but . . ."

Falloner dismissed the "but" with an indifferent hand and a wry grin. "I'm lucky to be down here at the Hold. I lost my birth mother when I was born, and my foster mother died of a fever the healer couldn't cool down, and there's no one up there I *want* to see."

"Not even your father?"

Falloner cocked his head at his friend. "No more than you want to see yours."

"I never said anything like that . . ."

"But you never mention him, do you? So you don't miss him, do you? Besides, I prefer to stay out of Carola's way and Lady Hayara's fairer to me than even Stolla . . ." His voice altered to a kinder tone. "But she's nice, even being head-woman in the Lower Caverns and all. *She's* the one made S'loner send me down here until it cooled off—" He stopped short, making a horrible grimace as if he'd let his mouth run away with him.

"What cooled off?"

Falloner's expression turned to bland innocence. "Cooled what off?"

"You just said . . ." And then Robinton stopped, shrugged, and dropped the subject.

It was Lady Hayara's intervention that saw Falloner going with Robinton.

"For the company," she told Merelan. "Falloner will show Robinton around without letting him go where he shouldn't." She fixed a stern look on Falloner, but let it turn into an understanding smile. "But I expect you not to tease Larna so much anymore."

"She follows me *everywhere*," Falloner complained, screwing his face up. "Larna's Carola's daughter," he explained to Merelan, "and a real pain."

"Now, Falloner," Lady Hayara said, wagging a warning finger at him, "I know that Rob will be asked to sing, but it's good for an upcoming harper to learn more about the Weyr than what is sung."

The brown dragon who collected the invited guests did not quibble about adding Falloner to his back. Nor did his rider, who greeted the boy with a wry grin.

"Allowed back, are you, weyrling?"

"It would seem so, C'vrel. Thanks, Falarth," Falloner added to the brown as he competently mounted and settled himself behind Robinton.

Robinton would have given anything to know exactly what that meant, but he suspected he'd never be told by Falloner. Before he could reflect further, he felt the brown launch himself off the ground with the usual neck-snapping lunge and Robinton braced himself for *between*. He was especially grateful when he felt Falloner's hands grip his arms and tighten the moment they went into that bone-searing cold. In *between* he could feel nothing, but he *knew* that Falloner still gripped him. It wasn't as bad, now he knew what to expect—and then, suddenly, he had the incredible good fortune to see a Weyr from on high.

Benden was unusual in that it was situated in an old double volcanic crater. As Falarth swung round, almost on wingtip, Robinton saw the watch dragon and his rider just beyond the massive Star Stones, which would bracket the Red Star on its next return at solstice. He saw dragons lying on the western facing ledges, asleep in the sun . . . and then the several black maws that gave into the Hatching Ground where a queen's clutch of eggs hardened until it was time for the weyr-ling dragons to Hatch and Impress their lifelong partners. As Falarth glided downward, Robinton saw the great golden bulk of Feyrith on her ledge, Chendith lying just above her, his eyes whirling in slow circles as he watched Falarth land lightly in front of the Lower Cavern.

Chapter 7

▼▼▼▼▼▼▼▼▼▼▼▼▼▼▼▼▼▼▼▼▼▼▼▼▼▼▼▼▼▼▼▼

So here he was. Falloner had diplomatically slid down the off-side of Falarth, thus avoiding a meeting with Carola who, with S'loner, greeted their Harper guest and her son, thanking them profusely for accepting the invitation.

"Come to Benden?" Merelan laughed. "I've been dying to."

Then she was introduced to Stolla, the headwoman of the Lower Caverns, a tall woman of middle years who, in turn, introduced the MasterSinger to the blue rider, C'gan, who was Weyrsinger: a slight man whose boyish face was eager and earnest, and so obviously thrilled to meet the MasterSinger. The other woman waiting to be introduced was Miata, who handled basic lessons at the Weyr. Robinton made his best bow to them all, and then S'loner took him by the shoulder.

"Go off with Falloner, Robinton," he said, grinning broadly. "We'll take good care of your mother, never fear."

"I don't worry, not when she's in the Weyr," Robinton answered boldly and, before his mother could reprimand him, he slipped around behind Falarth to meet up with his friend.

"C'mon, there's a lot to see," Falloner said and led the way, running across the Bowl to the black maws of the Hatching

Ground. "This is the most important place in the Weyr. Any Weyr . . ."

"Is that son of yours to be a harper, Merelan?" Robie heard S'loner asking.

He didn't hear his mother's exact answer and he wondered, once again, if maybe he could possibly be harper *and* dragonrider. And he'd Impress a bronze, too. Well . . . he'd settle for a brown and be in Falloner's wing and fight Thread when it came back.

Falloner showed him everything. The Hatching Ground was awe-inspiring, with the great vaulted roof, the steep rank of seats where guests could watch Impression, and the raised stone couch where the queen stayed, guarding her clutch and viewing the Hatching. Then there were some places that Robinton wasn't sure visitors were ordinarily shown. Falloner took him up steps at the side of the Hatching Ground and pushed through a door into what had to be the Weyrwoman's quarters. Robinton gulped, hoping that Feyrith was still fast asleep on her ledge and that Carola did not take a sudden urge to leave his mother. He walked on tiptoe and noticed that Falloner was putting his feet down more quietly than usual. From there, they went to the Council Chamber, with its immense stone oval table and the massive stone chairs where the Weyr leaders and wingleaders sat for meetings. Then down into the musty-smelling rooms that housed the Weyr's Records.

"Our Archives smell exactly like this, too," Robinton remarked, feeling a little safer this far from the weyr and Feyrith. As he ran one finger across the spine of one bound volume, leather rubbed off, and he hastily cleaned his finger and hoped the mark wouldn't show. The Weyr really needed to have these seen to; they were in far worse condition than those Master Ogolly worried over.

Falloner had noticed and now snorted. "That's another thing I like about Benden Hold—they keep their Records in good condition so you can actually read them."

Which Rob allowed as true enough. There was one drudge whose sole job was to dust and oil the leather-bound Records, and check that no insects had burrowed into the hide pages.

His mother had shown him some of the oldest ones, the ink still bright and who-knew-how-many-hundreds-of-Turns old.

They went back up and out the way they had come in to the Weyrwoman's quarters and only then did Robinton draw a sigh of relief. He did wonder why Falloner was venturing up here: did he do it because it was a way to annoy or get back at Carola for not liking him? Sneaking into her private quarters was a bit silly, Robinton thought, but he was glad he had had the chance to see the Council Chamber. This was where the bronze riders would assemble before a Threadfall. But those Records . . . Wouldn't they be needed then, too? And in much better condition than they were in now?

Moving quickly across the warm sands, Robinton expected to go back to the main living area of the Weyr, but Falloner beckoned him toward the top of the Bowl, a wicked grin on his face.

"Show you something not even many weyrbred know about," he said. Casting a glance around to be sure that no one was looking in their direction, he ducked around a large boulder. When Robinton hesitated, Falloner hauled him along by his sleeve.

Though there was still a good deal of spring daylight, the space was dimly lit, only showing a cleft in the cliffside through which Falloner disappeared. A moment later, a light sprang up inside, and Robinton nervously gulped as he bravely stepped toward whatever new surprise Falloner had in store for him.

Falloner held a small glowbasket over his head, the glows still bright enough to make shadows on the walls of the narrow fissure.

"Don't talk loud," he whispered, his mouth close to Robinton's ear, "because there's an echo and anyone near the Ground will hear it."

Robinton nodded vigorously. He didn't want his mother to discover that he was doing something possibly forbidden, maybe even dangerous, at Benden Weyr. Falloner led him down the twisting passage. Anyone even two hands taller would have had to duck, and it was as well both boys were slender, because once or twice they'd had to suck in their guts to get past protrusions.

Then suddenly, there was a dull light ahead and they came to an uneven crevice where they could stand erect and look directly out at the Hatching Ground.

"This is where we come to watch the eggs while they're hardening," Falloner murmured. "I even got out there and touched the eggs last time we had a clutch."

"You did?" Robinton was truly impressed by Falloner's daring. "Did you get caught?" Would that be one of the reasons the Weyrwoman didn't like him?

"Naw," Falloner said, flicking his fingers in dismissal.

"What do eggs feel like?" Robinton couldn't resist asking.

"Sort of rubbery at first . . ."

"At first?" Robinton was shocked.

"Yeah, they get harder every day." Falloner shrugged. "More fun checking every day or so. They get warmer and then the shells begin to feel thin under your hand. The dragonet eats the stuff around it in its shell, you see, while it's growing strong enough to hatch. You ever seen a wherry egg when the chick is only half-made?" Robinton hadn't but he nodded anyway. Lorra had once told him that some of the poultry eggs did that when they weren't used quickly enough. "Same thing. That's why dragonets come out of their shell starving to death."

"But they don't ever die. Do they?"

"S'loner says some do, but I haven't seen any eggs that didn't hatch." There was the implication of long experience in his tone. "Not that we have that many in a clutch." Falloner sighed. "We'll get more, though, nearer to the next Pass."

"We will have one then?"

"Sure, we will. There's been Long Intervals before. You're Harper Hall. You should know that."

"Sure," Robinton agreed hastily. He did know that—sort of. But he was going to check up on it once he got back to the Hall. "But none," he added as he suddenly remembered, "when there weren't all six Weyrs waiting for the next Fall."

Falloner was thoughtful. "We'll be all right," he said with more conviction than his expression implied. "We keep replacing the old ones who die off. Benden's at full fighting strength."

"But there's only Benden," Robinton said, whispering, as a sudden pang of fear shot through him.

"Benden will be more than enough," Falloner said proudly, and then covered his mouth with one hand, for he had spoken more loudly in his surety and his words echoed across the empty Hatching Ground. "C'mon, let's get out of here. I'll show you the barracks and have you meet some of my friends."

They carefully retraced their steps and Falloner hid the glowbasket under a protrusion. Then the weyrbred lad took to his heels and raced toward the right-hand side of the Bowl, beyond the Lower Caverns, where there was a great deal of talking and laughing and general noise. As they flashed by, Rob caught a glimpse of his mother talking to some of the old aunties and uncles at one of the tables. Well, that duty would be over, so he wouldn't have to nod and smile at the oldsters. The look of them, not to mention sometimes their smell, distressed him. People shouldn't get *that* old. When harpers could no longer work, they went back to their birthplaces or down to the warmer, southern holds.

The weyrling barracks were empty, since members of the last clutch had long since graduated to individual weyrs, but the place looked in good order for the next hatching. Falloner knew a back way out of the barracks complex, too, which took them into a broad corridor that he said led to the supply caves.

"There're lots of them," he said proudly. "Benden, Lemos, and Bitra still tithe properly every year, and the Telgar and Keroon Lord Holders tell us where the dragons can hunt, culling the herdbeasts for them."

Through other narrow aisles, Falloner led Robinton to the living quarters, showed him the alcove he had shared with three other lads, and then the bathing area: the Weyr's main bath, steam rising from the water, was big enough to swim in, Rob thought enviously. Beyond, Falloner said, were more storage rooms.

"And a maze of old hallways and too many locked rooms. I'll get in to see them when I'm Weyrleader." He chuckled.

Over his laugh, they heard the muted tones of an enthusiastically rung bell.

"Supper!" And Falloner wasted no time leading Robinton back to the Lower Caverns.

"Are all the Weyrs the same?"

"Well, I've only been to Telgar once, and they've got the same sort of places, like a Hatching Ground and a queen's weyr and records hall and stuff like that. Haven't you ever been up to Fort Weyr?"

"You're not allowed," Robinton said cautiously, with a sideways glance at his companion.

Falloner laughed. "Since when did that keep someone from doing something? I'll bet it's visited a lot."

"Well, actually, I think it is, but . . ."

Falloner put a finger over his lips and winked. "No two Weyrs are laid out quite the same, but"—and he gave a shrug—"you been in one, you'll find your way around Fort after this."

"I know, and thanks, Fal."

"Sure thing, Rob."

They swung into the Lower Caverns then. His mother was standing on the slightly raised platform where a long table had been set up at right angles to the rest of the dining area. There was another dais, too, with music stands, stools, and chairs; that was where they'd perform.

"How many players does the Weyr have?" Rob asked, counting up to fourteen places.

"We got one *good* gitarist, C'gan, one decent fiddler, and the usual pipers and a drummer, though you're much better than he is."

Rob considered this and then noticed that the top table was filling up with riders, and not all bronze to judge by the shoulder knots they wore on their Gather shirts.

His mother, seeing him, made a gesture to indicate that he could stay in Falloner's company. He was delighted. The weyrfolk, summoned to the dining area by the bell, took whatever seat they fancied. Falloner, hauling on Rob's sleeve, took him to a table occupied by six boys more or less Falloner's age. He waved vigorously and held up two fingers—in time to prevent some smaller lads from taking the vacant chairs.

"Just made it," said a black-haired lad, whose curls covered his forehead to his eyebrows. "Go on—there're plenty of other places," he added to the nearest of the small lads.

"This is Robinton, from the Harper Hall," Falloner said, flumping himself down. "That's Pragal," he told Robie, pointing to their greeter, "Jesken, Morif, Rangul, Sellel, and Bravonner. He's my younger brother."

Robinton thought there wasn't much resemblance, except for the unusual color—a bright amber, almost gold—of the eyes, but then, they must have had different mothers, since Falloner had said his was dead.

"How come you got back?" Bravonner asked.

"I told you I'm only at Benden for more schooling." Falloner said in a kindly manner to his sibling. "You been okay?" He glanced accusingly around the table at the others.

"Sure . . ." Bravonner began.

"I promised ya, didn't I?" Pragal said, bridling. "No one's bothered him."

"'Cepting you," Bravonner said with a wicked sideways look at Pragal, who promptly socked him on the arm with mock-ferocity. "You see?" Bravonner added, appealing to his older brother.

"Yeah. I can see that. Something good for dinner?" he asked Rangul.

This lad was of stockier build and well-fleshed, with eyes that darted from one speaker to another. He reminded Robinton of one of the apprentices whom he didn't much trust, a boy who lied bold-facedly after a dispute at his table and then laid all the blame on another apprentice.

"Roast herdbeast," Rangul said, smacking his lips. His expression altered to disgust. "And lots of tubers."

"You should know," said Jesken, a thin-faced lad with a close-cropped head of hair, "since you had to peel so many of them." And he laughed.

"Whatcha do to get that duty?" Falloner asked, his expression eager.

"No one's business but mine," Rangul said sullenly, with a fierce scowl across the table at the laughing Jesken.

"He pushed Larna in the midden," Jesken said, raising a protective arm when Rangul reached across the table with his fork to poke him.

"Enough of that," Falloner said in a crisp tone of command that indicated he often had to intervene between this pair. He glanced quickly around to be sure no one had noticed. "Not that Larna doesn't need to be taught some manners . . . but you only get in trouble. Who's minding her now?" He looked around again, and his eyes paused at a table on the other side of the room, occupied by young girls. "Oh, Manora *would* be stuck with her." He turned back to the other boys. "Didn't anything interesting happen since I left?"

The report that followed didn't mean much to Robinton, who didn't know the weyrfolk named. But shortly a platter of sliced roast was shoved at Falloner, ending the discussion.

"Back, are you?" the serving woman asked sourly. "Make sure there's no trouble at this table. You hear me?"

"As ever, Milla," he replied with an innocent smile.

"Rangul, go fetch the tubers," she added.

"I had to peel 'em," he protested.

"All the more reason to serve the product of your labors. Go. Jesken, you get the salad."

Grumbling under his breath, Rangul pushed back his chair and with no good grace collected the large, steaming bowl. Jesken was back before him with the basket of salad.

Falloner had by then served two big slices to Rob and himself, before passing the platter on. He gestured for Rangul to bring him the tubers. The lad complied, but sullenly: Falloner was clearly not one Rangul cared to antagonize.

"You're guest," Jesken said, offering Robinton the salad.

"And he'll be singing later, too. Good voice, good music." And Falloner winked at Robinton, who was then rather nervous about anyone finding out who had written the songs Merelan had told him were to be the Weyr's evening entertainment.

"I suppose we'll have to listen to you, too," Rangul said nastily to Falloner, his expression a mixture of irritation and envy.

"I'm the one who can carry a tune," Falloner said grinning snidely across the table.

"Those who can't sing play instruments at the Harper Hall," Robinton said, sensing this sort of teasing could easily turn nasty. Weyrlads were really no different from Harper Hall apprentices. "Hey, this roast is really good," he added, hoping to divert the conversation.

"Yeah, it is," Falloner said, chewing. "Not that we don't eat well here . . ."

"Most of the time," Jesken put in, his mouth so full that he had to push the gravy back in with one finger, which he then licked. "Real good tonight. Must have been younger than we usually get."

"We've got Robinton at the table, after all," Falloner said, grinning.

"You staying up here a while?" Sellel asked, glancing from Falloner to Robinton

"Tonight for sure," Falloner said. He nudged Robinton in the ribs. "They'll have you singing 'til dawn, you know."

"Then you'll be singing right with us," Robinton said, and put another forkful of the tender roast into his mouth. He sort of regretted that he'd have to eat lightly, but he couldn't sing properly with a full gut.

Sing he did, with Falloner, with his mother, and as a soloist. First, of course, they did the Duty Song, in which the entire audience joined, singing both chorus and verses once Robinton had sung the opening verse. There was applause for him through the first chorus. He rather liked that and took it for the compliment it was.

Then his mother mouthed "Question Song" at him. It was not next on the program, but as she was conducting the concert, he sang it—to a hushed and very thoughtful audience. S'loner was beaming with delight at the weyrfolks' surprise and attention.

Robinton and Falloner did several of his songs, without saying who the composer was, and these were well received.

The Weyr might not have a highly trained harper, but there were a lot of good voices and folk who picked up quickly on tune and chorus. This was a totally different audience from any Robinton had ever sung for—and quite possibly the best. His mother was responding to it, too, because her voice was joyous again, even in the more nostalgic melodies. They had established an unusual rapport with this audience, a new depth of "listening."

We listen, too, you know, harper boy, a voice said in his head, almost throwing him off his harmony.

That explained much to Robinton, but he didn't have time then to think it all through: he had to keep singing so as not to disappoint.

There were calls for old favorites from the gathering and it wasn't until Robinton's voice cracked with fatigue that Merelan called a reluctant halt to the evening's entertainment.

"We've imposed outrageously on you, Merelan and young Robinton," S'loner said, rising to his feet and scissoring his hands at the requests still being shouted from the tables. "It's late, even for a Weyr gathering, and you've been more than generous with your time and repertoire."

"The Harper Hall's tithe to the Weyr," she replied, dipping her knees in her elegant bow and spreading her left hand to include the entire audience. "It is a pleasure to sing for you."

"Our dragons have enjoyed it almost as much as we have," the Weyrleader said, and looked from her to Robinton, winking.

Suddenly the elation that had sustained him through a very long performance seemed to drain out of Robinton, and he wavered on his feet.

"Falloner, take young Robinton to bed," S'loner said arbitrarily, pointing toward the dormitory area.

"I'm near as tired as he is," Falloner said and, throwing an arm about his friend's shoulders, led him off.

"As for you, my dear Merelan, Carola will escort you to our guest weyr, one that should be occupied by a queen dragon. Well, soon enough, soon enough . . ." S'loner was saying as the two boys left for the Lower Caverns.

The next day, S'loner himself took them back to Benden Hold, Robinton and his mother quite conscious of the honor, even if they were both still fatigued by their exertions. Even Falloner was not his usual self, silent in his father's presence.

"I shall sleep all week," Merelan said as they waved farewell to the bronze rider and Chendith. "But what a splendid evening, Robie. *That* was a glorious performance. I know I've never sung so well before, and you were fabulous. I only hope that you keep that treble a while longer." She sighed and ruffled his hair as they climbed the steps into the Hold. "And have a mature voice, too, of course."

Lady Hayara arrived, waddling awkwardly since she was nearly at the end of this pregnancy. "I was sure they would keep you overnight when you didn't arrive at a decent hour," she said as she accompanied them into the Hold and toward the main stairs. "You look exhausted . . . did it go well? You have a glow about you, you know. Do you need anything? I won't go up the stairs with you today, I think." She gave a breathy sigh and fanned her face with her hand. "I had hoped to be delivered on time *this* time . . ."

Commiserating with the Lady and assuring her that they were all right, Merelan led her son up to their quarters, her shoulders sagging only when they were out of Hayara's sight.

"Singing like that sure takes it out of one, doesn't it?" his mother said as they entered their quarters. "Oh!"

They both saw the roll of a large message on the table, its origin obvious by the Harper-blue band spiraling its length. Her hand hesitated above the tube just a moment, but then grasped it firmly and broke the seal as she seated herself. She pulled out a sheaf of music and spread it open. Robinton saw her face pale, and her fingers shake a bit as she read the brief message attached to it.

"No, it's not *from* your father." She looked at the music before finishing the note. "It's from Master Gennell. Hand me my gitar, Robie."

He uncased it instantly, surprised at her urgency. It was then that he realized his mother had not sung any of his father's compositions in the Hold or in the Weyr. He knew that she was probably the only singer who could technically handle the difficult works his father wrote. Seeing her struggle a bit to stop the score from rolling up again, he planted his hands on the edges.

She struck the opening chord, paused to tune the strings slightly, and began again. Halfway through the first page, she looked up at her son, confused and surprised.

"This isn't at all like your father . . ." She peered closely at the script. "But it is certainly his writing," she said, and continued playing the notes.

Robie followed the music, and deftly shifted the pages from one to the next. He almost missed one turning because he, too, became touched by the plaintive melody, the minor chordings, the whole tenor of the music. As the last of the gitar notes died away, mother and son looked at each other, Merelan perplexed, Robinton anxious. He wanted her to like it, too.

"I think I can say," she began slowly, "without fear of contradiction"—a little smile turned up the corners of her mouth—"that this is the most expressive music your father has ever written." She wrapped both arms around her gitar. "I think he misses us, Robie."

He nodded. The music had definitely been melancholic, where his father usually wrote more . . . more positive, aggressive music, full of embellishments and variations, with wild cadenzas and other such flourishes. Rarely as simple, and elegant, a melody as this. And it was melodic.

She picked up Master Gennell's note. "Master Gennell thinks so, too. 'Thought you ought to see this, Merelan. A definite trend toward the lyric. And, in my opinion, quite likely the best thing he's ever written, though he'd be the last to admit *that*.'" Merelan gave a little laugh. "He'll never admit it, but I think you're right, Master Gennell." She looked at her son. "What do you think, dear? About the music?"

"Me?" Flustered, he couldn't find the proper words. "Are there any words to it?"

"Why don't you write some, dear? Then it would be a father and son collaboration. The first, perhaps, of many?"

"No," Robinton said thoughtfully, though he wished with all his heart right then that there could be a chance his father would use words he had written. "I think you'd better add the words, Mother."

"I think, my son, we'll both work on the proper lyrics." She ruffled his hair, her eyes sad despite the slight smile on her lips. "If we can find appropriate ones . . ."

Chapter 8

▼▼▼▼▼▼▼▼▼▼▼▼▼▼▼▼▼▼▼▼▼▼▼▼▼▼▼▼▼▼▼▼▼▼▼

R obinton didn't know what his mother wrote in her reply
to Master Gennell, but she did explain to her son that she
had to finish out her contract with Benden Hold. She also
wanted to give C'gan, the Weyrsinger, more training. He was
musically sound enough, but needed to develop more confidence in his harpering. She would also insist that a good, voice-
training Harper be assigned to Benden Hold when apprentices
walked the tables to journeyman status this summer. Benden
deserved the best there was.

"For a variety of reasons," she said. "However, I think we'll
bring Maizella back with us to the Hall. She'll profit more from
working with various masters now that she's learned the
basics." She gave one of her enigmatic smiles. "She can sing
with Halanna."

Robinton's opinion wasn't asked, but he would have much
preferred a longer term at Benden Hold and not just because of
his friendship with Falloner, Hayon, and the others. He didn't
really want to go back to the Harper Hall, even if, when an
excited Maizella started quizzing him about his home, he suddenly missed his friends there, even Lexey.

Maizella's parents were delighted to think that the Master-Singer even suggested the idea for their daughter. That was after Lady Hayara gave birth to a son.

"I'd have preferred another girl," she admitted to Merelan when she and Robie dutifully visited her. "It's so much easier to just marry them off suitably than have to worry about all the rivalry among boys to succeed. I mean, I know that Raid will make a good Lord Holder but . . ." And she never finished her sentence.

Falloner had spent one evening explaining to Robinton why it was better to be in Weyr or Hall because, if you were a male in line for succession in a Hold, you had to guard yourself against jealous brothers and cousins.

"But don't the Lord Holders all get together in one of their Councils and decide?" Robinton asked and got a snort for his ingenuousness.

"Sure, they decide, but it's usually the strongest one they pick, the one who's survived long enough to present himself as a candidate. Mind you, at the Weyr there's some scheming and displaying when there's a queen to mate." A shrewd look came over the weyr lad's face. "But no one dies, of course, because dragonriders can't fight to-the-death duels, and a real smart rider can make certain his bronze gets the queen ahead of the others."

"How?"

Falloner gave him a patient look. "There're ways, there are ways! That's how my father beat out all the other bronze riders when Feyrith rose the last time. Carola wanted C'rob in her weyr, but Spakinth wasn't as clever as Chendith. Not by half, he wasn't. *And* Feyrith's clutch by Chendith was much larger than her last one by Spakinth."

"I thought the Weyrleader stayed Weyrleader . . ." Robinton mentally reviewed all the songs he knew about dragonkind.

"Only as long as his dragon flies the queen," Falloner said, shaking his head.

"I wish you could come with me back to the Harper Hall," Robinton suggested shyly.

"No way," Falloner said. "I'll be back at the Weyr. I don't want to be away too long, you see."

"Why? There're no eggs on the Hatching Ground, and besides you're not old enough yet."

"Only another Turn to go," Falloner said, as cocky as ever. "Not that it hasn't been great getting to know you, and your mother's terrific. She's made sure I'll be more visible now."

"Visible?" It seemed to Robinton that Falloner would do better to efface himself instead of getting into so much trouble that he had to be sent away from the Weyr so the Weyrwoman would calm down. Robinton never did find out what his friend's offense had been.

"Yes, I can help C'gan now that I can read and copy music— almost as good as you can."

"You learn quickly," Robinton said generously.

"I have to," Falloner said, quite serious, "if I'm to be Weyr-leader in the next Pass. C'mon, I'll help you finish packing. You sure got more than you came with."

"Everyone's been very kind to me," Robinton admitted.

"Why not? You're stepping on no one's toes here."

Robinton had a lump in his throat the next afternoon when he had to say good-bye to all those he'd met at Benden— especially Falloner and Hayon.

"Don't worry, Rob," Falloner murmured in his ear as they stood by Spakinth's side, watching as the carisaks were heaved up and over the bronze's back. "As soon as I've a bronze dragon, I'll come visit. Promise."

"I'll expect you," Robinton told him, grinning broadly to keep the tears back.

"Up you get," C'rob said and flung him up the bronze's side.

Robinton knew the trick of grabbing a neck ridge and scram-bling into place. Then his mother, more gracefully, seated her-self behind him and waved to those on the ground seeing them off. When he heard her sniffing, Robie knew he wasn't the only one sorry to leave Benden. He did wish they could have stayed on.

It took a little longer to get Maizella up on Cortath, since she had so much baggage to bring with her for her Turn of training at the Harper Hall. Tears were streaming down her face—tears of joy, he knew.

Well, he thought with little charity, she'll find the Hall quite different from living in Benden Hold. And that thought kept him from sniffling.

Then they were off, Spakinth once more nearly shaking Robinton's skull from his neck with his skyward jump. He was becoming inured to the fright of *between* by now and felt only the cold, not the fear. He was rather proud of himself.

Spakinth was showing off: he emerged right over the Harper Hall courtyard, low enough to be on a level with the rooftops as he backwinged and delicately landed.

"Well done, Spakinth," Merelan said, clapping her hands.

"I'll kill him later," C'rob said almost grimly. "Pulling a stunt like that without permission."

"Oh, don't, C'rob," Merelan said, her eyes dancing. "What an entrance! And here comes Cortath with M'ridin and Maizella, rather more circumspectly."

Grinning, she waved at those gathered on the steps. Then she began to clap again as a chorus from the second-story assembly room sang a loud musical welcome.

We're glad you're home
We're glad you've come
We welcome you
With heart and voice
And hope you'll never leave.

Someone even provided a trumpet flourish and a roll of drums as a finale, which delighted Merelan even more. Only Robinton saw her sweeping gaze looking, just as he was, for his father.

Petiron was not among those standing on the Harper Hall steps, but maybe he was leading the singers. Master Gennell was there, waving enthusiastically along with Betrice, Ginia, Lorra, with her youngest daughter on her hip, Master Bosler, and Master Ogolly, who had an arm about Lexey and Libby. Barba stood on the step below them.

"Don't mention your father's melody, Rob, love. Not unless he does," his mother hurriedly whispered in his ear and then helped him dismount from Spakinth's high withers as Gennell and Betrice rushed forward to assist.

"My, you've grown," Betrice cried, giving him a big hug before Lexey and Libby could reach him. "And is that young Maizella?" she asked as Master Bosler and Ginia went to help the Benden Holder girl. "Another of Halanna's stripe? No, there's not much luggage, is there?"

"Maizella's all right, and she listens to my mother." Robie grinned as he opened the heavy jacket he'd worn for *between* and resettled his shirt.

"Didja miss us?" Lexey wanted to know, dancing about: his expression suggested that he had missed his patient friend very much indeed.

" 'Course I did, Lexey." Rob gave him a mock punch. "I learned some great new games, too, Libby," he added, turning to the girl.

His mother began to introduce her new student to the MasterHarper, his spouse, and the other adults, letting Betrice take charge.

"Robinton . . ." and his mother prompted him to thank Spakinth and C'rob for returning them home.

"Glad to do it, MasterSinger. Any chance of your coming back to sing at the Autumn Gather? I was asked to ask you," C'rob said, grinning from ear to ear.

"I'll see if it's possible, C'rob. I'd certainly like to." At her words, Robinton nodded vigorously, which made her laugh. "I can see that I'll be nagged to death until I do," she added, tousling her son's hair. "Can you not stop for some klah?"

C'rob shook his head with real regret. "Not today. But thanks!"

They stood there, courteously, while both riders remounted; then the dragons launched themselves into the air and turned eastward before disappearing.

Robinton caught the sad little sigh from his mother before she turned back and smiled at those who had welcomed her.

"Come now," Lorra was saying, taking Merelan by the arm, "I've put on a little something to take away the chill of *between* . . . And you lot be careful with the MasterSinger's things," she added, scowling at the apprentices who were halfway up the stairs, burdened with carisaks.

"We weren't *between* long enough to get cold," Robinton said.

"And who's the seasoned traveler, then?" Lorra asked, amused.

"Mother and I got to the Weyr several times a-dragonback, you know," he went on.

"Can we come in, too?" Libby asked, hovering in the doorway with Lexey and Barba.

"When were you ever refused food in this Hall?" Lorra demanded. As she resettled young Silvina on her hip, she waved them toward the small dining room with its table set with a huge bowl of her special fruit drink and plates of pies and cookies. "Even if you only just got up from lunch? Did Benden feed you just before you left?" she asked the travelers.

"Well, we were given lunch Benden time . . ."

"At least their timing's right," the headwoman said almost approvingly.

Merelan swung round from the table when she heard boot steps on the flagstones in the hall, but it was Masters Gennell, Bosler, and Ogolly coming in.

"I'd hoped that Petiron would make it back from Ruatha Hold in time," Master Gennell said apologetically to Merelan.

"Oh?"

"But he was certain he'd be here to greet you," Gennell went on, "so we didn't drum a message to delay your return until he was back." The MasterHarper looked toward the open Hall door as if he expected Petiron to be riding in at any moment. "It's not that long a journey, and I saw that the harpers were all well-mounted. Their summer Gather, and they'd particularly requested something special from us."

"Halanna went?" Merelan asked in a bland voice.

"Yes, and Londik, though I'd say," Gennell added with a frown, "his voice is about to change."

"That won't matter now," she said almost casually, and looked down at her son. "Robie can take over the treble solos. He did all that were needed at Benden, both Hold and Weyr, and it's not just as his mother I'm proud of him."

"No, of course not. And did you like visiting the Weyr, Rob?" Master Gennell smiled kindly down at him.

"It was fabulous," Robinton said. He was quite willing to describe everything; he couldn't remember if Master Gennell had been to the Weyr. "Isn't it?"

"Yes, a very special place indeed." Gennell gave Rob a pat on his head and then turned to Merelan. "So, tell me more about our new soprano, Lord Maidir's girl."

"She's a well-behaved young lady," Merelan said, chuckling as Master Gennell's obvious apprehension eased. "I'd scarcely inflict the Hall with another . . ." She cleared her throat and suggested that Robie might like to finish his drink with his friends.

Robinton went off, grinning to himself because he knew what she'd been about to say.

His father did not arrive back at the Hall until the long summer day had nearly ended. Two of the journeymen with him were leading mounts, one of which was very definitely lamed.

"Beast went lame, Mother," Robinton said from his perch at the front window. "Not Father's, though," he added as she hurried in from her bedroom to peer over her shoulder. "See. There he is!" And he pointed to his father's unmistakable tall, lean figure, dismounting from a Ruathan bay gelding.

He couldn't understand his mother's reaction. She'd worried about Petiron not being there, and now she didn't seem to care that he was safely home.

"It wouldn't be like Father to hurry on ahead unless everything was all right," he said.

"Sometimes, Robie," she told him, putting her hand under his chin and tipping his face up, "you're too forgiving."

He didn't feel so forgiving when it seemed to take an age for his father to greet his family.

"Trouble on the way, Petiron?" his mother asked, turning from the window and the brilliant sunset.

"Two lame beasts, because they thought to get home faster," he said, swinging saddlebags and instrument case to the bench. "You had the safer way to travel." He came over to her and gave her a peck on her cheek. "Londik's voice is gone."

"I can sing instead, then," Robinton piped up.

His father, almost as if just realizing his son was in the room, too, frowned slightly. "That's as it may be. But it is way past your bedtime, Robinton, and your mother and I have a lot to discuss. Good night."

"And you've no more welcome than that for your son, Petiron?" Merelan asked in such a tense voice that Robie was startled.

"It's all right, Mother. Good night, Father," he said and left, almost running out of the room in his dismay.

"Petiron, how could you?"

Robie shut the door on whatever reply his father made, glad that he couldn't hear anything through the thick wooden panels. He flung himself on his bed and wished he was back at Benden Hold. Even Lord Maidir was nicer to him than his father was. Why couldn't he please his own father? What had he done wrong? Why couldn't he do something right? He probably oughtn't to have said that he could take Londik's place. But he could. He knew he could. His mother had said that his voice was every bit as good as Londik's, and he was the better musician. And she didn't *just* say things like that to make you feel good—not about professional matters.

He muffled the sobs he could not control in his pillow. And when he heard some shouting later, he pulled the pillow over his head and pushed it tight against his ears so he couldn't hear anything except his own pulse.

He had to audition for the position of solo treble singer in front of all the masters. That made him a little nervous. The requirement had made his mother furious.

"Are you doubting my professional opinion, Petiron?" she asked when she heard what was proposed. All the windows were open, making it impossible for Robinton to avoid hearing.

"Any singer who is to be a soloist for the Harper Hall has to be auditioned," his father had answered.

"Only if he hasn't been heard by all the masters before," Merelan had said, tight-voiced.

"I do not wish anyone to think that I am pushing my son into a place that another also qualifies for."

"There *is* no other treble as qualified! Everyone but you knows very well that Robinton has a splendid treble."

"Then there is no problem in following protocol, is there?"

"Protocol! Protocol? For your own son?"

"Of course. For him more than any other. Surely you can see that, Merelan."

"I wish, Petiron, I do sincerely wish that I could."

Robie flinched when he heard the outer door slam. He felt his throat tighten and then reminded himself sternly that he had no time for that right now. He was harper-trained and he'd prove—especially to his father—that he was *well* trained.

Because he was, of course, facing his auditors, he caught the little reassuring gestures they made, and his mother's encouraging expression as she played the introduction to the music they had decided he should present first. He was to sing two songs, an optional piece and then a score he had not seen before.

"That," his mother had said in an odd voice, "is going to be very difficult because he knows all the music."

"There will be one he doesn't know," his father had said and given his head the one final nod that indicated this subject was closed.

So he sang the Question Song, and that made all the masters sit up, including his father. But the song suited his range and showed good phrasing as well as voice control, as he let the final note die away without breaking it off.

"Odd choice" was his father's comment after the warm applause had died. Petiron handed him a double sheet. "This would have been Londik's next solo. Not even he has seen it. You may have a few minutes to look through it." He held out his hand to take Merelan's gitar from her and sat on the stool, prepared to accompany his son himself.

With a sinking feeling in the pit of his stomach, Robinton turned his eyes down to his father's bold notations. But by the time he had to turn the page, he felt a surge of relief. If his father thought this would show up his unsuitability, he might even get a pleasant surprise.

"I'm ready," Robie said, turning the music back to the first page.

"You should take more time than that," his father said.

"I've read it through, Father," Robinton replied. His father didn't know how quickly he memorized music, even the complex tempi his father liked to use and the odd intervals he was fond of putting in: "To jar the audience awake," one of the journeymen had said in Robie's hearing.

"Let's not make the lad nervous, Petiron," Master Gennell said. "If he says he's ready, we'll have to take him at his word."

"I'll play the first measure, then go back to the top," Petiron said, as if conferring a special favor.

Robinton saw his mother's warning finger go up so he said nothing. But he was spot perfect coming in at the top. He didn't need to, but he kept the score in front of his eyes, not wanting to look in his father's direction. He had no trouble singing the unusual intervals, or keeping an accurate tempo, even when it changed almost every other measure. There was one run, which would have suited Londik's flexible voice, too, and a trill that Rob had no trouble with, either, his mother having used him to show Maizella how to deal with that sort of vocal embellishment.

"I do believe we have a more than adequate replacement for

Londik," Master Gennell said, rising and speaking over the applause. "That was very well done, Robie. Surprised you, too, didn't he, Petiron? You've been working the lad hard at Benden, Merelan, and it shows. It shows."

Petiron was looking at his son, his mouth slightly open, his right hand silencing the strings of the gitar.

"I do believe, Petiron, that you've forgotten that Robie turned ten while we were in Benden," Merelan said briskly.

"Yes, I had." Petiron rose slowly, putting the gitar carefully back in its case. "But you must read the dynamics of a new piece more carefully, son. In the fourth measure—"

Seeing Merelan's growing ire, Master Gennell jumped in. "Petiron, I don't believe you," he said. "The lad did not so much as falter once, singing difficult music—for you don't write any other kind—which he had never seen before, and you're quibbling about the dynamics in one measure?"

"If he is to take Londik's place, he must be accurate in all particulars," Petiron said. "And he will be. From now on, I shall oversee his musical education. There's a lot to be done . . ."

"Ah, but you're in error, there, my good Petiron," Master Gennell said in his mildest voice, his round face quite bland. "You"—he pointed his finger at the MasterComposer—"teach at journeyman level. We must follow the protocol, you know." And he beamed at a stunned Petiron.

Robinton heard a stifled noise and looked around at his mother, who gave him the oddest smile.

"Robinton is not old enough to be an apprentice, though as our lead treble, he is now definitely under Hall jurisdiction. But," Gennell went on in a very satisfied tone, "I think that he would benefit from special lessons with his mother, since obviously Merelan had brought his voice along this far with her usual excellent training." He nodded and bowed to her. "And, of course, he'll continue his regular lessons with Kubisa, for we can't short him on general knowledge and the basics, now can we, simply because he has a splendid treble? You did very well, Robinton." Gennell's beam now included Robinton and he awarded the boy a proprietary caress on his head and a final decisive pat. "Yes, and I think some of us here—I certainly—will be more than willing to oversee other elements of his training until he does reach apprentice age." Gennell then sighed abruptly. "Of course, when his voice breaks, we'll just have to see what his other musical qualifications are."

Robinton blinked when Gennell, whose wide shoulders shielded him from his father, gave him a solemn wink.

"Thank you, MasterHarper, I'll do my best not to disappoint," Robie said in the silence that fell.

Then everyone began to clear throats or shift feet or stand up. His mother moved to his side, hands on his shoulders, squeezing lightly to indicate her approval.

"Ah, Petiron, there's a drum message request from Igen for a repeat of that program you put on for them last year," Gennell said, taking the MasterComposer by the arm and leading him out of the audition room. "You might make it the debut for your son. Not surprised he did so well, considering his parentage. You must be proud of him . . ." His voice trailed off down the hall.

"The MasterHarper may appear to be asleep from time to time," Master Ogolly remarked in his dry, wispy voice, "but he doesn't miss much, does he, Merelan? What with summer schedules and all, I'm short of apprentices when I need them most. Robie, could you give me a few hours and help me catch up on copying manuscripts?"

Robie looked up at his mother for permission and she nodded.

"He writes the clearest hand, you know, Mere. Have you some free time this afternoon perhaps?" he added wistfully to Robinton.

"I'll be there after lunch," Robie said, grateful to be legitimately somewhere other than his own quarters for the rest of the day. Ever since he'd been considered old enough to feed himself, he'd sat at the younglings' table in the dining hall so he could avoid his father at noon. He'd get a copy from Master Ogolly of the work Londik had sung last year and memorize it. That way he wouldn't annoy his father.

If Robinton did not realize until he was full-grown how deftly the Harper Hall conspired to save him from his father's perfectionism, he was consumed with relief when "protocol" required him to join the other apprentices in their dormitory the day after his twelfth birthday. Instead of being on better terms with his father after two Turns of solo work, he seemed to annoy Petiron even more, no matter how hard he tried. In fact, it got so everyone noticed, and the other singers made a point of telling him how well he did, loud enough for his father—who gave him only a nod now and then—to hear.

He knew his transfer upset his mother, and yet he was positive it would make things a lot easier for her. It was only too obvious that his father couldn't wait to see the back of him. And his case wasn't the same as that of other apprentice lads: he'd lived in the Hall all his life, so he wouldn't be homesick in the dormitory. Although he would miss his mother's loving care, he was earnestly looking forward to leaving the family apartment.

"The boy is *not* going more than two hundred feet away," Petiron said as he watched Merelan taking great care in packing Robinton's belongings. Then he saw the thick roll of music she was stowing. "What's that?" he demanded suspiciously.

"Rob's done some exercises," she replied indifferently, and tried to place them out of sight in the carton.

"Exercises?"

"Classwork, I think," she added to stress the insignificance. She had it almost packed away when Petiron extracted the roll and pulled it open.

In the exasperating fashion thin hide can have, it resisted, and he was muttering under his breath with frustration. Merelan steeled herself and motioned surreptitiously for Robie to continue folding his clothing into the carisak.

Rob had so hoped that he could leave the apartment without any unpleasantness. Why did his father have to hang around

the apartment this afternoon when he could have been anywhere else in the Hall just then?

"Exercises? Exercises!" Petiron glared first at his spouse and
then through the doorway at his son. His tendency to use
scowls as facial expressions had already carved deep lines in
his long face. "These are copies of those ridiculous tunes the
apprentices keep asking to sing."

Robinton couldn't see his mother's face because she had
risen, hoping to retrieve the roll. Petiron looked from one to the
other and, for the first time in his dealings with his son, had a
sudden perception.

"You—" He waved the offending roll in his son's direction. "—wrote these."

"Yes . . ." Robinton had to tell the truth now, if never again.
"As exercises," he heard himself adding when he saw the deepening of the scowl on his father's face. "Sort of variations . . ."

"*Variations* that all the masters use in their classes. *Variations*
that the instrumentalists constantly use. And twaddle at that,
silly tunes that anyone can sing or play. Useless nonsense. Just
what has been going on behind my back?"

"Since you have heard the masters using Robie's songs in
their classes, and the instrumentalists using them, then nothing
has been going on behind your back, has it?" Merelan asked
calmly and retrieved the roll from her spouse's hand.

"He's been composing?"

"Yes, he's been composing. Songs." She did not add that Petiron was looking at some of their son's very early work. She
hoped he did not remember how long he had been hearing his
son's charming, happy tunes. "Wouldn't it be odd for him to be
tone-deaf as well as note-blind in this Hall, saturated by music
all the days of his life and two Harper Masters daily drumming
sound into his head? I'd say it is only logical that he would
write music and sing well. Don't you?"

Petiron stood, looking from one to the other. He watched
as Merelan rolled the songs tight and pushed them back into
the box.

"You hid from me the fact that he has perfect pitch, has a
good treble voice, and has been writing music?"

"No—one—has—been—hiding—a sharding thing from you, Petiron," Merelan said tensely, enunciating every syllable and using a swear word that shocked Robinton as much as it did her spouse, who recoiled from her controlled anger. "You—simply—did not hear, and did not see. Now, act the father for once in your life, and carry this carton to the dormitory. It's much too heavy for Rob." She pointed at the burden and then at the windows to the dormitory that Robinton would be using.

Without a word, Petiron picked it up and made his way out of the room.

Robinton looped two more carisaks over one shoulder and took one step forward, but his mother, her head turned toward the hallway, held up her hand.

"Wait a minute, dear." She turned back to him, her face drawn with sadness and despair. "I shouldn't have said that. I shouldn't have lost my patience with the man. But I can't keep on saving his self-esteem, catering to his enormous ego, and always at your expense, Rob."

"It's all right, Mother. I understand."

His mother reached out to caress his cheek—he was nearly her height now—shaking her head sadly, her eyes full of tears. "I'd be surprised if you really did, love, but it shows your good heart and generous spirit. Always keep that, Robie. It's a saving grace."

She let him go then, and though he didn't see his father on the stairs in the dormitory, the box was on the bed assigned him. He started unpacking, hoping that both the lump in his throat and the sense of having lost something important would go away before any of the other apprentices put in an appearance.

There were twenty-six in his class, quartered in three long rooms: he was lucky enough to be in the six-man one, so there was a trifle more space. By evening, he'd met them all, and they had been vetted by the older apprentices. He kept a suitable expression on his face when the head apprentice, a tall well-built lad from Keroon named Shonagar, rattled off what was expected of first-year apprentices, how they were the "lowest" of the "lowly" in the Hall, and the traditions of their new status. He also told them about the necessity of spending a night alone in the Weyr to prove their bravery.

"Harpers run into all kinds of problems and difficulties. This isn't just singing songs to folks in a hold in the evenings. It can be a dangerous life," he said, thoroughly solemn, "and you have to prove, now, that you can take it."

"But the Weyr's been empty for hundreds of Turns," exclaimed the skinniest of the new boys, Grodon, his eyes wide with anxiety. He gulped hard.

"We've all done it, lad. You will, too," Shonagar said firmly. He glanced over at Robinton, raising his eyebrows as he recognized the new apprentice. "All of you."

Robinton had rehearsed with Shonagar many times—Shonagar was a good second tenor. More important, he was fair-minded and really did keep good order in the apprentice dormitories. Though his position as head apprentice was not an official rank, Master Gennell encouraged his leadership. Shonagar would allow no bullying or improper behavior in the dorms.

Robinton hadn't mentioned his Hall background when the others were jabbering away about their homes, but it would soon become obvious. He hoped he could make friends in spite of having masters as parents. He knew how apprentices could behave. Fortunately, his innate modesty and good nature stood him in good stead as he settled in with the others. Grodon was terribly homesick the first sevenday, and Rob wheedled bedtime snacks from Lorra to ease his pain. Falawny, with sun-bleached hair and tanned skin, came from Igen. Shelline was a Neratian, also tanned; Lear was from Tillek and delighted not to have to become a fisher like the rest of his kin. Jerint was a dark-complectioned lad from southern Keroon who spent a lot of his time softly playing his pipes. He was good at it, too, Robinton quickly realized.

He did put himself forward ten days later when Shonagar entered their quarters after lights out.

"Right, now, who'll be first to spend the night at the Weyr?"

the head apprentice demanded, eyeing his victims sternly as they lay in their beds.

All save Robinton scrunched down further under their sleeping furs, trying to disappear.

"I guess I wouldn't mind getting it all over with," Robinton said, throwing back his covers.

"Good on you, Robie," Shonagar said, nodding encouragingly.

Robinton dressed in the warmest of his clothes and, grabbing his jacket, prepared to go.

Shonagar and his two deputies waiting out in the corridor led him down the back stairs and out the side door on the Hold side of the Hall. There were five runnerbeasts waiting there, held by a fourth apprentice. Robinton had always wondered how the round-trip to the Weyr was managed in the one night without all the masters knowing of the unscheduled excursion. He was glad he didn't have to hike up the long hill road that led to the Weyr. That would be scarier than being *in* it alone all night. Too many tunnel snakes across mountain roads at night. And other things.

They walked quietly across the huge Fort Hold square, up past the beastholds and cots, and then Shonagar led them through the tunnel that had been bored in the Fort cliffside, one of the minor wonders of the world that their ancestors had made, and through to the next valley. Across it—at a good pace now that the noise the runners made wouldn't be heard—and up the winding road that led to Fort Weyr. Again another tunnel had been bored by the amazing equipment the Ancients had once possessed, and through this they went. For Robinton, that was the scariest part, even though Shonagar opened the glowbasket he brought. Then they were out into the night, on the floor of the Weyr itself. Robinton could just about make out the openings to the Lower Caverns and a few of the individual weyrs in the weak light of a half-moon.

"You can build a fire if you want in the Cavern," Shonagar said, pointing and gesturing for Robinton to dismount.

One of the other lads laughed. "If you can find any firing, that is."

"Leave it," Shonagar said sternly. "We'll be back for you an hour before dawn. Have a good night."

With that he led the others, and Robinton's mount, away and Rob stumbled toward the black maw of the living quarters that had once teemed with weyrfolk.

His footsteps echoed slightly in the still night and he hugged his jacket closer around him. Well, it wasn't as cold as *between*. He did wish he'd had some warning so he could have saved a bit of his supper. Eating always made him feel better.

Once under the vaulting roof of Fort's Lower Caverns, he could see little but the hearths along its outer edge.

"If you can find any firing, indeed," he said with a snort. "And nothing to light it with." He thought he'd best get some matches and hand them out to the other lads so they could start a fire on their turns. Maybe see that there was some tinder for them to smuggle along. A glowbasket, even the smallest of them, couldn't be hidden under a jacket. Even the smallest blaze would be better than this deep black darkness. Not as dark, though, as *between*.

But there was light outside, so Robinton went exploring. He'd taken the precaution of looking at the plans of Fort Weyr in the Archives. He'd told his roommates to do so, as well, when they had a chance during their script lessons. So he found the steps leading to the rank of junior queen weyrs. They'd be warmer since they got their heat, as Fort Hold and the Harper Hall did, from deep inside the earth. No one now knew how that had been done, but that was why they all didn't freeze in the bleaker months of full winter. He was somewhat glad that this ordeal occurred in the early autumn.

He stumbled twice going up the stairs: the steps were slightly uneven, though wide enough to accommodate his whole foot. He found the entrance to the first weyr by almost falling into it—he'd been guiding himself along the ledge with one hand on the stone wall on his right.

Entering, still one hand on the wall, he once again almost fell inside when he reached the outer room, where the queen dragon had slept. As he moved cautiously into the room, he could smell the odd spicy odor that was so dragony.

Where had the weyrfolk gone to? There were so many notions about that, including the one that had all the dragon-riders and weyrfolk returning to where the Ancients had come from. If they had, then why had no one else come to Pern? Surely there would be interest in the dragons of Pern!

He barked his shin on the dragon's couch and let out an exclamation, rubbing his leg. He heard in the ensuing silence the faint rustle of tunnel snakes making their way out, he hoped, of the weyr. He decided he'd gone far enough into the darkness of the weyr, and sat down on the raised stone. Unexpectedly, he sat in a shallow declivity and felt around in it. Obviously, large and heavy dragon bodies had formed depressions in the stone, and he ran daring fingers in the dust, as if he could conjure the creatures that had made the hollows. That, more than anything else, reassured him. He grinned, and rearranged his body, swinging his legs around so he was facing the faint light coming down the hall, the wallow accommodating his still slight frame while he could pillow his head on his arms on the outer edge. He must remember to thank Falloner for taking him around Benden Weyr. Fort might be empty of its people and creatures, but it was still a Weyr and one of the safest places on his world. He could smell dragon, and dust, but mostly dragon. He went to sleep listening to the faint rustlings of tunnel snakes, but he doubted they would dare venture where dragons had lain.

It did him no harm with all the other apprentices that he had to be wakened in the dusk preceding dawn by some loud shouting. When Robinton emerged on the weyr ledge, Shonagar urgently waved him down.

"Where you been, Rob? We gotta get back to the Hall before they know we've borrowed the runners. We've been all over looking for you."

"It's warm in a weyr," Robinton said, yawning.

"Sorry to disturb your slumbers. Mount up. We're going to

have to *move!*" Shonagar had a respectful scowl on his face as he handed the initiate the reins. "And remember, not a word to the others. They gotta do it themselves, too."

"Oh, it's not so bad," Rob said, grinning.

"Just don't let me hear you've warned 'em about anything, Robinton!" Shonagar repeated, balling his hand into a fist.

"No. I'll obey."

Of course, Robinton realized he wouldn't actually tell them anything, but he'd show them the matches and tinder he'd put in their pockets.

As they cantered toward the tunnel, Robinton looked up at the Star Stones, immense black dolmens against a lightening eastern sky. He caught a flick of something and wondered if the ghosts of departed dragons still kept a watch on the heights. Looking again, he saw a wherry wheeling down, probably from its nest in one of the upper weyrs.

Robinton really liked being an apprentice. In this he astonished his roommates and the other twenty in his class. They would come to him for his advice and, often, comfort, and he'd help the slow ones with their lessons.

"Going to take over from me, Rob?" Shonagar asked him once.

"Me?" Rob grinned back. "You can keep the responsibility— for now. And I'm just one of them, so it's easier for them to ask me because I'm handy and know the place, that's all."

"For all of that, you've not had it *that* easy," Shonagar said with a wry smile. They'd just finished a long rehearsal for the Turn's End concert: Rob, as usual, was singing the solo treble parts. Halanna and Maizella were also soloists, but though Petiron remarked favorably on their performances, he had not so much as a nod for his son. The apprentices, being as astute as they were, did not fail to notice this. But if any complained, he'd shrug and remark that his father expected him to be note-perfect.

His mother kept up his vocal training, and he had now graduated to apprentice classes. He particularly enjoyed his stint in the drum tower, because at last he got to learn the meaning of the codes that he had been hearing all his life. Like everyone else, he knew that the initial beats indicated the final destination of the message and who had sent it, but it took time to get the sense of the actual message.

In fact, he was on duty the day Feyrith, Carola's queen, produced her last clutch—though no one knew at the time that it would be her last. The best news was that there was a queen egg, and the drum message added the extra beats for excitement and major news. A large clutch, too, with nine eggs that looked to be bronzes.

Robinton spent a few sevendays hoping that there would be a Search and he'd be found acceptable, and become a harper-dragonrider. But no dragons came on Search to Fort Hold or the Harper Hall, and no other Hold reported the arrival of dragons, looking for candidates. Robinton was bitterly disappointed. He had been so sure that the dragons liked him. Didn't they like him enough to come find him?

For fear of being ridiculed, he didn't tell anyone about his thwarted desire. He did ask a few questions of his masters, in case they knew how Searches were conducted, but the answers he got did nothing to assuage his anxiety or hopes. "That's always up to the Weyr, lad," or "Who knows what's in dragon minds?" "Sometimes the dragons don't Search. Don't need to. Didn't you tell me there were lots of lads your age at Benden Weyr?" Which was true enough, but it still didn't keep him from searching the skies for a dragon, in case he could get one to speak to him. His distraction was noticed in class, and he was given extra duties to encourage him to "pay proper attention to your lessons and stop daydreaming." He had time, while sweeping down the main court, to see the folly of his disappointment.

He was on drum tower duty again when the news of the Hatching came in. Swallowing the final vestige of his own disappointment, Robinton just *had* to find out if Falloner had been Impressed. After all, Falloner had a real right to be Impressed. Greatly daring, he asked permission of the journeyman in charge of the tower to find out.

"You see, I met a couple of the possible candidates. Falloner, he's the weyrling who was at the Hold for Mother to teach." Robinton was not above using what he needed to get to do something as important as this, and he knew that the Journeyman liked his mother. "I know she'd like to know if Falloner Impressed . . ." He let his voice trail off.

"Oh, go ahead," the Journeyman said with a smile. "Only keep it short."

Robinton worked out the message and the nonurgent coding, got approval, and beat it out himself. He hoped he'd hear back before his duty ended. But he didn't.

That evening, however, the Journeyman sought him out at dinner and gave him a slip of hide and a wink.

Robinton could barely restrain his hurrah! Falloner had Impressed a bronze. So had Rangul and Sellel—though that draconic choice surprised Robinton—and six others whose names he recognized from his visits to the Weyr. The Weavercrafthall lad from High Reaches, Lytonal, was now L'tol and rode brown Larth.

He caught his mother on her way to evening rehearsal and told her.

"I suspected that young rascal would make bronze," she said. "And Rangul. Nine bronzes is a good clutch. A queen egg is even better. It may well be that S'loner is right, after all." She hurried away then, without explaining her last cryptic remark.

Robinton wondered if Falloner, now F'lon, would remember his promise to him—that he'd come to the Harper Hall on his bronze so Robinton could meet him. Wouldn't his dorm mates be amazed! It was a fun thing to think about, but Robinton rather thought that F'lon, now being above a mere Harper Hall apprentice, might not consider he had to honor that promise. Anyway, it took a while for a dragonet to learn to fly.

He did his lessons in the Archives with everyone else, but mostly he copied special files for Master Ogolly, since he was the fastest and most accurate of them all. He had already made some instruments and had received the Harper mark, which allowed his work to be sold at Gathers. Now he learned how to repair broken frets and stems, and drum frames, and string harps and gitars and do fine marquetry. He was content in a way he had never known before, away from the tension that had become so constant in his parents' rooms. His mother, too, smiled more frequently at the head table or during her lessons with him. So his departure had indeed made life easier for her.

His treble voice lasted until the growth spurt in his thirteenth summer when his body, as well as his throat and speaking equipment, altered dramatically. He and his mother were rehearsing an Equinox duet when suddenly his voice made a dramatic octave drop.

"Well, now, that's that, I guess, dear," she said, resting her arm on the crook of her gitar. She smiled at the appalled look on his face. "Now, love, it isn't really the end of the world, though I daresay your father will be annoyed to have to make changes in the soloist so close to Equinox. Your voice won't last until then."

"But who'll—" In his dismay, Robie's voice broke again. "—sing it with you?"

"Recall that delicate-looking blond lad from Tillek who auditioned last week?" Merelan raised her eyebrows in a droll fashion. "He's not the musician you are, and I'll have to work him hard, but he has the range, if not your skill and experience."

"What's Father going to say?" Robinton asked fretfully. He really didn't want to be around to hear.

Merelan chuckled. "He'll consider that you did this on purpose, of course, to disarrange his concert. He'll rant a bit about your letting him down at a critical time, and then require me to take the lad on for special sessions." She regarded her son with a tilt to her head and an affectionate smile. "You'll probably end up a baritone, you know. You've the right facial structure. And your father's a baritone."

"I've never heard him *sing*," Robie protested.

Merelan chuckled. "Oh, he can. He just doesn't feel he sings well enough." She gave a little chuckle. "But, if you listen closely, you'll hear him joining the baritone line in the choral parts. He had a very good natural voice when he first came to the Hall. He just didn't think it was solo quality." She made a little grimace, followed by a light sigh. "He has to be perfect in anything he does."

"Mother," Robie began, because the problem was becoming more and more pressing, "what will I do when Father takes me for composition as a journeyman?" His unreliable voice cracked on the second syllable.

"Walk the tables first, love, and don't worry. Though I must be truthful and say that I wonder how we're going to keep from upsetting him over that. You already know as much as he does about theory, composition, and even orchestration. Fortunately, I think your particular forte is with vocal, rather than instrumental, music, so you won't be in direct competition with him. He may not see it in the same light, but neither of us can help that, can we? Let's go have some klah, shall we?" She put her gitar carefully back in the case and reached up to caress his cheek. "I still can't get accustomed to the sudden height of you. I wonder how tall you'll be. All the men in my family certainly are."

"I remember Rantou." Robie grinned, because he would never forget how upset his father had been at Rantou's preference for working as a lumberman, when he had the voice and musicality to be a harper. At least Robinton was not the only one whom his father expected to be perfect.

When his voice finally settled into the baritone range, he was nearly the tallest of the second-year apprentices. His father relegated him to the back row of the chorus, where Robinton was quite happy to be. His mother, however, beginning to instruct him in his new voice, was delighted with its flexibility and depth.

"It's a lovely voice, Robie." She flicked her fingers in an excess of delight, smiling at him. "Velvety and rich. Now, we won't force it but I think it's solo quality."

"Even if my father's isn't?"

Merelan made a face. "Yours has a totally different timbre, and a better range. We can work it into something special."

"Something appropriate for simple songs?"

Her grimace darkened and she slapped his arm. "Simple songs that everyone loves to hear, play, and sing! Don't you dare belittle what you do so very well. Far better than he ever could. The only real music he ever wrote—" She stopped, pursing her lips in irritation.

"Was the music he wrote while we were at Benden." Robinton finished the sentence for her. "And you're right. Speaking quite objectively as a harper, my father's compositions are technically perfect and demanding, brilliant for instrumentalists and vocal dexterity, but scarcely for the average holder and craftsman."

She waggled her finger under his nose. "And don't you ever forget that!"

Robinton caught the threatening finger and kissed it lovingly.

"Oh, Robie," she said in a totally different voice. "How different it all could have been." She leaned against him in regret, taking consolation in his tall, strong form and his embrace.

"Well, it wasn't, Mother, and we can't alter what has been." He patted her back soothingly.

Abruptly, and in another lightning change of mood, she pushed away from him, poking him in the ribs. "Will you ever fill out? I swear, you're nothing but bones."

"And there's Lorra complaining I eat twice as much as any other three apprentices. You're a fine one to complain," he added, noting a distinctive pallor in her complexion. She flushed, moving away completely.

"It's nothing." She gave a funny laugh. "Change of life, Ginia says."

"You're not that old, surely," Robinton protested, vehemently denying that *his* mother would ever age. "Why, your voice is better than ever."

She laughed with real humor. "Proof, son of mine, that I'm in my prime, not my decline."

The Harper Bell chimed the turn of the hour and she gave him a little push. "Your harp awaits you."

He kissed her cheek and was out the door to the accompaniment of another chuckle. But he knew she understood his eagerness to put the finishing touches on the lap harp that had caused him so much anxiety. It was one of the four pieces he had to finish creditably to become a journeyman, and he wanted it so that even his father could not find fault with it.

When his work was displayed anonymously with the others, his father passed it by without comment and dismissed someone else's instead. Of course, Robinton had been careful not to repeat patterns of embellishment that he had used on other items. It amused him that never did his father find fault with anything of his amongst those inspected.

The highlight of his second year as an apprentice came in the spring. Robinton was in the semi-basement workshop at the front end of the Hall rectangle when suddenly a bronze dragon landed in the center of the courtyard and the rider cupped his hands and yelled, "Robinton? Robinton! Apprentice Robinton!" That final call was almost a taunt, coming out in a singsong tone.

"By the First Egg! It's *you* the dragonrider wants, Rob," Master Bosler said.

Robinton peered up out of the half-window and saw nothing but bronze dragon feet and belly. "May I go?"

"My dear boy, if a dragonrider calls for anyone," the Master said, grinning, "that person had better hop it . . . Off with you!"

Robinton raced up the steps and out the right-hand door into the courtyard. *"I'm here, F'lon!"* he yelled, racing across the courtyard to the bronze, who had craned his neck around, eyes bright blue and whirling with excitement.

"I told you I'd come . . ." and F'lon modified his tone as he dismounted gracefully to meet his old friend, embracing him in his eagerness.

Once again, Rob was struck by F'lon's unusual amber eyes, which sparkled with delight.

"You also told me you'd Impress bronze . . ." Rob looked politely at the watching dragon. "What's your name, if you don't mind?"

The dragon blinked.

"Ah, he's shy." F'lon's wicked smile belied that. "His name is Simanith." The dragon put his head close to his rider's body, his eyes on Robinton. "You can always speak to my friend Robinton, if you want. He's going to be MasterHarper—when he gets old enough."

"Now, wait a minute!" Robinton exclaimed, holding up his hands defensively and laughing at the very thought. Master-Harper was not only a position he had no desire for but one his father would certainly veto

"Dream, man, that you make Harper. *I* dreamed and look . . ." F'lon gestured dramatically at Simanith, a broad proud grin nearly splitting his face in two.

"I was in the drum tower when the news came in, and I got permission to find out who Impressed bronze, so I've known," Rob told his friend.

"And never sent me word?" F'lon scowled in mock disgust as he stripped off the close-fitting riding helmet.

"Well, you're not supposed to send private messages. I got the whole list though, Rangul and Sellel . . ."

F'lon wrinkled his nose. "Yeah, R'gul and S'lel are bronze riders, too, though why they were picked out of those presented I will never know." He rubbed at his sweaty hair. "Hey, you've got tall."

Robinton stepped back to sweep his friend with an appraising look. "You're not short yourself."

F'lon turned sideways and tapped his shoulder. Obediently Robinton stood back to back with him. F'lon's hand proved their heads were on the same level.

"Going to grow any more?" F'lon asked.

Robinton laughed, partly out of elation that F'lon had remembered his promise and partly because they were the object of much attention from the windows overlooking the courtyard— including, Robinton realized, stifling a groan, the rehearsal hall where his father was working with the chorus. He also caught a glimpse of Lorra, standing on the steps of the Hall, beckoning to him. And then he saw her daughter, Silvina, running across the court toward them. She skidded to a stop and passed the dragon at a more decorous pace.

"Mother . . . says . . . he must have . . . hospitality . . ." she said, catching her breath and looking awed to be so close to dragon and rider.

"This is my friend from Benden Weyr who is now bronze rider, F'lon," Rob said, daring to clap F'lon on the back to show that a dragonrider would allow him such familiarity. "This is Silvina, whose mother makes the best cakes and cookies in the world."

"Well," F'lon said, rubbing his hands together appreciatively, "a dragonrider never refuses hospitality!" He paused, looking directly at Simanith. "He'll wait for me on the heights. Plenty of sun today."

Simanith sprang up after his rider and Robinton reached the steps, and his wings still flung dirt and gravel at them.

"Is riding a dragon as good as you thought it would be?" Rob asked shyly as they entered the Hall.

F'lon grinned and took a deep breath. "You've no idea how good it is." He slapped his friend on his back. "But I'll fly you anywhere you need to go, m'friend. Are you still singing?"

"Baritone now," Rob said with some satisfaction. "You? Not that it matters if you're a bronze rider."

"Oh, it matters," F'lon assured him with sufficient emphasis to reassure. "Dragons like music, and I guess I'm baritone, too." He did a descending scale in what Robinton professionally appraised as a light if pleasant voice.

"You're right—baritone. Too bad I'm not also a rider."

F'lon's expression changed as he caught the wistful note in his friend's voice. "There've been so few clutches that there were a lot of weyrbred to stand on the Hatching Ground. S'loner decided not to Search. Happens sometimes that way." F'lon's rueful smile was genuine. "You'd've made a good rider." Then he paused, his eyes unfocusing briefly.

I will talk to you, Robinton, if you wish me to, said a voice in Robinton's mind, a voice that had F'lon's intonation and texture. The double surprise, that Simanith was speaking to him and in F'lon's voice, caused Robinton to stumble on the steps. Grinning, the rider helped him regain his balance.

"Maybe it's poor substitute, Rob, but the best I can do for you," F'lon said.

"Simanith sounds like you," Robinton managed to remark.

"Does he?" F'lon considered this. "I hadn't noticed. We only hear them in our heads, after all, and not really out loud. Anyway, you can talk to him any time you want."

"Thanks, I will. When I can think of something appropriate to say."

"You will," F'lon said with great certainty.

S ilvina was waiting at the small dining room door and escorted them in. Robinton introduced his friend to Lorra. Though not as flustered as her daughter, she was clearly pleased to dispense hospitality to a dragonrider.

"I sent a messenger to your mother, Rob, because I know she's mentioned Falloner—excuse me, F'lon—as one of her pupils."

So a very cordial hour followed Merelan's entrance. All the cakes were consumed and most of the biscuits, and F'lon promised to fly Merelan anywhere on Pern she wished to go whenever she wished transport. Then she had to excuse herself to give a lesson, but she saw F'lon and Robinton to the entrance, where she assured F'lon she'd take him up on his offer.

"That is, if you're allowed," she said, glancing up at the tall young rider with a mischievous look in her eyes.

"I don't have much else to do. Even this," he told her, gesturing around the Harper Hall court, "is sort of work. We have to *know* how to get to any place on Pern, so actually, this is seen as a legitimate visit. I can come as often as I like."

F'lon had increased his assertiveness, Robinton noticed, exchanging a knowing glance with his mother.

"You can drum me if I'm needed," F'lon said, awarding Rob another of his affectionate punches before he leaped to Simanith's raised forearm and vaulted from there to the bronze's back.

"He's very much the rider, isn't he?" Merelan murmured to her son as they both waved farewell. "What a charming lad."

"You used to call him a devil, Mother," Robinton said chidingly.

"Shortening his name will have had no change on his essential nature, love. In fact, it's probably compounded the problem," she said tersely. "But I liked it in him that he would honor that promise to you." She gave his arm a final squeeze and a gentle push toward the workroom and his interrupted session.

Master Gennell did pause on his way to the head table to inquire if the visitor had been Robinton's friend at Benden Weyr. Robinton apologized for the interruption.

"No need, lad, not when a dragonrider favors you with his company."

Petiron, whose rehearsal had been interrupted by the dragon's arrival, scowled at him, but Robinton looked away as if he hadn't seen. It wasn't as if *he* had asked F'lon to visit. He disliked being discourteous to anyone, especially his own father, but he had learned, painfully, that anything he did annoyed his father, even when he did nothing. He tried not to remember things his dorm mates had said about their fathers, and special things their fathers had done for—and, more importantly in Rob's eyes, *with*—them. Harpers, of course, were different, and he shouldn't judge one by another's standards. Yet . . . that didn't make it easier being his father's son.

He completed all projects and passed all the examinations that would promote him to the rank of journeyman by the time he was halfway through his third Turn of training. Of course, he had had a head start, having begun his training sooner than any of the other lads in his group, who learned to come to him for help with any difficulties in their studies or their projects. Not even Lear teased him about his competence because, by the time they reached Third with him, they knew all about his problems with his father—and sympathized—and they all adored his mother. That was easier for Robinton to deal with: he adored her, too. But he knew, if his father didn't, that every performance took more out of her than it should. He even took his worry to MasterHealer Ginia, when Maizella told him his mother had fainted after one intense rehearsal prior to the Spring Equinox Gather at Fort.

"I really don't know what's ailing her, Rob," Ginia said, frowning slightly, "though I've made her promise to take the summer off and rest. Let Petiron handle whatever vocal training has to be done—" She shot him a searching look. "Or you." Her expression softened and she patted his hand. "You almost do anyway, from what I've heard."

Robinton sat up straighter in the chair, alarmed. All he needed was for his father to know about his coaching some of the chorus.

"Now, don't fret. Your father notices only what he wishes, and he certainly has not seen what's happening to Merelan."

"But you don't know what *is* happening," Robinton protested.

"I know that rest, a lack of tension—you know how your mother is before a performance, learning new music . . ."

He nodded, because she often worked herself as hard bringing the soloists up to the level Petiron expected as he did his instrumentalists and chorus.

"I think a summer down in South Boll with her family, with absolutely no performances and responsibilities, will see her right. It has been a very hard winter."

She patted Robinton's hand again. "You're a good son, Rob, and your concern does you credit. Now, I'll keep you informed, but you help me in getting her to take a good long rest, will you?"

"Have you spoken to Master Gennell?"

"Repeatedly," Ginia said, pursing her full mouth with

indignation. "But we all know that the Spring Equinox is important in our calendar and had better go off with no problems . . ." She rose, a signal that their interview was at an end, and smiled at him. "You should go with her and be sure she eats well and rests every day."

"I'll try." And he'd take F'lon up on his offer to fly Master-Singer Merelan anywhere.

As it happened, he didn't go with his mother: his father did. Merelan collapsed after singing the exacting solo at the end of the Equinox Ceremony, and Petiron could no longer ignore the fact that his spouse was ill.

Robinton did send the drum message, requesting F'lon's assistance, and he did help his mother onto Simanith's back. He had to step away as his father mounted behind her. The fact that his father looked distinctly nervous, anxious, and worried did not at all alleviate his own fears for her. Just this once, he sent his thoughts at his father, just this once, think of her first!

An hour later, F'lon returned and, over a cool juice drink and more of Lorra's light pastries, gave details of how he had installed Merelan in the cliffside dwelling with its splendid view of the sea, and how Petiron had hovered like an old wherry, fussing until F'lon was sure he'd drive Merelan insane with his attentions. Her youngest sister had appealed to her spouse to take the man away and let Merelan rest, and promised to see that Merelan did rest.

"She was upset when she saw your mother. I remember her being slight at Benden but not . . . not . . . frail," F'lon said, glancing at Lorra, who nodded.

"I spoke to Ginia, and she believes that a full summer off will restore my mother's health." Even as Rob spoke he caught Lorra and F'lon exchanging glances. "Now, look, if there's something I should know, tell me. She's my *mother*! I have a right to know."

Lorra turned to him, making a sudden decision. "Ginia doesn't know, so what can she tell you? But she's hoping the rest will help. Merelan has never been very strong . . ."

"You mean, after giving birth to a big lug like me?" Robinton demanded. He had overheard his father complaining that having a child had seriously damaged her.

"You weren't that big at birth, for all of you now," Lorra said in her droll fashion, "so don't cover yourself with midden dung in guilty reparation. *You* have never been at fault." She cleared her throat, realizing that her emphasis implied that she knew who was. "Merelan's always lived on nerve. It's the energy she uses to sing and perform at the level she does that drains her so. But there comes a time in a woman's life when she isn't as resilient as she was in her twenties."

"Mother would die if she couldn't sing . . ."

"It's unlikely to come to that," Lorra said sharply. "But she certainly will have to cut back on these exhausting performances. It isn't as if Maizella's not capable; or *he* can write for Halanna, who'd only be too happy to take on Merelan's First Singer duties." Her eyes flashed, and Robinton couldn't resist chuckling at her comment about Halanna. "Your father needs a scare like this," she went on. "He takes Merelan too much for granted."

"She's really the only one capable of singing some of his scores," Robinton said, oddly on the defensive.

"Well, he can just write simpler. Anyway, your songs are the ones anyone can sing and enjoy, Rob." When he started to demur, she flicked her fingers at him. "Oh, I know, I know, but it's the truth, isn't it, dragonrider?"

F'lon grinned, nodding vehemently. Then he rose, brushing pastry flakes from his lips and off his undershirt.

"Any time you want to visit her, give me a roll," he said, beginning to close the fastening on his jacket. "I've got to hunt Simanith on the way back."

W hen Merelan returned to the Harper Hall in the autumn, she was sun-browned and appeared much restored. Petiron continued to be solicitous and, as Robinton heard Master Bosler remark to a journeyman, he seemed to have mellowed. Well, he may have mellowed toward others, Robinton realized later, but never toward him. In fact, if anything, Petiron ignored his son more thoroughly than ever. There were not even any of the usual pithy complaints leveled at the baritone section. But then, because Robinton was more or less the leader of the baritone section, Petiron had no real cause for complaint. Everyone did better than their best at all times, as a sort of aid to keep him from his father's shafts of criticism. Petiron did smile more frequently, if mainly at the sopranos and altos, and he did praise the treble more often. Merelan did still coach his soloists, but she was given fewer voices to train.

Master Gennell called Robinton in one morning two seven-days after his parents' return. Sensitive to appearances now, Robinton thought the MasterHarper looked tired, as well as older.

"You've turned fifteen, now, haven't you, Rob?" Gennel began. Robinton nodded. "So how are we going to keep you busy this term?"

The question shook Robinton and he shifted nervously in the chair. "I'm not sure what you mean, sir." He paused, cleared his throat, and then blurted out, "Theory and composition are usually next term . . ."

"Ah, my lad, you've mastered those long since. I saw the orchestral piece you did for Washell, and none of us can fault it." Gennell smiled reassuringly. Then his expression altered. "But I cannot assign you to your father's class. And I must find suitable studies for you."

Robinton closed his eyes in relief at the knowledge that he would not have to endure a class with his father.

"I'll be plain, Rob, I've never understood your father's antipathy toward you, yet there's never been a word of complaint from you."

"He's my father, Master Gennell . . ."

"Well, we won't go into that any further since, in effect, the entire Hall has fostered you—and your talent." When Robinton ducked his head with embarrassment, Master Gennell prodded his knee. "Modesty is all very well and good, Robinton, but don't let it get in your way."

Robinton didn't know what to do and looked all around the comfortable office for inspiration. His glance caught the map, with its little colored pegs signifying the position of journeymen and masters across the continent. There were many places without pegs, which meant they were waiting to be assigned a harper.

"Sir, I like teaching," he said, pointing to the map, "and I've had good results with those I've tutored."

"Not that all those unassigned holdings would accept a harper if I had one to send them," Gennell said drolly. And when Robinton looked apprehensive, he added with a sigh, "There are some holds who profess not to require the services we provide."

"I find that hard to believe," Robinton said, appalled. Not want to learn how to read, and write, and reckon? How could people get along in life without such basic skills?

"Believe it, Rob," Gennell said, shifting in his chair. "At least, since there are so many still who do, we're not in any danger of going empty the way the Weyrs did." He cleared his throat, and moved records about on his desk. "You may discover that not everyone respects harpers as we would like them to. However, to a happier topic, would you take on a purely teaching assignment?"

Robinton shifted again, this time with excitement. He knew his dorm mates thought him daft to enjoy teaching—lighting the dim wits, they called it. But Robinton never saw the task as a chore. He looked for the end result, the bright smile of understanding on a student's face when knowledge suddenly seeped in.

"I think I'd like that, sir." He took a surreptitious glance at the map but then realized a fact. "But, Master Gennell, who's going to take instruction from someone only fifteen? I know I'm well grown, but . . ." He flicked his fingers out in a helpless gesture.

"If you're assigned to work under a more experienced teacher, you'd be welcome anywhere," Gennell said, rubbing his chin, "especially if you promise me to continue writing those songs and ballads."

Robinton flushed. "I can't seem to stop writing them," he said meekly.

"Good. We need to freshen up the repertoire with catchy tunes and musical nonsense. People like to whistle a tune, like to sing a new song and find harmonies. You're good at that. I expect you to continue."

"As long as it's all right . . ." Robinton said in an almost unintelligible murmur.

"It is more than 'all right,' Robinton, it is essential. Now, stop coloring up like a glowbasket. Learn to take honest praise with the same dignity with which you've received criticism." Abruptly, Gennell cleared his throat. "Well, that's decided, but I wanted to know if you wished to stay on in the Hall. We'd find something to keep you busy, if you did, though your mother's much better since she came back."

Robinton met Master Gennell's concerned grey eyes and gave a grateful smile. "I'm your apprentice, sir; you can assign me where you will. Where I'd do some good." What he didn't add hung in the air: *Because I can't do any good here.*

"Well then, that's settled. I'll see who can use an assistant harper."

Robinton was still trying to absorb this astonishing news when he found himself out in the corridor.

To be utterly truthful, he looked forward to leaving the Harper Hall and getting away from the constant censorious glances of his father. Privately he thought this was what was eating away at his mother: this tension and having to placate his father all the time. He wanted to get on with his own life—without constraint and with an enthusiasm he wasn't able to give scope to, here in the Harper Hall. He'd really enjoy being away—and as Master Gennell had promised to keep him informed about his mother's health, he could go with an easy conscience. It'd be so much better for her, too, if she didn't have to worry about him, had a reason to be proud of him.

He went back to putting the final coat of varnish on the lap harp he was making. He would take that with him, he thought, though originally he had made it to sell. He had already earned quite a few marks at Gathers with his output. When Jerint asked him what the MasterHarper had wanted him for, Robinton shrugged it off.

"Next term's duties," he said, which had the advantage of being the truth.

Robinton had become so adept at keeping emotions to himself that it had become a habit. And though he yearned to tell his mother, he knew she was busy with lessons this afternoon. He'd just have to hold his good news in. It was something to relish, anyway. As relieved as he was that he wouldn't have to take Theory under his father, he was most excited at the prospect of leaving the Hall on his first official assignment. He also knew he'd had a hint of something the oldest apprentices would die to hear: he suspected that Master Gennell was about to reveal who would walk the tables—the best of all the traditions in the Harper Hall. The announcement of who had made journeyman rank could be any day now; there was a lot of talk about its imminence in the dorms.

Sometimes the lucky ones were warned to pack what they'd need, but just as often, no clue at all was given until Master Gennell called out the names. That was always a great evening. The masters loved to surprise the fourths, make them sweat a little before giving them the reward for four Turns' work. At least he'd have time to warn his mother of his leaving; but he knew she'd be pleased for him. Even being assigned as assistant harper was an honor.

Robinton paused in his varnishing, whooshing the fumes away from his nose. The reek was stifling.

"That's the ticket," Master Bosler said, pausing by Robinton's work station. He gave him a quick pat on the back. "One of the nicer ones with all that careful inlaid pattern. And the skybroom wood! Very good! We can get a good price for it at the next Gather."

"With skybroom wood hard to come by, I think I might just keep it for a while," Robinton said, watching Bosler's expression. Would the Master have an idea of Robinton's immediate future? He knew that Master Gennell listened to the opinions of his masters. As an apprentice, Robinton's studies were governed by what all the masters—probably his father, too—thought of his progress, so maybe Master Bosler was aware of his good news. But no, the lined face and keen eyes did not alter.

So much for that, Robinton thought, and with a smile for his Master, he went back to applying the varnish. He wasn't using a quick-drying type because he wanted to avoid leaving any brush strokes.

By dinnertime, his mood had swung in the opposite direction and his stomach was churning. Maybe it had been his father's idea in the first place, removing the unwanted son from the Hall? His father was more likely to suggest he go drudge for someone in a back-of-beyond small hold, too far away for him to take time off and come back to the Hall. It'd be ironic if Robinton was assigned to Master Ricardy at Fort Hold. He already had three assistants, and another, elderly harper who did nothing but entertain for the old aunties and uncles of the Hold. No, definitely, Master Gennell wanted him to help teach. That had been the crux of the interview: would he be willing to teach?

Though the dinner was one of Lorra's better ones, Robinton found himself unable to eat, a fact immediately noted by his table companions, who were well aware of his voracious appetite.

"Inhaling varnish all afternoon has put me off," he offered as explanation.

Falawny gave him a startled look. "First time in three Turns it ever has," he remarked. "Ah, well, more for us, certainly, eh, fellows?" And he speared a third slice of roast from the platter being passed.

Robinton hadn't seen any packs in the hallway, so no one had been warned that tonight might be the night to walk the

tables. He sneaked a glance at the fourth-term table: judging by
the way dinner was being consumed, their appetites weren't
being affected. Determinedly, he mopped his bread in the
gravy and ate that, though his stomach roiled with either
hunger or nerves. He actually hadn't had all that much experience with either condition. He'd never gone hungry, and he
refused to let himself get nervous just over a hunch that tonight
might be *the* night.

He shifted about on his chair a lot, shooting glances at his
mother, but she was busy either eating, quite normally, or chatting with Master Washell and his father, who bracketed her at
the head table. Well, maybe she hadn't been told.

Because he spent so much of the dinner time looking about
the dining hall, he did notice that Journeyman Shonagar was
seated to one side. But there was nothing especially unusual
about Shonagar's presence: journeymen were constantly in
and out of the Hall, on errands, on reassignments, or to ask
advice of their masters.

The sweet and klah had been served, and Robinton managed
to get those down with no trouble.

Then he heard a chair being shoved back, and Master Gennell was on his foot, tapping his glass for attention. The room
was already still, breaths universally bated.

"Ah, I see that I have your attention." His grin swept from the
masters' tables, across the journeymen's, and toward the
apprentices. "So, Master Washell, send out for the extra chairs."

This task was customarily done by the first-term apprentices,
who scurried out and rattled back in, each carrying a chair
which they set in the spaces the journeymen made at their
tables. Twelve! Now, who would be seated in them in the next
few minutes? There were nineteen in the final term of their
apprenticeship. All of them managed to look calm and indifferent as befit trained harpers.

It was also the custom for those who walked to be escorted
ritually from their lowly apprentice bench to a chair at the
journeymen's tables.

Gennell took a list from his pocket and pretended to have
trouble reading it.

"Journeyman Kailey." The former apprentice jumped to his feet, and a grinning journeyman instructor immediately strode across the room during the applause. Then everyone had the beat and began the traditional singsong chant: "Walk, Kailey, walk. It's time to go ahead. Walk, Kailey, walk. Into your new life. Walk, Kailey, walk."

"You'll be going to Wide Bay Hold in Keroon," Gennell said, his voice rising easily above the chanting and the clapping.

And so it went for the next ten as well, ending with the popular Evenek, who had two journeymen jostling each other good-naturedly to do the honors. Evenek's lyrical tenor voice had often been matched with Merelan's in duet, and now she clapped loudly at the announcement of his assignment to Telgar Hold, a prestigious posting.

That left one chair—and eight more possible journeymen.

Gennell waited until Evenek was seated and he had been congratulated by those around him.

"To be a harper requires many talents, as you all know. Some of us are endowed—unfairly—" he put in, grinning charmingly around, "with more than a sufficient share."

Robinton looked over those remaining at the fourth-term tables. Really, Kailey and Evenek had been the top men: none of the others were "unfairly" talented.

"However, when the fundamentals of our craft have been well and truly learned, I insist that we hold no one back from the rank they are entitled to by knowledge and ability, and in this case, rare talent."

The room was buzzing, everyone trying to decide who the lucky one was. The fourth-termers were just as puzzled.

"Journeyman Shonagar, you claimed this right when you left the Harper Hall two Turns ago: exercise it."

Every head turned to watch Shonagar rise and, with the wicked half-grin for which he was well known, walk with measured step down the aisle to the third-term table.

When Shonagar stopped by him, Robinton felt paralyzed. His mouth dropped and his eyes nearly bugged out.

"Shut your mouth, pull your eyes in, and get up," Shonagar muttered in an undertone. "That gets you even, the only way you could." Even as he spoke to Robinton, Shonagar's grin widened at the surprise and shock that had hushed the hall.

Robinton was still trying to assimilate what he'd just heard—his name announced as journeyman—when Shonagar plunged a hand under his arm and, with a heave, got Robinton to his feet. "*Walk!* Walk, Robinton!" With that, Shonagar turned him and started propelling him to the journeymen's table. "Walk, Robinton, *walk!*"

"And none too soon," Master Washell shouted, jumping to his feet and smacking his big hands together over his head, urging people to join him. Bosler stood, clapping in rhythm with the reluctant Journeyman's stride. Betrice was up, as were the other Masters at the table, Ogolly and Severeid, and the kitchen workers crowded in at the serving doors, adding their noise to the general furor. The only two not on their feet were Robinton's parents: his mother was weeping, and his father seemed to be too stunned and stony-faced to be able to move. Robinton knew then, as Shonagar had told him, that he had gotten back at his father the only decent way he could—by success.

"Walk, Robinton, walk!"

Unashamed of the tears streaming down his face and swallowing the lump in his throat, Robinton walked the tables, bearing himself as proudly as he could, despite the tendency of his knees to wobble. Still steering him, Shonagar pushed him past the head table.

Through her tears his mother shot him an exultant look and a weak smile before she had to wipe her cheeks again. Neither of them looked at Petiron.

Installed in the final chair, Robinton was still shaking so badly that he could barely accept the congratulations of the other new journeymen. He noticed that they all had rank knots on their shoulders and then he felt Shonagar slip one up his arm and to his shoulder.

"Journeyman Robinton will go to Master Lobirn at High

Reaches, where it's hoped this sensible fellow will keep Master Lobirn out of more trouble," Gennell announced, and then called for glasses and wine for the new Journeymen. Sometime in that interval Petiron slipped from the room, but Merelan did not. And that was as it should be, Robinton thought.

Chapter 9

▼▼▼▼▼▼▼▼▼▼▼▼▼▼▼▼▼▼▼▼▼▼▼▼▼▼▼▼▼▼▼▼▼▼▼▼▼▼

And so Robinton headed off to his first official assignment with five full packs, even though he had stored some childish mementos in the Hall's vast cellars. His mother insisted that he drum a request to F'lon.

"It won't hurt your reputation at all for you to arrive on dragonback," she said firmly.

"It's showing off, Mother," he insisted.

"Others have requested conveyance," she went on, helping him pack up everything in his little room.

Whenever he returned to the Hall, he would bunk in the journeymen's quarters. He hadn't so much as laid eyes on his father since the night before, but that didn't surprise him. He was now separated from his father, both as parent and teacher. His relief was intense, his concern for his mother immense. She seemed so frail, and her hands trembled a bit as she wrapped his pipes and put them in one of the packs. Well, this parting was hard on them both.

"You'd need three pack animals to carry all this junk," she said, sniffing. But she gave him a big smile when he bent to see if she was crying. "Oh, I shall miss you, my dear son." She put both hands on his arms and looked up at him with misted eyes. "I shall miss you most frightfully, but I am also so very *glad* that you've been promoted out of your father's way."

"What—I mean, did he say . . . anything?"

"No." She gave a little laugh, turning back to stuff the last few things away. "He hasn't even spoken to me. And that's a sign of his total rejection of your making journeyman." She shrugged. "He'll get over it, though I don't think he'll ever forgive Gennell for doing it while he was out of the Hall."

"Shards! I hadn't thought of that!" Robinton cringed at the thought of Master Gennell plagued by his father's dislike.

"Now, now, Robie, Gennell's well able for your father's foibles. As I am. He'll simmer a while, and then go on and write it out in more music for me to sing."

Robinton clutched his mother's arm and made her look up at him. "You will be careful, won't you, Mother? And not give too much to his music?"

She patted his cheek lovingly. "I'll be good, and rest. How can I not? With Ginia, Betrice, and Lorra all at me—*and* your father. I didn't mean to scare him, but I think I have. He'll be much more careful of me. He does love me, you know, most possessively. That's what all this has been about."

Robinton nodded and then embraced his mother, feeling her thin bones and trying not to use his young strength to bruise her. But he wanted to hold her as tight as possible, for he was fearful he might never see her again.

"Oh, Robie," she said teasingly. "I'm much better. Don't fret. You *know* things will be easier . . . now . . ." she added apologetically. "I shall write or drum if I don't hear from you, young man. You hear me?"

"Indeed I do, MasterSinger. They've quite a good network of runners at High Reaches."

"They'd have to," she said with a patronizing sniff. "Living back of beyond like that."

The unmistakable trumpeting of a dragon reverberated through the courtyard.

"I believe your transport has arrived," she said, smiling, though her chin seemed to quiver.

He hurried to load up his packs, but was interrupted by the appearance of Masters Gennell, Washell, and Ogolly. They immediately pushed him out of the way and shared the packs among them, allowing him only the new harp case.

"I'm honored—I mean, you don't need to—" Robinton tried to protest, but he was overruled. Shrugging, he allowed them the duty.

Master Gennell winked at him as they walked out into the hall, and Robinton realized that this display of solid goodwill was as much for his mother's benefit as to make up for his father's absence. Their kindness touched him once again, and he had to swallow back tears.

"You made it, huh?" F'lon shouted as he slid down to Simanith's raised forearm and started piling luggage on the harness. "Congratulations, Journeyman Robinton! You've got greetings from all your old friends at Benden, Weyr and Hold." To the other new journeymen waiting in the courtyard for their conveyancing, he said: "Your dragons will be along shortly— and congratulations."

Loading took only moments and then Robinton had to make his farewells. His mother pulled his head down for one last kiss and embrace. He shook hands with the Masters and promised them that he'd do his best.

"Give my special regards to Master Lobirn," his mother called as he climbed up to Simanith's back. "He may remember me."

"Now who can forget you, Merelan?" Master Gennell said, putting a comforting arm around her shoulders.

That was how Robinton remembered his mother in the trying initial days under Master Lobirn's supervision. Fortunately, F'lon deposited him and his effects in the courtyard of the high and windy Hold and departed, seen by relatively few. And especially not Master Lobirn.

For that person was unimpressed with having so young a journeyman.

"Don't know what Gennell's thinking about, walking you up

at fifteen! Indeed, I don't, so don't go expecting any cosseting from me, young man." Lobirn eyed Robinton and scowled at the lean length of him.

It didn't help, Robinton thought, that he towered above the diminutive Master Harper. The man came not quite to Robinton's shoulder; he was heavy in the chest—he sang bass—and narrowed through the hip to short, skinny legs. His features were pulled together in the middle of his wide face as if they should have inhabited a much narrower one. He had a shock of heavy, wavy hair with bands of silver, making him look striped. All put together, he was an almost ludicrous figure. But no one snickered at Master Lobirn. He had too much presence, Robinton quickly decided, to ever be the butt of ridicule. His muddy brown eyes were shrewd, and there was no way that Robinton was going to underestimate him.

"I never expected to walk so soon," Robinton murmured, trying to be self-effacing.

Lobirn gave him a quick look, as if he thought Robinton was dissembling. "I shall expect much from you then, young man. Where were you raised? Who are your parents?"

Robinton was quite happy to answer since he hoped that would mollify his new Master. But if his mother met with Lobirn's approval, his father did not. Robinton was shocked—less at the blunt remarks about his father's sort of composing, which Lobirn felt was far too sophisticated to be of any use to anyone, than at hearing such criticism voiced, especially in front of the man's son. Not that it didn't mirror his own very private assessment of Petiron's ornate compositions, but to have mentioned such doubts would have seemed disloyal and a betrayal: as if his own songs merited more attention than his father's more ambitious works. It came as another shock that it *was* his music that Lobirn used extensively—though Lobirn did not know that Robinton had been the composer.

Robinton knew better than to make something of that approval, but it did much to help him endure Lobirn's crotchety behavior, his temper, his inconsistencies, and his general dislike of having to break in a "snot-nosed, wet-eared" novice.

Still, when the old Master saw how patient Robinton was

with some of the more backward students, he began to mellow a trifle. He delivered a word or two of appreciation. Lobirn himself was too short-tempered, and quick with a slap for the inattentive, so Robinton was given not only the slow but the very young, who had to be taught the basic Teaching Ballads. He didn't mind: in fact, it was a pleasure to sing those songs of his that Master Gennell had incorporated in the early Teaching Songs. It was quiet contentment to him that his songs were used and he could sing them without fear of Petiron's wrath.

He was also assigned the duty of spending several days of each sevenday going to the distant holds, often the only outsider they would see. These trips would end once the heavy weather settled in the high hills. So he copied out extra music for the holders to keep and study until his next trip. He had to write a report for each of his journeys; to his surprise, Lobirn went over these reports carefully.

Besides Robinton and Lobirn's three apprentices, there was another Journeyman Harper—Mallan, who was High Reaches born, and who handled other teaching routes and also some of the classes in the big Hold. The two Journeymen shared a small inner apartment on the Holder's floor, with two bed cubicles and a decent-sized day room, and shared the bathing facilities down the hall with the three apprentices who were quartered in one big inner room. Master Lobirn had an outside apartment with his wife, Lotricia, a faded woman with an enchanting smile and a kindly manner reminiscent of Betrice's. She had been an apprentice healer when she met Lobirn, but when they had become espoused, she had ended her studies and accompanied him to his posting at High Reaches, where she devoted herself to rearing the four children of their union. The one daughter had married a High Reach holder and occasionally visited her parents with her children. The sons had been apprenticed to other trades, although they returned now and again for a High Reaches Gather.

"None of them could carry a tune in a sack," Robinton once heard Lobirn say in total disgust. "Took after their mother's side. But they've done well. They've done well."

Lotricia was always bringing "her boys"—as she called the

apprentices and journeymen—extra food. "You're all growing, and you're all nothing but bones," was her happy complaint, and her offerings were always welcome.

With such constant travel and the busy schedule in the Hold when he wasn't traveling, Robinton had little time to compose. He took to writing the tunes that filled his head while on the road, stopping frequently to note, in tiny cramped script, the measures that he had piped or whistled or sung into being as he trudged up and down steep tracks. He barely missed injuring himself on several occasions when composing so distracted him that he strayed off the narrow runner traces that were sometimes all he had to follow to his destination. The advantage of composing as he walked was that he could sing and play as loudly as he wished—often getting an answering echo from the hills around him.

With the first big snowstorm, his traveling came to a halt. In fact, he was trapped for three days in Murfy Hold, which was cramped at best, and worse when the fifteen members of the hold were confined day and night.

Murfytwen, the twentieth man to hold there, broke trail for Robinton when the storm had died. He had an urgent need to collect supplies that he hoped were awaiting him at High Reaches, a trip he had delayed far too long.

"Easier to haul it all back on snow, though," Murfytwen said cheerfully as he lashed the supplies to the sled that had been loaned him for the trip. "See ya when I see ya, Harper. Thanks for them new tunes. We'll learn 'em good. An' Twenone will know his times tables by the time you're back again. Promise!"

With his gloved thumb up in a final gesture, Murfytwen started trudging back the way he had come.

High Reaches, set on its bluffs, like the broadside of a fishing ship, had weathered many storms, and its thick walls kept all but the most shrieking winds from being heard. But living in this Hold was quite different from living in the Hall or even in Benden Hold. As every Hold should be, it was self-contained, with journeymen in all skills and a Masterminer, Furlo, as well as his gangers, who mainly worked for copper, which was always in demand. Master Furlo had a double quartet among his miners who sang most evenings, at the drop of a hat, as Mallan put it, grinning. Furlo was good on the gitar, having had to accompany his chorus since he was familiar with their repertoire, but Robinton offered to take over and Furlo was only too happy to accede. High Reaches Hold had enough instrumentalists, thanks to Master Lobirn's efforts, to mount a considerable orchestra. The worst of the winter evenings would go by quite happily, with Lord Holder Faroguy and his Lady, Evelene, joining in from the head table. Three of their twelve children either played or sang creditably.

The evenings were not restricted to musical ones, but also to wrestling and other such physical exercises. Robinton joined in the Hall and Step runs with enthusiasm. His long legs and the lung capacity singing had developed in him gave him an advantage.

He hadn't ever heard of Hall running—at Fort, even in the worst winters, one could get outside for exercise. But here, where the holders were confined by weather and terrain, the long halls were put to use as sprinting alleys, or for long-distance running. The stairs were also utilized to see who could get to the top and back fastest—preferably without breaking a leg. Sprained ankles were common, as were strained shoulders from grabbing banisters in the effort to prevent more serious falls.

Robinton did well enough in the running, but he eschewed the physical duels. Harpers tended to be pacifists, with a few notable exceptions: Shonagar had been champion wrestler in his home hold and at the Harper Hall, besting the holder of the medium weight title at Fort Hold on three occasions. But harpers usually would not risk injuring their hands, and Robinton used that as a legitimate—and, to most, acceptable—

excuse. That did not keep him from the censure of the acknowledged wrestling and dueling champion, a young man in his
mid-twenties, named Fax.

Even on his first encounter with the young holder—a question of who took the steps first at a landing where several halls
met—Robinton felt uneasy in the man's presence. Fax was
aggressive, impatient, and condescending. A nephew of Lord
Faroguy, he had recently taken Hold of one of the Valley prop-
erties, which he ran with a heavy hand, demanding perfection
of all beholden to him. Some craftsmen had asked for transfers
to other holdings.

Robinton heard unsettling rumors about Fax's methods, but
it wasn't for a harper to criticize—or to take precedence over a
holder, so he had courteously allowed Fax to go first. All he got
for his deference was a sneer, and he noted that Fax, who had
been striding with urgency to get somewhere, now slowed his
pace deliberately. What that proved escaped Robinton completely, but it did give some of the rumors more credibility than
he had originally thought.

One evening Fax went out of his way to get Robinton on the
wrestling mats: not with himself but with one of his younger
holders.

"An even match, I'd say, pound for pound and inch for
inch," Fax said, his expression bland but his eyes challenging.

"I fear I'd be no match at all," Robinton said. "As a harper,
I've only the usual training in body sports. Now, if your holder
sings, then I'll accept a contest."

Fax regarded him a long moment and then, with a sneer,
swung toward Lobirn. "One phase of training that is so often
ignored, Master Lobirn."

Lobirn was able to give back as well as take and he did so
with a matching contempt. "Many a man has rued the day he
tried to best a harper, young Fax, for song and story last longer
than mere physical prowess," he replied. "Or is your lad still
complaining that my long-legged lad has bested him in the
Hall runs every time they've competed?"

Robinton was surprised that his Master was aware that

Robinton had won so many of those races and frankly amazed that his wins had disgruntled Fax. At the time, the runner-up had taken his losing in good part.

Fax awarded Master Lobirn a sustained and disturbing look, gave Robinton a final contemptuous glance, and left. Robinton breathed a sigh of relief.

"Watch him! He really wanted an opportunity to humiliate you in front of the entire Hold," Lobirn said. "I can't have that. Ruins discipline in the class. But if you wanted to do some work-outs with Mallan on the defensive moves you were taught at the Hall, it wouldn't be a bad idea. For you both. And the apprentices."

"I think I will, Master," Robinton replied soberly. There was little doubt that Fax had a personal grudge against him. Or maybe it was against all harpers. In any event, Fax did not request a harper for his holding. That was his decision and his folk would be stinted by the lack, but only Lord Faroguy could require his holders to provide education. Since Fax's holding appeared to be so much more profitable under his management, Lord Faroguy had little reason to question his methods. Somehow Fax managed to keep from his uncle the fact that his profits were obtained by whippings and threats of eviction.

Mallan and Robinton went through the drills on mats, and if Robinton was able to floor Mallan occasionally, the other journeyman was just as deft. At least they each were capable of quick, reflexive action.

W ith the pass shut by massive drifts, communication was now limited to the drums, and an eight-hour evening watch was one of Robinton's less agreeable duties as a journeyman. Even a blazing fire in the hearth did not keep the drum tower warm enough for comfort. The pacing of every drum-watch-keeper since the Hold had been carved out of solid rock had worn a trough around the perimeter of the tower. One had to be careful not to stumble. One good thing, though, the tower could be reached from within the Hold itself. Some Southern Holds had outside stairways to their drum heights.

Manning the drum tower was no sinecure and required close attention. Snowfall sometimes muffled incoming messages, and outgoing ones could cause minor avalanches, heard as distant thunders in the night and made eerier by the darkness. On clear evenings, when both Belior and Timor were full, he could sometimes see the seven spires of the abandoned High Reaches Weyr. He wondered how it varied from the other two he had seen. Probably not by much, but maybe he'd see if he couldn't get in that one, too, simply for comparison's sake.

All the new surroundings and experiences struck fresh chords within him. Rather boldly, he composed a song for the miners' double quartet that was more suited to their vocal skills than many available ballads: a humorous tale of six verses and a chorus about a miner and his love, just their style. It was so well received that Master Lobirn wanted to know where Robinton had been hiding it.

"Oh, well, it was among the stuff I brought up," Robinton said, caught unawares.

"Really?"

"Well, sort of. I mean, the melody was written out. I sort of rearranged it for the miners and added the chorus so everyone could join in."

"Did you now?" Master Lobirn eyed his Journeyman and pursed his lips thoughtfully. "Well, if you say so."

Robinton retreated as soon as he politely could. Master Lobirn had only glanced at the last packet to come in from the Harper Hall before handing it over to him. There were such good voices and players here, and a new song could liven evenings so much that Robinton hadn't been able to resist the temptation to sneak in his new song. He'd be more circumspect and just adapt other music, already in the repertoire.

He underestimated Master Lobirn.

"You wrote these," Lobirn said, stamping into his bed cubicle one evening, a sheath of neat music scores in one hand, his expression accusatory.

As Robinton was in the process of writing down yet another

tune, he could scarcely deny it when Lobirn snagged the hide out of his hand and began comparing them.

"You've written almost all the new music the Hall has been sending out, haven't you?"

Robinton struggled to his feet, a difficult enough maneuver due to the cramped space and Lobirn's proximity to his bed. He felt at an extreme disadvantage lying sprawled on his back. Then he realized that towering above Lobirn was not exactly a good tactic either, because it forced his agitated Master to have to look up.

"Master Lobirn, I can explain . . ." He squeezed past the man and gestured for him to exit into the larger living room. Mallan was not to be seen.

"By the First Egg, I am waiting to hear!" Lobirn said, his neck red and swollen, his eyes blazing. "All this time—it must be five, six Turns, I've been passing music around that was written by . . . you! It's bad enough you're a journeyman at fifteen, but a composer at—at *ten!*" Lobirn slammed the offending scores down on the table and then pinned them down with his fist, glaring around at Robinton, who had seated himself to be diplomatically lower than his Master.

"Actually . . ." Robinton quailed at having to tell the truth. "One or two were written when I was a little younger."

"A *little* younger?" Libirn's eyes nearly popped. Planting both fists on the table, he leaned menacingly over Robinton. "Just *when* did you write the first? How old *were* you?"

"I . . . I did some variations when I was three, my mother says."

Lobirn regarded him and then, in one of his characteristically abrupt changes, threw back his head and started to howl with laughter. He laughed so hard that he had to steady himself on the table edge, and then collapsed into the other chair, holding his sides. As the door was open, the laughter carried down the hall and brought Lotricia to see what had her husband in such a mood. Journeymen quartered next door also came to see what was happening.

"Whatever did you tell Lobirn?" Lotricia asked, eyebrows risen almost to her hairline. "I haven't heard him laugh like that since Fax got caught in the wine barrel." She was smiling. In fact, everyone, except the now concerned Robinton, was grinning.

"I . . . didn't *tell* him anything," Robinton said truthfully. The reason for the laughter was still spread across the table and hurriedly he tried to gather the sheets up.

Lobirn's hands stopped him, and his laughing abated as he stammered out an explanation to his spouse. "This one . . . is the . . . one who's written . . . all the new tunes."

"Oh, no, not all."

"No? Not all? You gave others a look-in?" And that set Lobirn off again.

Lotricia planted her hands on her ample hips. "You're not making much sense, Lobirn, and you usually do," she said with a hint of pique. "And if it's made you laugh so much, I want to hear the whole story. Do calm down. Rob, is there any klah in the pitcher?"

Robinton hurriedly poured lukewarm klah into a clean cup, which Lotricia took from him and passed to Lobirn. Still in spasms of laughter, Lobirn paused long enough to take a sip. This seemed to steady him. Wiping tears from his eyes, Lobirn beckoned for the onlookers to come closer. He tapped the music.

"Robinton, our newest and youngest journeyman, is the composer of most of the songs—which, by the First Egg, we both have been teaching you . . ."

"Did you write them, dear?" Lotricia said, her blue eyes wide with pleasure. "I told you he was a clever lad, and modest, too," she added to her husband. "Whyever isn't your name on the music?"

"As an apprentice, I'm not allowed . . ."

"That's what's so funny, Lotricia. Don't you *see*?"

"No, I don't, Lobirn, although I think his music is so singable."

"That's it! That's why it's so funny," Lobirn said, patting her hands for being so clever.

She regarded him blankly.

"His *father's* music isn't copied and sent to every Hold and

Hall," Lobirn said. "But Robinton's tunes have been since he was *three*! Get it now?" He was agitated further by his spouse's failure to see the humor and his neck reddened again, his face puffing out. "The joke's on Petiron! That conceited, condescending, consummate composer hasn't half the talent of his own son!" He rose then, chuckling and chortling: he managed to slap Robinton on the back and, taking charge of the music he had brought with him, he started out the door. Then he saw he had taken the unfinished sheet and, chuckling, he handed it back to Robinton. "Let me see it when you've finished, will you, Rob lad?"

He was still laughing when he closed the door on his own quarters.

"What was all that about?" one of the journeymen woodsmiths asked Robinton, still mystified.

"A Hall joke," Robinton said, smiling inanely and trying to close the door.

"Oh?"

After that incident, his relationship with Master Lobirn altered dramatically to an equal footing—or at least Lobirn treated his Journeyman with the respect he would give a peer. Robinton was delighted, astounded, and quite humbled by the compliment. His masters at the Hall had been benign taskmasters, encouraging and supportive, but they had treated him as a student. Now Lobirn treated him as an equal, despite the difference in age and experience. It was heady stuff for Robinton and he schooled himself never to abuse this status, working even harder at all the tasks Lobirn assigned him. However, this respect generated an unexpected side effect: it made him realize all the more keenly the relationship that Petiron had been unable to give him. In order to abate his bitterness, Robinton began mentally to refer to his father as Petiron, rather than "father." Maybe one day he could forgive the slights and the terrible hurt Petiron had inflicted on him—but not yet. Meanwhile, in his growing pleasure in Lobirn's continued good favor, painful memories of striving for an acceptance that had never come began to fade.

There was one last blast of winter in High Reaches, and then the spring melt occurred, turning the hills and tracks into rivers of mud. Trees budded out, and in the valley, farmers began seeding their fields. And Master Lobirn set up the schedules for his journeymen.

That was when Robinton noticed that there were no pegs on a wide area at the southwestern end of High Reaches.

"Surely that's where Fax has his hold," he said.

"It is," Lobirn said in a flat voice.

Mallan gave a droll grin.

"He has not requested a harper," Lobirn added in an acerbic tone.

Robinton sat straight up in surprise. "But . . . why not?"

"He doesn't like us muddling the minds of his holders with unnecessary information," Lobirn explained.

"Unnec . . . But everyone has the right to read and reckon."

"Fax does not wish his holders to be educated, Rob," Mallan said, crossing his hands behind his head and tipping his chair back. "Simple as that. What they don't know won't hurt them—because they also won't learn their rights."

"That's . . . that's . . ." Robinton struggled to find the appropriate word. "Can't Lord Faroguy insist?"

Lobirn grunted. "He has suggested that reading and figuring are considered assets . . ."

"Suggested?" Robinton shot out of his chair in protest.

"Now, lad, calm down. It isn't that we don't have more than enough students . . ."

"But he's denying them their rights under the Charter!"

"He denies there is a Charter, you mean," Mallan put in.

"The Charter also guarantees that a holder has autonomy within his holding," Lobirn pointed out.

"But his holders have rights."

"Don't be so naïve, Rob. That's exactly what he's denying them access to," Mallan said, dropping his chair to all four legs for emphasis. "And don't go putting your head in that snake's pit. You'd never match him in a fight, and you come on strong to him on that point and he's every right to challenge you. And be sorry that he just happened to break your neck!"

Robinton turned to Lobirn for support, but the Master Harper shook his head.

"I've warned Faroguy often about allowing Fax to have so much control. I've also warned both young Farevene and Bargen, Faroguy's eldest sons, to be on their guard. I'll say this for Farevene: he's a good wrestler and keeps himself fit. Bargen relies on the fact that the Council is unlikely to approve a nephew as long as there are acceptable sons. Both of them are, in my estimation. But I don't think they realize just how ambitious—and greedy—Fax is."

Lobirn gave another curt nod of his head.

"At that, we harpers have the respect our Hall deserves here in High Reaches, though I've heard"—his expression turned gloomy—"there're getting to be more and more places when harpers are barely tolerated."

Mallan and Robinton both stared at him.

"One of the northern traders mentioned something . . ." Mallan began.

"Let's not borrow trouble until it comes our way," Lobirn said firmly, and he went back to scheduling Robinton's assignments.

That discussion weighed heavily on Robinton's mind. He had been taught his Charter, and had even seen the original, carefully preserved between glass panes, its ink and precise lettering a marvel even after all the Turns since it had been written. The Charter was taught first as a Teaching Ballad to the youngest children, and then with more detail as the students grew old enough to memorize its provisions and to understand the meaning of each clause. A holder was not doing his duty by his people to deny them this information.

On the other hand, there was no provision made to punish holders who did not disseminate the information contained in the Charter. This was one of the shortcomings of the document. When Robinton had queried that in class, Master Washell had responded with a snort and then the notion that it must never have occurred to the writers of the Charter that anyone would be denied such basic human rights.

Robinton hoped that those who had learned their figures and letters under the previous holder would pass them on—however illicitly—to their children. Knowledge had a way of permeating any barriers set to exclude it. He could only hope that held true in Fax's hold.

Chapter 10

▼▼▼

The three Turns that Robinton spent at High Reaches seemed to go by very quickly, punctuated by the rigors of the seasons. But he learned a great deal more than harpering, and considerably more about how a Hold, controlling a population of many thousands of lives, was managed. At the head table in the evenings, Lord Faroguy seemed mild, gracious, and inoffensive. But, in his office, directing his sons and stewards in Hold management, he was incisive and efficient. There wasn't much the man didn't know about what went on in his Hold—except for the "blind spot," as Lobirn put it, about Nephew Fax.

"Oh, Fax is clever," Lobirn had told Robinton. "He did his time with Faroguy, same as the sons are doing, but you'd almost think Fax was a pure Blood relative."

"Maybe he is," Mallan put in, raising a critical eyebrow. "They do resemble each other."

Lobirn dismissed that notion. "Faroguy has always adored Evelene. It's only a family resemblance."

Mallan lifted one shoulder. "Fax's mother died at birth, so we'll never know, will we? There's always the possibility that, with Evelene pregnant so often, he might well have taken his ease elsewhere."

"Strike that," Lobirn said roughly. "And keep such notions to yourself."

"I have, but Faroguy's preference for Fax makes me wonder. He was born when Evelene had all those miscarriages. Before Farevene was finally born." But Mallan had let the subject drop.

The disturbing conduct of Fax ended up being the only unpleasantness Robinton encountered during his Turns at the big Hold. He even had his first experience with a woman, thanks to Mallan's conniving. Robinton had never thought much about his appearance, looking into a mirror only to be sure his hair was neat: he wore his dark brown hair long and braided, as many young men were currently doing. But he was putting flesh on his long bones, filling out, thanks to Lotricia's generosity with her "treats," and striding up and down the hills had added muscle to his lean shanks and chest.

As harper, he usually played *for* the dances, rather than taking part in them. Then one day when Mallan noticed him chatting with three of the young holder girls between dances, he nudged Robinton.

"I'll take the next set for you. Time you picked out a partner." Another nudge to Robinton's ribs was accompanied by a wink. Then he stopped Robinton's protest by turning to the first girl. "Sitta, he's shy. Spent so much time playing for dancers, he doesn't know the steps."

"Don't know . . . of course I know how to dance," Robinton protested, and he made haste to invite Sitta to dance. It wasn't that he hadn't noticed her, with her delicately slanting eyes in a charming face and her tiny figure, set off by the bright dark blue of her Gather dress. It was more that he didn't quite know how to strike the right note with those he fancied.

"I thought you'd never ask," Sitta said demurely, setting her tiny hand among his string-callused fingers.

"I've *wanted* to," Robinton replied sincerely.

"It's about time you did, Harper," she replied pertly, and

then they were on the dance floor, saluting each other as the other couples did, before the music began—adagio this time, so he did not have the chance to embrace her.

Sitta was a nice child, and after two dances with him, suggested that he partner one of her friends so as not to give anyone cause for talk. Quickly Robinton agreed; as a harper, he certainly shouldn't publicly indicate a marked preference— yet. And secondly, he really did want to dance. It was exhilarating. He also danced with Triana and Marcine. Triana was jolly and seemed more interested in being seen to dance than who she was partnered with. Marcine was pleasant and attentive. Then it was time for him to take up his instrument again.

Triana went off in search of another partner, though she said he was one of the best she'd had here, while Sitta and Marcine hung about the players' platform and were quite happy to wait until he was free again.

The next few days he seemed to meet Sitta and Marcine accidentally wherever he went. Then he was off on his rounds for the next four. When he returned late in the evening, Sitta was somehow in the main Hall, so it was natural for her to make sure he had something warm to eat and drink. And something warm in his bed to welcome him home.

Robinton used the same sign to Mallan that the older journeyman did—tipping one of the chairs against the table to indicate that he was not to be disturbed in his room. So he and Sitta discovered each other, and he found this aspect of life very good indeed. Sitta made every effort to waylay him in the Hold until he thought her as clever as a dragon to be able to find him so easily. Marcine pouted for a week or so, but both she and Triana continued to seek him out as a dance partner. Never more than two dances at a time, however.

Sitta might fancy being a harper's spouse, but until he had a more permanent placing, he could not entertain the thought of any serious long-term partnership. But it was very pleasant to have a loving friend. It was very different from a loving mother.

The news he had from the Harper Hall was that Merelan was in fine voice and very good health. He heard from her whenever the runners brought in letters, and he always had one to send back to her.

F'lon and Simanith came with the word that Carola had taken ill and MasterHealer Ginia had been sent for. The entire Weyr was upset because Feyrith was a relatively young queen. Any dragon's death was a shock to the rest of the Weyr, but to lose the queen was disastrous.

"I've never cared that much for Carola as a person, I know, but she is a dragonrider . . ." F'lon looked glum.

"Feyrith would just go?" Robinton exclaimed. "But the Weyr has to have a queen!"

"We do," F'lon reminded him. "From the last clutch, even if she is very young. Mind you, I could wish there'd been more choice for Nemorth than that Jora!" He exhaled in exasperation.

"Why?" Robinton asked, his mind more fixed on the enormity of the loss of a queen than what annoyed F'lon about Jora.

"Why? Because she's afraid of heights. Can you imagine that? Won't matter. Simanith fancies Nemorth, and I'd rather have a plump body than the rack of bones Carola's become."

"You don't think your father's bronze will give way to yours?" Robinton asked, startled. He knew how ambitious F'lon was, and how competitive bronze riders always were about mating flights, but wasn't F'lon ignoring the fact that his father was a good deal more experienced?

F'lon had the grace to look abashed. "Well, even S'loner can't last forever, you know. And Simanith is a very good bronze!"

"I'm sure of that," Robinton replied quickly.

Thank you, Harper.

Robinton beckoned for F'lon to lean closer. "Doesn't it upset him?"

"It won't until it happens. Dragons don't much worry about tomorrow, you know. It's why they need riders."

Three days before Turn's End, the Weyrwoman died, having

valiantly fought to live. In the Harper Hall, Robinton was instantly aware of Simanith's grief at the loss of Feyrith, although he said nothing until the drums confirmed the deaths. It certainly was grim news for all the celebrations. Everyone mourned the loss of both dragon and rider. Robinton was especially devastated, as he was one of the few people in High Reaches Hold who had known both weyrwoman and dragon in the prime of life. But he didn't have much time to mourn, for Lobirn told him that Master Gennell wished him back in the Harper Hall for a new assignment.

"You've learned a lot here, Rob, and I'm sorry to see you go, but you've more talent, both as a teacher and a musician, than is needed here. And there are other places where you can do more," Master Lobirn said when F'lon and Simanith arrived to convey Robinton and his effects. Then he embraced the young man firmly, despite the disparity of their heights, and turned quickly away.

Lotricia also hugged him, weeping and telling him to be careful, and to come back and visit whenever he could.

Robinton had already taken formal leave of Lord Faroguy, who had unexpectedly given him a fat purse of marks.

"You've been a fine worker, and all reports of your conduct and effectiveness have been full of praise. You deserve something to see you comfortable in your next position. Give my regards to Master Gennell, and of course, to MasterSinger Merelan." Faroguy had extended his hand, and Robinton had been happy to shake it enthusiastically, even though he had to soften his grip when he noted Faroguy wincing.

Now Mallan shook his hand, grinning, and at last Robinton was ready to leave.

"When's the mating flight?" he asked F'lon when he settled on Simanith's back behind his old friend. He spoke teasingly.

"I'm not sure Nemorth'll ever get off the ground the way Jora acts," he said in disgust. "The girl *is* afraid of heights. She only takes the steps to her weyr if someone walks on the outside to keep her"—he altered his voice to a squeaky falsetto—" 'from tipping off.' "

"But doesn't she . . ."

"Fortunately," F'lon went on, "when Nemorth's lust is up it won't matter a pile of old ashes what Jora wants." He grinned wickedly back at the harper. "Nemorth's blood will be up, and nature will take its course."

"And S'loner?"

"He'll take his chances with the rest of us."

Just then Simanith, who had surprised Robinton by *walking* to the edge of the High Reaches court, scared him half to death by falling off the edge into the long drop down to the valley floor. His stomach dropped and he clutched frantically at F'lon, wondering what ailment had taken the dragon so suddenly.

F'lon was howling with laughter at his reaction, and then they were *between* and the chill was almost welcome as the alternative to being dashed on the rocks.

"That was a damned nasty trick," Robinton said, leaning forward so that F'lon could hear him as they circled above the Harper Hall. He also gave F'lon an angry punch in the shoulder blades to show his displeasure.

"Why should Simanith waste energy leaping when he can glide off?"

"You might have warned me."

F'lon's chuckle whipped back to Robinton's ears and he knew it was useless to complain.

Simanith, the next time F'lon does that, would you please give me a second's warning? Robinton asked. He'd had little occasion to initiate conversations with Simanith, so he wasn't sure if the bronze would hear him.

I will try to remember since you don't like falling. At least Simanith sounded apologetic, which somewhat mollified Robinton.

Not above another display, F'lon had Simanith gliding in a lazy spiral down to the Harper Hall courtyard, making certain that their arrival was witnessed. By the time Simanith had folded his wings to his back, a welcoming committee had gathered on the steps. Robinton would really have preferred a less public arrival. His mother, who did look well to his searching gaze, was standing by Lorra, who had her arm about the shoulders of a very pretty, tall brunette who looked somewhat familiar. Kubisa and Master Ogolly completed the smiling group. Glancing up at the rehearsal room where Petiron spent so much time, Robinton could neither see nor hear any activity. He breathed a sigh of relief and then dismounted, striding to the steps to embrace his mother.

She was not quite as frail in his arms as when he had bid her good-bye three Turns before, but there were a lot of white streaks in her carefully braided hair and he thought her face looked more lined. Those marks of aging disturbed him terribly—he didn't like to think of his mother growing old. But he hid his fears with smiles and all the glib, silly phrases people say when renewing contact.

In the fuss to thank them all for coming, he kept glancing at the very pretty adolescent brunette, who was also pretending to be composed, a state belied by the flush that kept coming and going on her cheeks. Then he put a name to her face.

"The Turns have done you well, Silvina," he said, holding out a hand to his childhood playmate while still embracing his mother.

"And you're not so bad yourself now, Harper," she said pertly, grinning.

"You've filled out a great deal," Merelan said, patting his chest and feeling the muscles in his arm. "You're even taller," she added with a sort of accusatory wonder, as if he had no right to alter his appearance while separated from her.

"Master Lobirn worked me hard," he said, pretending weariness.

"Nonsense," Kubisa said in her forthright fashion. "You look in fine shape. In fact, you've improved quite a bit."

Betrice appeared in the doorway. "Ah, he has come. Good. Lorra's laid a spread for you, and we're all waiting to see if she's done you proud. Come in, come in, Robie." She grabbed his hand away from Silvina and led him in.

Robinton released his mother only when they were in the small dining room and he could settle her in a chair. Just as he was about to seat himself, Master Ogolly came rushing in.

"Oh, I did want to be on time," the Archivist said peevishly. "My dear boy, it's so good to see you!" Then he looked at the laden table and beamed. "How marvelous. I'll just stop for a cup of klah, and maybe one of those little cakes, but I've got such clumsies as apprentices this Turn. You don't know how much I miss your neat copying, Robie. Oh, I should give you your full name now, shouldn't I, Journeyman Robinton?"

"You can call me what you will, Master Ogolly. I'm always yours to command."

"Master Gennell will want to see you sometime this afternoon, Rob," Betrice said, "when his class is over."

"Any ideas about where I'm to be posted next?" He winked at Betrice to assure her that he didn't expect her to tell him.

"Oh, we'll keep you busy enough," she assured him with a mock scowl.

The conversation went to general topics, such as who had been posted where, and Robinton asked after his old dorm mates who now were journeymen, too, and heard about Shonagar's latest wrestling successes. That made him think of Fax.

"What's wrong, Rob?" his mother asked, a gentle hand on his arm, as she caught his change of mood.

"Nothing," he said. His response didn't fool her, but he didn't feel that Fax's delinquency in educating his holders was a subject for this table.

When he did have a chance to bring the subject up to Master Gennell during his interview with the Harper, Gennell nodded soberly.

"Lobirn has acquainted me with that situation. Unfortunately, without Faroguy's consent, the Hall can do nothing."

"But that's not right," Robinton protested.

Gennell nodded again, sympathetically. "We can only do so

much, Rob, and are wiser not to trespass where a harper's life might be endangered."

Robinton blinked in surprise. "Endangered?"

"There have been such problems before, lad, and there will again, but somehow it comes right. As long as Fax keeps his ideas to his own hold, I can do nothing. Nor is it wise to. That's something you learn as you go on. Cut your losses when you have to. One small hold in the northern lands is not as vital as a larger one nearer home, as it were. But I'm assigning you to where you will do the most good. Now—" Gennell swiveled and pointed to a peg. "—that's your new assignment. And I think you'll do quite well there. You got a fine recommendation from Lobirn, and he's not easy to please. But first . . . Petiron is away for several days, so you might like to relax and spend some time with your mother."

"She's not well?" Robinton leaped on the wording.

"Yes, yes, she's fine, lad. No need to fret about her as you'll discover," Gennell said. He sounded so sincere that Robinton relaxed. "There's a ship due in at the Fort harbor and you can take passage on that . . . and let's not prevail too much on a dragonrider's favor for transport."

"F'lon insisted . . ."

"Now, now, I'm not faulting you, Rob, but I think it better that you arrive at Benden—"

"Benden?" Robinton couldn't believe in such luck.

"Yes, Benden—but arrive this time without benefit of Simanith's wings. That young lad is a thorn in Lord Maidir's side, both he and that father of his, the Weyrleader."

"But, when Mother and I were there, Lord Maidir—"

Gennell held up his hand. "As I said, it would be better if you didn't arrive on dragon wing. I don't want you considered an alarmist, too. Harper Evarel is looking forward to your assistance. He's retiring soon, and if you suit Lord Maidir—in fact, he asked if you were available now—you'd probably stay on there."

Robinton forbore to ask further questions, knowing that he could find out for himself what the situation was. It was very odd that the Weyr's own Hold was doubting the Weyrleaders.

F'lon had expressed himself on this score during the informal party. The young bronze rider had also given him something more to think about as they crossed the courtyard to the waiting Simanith.

"That pretty girl—Silvina—fancies you, lad," he said. "She wouldn't give me the time of day, but she couldn't keep her eyes off you. Don't let a good opportunity pass you by, Rob." And F'lon winked as he clapped the Harper on the back before taking the jump-step he always used to reach Simanith's forearm. And then he was waving farewell from his bronze's back.

Robinton was so surprised by the comment that he had no time to tell F'lon that he'd known Vina as a playmate and she was probably just happy to see him again. He retreated a good dragon-length to avoid getting dust and grit in his eyes when Simanith leaped upward.

But, later that night, after he and his mother had caught up on some of his more amusing adventures at High Reaches, he was too restless to sleep. Though she had told him his room was ready, he had insisted that he sleep in the journeymen's accommodations. He knew she was disappointed, that she wanted to see to his comfort herself and enjoy his proximity. What he couldn't say was that his old room would bring back far too many memories he had no desire to recall. Or maybe she understood that, because she didn't press him. Casually she mentioned that Petiron was doing special music for a Tillek Holder espousal, and that was why the Hall seemed almost deserted. She had also noticed Silvina's intentness.

"She's grown into such a lovely young woman. A nice rich contralto. Have you written any songs for that voice?"

"Yes, actually, I have," Robinton said, reaching for the leather folder that contained his scores. It gave him something to divert her from thinking more about Vina's so-called interest in him. "In fact, I've copied out the best of my new tunes for you." He put an emphasis on the word "tunes"—Petiron's sarcastic name for them.

"Now, Rob . . ." His mother gave him a reproving look.

That was when he told her about Master Lobirn's laughing

fit, and she was appropriately amused by the incident. Then she insisted on looking at all his new songs, and played them, singing along half-voice, although occasionally singing out fully for the ones she particularly liked. He hummed along with her because he couldn't help himself: singing his own songs with his mother was a pleasure long denied him.

"Ah, dear love, you have such a knack for song and ballad," she said when she had gone through the lot. "And you've developed so much . . ." She sighed. And Robinton, deciding she was tired, gathered up the scores and insisted that she rest now.

There was something about his mother that was different, not quite right, despite all the assurances he had been given. He gave her a goodnight hug and kiss.

"I've several days before I have to take ship," he told her.

"Where did Gennell assign you?"

"You didn't know?"

She laughed. "Gennell keeps his own business to himself, but he did assure me that it was a posting worthy of your abilities."

She was delighted when he informed her that he'd been assigned to Benden.

"I'd hoped that you might. I know Evarel is thinking about retiring," she said, hugging him fiercely. Then she gave him a mock coy glance. "Why, I'd even thought of asking Gennell if he wouldn't consider you, but that would be favoritism."

"And my mother wouldn't stoop to that?" he said, teasing her lightly. "Even for her own son?"

"I have my scruples, dear," she replied, affecting a prim manner.

Silvina served him his dinner first at the journeymen's table, gave him larger portions than she gave the others, and hung around, asking him about High Reaches and being not quite a nuisance. Two or three harpers he didn't know very well grinned at him until he became a little uncomfortable about her attentiveness.

She *was* pretty—prettier than Sitta or Marcine—but he wasn't going to be around long enough to get to know the adult Vina.

Anyway, Master Gennell rose to his feet and started the ceremonies that made apprentices into journeymen—always a marvelous occasion. His new posting was included, and he saw how proud his mother was when it was announced. He wondered what his father would have said.

So he traveled by ship, runnerbeast, and foot to Benden, a journey that not only made him appreciate the speed of transport a-dragonback, but also impressed on him the size of the continent, which until then had only been a map, not actual lengths he had set foot on.

He discovered that he could sail without getting seasick—which pleased the captain no end when a storm made half the crew too nauseated to work and Robinton was pressed into service. And he saw the Dawn Sisters for the first time.

He'd come on deck just at dawn and noticed the bright spark in the sky.

"That can't be a star," he said.

"Ent one," the dog-watch sailor said with a grin. "We calls 'em the Dawn Sisters. Why, I dunno. We sees 'em just as clear at dusk, too. Only from this latitude, though. You won't see 'em up north where you comes from."

"Amazing," Robinton said, leaning against the cabin housing, unable to take his eyes from the shining spot. Then, abruptly, the sun raised itself above the horizon and the spot winked out. He meant to come back and test the sailor's word that the phenomenon occurred at dusk as well, but he forgot about it.

He liked Ista Island—what he saw of it sailing past the coastline—and admired the black diamond beach around the little off-shore island, which was no more than an old volcano sticking its crater head up out of the water. He found he could manage a runnerbeast adequately to help drive burden beasts and other runners to their destination, and all his travels up the High Reaches mountain tracks made the rest of his journey more of a delight than a problem. Especially since, as a harper, he was welcome in any small hold, where, in return for an evening's songs, he got the best meal available, as well as the best bed.

Except for one night when he had left the drovers who'd sold him an elderly but sturdy packbeast to carry his possessions and was proceeding on his own. He was nearly to the Benden Hold borders, the head drover had told him, and recommended the inland road as being the shorter way. He'd passed a Runner Station midafternoon but decided to travel as far as he could that night. As the sun was nearly down over the mountains, he was beginning to look around for any shelter, even an old Thread halt, when he came across a runner trace. These were always laid out as the straightest distance between two points, so he switched to the narrow, mossy trace. He was ascending a hill when he saw lights ahead, off to his left, snug against a forest. The trace was bisected by a wider road that appeared to lead directly to the hold so he turned, his elderly pack animal moaning a bit.

"It's nearby. Not much further, and you can eat, too."

The animal groaned on a different note. If Robinton hadn't been so tired and hungry, he'd have been amused at the variety of sounds the beast could make.

As he approached the cothold, he smelled tantalizing odors coming from within and his stomach growled. So did several canines within the cot. The packbeast gave off a loud, slightly fearful protest.

"They're inside and can't hurt you," he told the beast as he resettled his tunic, pushed his hair neatly behind his ears, and courteously rapped at the door.

"Who's there?" a sharp male voice demanded, and then told the canines to shut their fuss. "Can't hear over the noise."

A female voice murmured something.

"A traveler, in need of a night's lodging," Robinton said.

"Can you pay?"

"Certainly." A harper was expected to sing and entertain for supper. He would usually offer a half mark, but was always refused.

The door opened a crack, and he couldn't see the face of the man, the light being behind him.

"Who be you?" the man asked.

"Robinton's my name," the journeyman replied with a slight bow and put his hand to his belt pouch. "I have good Harper Hall marks—"

"Ha! Harper Hall." There was contempt in the voice.

"They're good at any Gather," Robinton said, more than a little taken aback by the response.

"Do let him in, Targus. We've more than enough stew," the woman said. She pulled the door open, peering out at him. "Why, it's only one man, Targus. And carries no weapons but an eating knife." She swung the door wider and Robinton could see four large men seated at the table. "Sortie, boy, go put his packbeast in the lean-to, and come in. Robinton, you said your name was? I'm Kulla."

A gawky lad appeared and slipped past Targus, taking the lead rope from Robinton's hand and clucking encouragingly at the packbeast. The beast started to resist, but Robinton swatted him across his stubborn rump and he followed the boy.

"I really appreciate your hospitality, lady," he said, ducking his head to step into the room. He nodded impartially around at the others. "I'm on my way to Benden Hold."

"He's a harper, Pa. That's blue cords on his shoulder," one of the diners said, pointing with his knife at Robinton's left arm.

Targus, scowling deeply, hauled Robinton around so he could see the offensive cords himself.

"Now, you see here, Targus," Kulla said, planting both fists on her ample hips and glaring at her spouse. "You keep me from Gathering, but if a harper comes to my door, I'm not turning him out. Not that I'd turn anyone away so late in the night."

She grabbed Robinton's other arm and pulled him away from Targus's grasp and toward the table.

"Brodo, get a plate. Mosser, a cup. All we've got's beer, but it'll quench a thirst." She angled Robinton toward the table and pushed him into what he took to be her own chair. Taking the plate from Brodo, who was grinning as he passed it to his mother, she filled it amply and gestured for him to be seated. "Erkin, the bread's by you. And, Targus, you sit. I'm so eager to see a smiling face that I'd eat with a watch-wher who did."

Jutting his jaw out, Targus held out his hand to Robinton, his eyes suspicious. "Said you could pay?"

"Indeed, and I can," Robinton said, half-rising to reach his pouch.

Kulla pushed Targus' hand away. "Harpers shouldn't have to pay, Targus. You weren't ever brought up right by that family of yours."

"I insist," Robinton said earnestly because he didn't like the expression on Targus's face. He kept only a few small pieces in his belt pouch—the rest were in a sash inside his shirt—and he displayed them all. "This one is smithcraft. Will that be preferable?"

"Preferable?" sneered Targus as his thick and slightly greasy fingers gathered the mark piece from Robinton's palm. "Harper words. What's wrong with 'Is that good?' Or do you always have to show off your larnin'?"

Kulla pulled Robinton back down. "Eat. You look peaked, and don't mind Targus."

Robinton decided to concentrate on eating. There was nothing wrong with the flavorsome stew, or the quality of the tubers and greens that accompanied it. The bread had been made fresh that day, and when the last piece was taken by Erkin, or maybe that was Mosser, the woman sliced up another loaf and filled the dish. Though his hunger would have been sated by the first helping, she served Robinton a second, equally large portion while Targus grumbled.

"I'll feed whoever I choose in this house, Targus. This hold has always been hospitable. You can dislike harpers all you want, but I don't," she said fiercely. Then in a completely different tone of voice she turned and smiled with genuine appeal in her eyes. "Would you mind playing for us after?" When Targus started to growl, she turned on him. "And you shut your face, Targus. I haven't heard any music since last Solstice, and I promise you'll eat nothing but cold porridge for the month if you say another nasty thing."

The young boy had slipped back in and helped himself to more stew and bread, shooting glances at the other end of the table where Robinton ate, solidly protected by Kulla.

"Music!" Targus did growl when Robinton brought out his pipes.

"You've no gitar?" Kulla asked plaintively. "I was hoping you'd sing for me."

"It's on my pack animal . . ."

She sent the boy, Sheve, for the instrument. "And handle it careful, y'hear?"

The moment Robinton started playing, Targus stamped toward a half-open door, turned, and glared at his sons expressively, but all of them pretended not to see and he slammed the door behind him.

Robinton played and sang far more softly than was his habit. When he finally made a few bad chords from sheer fatigue, Brodo touched his mother's arm. "He's sung for a week of suppers, Ma."

"Why's Pa hate music so?" Erkin asked.

"He says harpers sing lies," Mosser said, malice in his twinkling eyes.

"Didn't hear a one," their mother said stoutly. Then she waggled her finger at Mosser. "Nor you, neither, or you'd've stirred yourself out of the room when your pa left. You'll sleep in here, Harper. Erkin, get the furs. Sheve, throw down that spare mattress from the loft. I'll just bank the fire."

His bed was quickly organized and the final nighttime chores completed, leaving him in sole possession of the main room. He was relieved to see the canines follow the boys out to another part of the cot.

The thud of wood going into the fireplace roused him from a

deep sleep and he saw his hostess taking the porridge pot from the back of hearth where it had simmered all night.

"You'll want to travel soon's it's light, Harper," she said in a soft voice.

"He hasn't given you any trouble . . ." Robinton began.

Her snort of denial was soft, but he could see her lips were smiling. "He knows better," she said, still quietly, and then reached for a cup to pour him klah.

It was thick and very strong; the jolt of the liquid in his belly woke him up completely. She set a bowl of porridge on the table and began to slice more bread, which she then covered with a worn but clean napkin.

"The beast'll be to the left as you leave the cot," she said.

He finished his breakfast quickly, accepting her haste, hospitable though it remained. With the bread in one hand and his gitar in the other, he murmured his thanks again and left.

The sun was not yet up, but there was light enough to show him the beasthold. He'd had plenty of practice now in settling the pack so that he was off down the road again within minutes.

"And let that be a lesson to you," he murmured to himself. "Harper lies? Whatever would he mean by that?"

He passed over the Benden border late that morning, and that night stayed at a friendly Runner Station where harpers were always welcome.

When he finally arrived at the Hold, no one was on the steps waiting to welcome him. Just as he was climbing up to the entryway, a party of riders clattered in on the northern road and he recognized Raid, Lord Maidir's eldest son.

"Ah, Journeyman, we've been expecting you," Raid said, swinging down from his mount and throwing the reins of the tired beast to the holder who came running up from the beasthold.

"Raid, it's good to see you again," Robinton said genially.

Raid peered up at the harper. "I know you?"

"Robinton. MasterSinger Merelan's son," Robinton said, taken aback.

But Raid responded with a wide grin and an extended hand,

then a clout on the arm. "I wouldn't have recognized you from that scrawny kid!"

Robinton had to laugh—Raid was in no way altered from his memory of the young man.

"I have earnestly tried to improve myself," he admitted.

"Glad to hear that," Raid said, characteristically unable to spot irony. "Come, there'll be hot klah or wine, now that you're old enough, to wash away the travel dust. Been long on the way?"

"Yes, and fully appreciate the size of this continent now in a manner I had not experienced."

"Yes, well, there's that, isn't there?"

Robinton reflected that Raid had been born in a mold and not altered the framework one bit in his nearly thirty Turns. Well, there is something to be said about predictability, for a harper's purposes, he thought.

"Your father's well? And Lady Hayara?" he asked politely.

"My father is much bothered by joint-ail." Raid frowned with concern. "Our healer can relieve the discomfort only for short periods of time." He sighed and, also characteristically, did not mention his father's second wife.

But she had been alerted by the return of the work party and was sailing into the Hall, a woman whose proportions seemed to be a permanent appearance of late pregnancy. Her smile when she recognized Robinton—and she had no trouble doing so—was all he could wish for, both as a returned guest and a new harper.

Talking away furiously, which permitted her to ignore Raid beyond a brief nod, she called for a drudge to take Robinton's carisaks to his quarters, then urged him into the Hall where food and drink were being brought in and set on a table. She ordered chairs to be set for her and the harper, and apologized for Lord Maidir's absence, and told him that Maizella was about to be espoused to a fine young holder, and said that she was so glad he had come so that he could plan the music because she really didn't have anything new, and if Robinton did, that would be splendid but only music that had a tune that people could enjoy. Then she realized what she had said and started apologizing about his father's *sooo* impressive music, but really that sort of thing wouldn't do for such a happy occasion, would it?

At some point during that monologue, when she stopped to draw a breath, Raid said that he would inform Lord Maidir of the harper's arrival and see when it would be convenient for Robinton to officially present himself to the Lord Holder. He would also apprise Harper Evarel that his Journeyman had arrived.

Breath taken, Lady Hayara, whose ebullience had not altered, brought him up to date on how many students there were currently, and told him that Maizella, in her spare time, was conducting lessons with Harper Evarel, who was nearly as crippled with joint-ail as her spouse but carrying on bravely until Robinton could arrive, and exclaimed at how happy Evarel would be to have a trained assistant because—she didn't know why—the holders seemed to be breeding enormous families.

Robinton managed to stifle a laugh. He had counted up the number of offspring she had presented Lord Maidir in the Turns since Rob and his mother had been at Benden Hold: she was a fine one to talk about large families, with seven more in the intervening years, making a total of ten. Small wonder that Raid said little to her. She was presenting him with problems; although, undoubtedly, Raid would delegate the more responsible males to assist him, while espousing the girls as creditably as possible. Robinton just hoped there wasn't an ambitious and scheming nephew in Benden Hold, too.

Then, his klah finished, he said that he would go to the schoolrooms and see if he could help Master Evarel.

"But you've just arrived from a long and terrible journey. He won't be expecting you to pitch in . . . right away!"

"I shall see what Evarel wishes, Lady Hayara, but I assure you that I have traveled at a leisurely enough pace and been well treated by everyone on the way."

So he thanked her again for the welcome and the refreshment

and would have used the backstairs when she called him sharply back and pointed to the main ones at the side of the Hall.

"Journeyman Robinton, kindly remember your new status," she said with a hint of dismay. "You are *not* a child anymore." It was the closest he had ever heard her come to disapproval.

He bowed and, muttering something about old habits dying hard, strode across the floor to the appropriate staircase.

Master Evarel was quietly delighted at his arrival—and at his willingness to get right to work if that was required, for the older man's hands were badly gnarled with the joint-ail and obviously paining him.

"Maizella usually plays for me, but she's away this morning," Evarel said gruffly, leading Robinton to suspect that the harper's voice was also going. He had sung bass: it was the tenor range that was apt to go first. "That is, if you're not fatigued . . ."

"I'm fine, Master Evarel. I'd be happy to assist. Perhaps I should have pushed on last night . . ."

"No, no, the last part of the track could be dangerous at night." Evarel put up a hand to reassure Robinton even as he passed the gitar over.

The youngsters in the room giggled and squirmed in their seats at the changeover, looking over the lanky journeyman with eager expressions.

Just as he was singing them through the first verse of the first Teaching Ballad, he heard the drums and paused to listen to the brief message: "Harper Safe."

It took him a moment to realize that the message concerned him. That made him feel even more welcome than ever—to be the subject of drum talk.

And thus began Robinton's second stay at Benden Hold.

At Evarel's request, Robinton's effects had been put in the room he had shared with his mother during their previous stay at Benden Hold. It was Evarel's apartment, which he apologetically offered to share, if Robinton had no objections. His spouse had died some years back and he felt odd about having such a large apartment all to himself. Robinton was more than pleased because, while the inner rooms at High Reaches had been only one corridor away from outside, he much preferred having outer wall accommodations. It was silly to feel the constraint of rock when that was actually all he'd known in his life, and when so many folk lived long, healthy lives quite contentedly in the inner passages of the bigger Holds and Halls, but he did like to be able to look *out* whenever he chose. He also felt closer to his mother in rooms they had occupied together in one of the happiest spells of his boyhood.

Being Journeyman in a busy Hold was a considerable change from that earlier time, and yet Robinton was not the sort of personality who could abide idleness. If he wasn't instructing, taking his drum tower watches—Hayon, the oldest of Hayara's brood, was technically in charge of that part of the Hold's routine duties—or taking a few days to travel to the corners of the Hold to tutor small holder groups, he busied himself mending instruments, repairing music sheets, and copying those that Evarel's pain-wracked hands had been unable to keep in good shape.

When the cold weather deepened, Lady Hayara arrived with the Hold's healer, Master Yorag, bringing a basin of warm wax to ease the frozen joints of the old Harper's hands and knees. She helped rub in the herbal oils that increased daytime mobility.

"I do wish you'd reconsider the Neratian offer," she would invariably say when she entered. "It is freezing here, and the cold is simply not good for your joints."

"I'll be fine, Lady Hayara, I'll be fine," old Evarel insisted, adding most mornings, "now that Robinton's here to assist."

Then he began to add, "And he's halved my work and taken over all the difficult tasks."

By Turn's End, when a chest congestion kept him in bed for six days running, and Robinton was beside himself to keep the water bottles warm enough to give him some comfort, Evarel succumbed to the inevitable and said that perhaps he ought to spend the rest of the winter where it was a trifle warmer.

Lady Hayara ordered up the travel wagon and had Robinton send drum messages to holds on the southern route to have team changes and fresh drivers ready so that Evarel would make the journey in the most comfort she could secure for him. Maizella and Hayon were sent along as his escort.

As Robinton carried the gaunt old Master Harper down to the conveyance, he wondered why Benden hadn't requested a dragon and rider. He had seen dragons in the sky, but none had touched down at Benden Hold as they used to do, and none had been invited for any of the dinners that Lady Hayara loved to give with the least excuse. Robinton had been too busy to visit the Weyr on his own, to discover the dragonriders' viewpoint on the coldness between Hold and Weyr. Then he answered his own question, as he realized that the cold of *between* would have been the worst possible course for the sick man, not to mention the difficulty involved in hoisting him to the dragon's back without additional pain.

The travel wagon's narrow body was well-sprung and well-padded and would pass on most of the normal trails. Such vehicles had become quite popular during the Long Interval. And most holders kept good teams ready in the beasthold or in a nearby paddock for travelers' needs. This wagon was also comfortably sized: "Lady Hayara wide, which means the two of us will fit," Maizella said with a touch of malice, although Robinton had noticed that she was now on better terms with her father's second spouse than Raid was.

Robinton watched with a lump in his throat as the old man left. Lady Hayara was openly weeping.

"He's taught all my children, you see," she admitted as Robinton gave her a steadying hand up the steps to the Hold. "And I really don't think he should come back—even in the warmer weather."

And so it was that Evarel did not return to Benden Hold. Robinton slid into the vacancy and started quietly training three of the brighter hold children to be his assistants. One lad was harper material, unless he missed his guess. Robinton had a sixth sense for that: he likened it to a green dragon's ability to perceive rider potential in youngsters. He did wish that somehow or other he could find a girl as talented. His mother would so enjoy having another voice to train as she had Halanna and Maizella.

A Turn and a half later, S'loner's Chendith flew Jora's Nemorth and a clutch resulted. Not a large one, but six bronzes, three browns, five blues, and six greens were hatched.

F'lon had been quite caustic about the long wait for Nemorth to come into season. He blamed it on Jora's own immaturity and fearfulness.

"This business of Jora's being afraid of heights is inhibiting her queen, of all stupidities!" F'lon paced up and down Robinton's apartment, waving his arms about in frustration. "I personally know that Nemorth was glowing as bright as a gold nugget when Jora took it in her head to be violently nauseated and faint. Naturally that put the poor queen off, making her nearly frantic with worry over her rider." F'lon kicked at a chair in his way, venting his disgust with the Weyrwoman. "Frankly, I'll be surprised if we ever get Nemorth in the air to mate."

When the mating flight did occur, Robinton tactfully did not ask for any details the next time F'lon appeared at Benden Hold. F'lon made only one reference to the event.

"S'loner had no great joy of the day. We all hope Chendith had more." He spoke in such a neutral tone that Robinton couldn't tell if F'lon had gotten over his disappointment; but the bronze rider had an infinite capacity to ignore what he wished.

F'lon was shortly able to report that Nemorth was showing unmistakable signs that she was in egg. He even appeared happy to be able to make such an announcement.

"All in all, considering the way Jora carries on, I'm just as glad that I don't have to put up with her nonsense and carryings-on. S'loner's welcome to them." He grinned maliciously.

In his capacity as Hold Harper, Robinton was invited to the Hatching and the Impression. And impressive that was for the sensitive Harper. He had never seen such joy, or felt so touched by another's elation. Each new bonding added to the impact, and he found himself wishing desperately that somehow he *could* have been both harper and rider. He was in tears, and unashamed, by the end of the Hatching. Even F'lon, collecting him from the spectators' seats above the Hatching Ground, was blurry-eyed with unshed tears.

"Gets to you, doesn't it?" the bronze rider murmured, wiping his own eyes.

"I didn't realize it was like . . ." And Robinton spread his hand helplessly over the hot sands—which made him speed up his pace lest he scorch the soles of his feet even through good harper boot leather. "The most incredible moment in a man's life . . . isn't it?"

"Indeed." F'lon glanced fondly over his shoulder at Simanith, who was leaving the Hatching Ground by the upper exit. Most of the dragons were already on their way to their own weyrs, and Robinton was awed by the sight of their deft insertion in the dark hole at the top of the immense cavern. He was amazed at how gracefully imminent collisions were avoided as the flying dragons filed out.

F'lon draped a careless arm across Robinton's shoulder. "Now is the good time. In the euphoria of an Impression, all old insults and agitations are put aside. Even Raid came today."

"Wasn't he supposed to?" Robinton asked, hoping that tonight he might at last get some answers to explain the estrangement between Raid and F'lon. They had once been very good friends. Robinton hadn't noticed at first that the two were never in the same room together. But F'lon could be caustic, and Raid had his own foibles. "Maidir and Hayara have talked of nothing else since the drum message came about the clutch."

"And Maizella and that fish-faced spouse of hers." F'lon grimaced. "She's pretty enough to have done better than that."

"Cording's got a large and prosperous hold on the Eastern Sea. He gives her sea jewels and goes goggle-eyed when she sings to him," Robinton remarked, keeping his tone nonjudgmental. He liked Maizella much better now than he ever had as a child. He also rather liked Cording, who was solicitous of his love's parents and the brood of younger children, and courteous to his Lord Holder, but he did have a distinct resemblance to a fish, with that shock of sun-bleached hair, flat face, and rather blunted features. But a harper had to be careful of admitting to anything at all improper—even in confidence to a friend.

"That's as may be, but he doesn't believe in Thread," F'lon said in a flatly disapproving tone.

Since that would have caused F'lon to dislike anyone, male or female, Robinton declined to comment further on Cording's good points. And now he'd been given a lead-in to the problem he'd been dying to address.

"Is that the basis of your argument with Lord Maidir and Raid?" Robinton asked. After all, one of his duties as harper was to act as mediator whenever necessary. Not that he felt himself an expert, but he could at least try to understand the dispute from both sides.

"Of course." F'lon actually ground his teeth. "Neither of them will listen to S'loner or me. And it's not as if we were the only riders of that opinion. M'odon is adamant that we'll see Thread within the next three decades. And I've checked his figuring time and again. He might be out a Turn or two, but not by more than that." He glanced about irritably, as if hoping to find something he could at least kick. A stone lay across his path and he kicked that across the Bowl so that both of them heard it connect with the cliff and shatter. F'lon grunted at his success. Then, in one of his abrupt changes, he pointed to a table not far from the entrance of the Lower Caverns. "Let's take that one before anyone else can settle."

Robinton decided to wait for a more propitious opening to obtain further details. F'lon was not the most tactful of riders—nor, for that matter, was his father—but perhaps, in the aftermath of the Hatching, he could make some progress in healing the breech.

Most of the invited guests were still on their feet, wine glasses or klah mugs in their hands, while the aromas of the upcoming feast wafted in tantalizing waves from the busy kitchen. In the distance, by the weyrling barracks, Robinton caught sight of the newly Impressed riders feeding their dragonets, who raised squeaky but imperious voices, protesting the slowness of the service. Once sufficiently full, the dragonets would be bedded down, and then the new riders would join their parents for the festivities, elated with pride at their success. Robinton had noted that a Benden holder lad had Impressed a bronze—a talking point with Maidir. There was such an air of rejoicing, of gladness, of accomplishment, that Robinton had trouble restraining himself from grabbing up his gitar and making appropriate triumphant music. His turn would come soon enough, and meanwhile here was C'gan, his oddly boyish face smiling, making his way toward them, carrying a tray of glasses, a skin of wine looped over his shoulder.

F'lon waved for C'gan to hurry. Robinton had had a chance on his arrival to quiz C'gan on how many musicians he would have to supply music, and what special songs might be requested. He had brought some new songs, as well: three of his own and four from the Harper Hall. He had learned that he didn't need to tell anyone who had composed them. If the songs were good, they were sung again and again, and those that failed to catch on, he could simply forget. There were few of his in the latter category. A march from Petiron's pen was included in those from the Hall, and Robinton deemed it a new departure for the MasterComposer: rhythmic and solemn, but stirring.

Eventually those at the head table took their places, a signal for the weyrfolk to serve their guests, green riders helping to cater to the extra numbers. Bronze and brown riders were not required to serve guests, so R'gul, S'lel, L'tol, and R'yar, the lad who had been Searched from his first apprentice year at the Harper Hall, joined Robinton's table.

Robinton was close enough to the head table to get his first good look at the young new Weyrwoman. She was not at all as attractive or sensual as Carola had been. But that was not relevant—no matter what her looks or personality were like, S'loner's bronze had to fly her queen to keep him in the Weyrleader's position. From the scowl on S'loner's face, he wasn't too pleased with his new Weyrwoman. He was, in fact, leaning away from her, idly rubbing his left shoulder and arm, and not directing much conversation in Jora's direction. She was pretty enough, in a sort of overblown way, but was already getting more plump than was healthy for a rider, not to mention for a young woman. She was flushed with the success of her queen, Nemorth, and making what appeared to be giddy confessions to Lady Hayara, who merely listened with a polite smile plastered on her face. Lord Maidir exchanged a few comments with S'loner, but for the most part concentrated on the excellent food served and the fine Benden wines.

Robinton considered that wine one of the fringe benefits of being a Benden-based harper: they had the best vineyards on the continent, and the main Winecrafthall was in the next valley over from the Hold itself. The whites were crisp and light, sometimes with a citrus tang, sometimes an almost floral taste. He had been used to the foxy sauternes of Tillek, the other large wine-producing Hold, and the variety produced by Benden fascinated him. The reds, especially the clarets and the burgundies, were full and wonderful to hold to the nose and savor through the mouth. Robinton had discovered that he could drink the whites all night long and generally rise up from his bed the next morning without a heavy head or sick stomach, but he had to be careful with the reds. And he dreamed of tasting the sparkling wine that once had been produced at Benden. MasterVintner Wonegal was still trying to reproduce it, but the vine blight of two hundred Turns before had wiped out that varietal, and cross-pollinating of the better white grapes had not yet produced an adequate replacement.

The feast was superb. There was roast herdbeast, flavorful with herbs and done to pink, though there were crusty top slices available to those who liked it well-done. Wild wherry in quantity, and so tenderized as to slide down the throat with its accompanying wild-berry gravy. There was also a variety of fish, grilled and baked, with enormous bowls of tubers and vine beans; breads, both flat and raised; and fresh greens that had been grown in tropical Nerat. Fruits, too, and nuts from Lemos. Though most of the candidates had been weyrbred, some had come from nearby Holds, and their families had probably brought offerings. Only two lads had been injured—slightly—when the dragonets lurched out of their shells and looked around, keening, for their mind mates. And a bronze had hatched first.

"The best omen we could have," F'lon remarked.

"Why is that?" Robinton asked.

"Bronze is the best, of course," F'lon said with a slightly drunken grin on his face. "A bronze first means the clutch is strong, even if not as large as some would have made it. Jora's useless as a Weyrwoman." His tone turned disdainful. "Not only is she afraid of heights, but she's nervous with Nemorth, and if S'loner hadn't been helping, she'd've let the queen eat before her mating flight." He snorted in contempt.

"That wouldn't have kept you from edging S'loner out, though," R'gul said, a disapproving frown on his round face.

"Tchaaa!" F'lon waved aside the rebuke. "So he sired me, but bronze riders are all equal in the air at mating time. The queen should have the best available—more to make up for her short-comings than anything else." And he made another contemptuous noise and unslung the wineskin from the chair back. "So, Harper Robinton, with what songs will you regale us tonight?" He waved toward the top table. "Everyone's eaten, and let's not have another brawl between our Weyrleader and our Lord Holder."

Robinton got to his feet, his height making him visible to the head table, and he waited until he could catch S'loner's atten-tion. The Weyrleader had bent his head to listen to something one of the weyrgirls was saying, a girl Robinton had noticed himself because of her quiet dignity and gracefulness. S'loner shook his head, and then the girl pointed toward Robinton. Spotting the harper, S'loner raised his right hand to give him the signal to begin the entertainment.

C'gan had been watching, too, and he stood, which told the players to gather on the dais.

"I've a few new ones for your ears," Robinton told F'lon. "And a fine march. Enter-the-new-riders sort of thing."

"Great!" F'lon waved a loose arm in command for the music to begin. He was fairly well gone in wine, so Robinton did not take offense.

Looking closely at the head table as he made his way to the players' raised dais, Robinton did not see any signs of an imminent dispute between Leader and Holder. But the two were looking away from each other and neither was talking. It was indeed time for diversion before the silence became unbearable. Jora was still talking to Lady Hayara, who was all but slumped down in her chair with boredom. Now, seeing the Harper gathering his instrumentalists, Hayara sat up straighter and waggled her fingers at him—doubtless from gratitude, unless Jora would talk through music, too. But then Lady Hayara would have a legitimate excuse to request her silence.

Robinton started off with Petiron's march; it had a few feet stamping and some clapping in rhythm, so he was subtly amused that his opinion was now verified. Then he called for the Duty Song, followed closely by the Question Song, which he played whenever he could. But this time it was not as well received by either Weyrleader or Lord Holder, and he was almost sorry he had included it.

So he did a rendition of one of his newer songs, backed by C'gan on gitar, and two pipers and the hand drum. The song was appreciated enough to require him to repeat it immediately, and there were many voices lifted in the chorus with him. Riders were not as inhibited as most holders, and whether they had the voice for the song or not, they were lusty in their singing.

C'gan took turns with him and then called forth some of the solo voices. Maizella sang, as did R'yar, who had an excellent light baritone and hadn't forgotten any of his repertoire in his Turns as a rider.

Robinton never knew when Lord Maidir and S'loner left the table, for night had fallen, and although there were plenty of glowbaskets on the poles around the Bowl, there were so many coming and going with wine or to answer nature's require-ments, and so much for him to oversee as Harper, that he noticed their absence only when Lady Hayara rose and left the table, escaping a Jora slumped drunkenly across it.

No one would ever know exactly what did happen that night, but suddenly a piercing scream from Nemorth roused everyone. Especially when every other dragon voice augmented her heartrending, piteous scream. It seemed to go on and on, as if none of the dragons need pause for breath. It cut through the night air, worse than any tormented watch-wher's cry—a knife to the ears and to the heart. He thought his heart would stop at the anguish that reverberated in the Bowl.

He was by no means the first person to clap hands to his ears to muffle the awful screeching. It was the look of shock on dragonrider faces that gave Robinton his clue to the tragedy that had just been announced in dragon voice. The entire Weyr was mourning the death of a dragon.

Robinton grabbed C'gan and turned the stricken rider to him. C'gan's nerveless fingers slipped off the gitar neck as tears sprang from his eyes.

"What is it, C'gan? What's happened?"

Gulping to clear his throat, C'gan turned anguished eyes to the Harper. "It's Chendith. He's dead."

"Chendith?" Robinton whirled around, trying to spot S'loner in the crowd of shocked people. He saw F'lon, miraculously sober, running first to T'rell, the Weyrlingmaster, because the keening had aroused the dragonets and T'rell needed help in rounding up the new riders to go comfort their distressed beasts. Not a young man himself, T'rell looked haggard with grief and staggered as he moved about the tables.

"Dead? Why? How?" Robinton demanded. "He didn't look sick or anything during the Hatching." He lost sight of F'lon, then saw him again, hauling the Weyr Healer into the light.

Then Lady Hayara gave a shriek that pierced through the keening. "Maidir? *Maidir! Where are you?*"

It was the watchrider, circling down on his dragon, who told them that he had seen Chendith, with two aboard him, going *between*. He couldn't see too well in the darkness above the lighted Bowl, but he thought that Chendith's passenger had been Lord Maidir. He'd caught the shine of white hair and the green of the man's garments. Lord Maidir had been wearing green.

"But why? What could have happened to them? S'loner wouldn't take Chendith's life. Nor his own," C'gan said, sunken in despair. "What *could* have happened? He was in such high spirits over the Impression. And twenty dragons."

They had to try to rouse Jora from her drunken stupor, because Lady Hayara had not seen the two men leave the table.

"They have been estranged so long," Hayara said through her tears, "and it was only after that song of yours, Rob, that they started speaking to each other. I thought it was such a good sign, but I couldn't *hear* what they were saying because—" She cut off what negative comment she had been about to make, though her disgust with the Weyrwoman was plain.

F'lon, R'gul, and S'lel were trying to sober Jora up with strong klah, but she was boneless and kept sliding down the chair and having to be propped up to get any of the restorative liquid down her throat.

Healer Tinamon, assisting, put forward a tentative theory. "S'loner may have looked strong and healthy, but he was having chest pains far too frequently," he said. "I'd given him the usual remedy, although I wanted him to call in a Master-healer or at least visit the Healer Hall. He said he would after Impression."

That did not explain why Maidir had accompanied S'loner on what was his last flight, although Lady Hayara said that her spouse was very tired and might have requested either a place to rest here at the Weyr or the courtesy of a return to Benden Hold.

"Oh, please will someone take me back to the Hold immediately?" Lady Hayara asked piteously. "Maidir may be there and have some explanation for us."

R'gul promptly volunteered, and the quiet weyrgirl who had spoken to S'loner earlier had the good sense to bring Lady Hayara's riding jacket. Together they escorted her into the darkness of the bowl, where Hath, still keening, waited.

C'rob, M'ridin, and C'vrel, the oldest of the wingleaders, were holding a conference, which F'lon joined as if he had the right. Plainly the other riders did not think so.

"The next mating flight will decide that, F'lon, so let's not jump to any premature assumptions. And with Jora the way she is, that's likely to take a few Turns," M'ridin said in a low but angry voice.

"I suggest we clear the Weyr of all visitors," C'rob said. "This Impression is over."

"And marred by a death, which is not good, not good at all," C'vrel added, shaking his head.

"Keeping the dragons busy is the best thing for them," M'ridin went on. "Only be bloody sure to remind riders to give the clearest coordinates they ever had in their minds."

"Wouldn't it be better to let people stay . . ." C'vrel said.

"No, the Weyr must mourn its own," C'rob said. "I'll ask only the older riders to convey passengers." He ignored F'lon and went to choose those whom he considered responsible enough.

S'lel and another stalwart weyrman were now carrying Jora up the steps to her quarters, having failed to rouse her. On the ledge, Nemorth was still keening loudly for her mate, swaying her head and neck back and forth, her eyes whirling with the muddy reds shot with orangey yellows of extreme distress. It was then that Robinton realized the sides of the Weyr were punctuated by many pairs of whirling, distressed dragon eyes, like colored glowbaskets of unusual size. He remembered that long after other details of that terrible evening faded: the whirling eyes and the sad, bone-shaking keening from several hundred dragon throats echoing back and forth across the Bowl, all night long.

A drum message brought the information that Lady Hayara had not found Maidir at Benden Hold. The fatal accident had taken all three in that brief instant *between*. Robinton asked C'gan to convey himself and Raid, who was probably now the Lord Holder of Benden, back to the Hold. His stepmother would need his support and what comfort could be given her.

Robinton was packing up his music and instrument when F'lon came up to him.

"You'll want to go back," the young bronze rider said in a weary voice.

"I've asked C'gan . . ."

"Why him?" F'lon was angry.

"You've just lost your father, man," Robinton said, gripping the rider tightly on the arm. "I could scarcely impose on you . . ."

F'lon brushed hair back from his forehead in an irritable gesture and swung this way and that. "It's not as if we were close—weyrbred not taking that much store in relationships— and *shards!* But he's messed things up dying like this!"

Whether or not that outburst was F'lon's way of expressing his grief, Robinton was never sure, but the dragonrider was certainly furious. Robinton knew that the young bronze rider had been proud of being the Weyrleader's son. He'd always affected an attitude of disdain for the relationship, but at least he had *had* one with his father. Robinton envied him that.

"The others are too nervous as it is," F'lon went on savagely, looking every way but at the Harper. He kicked at the dirt of the Bowl and kept shaking his head. "I told him he was chancing it with those chest pains. Listen to his son? Oh, no, he knew it all."

In the glowbaskets, Robinton now noticed the wet streaks on F'lon's cheeks and he wished he could find something to say that would ease his loss. There was nothing.

"Oh, go on, Rob. You're safer with C'gan anyway. At least right now."

"Keep me posted how things are here, will you, F'lon? I know you can drum."

He gripped the bronze rider's arm in what he hoped expressed his sympathy and regret and then, picking up his carisaks, made his way out of the brightly lit area to the blackness of the Bowl, the silhouetted shape of C'gan's blue Tagath, and the glimmering shine of sad dragon eyes, dotting the wall of the Weyr.

Chapter 11

▼▼

His first act on returning to Benden was to search for Maizella and find out how Lady Hayara was doing. The girl looked almost as haggard as her mother had.

"She's had a healer's draught and will sleep her grief out," she said. "And I'm about to take one myself. I still can't believe what's happened. Couldn't there still be a chance they'll emerge from *between*?"

Robinton shook his head. "The dragons would know. And they know that Chendith is no more. I'm so sorry, Maizella."

"I know you are, Rob," she said, touching his arm. "And Raid's taking charge," she added with a touch of bitterness. "Could he not have waited until morning? Oh, he wants you on the drum tower . . ."

That was Robinton's second act, sending out the sad report of the double tragedy. Raid had already composed the message and thrust it abruptly at Robinton the moment the harper reached the top of the tower. As he got his wind back, Robinton read it. Different temperaments responded to tragedy in different ways, he reflected. He did not, as Maizella evidently did, think that Raid was heartless and unaffected. Rather he was proceeding with what he had been trained to do: take over the Hold and do whatever that new responsibility required of him.

The Lord Holders of Fort, South Boll, Tillek, and High Reaches, where it was only early evening, immediately drummed requests for dragons. There were messages later that long night from Telgar, Ista, Igen, and Nerat as men were roused with the tragic news.

By morning, all the major Holds knew and had responded. And by morning, a stream of Benden holders started arriving, some with wine or food. The women went either to the kitchens to help or upstairs to the family, to express their grief. The harpers from the outlying holds arrived to spell Robinton at the drums: his hands were swollen from constant use of the sticks and he could barely concentrate on incoming messages, much less reply confidently.

With the tower manned, he collapsed for a few hours' needed sleep and was roused when F'lon, looking pale and exhausted, woke him with klah and slabs of bread.

"I brought Faroguy in, with two of his family," the bronze rider said. "They didn't know I was S'loner's son." He gave a snort as he collapsed on the foot of the bed, slumping against the wall and nursing the hot klah on his chest. "You learn a lot more that way."

"What more?" Robinton struggled to a sitting position. "*Who* came with Faroguy?" he asked, the mere fumes of the strong klah sparking his instincts.

"Oh, that nephew and the son."

"Fax?"

F'lon frowned. "I think that was the name he said."

Robinton swore under his breath. "Watch that one."

"Oh, I intend to," F'lon said, cocking his head, his expression fierce. "He doesn't think much of dragonriders, and he doesn't think much of harpers, for that matter."

"I know. I would have thought he'd abstain."

"Shards no! He was grinning from ear to ear. Although . . ." And now F'lon paused, knitting his brows. "I think that his coming was a last-minute addition. There were just Faroguy and his oldest waiting for me. Then Fax came rushing out. He was up onto Simanith before I could speak."

Robinton continued to swear under his breath. He had no desire to confront Fax. He wondered how—and why—Fax had inserted himself into the group from High Reaches. He wasn't a member of the Council of Lord Holders and Masters. He couldn't vote on the matter of Raid's suitability.

"Oh, I also picked up MasterHarper Gennell and Lord Gro-gellan from Fort. Gennell's asking for you."

"Yes, he would be." Robinton drew his knees up so he could throw the covers off his legs. He had not bothered to strip off his clothing, and now he could scarcely appear in such wrinkled garments.

"Take your time. Have a quick bath. You need it." F'lon's ever whimsical sense of humor prompted him to hold his nose in demonstration.

"Yes, I do, don't I?" Robinton was aware of the reek of wine and sweat about his person.

"Gennell didn't seem in a hurry. Just asked where you were. Hayon said you were catching some rest. How's he taking his father's death?"

"He's been marvelous with Lady Hayara and the others but I can't think he likes having Raid in charge now."

"Don't think I would either," F'lon said bluntly and left the room.

Robinton stripped off the dirty clothing, grabbed clean garments from his chest, and strode to the bath, grateful that he didn't have to vie with others to use the common one down the hall. The hot water was stimulating, and he felt much better as he pulled on trousers and wriggled his arms into the clean shirt. He took his shoulder cords from the old shirt and attached them, making certain they were properly hung. Then he rough-dried his hair before he gathered it back with a thong. He really should have it trimmed. Later.

F'lon wandered in just then, having filled Robinton's klah mug. "Now you look respectable, as befits the Hold Harper."

"Why don't you get some sleep?" Robinton suggested, pointing to his empty bed.

F'lon looked in that direction and sighed. "That's the best idea you've had so far. Call me if you need me," he said, gulping down the last of his klah and beginning to roll down the tops of his flying boots.

Robinton heard the thud of the first one as he was closing his door.

The Hold was teeming with quiet people, talking in the corridors or in small groups in the Hall as Robinton descended the front stairs. Trestle tables had been set up and were loaded with plates of bread and bowls of fruit and slices of meat that had been rolled up for easy eating. He spotted Master Gennell talking to other Masters, flown in from their Halls to attend to the sad duty of succession. Gennell saw him and waved for him to join them.

As Robinton obediently wove his way through the assembled, he looked about for Fax, or at least Faroguy and whichever son had accompanied him. He assumed the Lord Holders must be convening somewhere else, but he did spot Farevene, standing in the entrance hall, looking around uneasily. Then Naprila came up to the young Holder and Robinton had reached the Masters.

Gennell introduced him to the Masters surrounding him: Smith, Weaver, Fisherman, Farmer, and Miner. He already knew MasterHealer Ginia, and she nodded soberly in greeting. More Masters would assemble for the Council meeting; these were but the first arrivals.

"Give us your account of what happened last night, Robinton," the MasterHarper said, and Robinton did, pleased that his wits had been aided by the klah and the bath so that he was able to make his report concise.

"Dreadful thing!"

"Terrible tragedy to lose both a Lord Holder *and* the Weyrleader."

"And at such a time—right after a Hatching!"

"Who will take over at the Weyr?"

They all looked at Robinton.

"I believe that will be decided in the traditional way when the queen mates again," the young harper replied.

"But the Weyr can't be without leadership for several Turns," the Fisherman protested.

"There are older riders: C'vrel, C'rob, and M'ridin," Robinton said. "They were taking charge last night."

"It's not as if there were Threadfall to worry about," the Miner said.

The Weaver snorted. "All too true, not that that S'loner wasn't drumming up alarms. Didn't take any serious notice of that, I can tell you."

Robinton forbore to speak up in such company, but he did notice that all the other Masters but his own seemed in agreement on that point.

"Jora is a young woman," the Farmer went on. "I wouldn't be concerned with Weyr management if Carola were still alive. She knew what was what."

"Weyr management is," Master Gennell pointed out politely, "the concern of the Weyr. Not ours. I presented my condolences to the bronze rider who conveyed us."

Robinton nodded. "That was F'lon, a son of S'loner."

"It was?" Ginia exclaimed in surprise. "Amazing. I don't think we need worry about the Weyr if that is the standard of rider presently handling its affairs."

Robinton told himself to remember to tell F'lon that he had one admirer among the Masters.

Just then, Raid approached and greeted them all with weary courtesy, thanking them for coming so quickly. "I've had seats for the entire Council placed in the small dining room, if you'd like to proceed," he said. "Robinton, will you show them the way?"

"Are we all present and accounted for then?" the Weaver asked, glancing about the crowded room.

"The last have arrived and are prepared to proceed," Raid said, bowing and moving off toward the refreshments, where

Maizella was pouring wine, assisted by Cording. Hayon was standing nearby, looking dolefully into his glass, Rasa and Anta beyond him.

Robinton duly led the Masters to the small dining room, which was just about large enough to accommodate the numbers.

"Wait here, Rob, in case we need to send for someone," Gennell said, pausing as the rest of the Craftmasters filed in.

Robinton nodded. Send for whom? There were no other Weyrleaders who traditionally officiated at such a meeting.

"It's started?" a familiar voice asked with a touch of amused malice.

Robinton turned his head slowly to regard Fax and gave him a cool look.

"I believe so," he said in a flat, unequivocal tone.

"You're Harper here, are you, Robinton?"

"Yes."

Fax regarded him steadily, amusement still keen. "And no corpse to lay to rest, either. Convenient that."

Robinton refused to rise to the bait and looked straight ahead, hoping Fax would leave.

"I'll leave you to your duty, then," Fax said. Swiveling on one heel, he made a leisurely return to the Hall.

Raid was confirmed within the hour, and then Robinton was sent to find out if any of the dragonriders he had named were present in the Hold. The Council begged the favor of a few words with any of the bronze riders. Robinton wondered as he went on search if he should send someone to wake F'lon. But he found M'ridin, C'vrel, C'gan, and C'rob in the courtyard, as well as the girl he had seen speaking to the Weyrleader.

"Manora here," C'rob said, indicating the girl, "says that the Weyrleader was unwell at dinner. She overheard Maidir asking to be conveyed home and S'loner said he'd do it because he wanted an excuse to leave. He's been having pains in his arm rather more often than he admitted, even to Tinamon."

She looked both uneasy and dignified; her eyes were still red from tears. But she nodded, confirming what C'rob reported.

Robinton escorted them all to the Lord Holders. Fax sauntered along in their wake, smiling enigmatically when Robinton firmly closed the door in his face.

When the Lord Holders concluded their interview with Manora and the bronze riders, most of them left the small dining room for the refreshments available in the Hall. But Robinton saw Lord Faroguy in the group that remained, and was startled by the change in the man. He looked almost bloodless with fatigue, as if he had little energy and substance, barely responding to whatever Lord Melongel, of Tillek Hold, was saying to him.

Then Farevene bustled down the hall, carrying a tray of food and drink. Giving Robinton a nod of recognition, he hurried up to his father and Lord Melongel. Melongel took the nearest glass of wine and passed it to Faroguy, then watched anxiously as the older man sipped and smiled in appreciation of the courtesy.

"There may be need for another Council, soon, Harper," Fax commented, appearing at Robinton's elbow. "Mark my words."

Robinton made no reply, managing to keep his expression bland though he seethed inwardly at Fax's pretentiousness. He could not help but worry about Faroguy, though it irritated him to give any weight to something Fax might say. Especially since both Melongel and Farevene seemed so concerned over the High Reaches Holder.

There was little a harper could do, Robinton realized philosophically, but he'd have a word with Farevene if the opportunity arose. Then what Farevene was saying to his father reached his ears.

"MasterHealer Ginia would be glad to give you a consultation, Father, as soon as you feel able."

"It won't do any harm," Melongel agreed heartily.

"Very well," Faroguy said with a heavy sigh and a flick of his pale hands where they rested on the arm of the chair. He managed a weak smile. "I'd rather another Council was not called sooner than necessary. And on my account." He took another drink of the wine, then looked at the glass. "Benden wine is, I fear, superior, Melongel."

"Just give us the time Benden has had with vine-culture and you'll see a comparison in our favor," Melongel replied with a hint of challenge.

"Robinton?"

The Journeyman turned at the touch on his arm to see C'vrel standing there, frowning.

"Simanith is on the heights, but I can't find F'lon anywhere."

"He's asleep in my quarters. He was reeling with fatigue," Robinton replied.

"Yes, well, we all are. But I'd rather you either kept him in your rooms or woke him now. Fax is wandering around, and I have a good suspicion—confirmed by Farevene in there—that he's probably looking for F'lon." C'vrel shifted his weight anxiously. "There's no doubt in my mind that F'lon would start trouble. We've had enough."

"I'd agree to that."

C'vrel gave a short bark. "S'loner sent F'lon out on quite a few *unwise*"—he lifted one thick black eyebrow—"errands which, quite frankly, were not conducted to the Weyr's advantage. I, for one, did not condone some of S'loner's methods or aims. Candidly, it's almost as much a relief to us—" The wave of his hand was meant to indicate the other older bronze riders. "—that S'loner's no longer leader as it is to the Council. So do us all a favor, Harper, and keep F'lon out of Fax's way. I'll take the High Reaches party back myself. I didn't know, in fact, that F'lon had been to that Hold today. M'ridin was to make that transfer."

Robinton nodded. Odd: F'lon had wished Robinton to think he didn't know Fax, and yet the young rider had seemed almost eager for a confrontation with the holder. It was fortunate indeed that exhaustion had intervened.

As he made his way to the front staircase, Robinton stopped

by Hayon. "I'll be in my quarters if I'm needed. I've been advised to keep F'lon and Fax separated."

"Oh, F'lon's in your rooms?" Hayon heaved a sigh of relief. "We've all been wondering. Especially that Fax. I don't like that man."

"Perceptive of you, Hayon."

"I'll cover for you. There're enough harpers here, as well as Master Gennell."

Robinton wished he could have been in two places at once, but it was far more important for him to keep F'lon asleep until the Council had departed. He wondered just what had transpired between the two. F'lon was known to be a clever fighter . . . but no rider should put his life—and that of his dragon—in jeopardy. Which was why it had been irresponsible of S'loner to fly when he was unwell. Robinton knew that a man's heart could stop from one second to another. Chendith would have known in that instant that his rider had died, and the presence of a passenger would not have deterred the dragon from suicide. And the grievously tragic death of Lord Maidir.

F'lon was asleep, sprawled out on the bed. Carefully, Robinton laid a blanket over him lest a chill wake him prematurely. The sun was well west by now, and the room was cooling down. He locked his door, pocketed the key, and, taking a light fur from the closet, laid himself down on the little bed in the room he'd occupied as a child. He was asleep almost as soon as he closed his eyes.

"All right, where's the key?" a voice said in his ear as a hand shook him roughly.

The little room was dark, and only one glowbasket was open in the outer chamber, but the long boots on the figure by his bed told him that F'lon was up and anxious to leave.

"Oh, sorry, F'lon."

F'lon snapped his fingers for the key as Robinton fumbled for it in his pants. "If I find that the High Reaches contingent took another dragon back, I shall be quite annoyed."

"If one hasn't," Robinton replied, "*I* shall be."

He gave the key over and lay back, wishing he'd been allowed to sleep round the clock as he heard F'lon stride noisily across the outer room, fumble the key into the lock, and swing the door open so roughly that it crashed into the wall.

"I'd better go after him," he murmured to himself, but he consoled himself with the thought that C'vrel would have whisked the High Reaches trio off long before now.

He was right. F'lon must have just received that information from Hayon when Robinton reached the top of the stairs, for the bronze rider glared fiercely over his shoulder at him. Then, in one of his lightning changes of mood, F'lon smiled and waved a hand. The tension drained out of his figure, and he sauntered over to see what he could find on the depleted refreshment table. Hayon and his younger sisters and brothers formed a disconsolate group to one side of the hearth; on the other, Lady Hayara sat with her sisters and brothers who had come to bear her company.

Robinton made his way down the stairs and stopped one of the drudges. "Would you know if the MasterHarper is still here?"

She pointed to the hallway and then crooked her finger to the left to indicate the small dining room.

He found Master Gennell with Lord Grogellan and the MasterHealer.

"F'lon is up," he told them, "and I gather the High Reaches folk are long gone."

Grogellan chuckled and Master Gennell grinned. "Master Ginia, did you get a chance to assess Lord Faroguy's condition?" Grogellan asked.

She nodded. "His son will see that he has the best of care for however much longer he is with us," she said solemnly. "It is a condition of the blood for which there is no cure for a man his age."

"Does Fax know this?" Robinton asked bluntly.

Grogellan snorted and Master Gennell looked about to reproach his Journeyman, but Ginia raised her hand.

"That young man knows a great deal too much about too many matters that are not actually the concern of a *small*"—and she stressed the adjective—"holder."

"Who might not remain small," Robinton said. "That's a very ambitious and greedy person."

"You had a run-in with him at High Reaches?" Gennell asked.

"Not a run-in, Master, but, as I felt obliged to tell you when I returned from that contract, he does not permit harpers to teach his holders basic skills."

Grogellan raised his eyebrows in surprise and turned to Gennell. "Is that true?"

"Yes, I fear it is."

"But surely someone as thorough as Faroguy would have insisted."

"Faroguy is old, tired, and sick," Robinton went on, "and remarks that the Charter allows autonomy within a hold."

"Which begs the question of whether the hold in question allows the Charter in," Master Ginia said, catching the point. At Robinton's nod, she went on. "Frankly, I don't like such an attitude. Intolerant and high-handed."

"An educated cotholder is far more useful and productive," Grogellan said.

"From what I understood, Fax's cotholders had better produce as much as he expects them to," Robinton said, "and no excuses allowed."

"I shall give the problem considerable thought," Gennell said.

"As will I," Lord Grogellan said. He glanced over at the door and rose. "I see our rider has come. Will you be back at the Hall soon, Robinton?"

"I'm contracted here, Lord Grogellan, but it's nice of you to inquire."

"Keep me informed, Rob," Gennell said, not needing to make specific what information he wanted.

Master Ginia, however, startled the Journeyman by standing on tiptoe to plant a kiss on his cheek. "I promised your mother I would," she said, and then left him gawping after her.

As he felt his cheeks reddening, he could only hope that no one else had seen her salutation. That wasn't his mother's style, but he smiled as Ginia disappeared down the hall.

R aid took Hold with no faltering and no hesitation. He called all his craftsmen to a meeting the next day and asked if there was any business that he needed to go over with any of them. Then he announced that his sister, Maizella, would exchange her espousal promises after the usual period of mourning, and that Lady Hayara would remain in the Hold until he could find a spouse of his own. He naturally would arrange suitable employment for his numerous half brothers and sisters.

If the speech was stuffy and stilted, there was no question that Raid would not honor his commitments. But Robinton quietly seethed at the awkward way the young man went about it. There were so many ways in which a bitter pill could be sweetened, and Raid seemed to know none of them, with all his blunt speaking and total disregard for the feelings of others. Only Maizella could rebuke him. Lady Hayara merely regarded him with filling eyes and numbly accepted his orders. Fortunately she was a capable woman and the ordering of the Hold had long been hers so there was no friction on that score. Even Raid knew her value to him. He didn't even begin looking about for an appropriate girl until his father had been gone three full months.

But something had noticeably gone out of the Hold that Maidir had managed so capably and . . . circumspectly. Holders with problems did not discuss them with Lord Raid: he told them what they had to do and that was that. Robinton did what he could to soften the Lord Holder's unequivocal statements, obliquely suggesting that Raid was still numbed by his father's tragic demise; and that, while he was well-trained and competent, he still lacked the touch that only experience would give him.

One day just before Robinton would have been at Benden two full Turns, Raid called him to his office.

"I hear a few things about you, Journeyman, that I do not like," he said, coming to the point immediately. "I am Lord Holder and what I say is how things will be. I do *not* need you soothing down disgruntled holders or denigrating my efforts behind my back. You may leave."

"Leave?" Robinton felt as numb as he had suggested Raid was.

"Leave. I hereby release you from your contract." Raid tossed a pouch of marks across the table to Robinton. "I shall request a replacement from the MasterHarper. Without prejudice, of course, since you have discharged your duties with efficiency and energy."

"Efficiency" and "energy" were two of Raid's favorite words. "But I . . ."

"You may drum that bronze rider friend of yours to convey you back. Give this"—he fielded a little roll of hide to join the pouch—"to Master Gennell. You do not suit me as the Hold Harper." Then he rose to his feet, to indicate the meeting was over.

For once robbed of words, Robinton scooped the two items off the table and, pivoting on one heel, strode out of the office, wanting very much to slam the door behind him.

Without a word to anyone, embarrassed and furious about his dismissal, he went up to his rooms and packed his things. He had to visit the schoolroom, where Maizella was rehearsing the secondary children; she must have known about his dismissal, because she only glanced up to see who was entering the room, then averted her eyes, saying nothing to him, continuing to listen to the recitations. He collected all his music and notes, and though he smiled at his former pupils, he said nothing.

Better to leave it at that, he thought as he ran up the tower steps three at a time. He was breathless at the top, but he had also worked off some of the frustration and anger he felt at such an unfair dismissal. Raid was just too inexperienced to realize how he offended his holders, or that a harper could be a good resource for management.

Hayon was on watch and smiled as Robinton entered. But whatever he was about to say by way of greeting died before he could sound it.

"I'm allowed to send a message," Robinton said, unable to keep the edge out of his voice. He picked up the sticks and rattled out a terse request for conveyance. Hayon's eyes widened and he looked about to speak again, but held his peace.

It was awkward, waiting there for a response from the Weyr, but Robinton was not in a mood to placate anyone and Hayon was sensitive enough to feel it. The Journeyman sank back down on the stool and waited, sipping at his klah during the interminable time it took for the distant drums to sound. A dragon would be there presently.

"All right, what's wrong, Rob?" Hayon asked finally.

"Your brother does not find me a suitable harper."

Hayon regarded him steadily. "My *half* brother," he said with a deliberate emphasis on the degree of the relationship, "sometimes does not use the wits he was born with. If he was. Does he *know* all that you do to calm down the experienced holders he keeps insulting?"

"That is precisely why I am to leave, Hayon. Tell Lady Hayara I'm sorry to go . . ."

"She'll really miss you," Hayon said staunchly.

"I certainly don't envy her. Nor you."

Hayon gave a little smile. "I'll survive. At least, I've always known that I would have to."

"There's that," Robinton said and extended his hand, which Hayon clasped heartily in both of his.

"Tell you one thing, Maizella's going to miss you at her espousal."

"I think not," Robinton said, but he smiled without rancor.

"Here comes your dragon. Oh, and if it's F'lon, warn him that my brother's raging over him paying so much attention to Naprila."

"Oh?" Robinton had missed that. No, Lord Raid would not want his half sister seeing too much of a dragonrider, though he rather thought that Lord Maidir would have been receptive. Maidir had known that life in a Weyr could be preferable to working a hold.

When Hayon rose to escort Robinton down the stairs, the Journeyman shook his head. "Let's not give Raid any cause for complaint about my departure. I want *out* as quietly and inconspicuously as possible."

Hayon chuckled. "You will have to work hard to be inconspicuous, Rob. I shall miss you badly."

With a final nod of thanks, Robinton started down, collected his carisaks from his room, and made his way down the main stairs and out the door without seeing anyone.

F'lon and Simanith had come for him. Robinton did see Raid at the office window, watching him sling his things up to F'lon to arrange on Simanith's back. Then, with a good leap of his long legs, he made it to Simanith's cocked forearm, and grabbed F'lon's gloved hand to help him the rest of the way.

"Sacked you, did he?" F'lon said, grinning and tossing an airy wave in the direction of the office window.

"Did you know he would?" Robinton asked, wondering how he had missed the change in Raid's attitude.

"I hoped he would. You can do better elsewhere."

"Benden's a good Hold," Robinton protested out of loyalty and truth.

"Under Maidir, yes. Raid's going to have to learn some tact."

"You heard talk about that?"

F'lon gave a shrug. "Hang on." And Simanith gave the head-snapping leap skyward.

Robinton did feel a lump in his throat at leaving Benden Hold. He had been happy there as a child, and so proud to have been asked to come back as a journeyman for Maidir. Really, he had done his best as he had been taught. Where had he gone wrong?

"Nowhere, as I interpret the matter," Master Gennell said when Robinton had his interview, "Young Lord Raid has a lot to learn about handling his people. "The MasterHarper sat with steepled fingers and a sympathetic expression on his face. "He will, though. He had good training. And the results of his current practices will show him the error of his ways."

"Really?" Robinton gave a snort of disbelief.

"Oh, I think so." Then Master Gennell grinned. "Actually I can use your talents in at least six other positions. You may choose."

That was how Robinton came to spend the next two Turns at Tillek Hold. And found the first love of his life. The only two drawbacks to the posting would be the awful weather that never seemed to include many sunny days, and the very sharp, foxy white wine the slopes of Tillek hills produced. He would also start the extra study for his Mastery, which included Applications of the Charter and the Precepts of Arbitration and Mediation, advanced aspects of the Harper Hall's purview. The Tillek Hold Master Harper, Minnarden, had agreed to undertake his tuition, since Minnarden attended the Hold's court sessions. Robinton was looking forward to working under Minnarden, and his mother thought well of this Master.

"Solid man for basics, and a kind person, too," she'd said. "You'll have no trouble with him." She'd added one of her mischievous smiles, slanting her gaze up at her tall son. "He dandled you on his knee at one point." She laughed as Robinton grimaced. "Don't worry, love. He won't embarrass you by remembering."

Robinton certainly hoped not. He didn't think such a reminiscence would be good for his authority over a class.

He, and young Groghe, Grogellan's third son, made the trip on runnerback: some of the good Ruathan stock which were so popular, plus a pack animal for their supplies and effects.

Groghe was going to spend a Turn in Tillek Hold, stewarding for Lord Melongel. Lord Holders often rotated their sons in hold management, or fostered them outright from time to time. Groghe was Rob's age, an energetic young man who resembled his mother, Lady Winalla, more than his father. He made the arduous trip pleasant for, despite a tendency to make all the decisions about camping and hunting and duties, he was a sturdy traveler and a good companion. His taste in songs leaned to the bawdy but Robinton didn't mind obliging him in the evenings, especially when they sheltered overnight in one of the all-male holds—miners, herders, and foresters—on their way. For the simpler melodies, Groghe sometimes accompanied him on a pipe.

On the way, Groghe had a small errand to do for his father. One of Lord Grogellan's high mountain holders was having trouble with a neighbor who was on Tillek Hold lands, not Fort's. Groghe was to see what he could do to solve a problem that had now existed for several Turns.

"I'm fed up with his complaints, both written and at Gathers," Lord Grogellan had said. "I've sent messages to Melongel, who's equally disgusted with the case. With Journeyman Robinton along, you should be able to solve the problem. A matter of a mutual wall, I understand. Making a mountain out of a very small pile of dirt."

When they came down the side of the mountain, heading north, they saw the two cots, both substantial in size. The Fort man was a herder, the Tillek man a forester. The cots were separated by several dragon-lengths, and in plain sight was a collapsed stone wall, five or six dragon-lengths long, which separated field from forest. Perhaps a storm had brought down a swath of trees, smashing into the structure and damaging a long stretch. They could also see the shaggy coats of herdbeasts being driven from the forest, with angry shouts by the men doing the driving, and furious cries from three men waiting on the field side. The drivers were not sparing of their clubs in getting the woolly beasts back on their own side of the wall.

"Fix that sharding wall, Sucho, or I'll kill the next ones that come into my plantation!"

The driver's bellowed threat carried easily to the two travelers.

"We *would* arrive in the middle of it," Groghe said to Robinton with a grimace. "Ah, well! It's to be done!"

They had indeed hoped to arrive before dark, so they could have a quick assessment of the problem. Now the issue would have to be met immediately.

"A wall has two sides," Robinton remarked and grinned.

"Good evening to you," Groghe said, raising his voice.

The driver had stopped at the pile of stones and, shielding his eyes from the glare of a sun close to setting, peered at the two riders. The holder whirled, raising a sturdy staff, and his sons—they resembled him too much to be anything but—assumed defensive stances.

"Groghe of Fort Hold and Journeyman Harper Robinton," Rob called out, raising his hand high.

The two older men exchanged glances. "You've been complaining again to Lord Groghe, Sucho?" the forester shouted, grinning maliciously. "Welcome, Holder and Harper. You must spend the night with me and mine." He gestured to his own two sons.

"We'll be grateful for shelter, I assure you," Robinton said at his most gracious, close enough to the wall now to halt his runner and swing down from the saddle. He was taller than any of them, and he would use that to his advantage.

Groghe dismounted as well, and stood firmly at Robinton's side. "My father, Lord Grogellan, wants this settled and has sent me and Journeyman Robinton to be sure that this time the matter is finished."

That was all that was needed to send both men into loud and conflicting claims: Tortole insisted that the wall had fallen on Sucho's side, so it was up to him to repair it; Sucho claimed that if Tortole hasn't been so clumsy in felling the line of trees so that they damaged the wall, there wouldn't have been a problem. Robinton then noticed that the remains of the uprooted trees on Tortole's side were well covered in moss, suggesting that the stumps had been there for many Turns. That the storm had done more damage to the forestation, knocking down a swath that continued on up and down the hillside, than to the meadows of the herder was clear, but why two isolated families would not combine to replace the dividing wall was not.

"*Enough!*" Groghe shouted.

"Quite enough," Robinton said into the sudden stillness. "A wall has two sides, my friends."

The response was blank looks. The younger men muttered together.

"Of course a wall has two sides," Sucho said, scowling.

"Your side and his side," Robinton said patiently. "You build your side and he will build his side."

Sucho and Tortole goggled at him. Groghe turned a chuckle into a cough.

"The wall was not one stone thick, was it?" Robinton went on, looking sternly over the group. He could see that the wall had been wide and high enough to keep the herdbeasts from easily jumping over to reach the lush grass where the swath had been cleared.

Sucho shook his head. "That wall's been there since my hold was built."

"Since *my* hold was built, you mean," Tortole said.

"Then it's small wonder that it has fallen. The mortar would have deteriorated over the Turns," Robinton said. "But that does not keep it from having two sides. You—" He pointed over the fallen wall at Tortole. "—will build your side, smack up against Sucho's." He turned to the herder. "And you will be sure to build your side smack up against Tortole's. You alternate putting in the mortar to be sure that both sides are bound together."

"And we will see you started in the morning," Groghe said.

"But we've other work to do!" Tortole shouted, outraged.

"I've herds to tend," Sucho bellowed simultaneously.

"I notice that you each have two sons," Robinton put in. "Strong fellows, and you have the stones to hand. I wonder which of you, working three to a side, can finish your side first."

"Why, my sons and I . . ."

"My sons and I . . ."

Tortole and Sucho glared at each other.

"Then we will see just who does win tomorrow, won't we?" Robinton said as pleasantly as possible, smiling amiably.

"You'll stay with *us*," Sucho said, jerking a thumb at his chest.

"No, they'll stay with us in a decent cot—" Tortole replied.

"*No!*" Robinton's well-trained bellow silenced them both. "Since Groghe is Fort, he will stay with his holder. And I, not being beholden to either Fort or Tillek, will stay with Tortole. However, if this evening, anyone will care for a song or two, I will sit on that post—" He pointed to the one still standing, where a gate of sorts must once have been, allowing access from one holding to the other. "—and sing *for both families*. Since a harper is obliged to be impartial."

Then, before the astonished men could argue further, he swung up on the Ruathan runner and urged it forward, finding a narrow place where the animal could hop easily over the scattered stones.

"Will it be possible to have a wash before dinner?" he asked his appointed host as he paused by him.

Groghe was drawing Sucho with him toward the cot, where several more figures had appeared in the doorway. Groghe was initiating pleasantries, and Robinton heard the grumbles of answers.

"I do hope that we will not put you out for our dinner. We have our own provisions," Robinton said. "A nice plump wherry that I took off its branch this morning." He patted the carcass, which he had fastened to the back of his saddle.

"How'd you get it?" one of the sons asked, peering at the beheaded avian.

"Knife throw," Robinton said indifferently. It wouldn't hurt to suggest that he was proficient with a blade. He was, but it bore repeating with these rough-living folk. Tortole was bigger than he, and massive. His sons, while younger, were no less substantial. It amused him that the herders looked equally able to take care of themselves, which probably contributed to the stand-off.

"And you a harper?" The son sounded surprised.

"Oh, I have to travel long distances on my own," Robinton said as they reached the forester's cot. He nodded pleasantly to the three women who came out, their curiosity getting the better of their shyness. "Hunting's necessary from time to time." He gave a courteous bow to the oldest of the women, dressed in rough skin pants and clearly embarrassed to have a visitor. "I have begged shelter from your spouse. And bring this to add to the supper pot." He bowed again as he handed over the wherry.

She opened and closed her mouth several times without getting a sound out.

One of the others took it from her, examining it with a knowledgeable eye, and managed a grin. "Young and fresh. Thanks, Harper." She nudged the other, who was too surprised to respond to his smiles in any way. "It'll do just fine. If these louts would do more hunting instead of herding, we'd not take yours from you." She gave the men a withering smile and then, grabbing the old woman by the arm and prodding the other with the wherry carcass in her hand, she propelled them all into the cot.

"I'll get the loft ready for you, Harper," one of the lads said, remembering the duties of hosting.

"I'll do your mount. Ruathan, isn't it?" the other said, taking the reins from Robinton's hand and casting an approving eye over the runner.

"I'll just . . . take my things," Robinton said, slipping open the knot that tied the saddlebags and grabbing them and his gitar.

"You'll play for us this evening?" the first lad asked, eyes glinting with hope.

"I said I will. And I will. On the post so *both*—" He paused for emphasis. "—can enjoy."

The cot, while somewhat primitive, was larger inside than it looked outside. The main room was obviously where most interior work was done, but it was separated into sections:

one for the women's tasks, another for the men's, with an eating area and well-made chairs set near the fireplace. There were rooms off each end, and off the long wall that the hearth dominated; ladders led to lofts on both sides. If he were to be accommodated above, Robinton decided, he'd best remember to keep his head down.

But he was escorted to one of the side rooms, which contained one large bed. The son cleared clothing from the two stools and one chest, where he gestured for Robinton to place his bags.

"Who am I displacing?" the Journeyman asked.

"My father and mother." The son gave a chuckle. "The honor is theirs, and ours, to have a harper as guest. I'm Valrol. My brother is Torlin. My mother's name is Saday; the girl who took the wherry is my spouse, Pessia, from Tillek Fisher-crafthall. My sister is Klada. She would like to spouse Sucho's son, but my parents won't let her because of the wall. But, if she spouses him, then Pessia and I will have a room to ourselves."

Valrol spoke in a low voice and quickly, trying to give Robinton all the necessary information before an extended absence brought his father to see what was delaying them.

"I'll show you where the bath is," he said, and Robinton murmured thanks, rummaging in his pack for his towel, soap, and a clean shirt.

The bath was actually heated by some connection with the hearth, so it was not the cold wash that he could have expected. He did not loll in the warm water, though he would have liked to soak the aches of travel out of his bones, but he was grateful for the luxury.

A trestle table had been set up, but Robinton had the impression that the family usually ate in the chairs by the fireplace. Pessia was putting the last of the wherry sections into the bubbling cauldron swung over the fire. Saday was busy tearing greens into a beautifully crafted wooden bowl, while Klada, still in shock from being in the presence of a stranger, and a harper at that, was trying to put cups on a tray without dropping them. With an exclamation at her awkwardness, Torlin took the tray from her and, grabbing up a wineskin, gestured for the harper to take a seat at the table.

Foxy though the wine was, Robinton was grateful for the cup and gave a proper Harper toast to his hosts, smiling at Saday when she shyly placed the salad bowl on the table.

"That's beautifully done, Holder Saday," he said pleasantly, rubbing a finger along the rim. "Local wood?"

She nodded, managing a smile, and then looked anywhere but at him, taking a long drink from her cup.

By the time dinner was served and eaten, she had grown accustomed enough to him that she suddenly blurted out that she had turned the bowl herself.

"Do you send your wares to the Gathers?" he asked. Many people made a few extra marks from their homemade things.

She shook her head vigorously. "Not good enough."

"I think so," he said kindly, "and I've worked in wood. I make my own instruments."

She bent her head, and that was the last he heard from her in conversation. His reassurance sat well with Tortole, though, who was far more amiable as the meal progressed. The men dominated the talk, asking questions and listening eagerly to Robinton's answers; their original rancor over his solution to the wall problem was easing. Pessia, having been reared in a large community, felt comfortable enough to break in several times with cogent queries about the rest of Pern, and Valrol beamed proudly at her. Seen in a less threatening posture, Valrol was a good-looking young man. Robinton noticed the fond glances exchanged by the two and understood why she had taken him, despite the hold's isolation. Klada was attractive, too, or would be if she looked up at anyone.

The pleasant after-dinner talk was truncated by a knock on the door. All three men lurched to their feet and Saday gave a fearful squeak, but it was Robinton who reached the door first, forestalling further unpleasantness.

Groghe stood in the doorway, a glowbasket in one hand and his pipe in the other.

"Damned near broke my neck over that sharding wall," he muttered under his breath. "Are you finished eating, Journeyman Robinton, so that we can have the soothing benefit of new songs?"

A glowbasket appeared in Tortole's hand. Shawls and jackets appeared on the Tortole contingent as they all stepped out, forming a sort of cordon that moved with Robinton.

"Pessia, grab my gitar, would you please?" he asked, pointing to the side room where he had put his things.

Once she returned, smiling at being given such an honorable task, he joined Groghe and they all made their way to the post where he had said he would sing. The Sucho group had brought out chairs, and instantly Tortole ordered his sons to bring seating for his folk.

"Lovely evening," Robinton said as Groghe found himself a seat on the broken wall and settled down. The harper returned the Holder's wink with a nod and a grin and tuned his gitar.

Despite this being a very small gathering, he started off with the Duty Song, Groghe joining him with his pipes.

The look on the faces lit by the glowbasket, their hunger for music, for companionship—which made this estrangement over a wall even more ridiculous—was a scene that Robinton doubted he would forget. And one that made his profession all the more important in his own eyes. He had taken so much for granted in his own life.

He played and sang until he went hoarse. As the gathering progressed, one after another of his listeners began to sing choruses with him. In fact, by the time he could sing no more, he had quite a good chorus going, with three-part harmony in places.

It was Groghe who called a halt. Robinton could no longer feel his own buttocks, they'd been mashed against the post so long.

"We have had a long day's travel, my friends, and you have a wall to build tomorrow," the Holder said. "You have sung in harmony this evening. Continue that mood tomorrow."

"I'll only build my half of the wall," Tortole said, unwilling to concede.

"And Sucho will build his," Robinton said quickly, pointing

at Sucho, who hesitated briefly before nodding. "Your women don't need you two fighting," he added. "They are lonely enough up on this hill without being able to share their lives with another family."

The women agreed loudly.

The two families were already at work—the women of both working together to mix mortar and crack the old off the stones—by the time Groghe and Robinton were ready to mount. Robinton's parting gift was a sheaf of songs, which he gave to Pessia.

"You have a good, strong alto. Get them singing again."

"I will. I've missed it fearfully," she said, holding onto his hand a moment before taking the music. "Thank you," she added under her breath.

By the time they had reached the trail winding through the forestry, Groghe kicked Robinton's stirruped foot, grinning. "A wall has two sides, indeed! You've a glib tongue on you, Harper, but what a great notion! My father will howl with laughter."

Robinton grinned, though the image of the dignified Lord Grogellan howling with laughter was more than he could manage. He was, in truth, rather pleased with himself for the success of their interference.

Chapter 12

▼▼▼

By the time they got to Tillek Hold, however, he had tired of hearing Groghe repeat the tale of their little foray into arbitration at every hold they sheltered in on the long coastline leading to the tip of Tillek and the Hold. Lord Melongel was relieved to hear that the situation had been remedied—and very pleased to procure Journeyman Robinton's addition to his staff with such an instance of his abilities in the field. To offset this minor success, Robinton felt obliged to explain the circumstances under which he had left Benden Hold.

"He'll learn, young Raid will," Melongel said after Robinton had been candid with him. "His loss, Tillek's gain. Come, meet my Lady and my tribe of promising Bloods. Master Minnarden's off doing an arbitration service for me, so you'll have to wait to hear what your precise duties are here. However, I'll warn you now that I like to change journeymen every three to four Turns, so don't take it personally when either Minnarden or I suggest we make a change."

Robinton grinned back, liking the man's manner: a refreshing change from the two much older Lords he had served, and a decided relief after Raid's didacticism. Melongel was in his prime, active, vigorous, with rugged good looks, though not quite as tall as his Harper. He seemed to have time to attend to all his duties and still go out with the fishing fleet from time to time. Since Tillek Hold not only hosted the Fisher-crafthall but the MasterFisher, *and* did most of the western shipbuilding, Melongel thoroughly understood the needs of that Craft as well as the agriculture and forestry that made Tillek a profitable Hold. He had even qualified for his captaincy, but had never taken a command. On one cruise around the Southern Sea to Nerat, Melongel had found a major Holder's daughter, espoused her, and carried her back to his Hold. Robinton heard him call that the most profitable journey he'd ever made.

When Master Minnarden returned two days later, he welcomed his new Journeyman effusively, with reminiscences of earlier days spent at the Harper Hall, and duets sung with the MasterSinger Merelan. Robinton held his breath, but the Master Harper did not embarrass him in front of the other two journeymen with tales of Merelan's little boy.

"I understand you're very patient with the slow and I've several here I'd like to see you bring up to the level the others are at. With one it may not be possible. But if you can do anything, his parents and I would be grateful."

Robinton murmured something polite.

"To offset that chore, I'd like you to take the singers of the Hold for choral practice. I've had to do so much mediation lately that I've had to give up a steady progression for them. You'll stand the necessary drum tower watches." At that, Minnarden grimaced, for the long hours of listening and little action were a penance for most harpers, who tended to be gregarious by nature. "If you can find a couple of lads in the Hold to train up to drumming, I'd be grateful. Shorten our hours. I've not had the time, and neither Mumolon nor Ifor have the top rating you got from the Hall Drum Master."

Again Robinton nodded. He had had the advantage of being raised in the Harper Hall and learning to decipher messages long before he took the actual course.

"The usual evening divertissements, but we trade off." Then

Master Minnarden looked quizzically at him. "Bring any new songs with you?" When Robinton smiled in assent, Minnarden sighed with relief. "Both Mumolon and Ifor are good harpers, excellent teachers, but couldn't compose if you gave them words and music to put together. That's your special skill, I understand . . . and don't turn modest on me."

Robinton chuckled.

"You're quartered well?"

Robinton bowed his head gratefully, for he had an outside room, small but private, with a window facing east, and a bath next door.

"Need anything?"

Robinton shook his head.

"Good. Tillek is not as much a warren as many big Holds. But that's because the cliff doesn't have that many caves, so they've used the local stone to build sturdy, Threadproof housing."

Robinton looked at him sharply. This was the first time anyone had mentioned Thread.

"Hmmm, yes, young Harper, I believe we'll see Thread again," Minnarden said solemnly. "I've read too much in the Archives to think Pern will escape its return—in due time. Are you of my mind? Which, I must add, is not shared by many, including Melongel, though he's a well-read man."

"The dragons told me. And I've friends in the Weyr . . ." Robinton admitted hesitantly. But if Minnarden believed Thread would return, he wouldn't object to Robinton's friendship with a dragonrider.

"Keep them. Cherish them," Minnarden said. Then he cocked his head to one side. "Is that why young Lord Raid let you go?" He held up his hand when Robinton moved uneasily in the chair. "I know, I know. If you believe in anything—*anything*— keep that faith. Now," he went on, rising, "if you've any questions after you've settled in, I prefer my harpers talking to me rather than complaining to each other. One last item, though, since this Hold's main source of income is from fishing, I'd like it if you could see your way clear to learn as much of this different lifestyle as you could. Never hurts. Even the hull of a ship has two sides."

Robinton groaned: he was getting mighty tired of that reference! But he had to grin at Minnarden, who was clearly delighted with his new Journeyman's adventure.

Minnarden then retrieved from the shelf behind him a squared-off leatherbound record book and slid it across the table to Robinton. "If you haven't memorized the Charter, you'd better, and study the examples of some of the more common infractions." Minnarden grinned. "That aspect of our job can be quite interesting at times . . ." He paused to sigh. "And at others, about as infuriating as dealing with the dumbest, most insubordinate, mentally deficient adolescent male."

Melongel's middle children—he had nine—were part of the chorus group that Robinton was to rehearse. Bright, intelligent, and curious, the two boys and one girl were musical enough so that any of the three could have apprenticed in the Harper Hall. His oldest, just a year younger than Robinton, was Oterel, a rangy awkward lad needing to grow into his bones. Oterel was delighted to have Groghe share both his room and his duties, for he already had stewardship responsibilities, which went more swiftly with help.

And then there was Kasia, Lady Juvana's youngest sister, who was living at Tillek Hold.

Robinton felt a decided attraction in his first meeting with the attractive young woman. In the previous Turn, she had tragically lost her lover to a storm at sea off Nerat coast, half a month before their espousal. Her parents had sent her to Juvana to ease her grief. It was the aura of sadness that caught his eye, the sorrow that lurked in her lovely sea-green eyes. And the tremulous smile that, only occasionally, briefly lifted it. But she was cheerful, helpful, and kind, with a real understanding of the trials of her younger nieces and nephews. She was obviously their confidante, as well as her sister's. She had a comprehensive memory and was able to come out with astonishing bits and pieces of information that she had tunneled away.

"I just remember things," she said with a little shrug when Robinton asked her if she knew all the words to an old Teaching Song, one he was revitalizing. Which she did—word-perfect. "I can't say why I know that particular ballad, but you'll find it on the second shelf from the top of the right-hand side of the library."

And sure enough, there it was, with Kasia grinning with delight at her accuracy: an occasion when the sadness disappeared. He became determined to lift the shadow completely. He was chagrined to discover that he was not the only young man in the Hold who had the same ambition, including his fellow harpers.

Robinton was only twenty, a fact he kept hidden since he didn't look so young and could cite five Turns of active Harpering. Neither Mumolon nor Ifor knew that he had been fifteen when he walked the tables to collect his Journeyman's knot. Minnarden knew, and probably Melongel, but his youth was not a factor in assigning him difficult tasks. Especially after the Wall Incident. If Ifor and Mumolon suspected, it didn't matter to them, as he performed his duties too well to require criticism.

Kasia was several Turns older and looked younger: except for the harbored grief. However, that age difference, as well as her continued mourning for her lost lover, were the reasons why Robinton was hesitant in discovering if the sudden, keen attraction was mutual. Their ordinary tasks often brought them together. In that he was luckier than the others who sighed over her.

He contented himself with enjoying her company, her bright humor, her lovingness, and sparring with her in duels of memory and, often, song. She had had excellent training: she sang with a sweet light soprano and played fiddle and pipe. She was envious of his harp, which she played middling well, not having an instrument of her own. So he concocted the notion of making one for her in his spare time. Tillek's port shipped quantities of timber, as well as storing it for the building of hulls. He made himself agreeable to the local MasterWoodsmith, an accomplished carver named Marlifin, who was only too happy, when requested, to find him well-seasoned and unusual woods. Tillek Hold had a well-equipped workshop, as most large establishments did, so Robinton had only to start his project. He did ask Marlifin to do the carving of the forepillar patterns of the flowers that Kasia had said she loved. Robinton couldn't carve fancywork without ruining a lot of good wood, and this harp had to be special. It was going to take long enough as it was. He did manage, after several faulty starts and not a few cuts on his hands, to carve the harmonic curve and the neck, which would hold the pegs to tune the strings of the harp . . . when he got that far.

He also took Minnarden's advice to learn more about a fishing hold and found great favor with Melongel, and incidentally with Kasia, when he volunteered to go out on a fishing run with Captain Gostol, whom he had met at the Harper Hall. Kasia shipped out on the same voyage, as galley cook and companion to Gostol's daughter, Vesna, who was going for her second's ticket. There were two other women in the crew of fourteen, for the *Northern Maid* was the length of a queen dragon. The female sailors surprised Robinton. He was accustomed, being Harper-trained, to women having equal status as performers and composers, but it had never occurred to him that other Crafts also promoted women to positions of trust and responsibility. He was astonished to find them fishing, since that was a hard life. He discovered just how hard on that trip. Fortunately his immunity to seasickness was a great mark in his favor. He struggled to help lower and haul in the trawling nets, slipped on fish guts, laughed when he got up covered with gore and slime—and was teased for the stench of him until the job was done and he could change. If he wasn't considered able to stand a watch, he was available to heat soup or klah in the galley for those who did.

Of course, Kasia's post was the galley, though she was also a dab hand at gutting and salting the catch. So they had time to talk. He was as subtle as he could be, lighthearted, and finding odd bits and pieces of humorous things to tell her, to dispel the sadness that still lurked. And, of an evening, or sailing to another likely spot to fish, he would manage to place himself close to her while they helped pass the time by singing. He toned down his heavier baritone to blend with her light voice in duets or choruses. He also picked up a few local worksongs, favored by the Tillek Fishermen.

The most vivid memory he had of that sevenday was of the shipfish who were in the habit, Captain Gostol said, of accompanying the fishing vessels.

"That's old Scarface, that is," the captain said, pointing to one whose bottle-nose was indeed scarred. "Got hisself caught somewhere."

"Are they singing?" Robinton asked, hearing sounds when the leaping shipfish were airborne.

"Naw, just the sounds they make, shooting the air out of them blowholes," Gostol said. "Though I've known instances when a man blown overboard's been rescued by 'em." He paused and tilted his head midships. "Storm was too fierce to save that 'un's man. Shame, too. Good fisher. Nice girl. She shouldn't pine too long, ya think?" And now he cocked his head at Robinton, a sly grin on his rugged, weather-worn face.

Robinton laughed. "Considering how many fellows come round to see her at Tillek Hold, it's only a question of her pointing a willing finger."

"So you say, do you?" Then Gostol pointed. "She's got another young'un since last time I saw her. That one with the mottled rostrum. See her?"

The shipfish was in fact almost hovering in the air, squeaking, crackling at the humans, whom she knew were admiring her. Her baby, half her size, was doing its best to match her leap.

"Do the same ones swim in these waters all the time?"

"Think so. Recognize 'em certainly." The captain gave an uncharacteristic sigh. "Like watching them. Sometimes," he said, leaning his forearms on the rail, "I think they sort of—" He made a slanting motion with his thick-fingered right hand. "—ease us one way or t'other, and we follow, 'cos they seem to know where the fish are schooling."

"Really?" Robinton leaned his arms on the rail, too, as if he could get closer to the leaping shipfish who were still clicking and squeaking at him, almost as if they were saying something he just couldn't quite catch.

"They're good luck, they are. No fisherman ignores them. Always give 'em something from each net." The captain stood up, peering over the rail, his stance alert. "Watch! Yup! We're sailing right into a mess a' bordos. Good eating, bordo. Good for saltin'." And he started forward, shouting orders to the crew to be ready to drop the nets.

Robinton could actually see the school over the starboard side of the *Northern Maid*. The sleek thick bodies were gray-striped, as long as his forearm, with bulging eyes on either side of their blunt heads. He'd never seen such a concentration of fish. Oh, he'd fished as a child down at Pierie Hold but had never seen a multitude of fish. However did they wend their way without accident? Did they have a leader, the way some of the herdbeasts did? Or an instinct similar to dragons, who never interfered with each other even when they came out of *between* in wing formation? He was fascinated.

Then Gostol roared out the command to lower the nets, and Robinton went forward to lend a hand.

That was actually the last fair day of the run, for the clouds closed in and they had to work in a driving rain, making a difficult job even more arduous. Robinton was exhausted, his muscles protesting their abuse and his hands raw. So, when they finally had time to relax over a late meal and he was asked to play, he brought out his faithful pipe as being the easiest for his sore fingers.

He could not help but be relieved when they sailed back into the deep natural harbor that made Tillek the best port on the long western coast. There were long rows of terraced cots carved out, or built out from, the several levels of cliff above the harbor. Some fishermen could anchor their ships right in front of their cotholds. Floats that rose and fell with the tides gave access to stairs, some cut deeply into the cliffside.

As the *Northern Maid* slid past the breakwaters that extended the arms of the U-shaped harbor, folk waved to the sailors who were making right and tight the sheets and lines, preparatory to docking. Gostol was allowing his second to bring his ship in, and Robinton, knowing how important it was for Vesna to complete the maneuver satisfactorily, was holding his breath for her when Kasia joined him. She had changed from her rough-weather gear into a long skirt and a thick woolen jumper against the chilly wind; her hair was newly braided. Her eyes didn't seem quite as shadowed. Maybe she had sailed with them to dissipate the last vestiges of her sorrow for Merdine. She had actually mentioned his name at one point during the voyage.

"Breathe, Rob," she said, laughing at him and lightly clasping her hands around his left arm.

The use of a short name for him made him catch his breath twice in a row. Did that mean she liked him?

"Will she make it?" he asked. Kasia had more experience with such things than he.

"The ship's making just enough way so that I think she'll nudge the dock and come to a full stop. Which is exactly what she should do."

The *Northern Maid* did seem to be moving but imperceptibly, the smallest hint of a wake visible on this side of the bow.

Kasia laughed, leaning into him, as he unconsciously exhaled as if his breath could give the ship just that touch more forward motion. They were nearly broadside of the fishing dock, their destination. Seamen stood fore and aft on the *Maid*'s deck, ready with mooring lines. They'd already put out the buffers. Men and women on the dock were edging forward, to catch the lines and snag them on the bollards, eager to proceed with unloading the perishable cargo.

Time seemed suspended as the *Maid* drifted more and more slowly until she just barely touched the dock and slid along it, the protective bumpers kissing the dock edge, coming to a final halt as the mooring lines were secured with deft loopings that stopped all movement with just the least little jar.

Kasia let go of Robinton's arm and clapped, shouting a "well done" in the direction of Vesna at the wheel. There were other congratulatory roars, and Robinton grinned at Vesna's pantomime of wiping sweat from her brow. She was smiling happily.

"Gostol's a hard taskmaster, but I'd say she's passed this test," Kasia said. "Let's go. They'll be at the unloading for hours, and I'm dying for a long hot soak. My hair must reek of fish and cooking oils."

Since she hadn't spoken a word of complaint throughout the voyage, Robinton was surprised at the return of fastidiousness. Not that he wasn't just as eager for a bath as she.

They'd given Gostol formal thanks and made farewells as the *Maid* was on her final tack into the harbor, so now they were free to disembark, carisaks of wet and dirty clothing over their shoulders.

"There're worn spots on this wharf, Rob," she said as they started across the wooden expanse. "Watch where you go."

"A mere several hundred Turns old, Minnarden said."

"A mere?" She tossed her head sideways, laughing at him, her sea-green eyes sparkling.

They wove past the fish factory workers guiding their carts to the ship, and strode up the wide steps to the right and on to the wide road that led to the Hold.

The day was overcast, rain threatening, but the roadway was bustling with people on their everyday activities. Many greeted the harper and Kasia without interrupting their progress. Occasionally their free hands touched, and Robinton was aware of each brush. He didn't dare look down at Kasia to see if she noticed the contact, but he did feel that the trip had been very worthwhile in cementing a relationship. A glow of satisfaction added to his contented sense of accomplishment.

"Let's do it again, Rob, and soon," Kasia said, her face glowing. "You're a good sailor, and Captain Gostol said he'd take you onboard any time you wanted to lend a hand."

"I'll sail again, anytime, with you," he said, grinning down at her and, daringly, caught her hand in his, squeezing it a trifle and eager to see her reaction to such a familiarity.

She squeezed right back. "I can't wait to get clean," she exclaimed and raced up the Hold steps so he had to follow with more haste than dignity.

In fact, she seemed intent on leaving him behind, as she careened into the hall and then around to the first flight of steps. They had two more to go before they were on their level. She was half a step ahead of him as they reached the top landing, breathless with laughter and the climb. She turned, grinning at her success, and he paused on the next to last step, their faces on a level. He didn't think—he just caught her about the waist, pulled her to him, and kissed her.

He hadn't known he was going to before he did, and as she leaned into him, arms about his neck, he was thrilled that she didn't reject him. It was the sweetest of kisses but far too short because, hearing steps coming down one of the halls, they broke apart. Kasia whirled, flashing him a brilliant smile, and dashed off to her apartment, leaving him more breathless than ever but surely the happiest man in the Hold at that moment.

All during his bath, which he was half tempted to shorten so he could search Kasia out that much sooner, he fantasized about their possible future together. After all, a journeyman harper who was going for his Mastery was a good match to make, even for a Holder's Blood. And his father had Telgar Blood. They couldn't fault his mother's achievements as a MasterSinger. He could always make instruments for extra marks. His contract with Tillek Hold was fair enough for a single man. He felt he could rely on Lord Melongel's basic sense of fair play to make an adjustment for an espoused, especially one espoused to kin. He could finish his contract here and make certain his next one improved enough to support a spouse. Since Kasia was Blood kin to the Lady Holder, they could expect to receive larger quarters for an espoused pair and there were rooms available. He chided himself for such thoughts on the one hand, and on the other, relished the joy of having them.

Since he suspected Kasia would take her time bathing off the brine and fish oils, he forced himself to be as thorough. The color of the water and the thin slick of oil suggested that he was wise to soak. His hands stung a bit from the sweetsand and he'd several broken nails as well as various scrapes and nicks. Nothing that wouldn't heal. Saltwater was good to clean wounds, even little ones. So he tended to his appearance and nails as he dressed in clean warm clothes. He must see about getting some new things. These were all old: serviceable, but not exactly stylish. Clostan, the Hold Healer, was always so well turned out that he might ask the man which tailor he used in Tillek. Clean at last, Robinton became conscious of the reek from the carisak of dirty clothing. He'd take it down to the wash room himself rather than have it contaminate his quarters. After all, maybe Kasia . . . and he cut short that delightful thought, although the prospect might be possible.

He was apologizing to the old Auntie in charge of the laundry drudges for the state of his clothes and she was grinning toothlessly up at him, when light steps on the stairs alerted him to Kasia's arrival with her bundle. Their eyes met, and he was sure he was blushing at the intensity of her gaze. That her cheeks reddened, too, was an excellent sign.

"Juvana wants to hear how we fared, Robinton," Kasia said, almost formal in manner. She passed over her clothing to the Auntie, all too casual, and the Auntie's grin broadened as she looked from one to the other.

"Well, by all means let us relate our adventures," he said as blandly as he could, and taking her arm in his with a grand gesture—at which Auntie cackled—he led her up the stairs.

This time they did not race but walked slowly, eyes meeting when their legs brushed as they climbed the steps. At the top, Robinton was almost trembling. Oh, he'd sung love songs and knew the various degrees of loving as well as the next harper. But to be himself immersed in precisely what the lyrics described was another experience entirely. To see Kasia responding to him was an even greater miracle.

They spent an hour with Juvana and helped her to sort mending yarns, allowing their hands to meet in the process. Robinton knew how to spin out a good tale about his inadequacies on board a working ship, while Kasia loyally corrected him with her version of the matter.

"I have considerably more respect for fishermen now, I assure you, Lady Juvana," he said when the bell sounded for the midday meal.

"D'you think Gostol will give Vesna her ticket now?" Juvana asked Kasia as they made their way down to the dining hall.

"I know he was pleased with her docking . . . stylish and accurate," Kasia said after a pause to consider her answer. "And she certainly knows her craft. Is she after the new hull in the shipyard?"

"Which journeyman isn't?" Juvana said in a droll tone. "Now you're back, will you help me with fitting the children's new clothes?"

"Did you get the borders all done?"

"I didn't waste my time while you were having fun sailing . . ."

"*Fun?*" Kasia protested, giving her sister a stern look. "In the weather we had?"

Robinton felt left out of this exchange but told himself not to be silly. Just because he was besotted with Kasia, it didn't mean he could expect her undivided attention. And she might not wish to ascribe more to that quick kiss than the whimsy of the moment. Gloomily he added to himself that it might only have been the elation of getting home. There were other men, as he'd told Gostol, who showed a keen interest in Kasia. What did he, a journeyman harper, really have to offer a girl of good Blood?

So he plunged back into the work he was contracted to do and tried not to think of ways to intercept Kasia in her daily rounds. But it was hard and they did seem to keep meeting—in the halls, on the steps, certainly in the schoolroom, and for meals. She accepted his company at table as readily as she accepted that of Valden, who was soon to take over a new hold created in the forested lands above Tillek—which Robinton devoutly hoped might be too isolated to attract a socially active girl. Or Kalem, who was a journeyman shipbuilder with a cot of his own up the hill, so that Kasia would be near her sister. Emry was exceedingly handsome and managed one of the Storage and Shipping holds for Melongel. He evidently made plenty of marks, judging by the fine clothing he wore: even what he wore bringing reports to his Lord Holder was better than Robinton's best Gather wear. And during the evenings, when Rob might have monopolized her company, he had to play or sing with the other harpers. He only had one or two dances with her, when Mumolon or Ifor took turns. The other men had the whole evening in her company, with no responsibilities.

It was frustrating. He worked on the harp. Her birthing day was in early spring and he wanted it ready by then, but he had to restrain himself from slighting any of the steps required in its making. The glue had to harden on the sound box; he had carved the pegs and set the sharping blades, which would permit modulation and even changing keys. He intended to tune the harp to C major. He had to wait for the strings to arrive from the Fort Smithcrafthall, which specialized in extruding the fine wire needed. Still, he spent less time working on the harp than he did looking at it—and thinking about how it would look in Kasia's lap, being touched by Kasia's hands.

Everyone in the Hold seemed anxious to celebrate Kasia's day with her, and Robinton wanted desperately to have privacy when he presented her with the harp. He was beginning to think that such a gift would establish the depth of his feeling for her. Which was what it was supposed to do, really. It was scarcely on a level with the casual gifts that were generally presented on a birthing day. Presenting it to her publicly would leave him open to teasing, as well as speculation about his affection for her. Affection? His love! And the harp was a fine one. He gave himself that much credit. He did do good work—especially when his heart was in the doing.

So he did not appear empty-handed in public, he had found some early berries in the woods above the Hold. She made much of his thoughtfulness and exclaimed a lot over the pretty basket he had woven to hold them. He managed to get a private word in her ear, because, fortunately, it was customary to give a birthday girl an embrace and a quick kiss—if you were so inclined. In Robinton's mind, there were too many so inclined. He watched to see just how long she permitted the familiarity and rather thought she had clung just a moment longer to him. So he took that chance to murmur in her ear that he had something special to give her but not in front of everyone. Could she meet him in the workshop?

She nodded, her eyes dancing, and murmured, "After the meal," before releasing him and turning to accept other tokens. For she was popular. There were presents from everyone, including a lovely comb, which Vesna had scrimshawed on the *Northern Maid* for giving her the moral courage she needed in getting her second mate's ticket. There were the usual lengths of cloth, and scarves and bracelets. Valden had presented a slim little belt knife with a blue leather sheath. The most impressive gift was from her parents: a beautiful Gather outfit in a shade of delicate spring yellow, with stiff silver thread embroidering neck, hem, and cuffs. Various sea captains had obliged by passing it on around the continent on the Great Western Stream from Mardela Hold in Nerat until it arrived at Tillek, three days before her party. Juvana had kept it hidden in her closet.

"You must wear it tonight," Juvana said.

"Not tonight," Kasia protested, her fingers running along the stylized embroidery. "I'll save it for the Gather."

"Well, just try it on and let's see you in it," Juvana insisted.

"Later, not now," Kasia said firmly and arranged her presents in a pile before sitting down to the midday meal. As was customary, all the food offerings were known favorites of hers.

"Everyone's making such a fuss over just a birthing day," she said, coloring with embarrassment.

"But it's *your* birthday," her oldest niece protested.

Robinton could hardly eat. But eventually the meal was over and he made a leisurely descent to the workshop. And then paced and paced, waiting for Kasia to arrive.

When she did, she was flustered.

"I couldn't get away!" she said. "Now what—*oh!*"

He hadn't been able to think of anything appropriate to say to introduce the gift so he had been standing in front of it. He moved aside and, with his best and most elaborate gesture, indicated it was hers.

"Oh, Robie . . ."

His name, said in just that voice and tone, was more than compensation for all his hard work. On seeing it, her eyes had widened and then filled with tears as she stepped forward. Almost hesitantly, she reached out to touch it, a fingertip following the line of the neck progressing around the ornamentation down the forepillar before she let her fingers run up the strings.

"Oh!" she gasped again at the delicate sound it gave.

Impatient for her to use it, to hold it on her lap and give it voice, he pulled a chair over to her and practically sat her down, lifting the harp to her knee.

"Oh, Robie, this is the most beautiful thing. I've never had such a magnificent gift. Even—" And she stopped short. He suspected she might have been about to cite something Merdine had given her. She gave him a quick glance and he smiled encouragingly back, though his mouth had gone very dry and he had a sick feeling in his stomach. Then she lifted her hands, as he had seen her do in his mind during the long hours of woodworking, and struck a chord. He had tuned the harp very carefully so the chord sang tremulously on the still air of the empty workshop. "This is not just a birthing gift, is it, Rob?" she asked, turning to him, her wide eyes soft. No shadows. When he didn't—couldn't—answer, she said in the tenderest possible tone, "Is my eloquent harper wordless for once?"

He swallowed and managed a sharp nod. "Absolutely," he said, opening his arms in his helplessness, knowing that his smile must appear inane.

Her lips curved in one of her gentle and delicious smiles. "Oh, Robie," she said, turning her head from side to side, a look of wonder and joy on her face. "Haven't I done my best to *show* you how I care? Even braving the sea to fish so we'd be together?"

His paralysis ended at her gentle reprimand and he pulled her into his arms. Her arms went about his neck, her hands catching in his thick hair as she pulled his head down. "I want a proper kiss from you now, Harper Robinton! Not a polite birthday peck."

He was as properly improper as he dared. Only she dared more, and before he could fret about any inadequacies as a lover, she was responding in such a way that it fueled his ardor out of bounds. Always, afterward, he remembered that moment any time he smelled the pungency of varnish or well-seasoned wood.

In the loving aftermath, Kasia told him that Juvana approved and would support her choice with their parents.

"How does she know?" Robinton demanded, startled to think that Lady Juvana had been discussing him with Kasia. And possibly with Lord Melongel.

"Because I've been filling her ears with Rob this and Rob that," Kasia said, grinning at his reaction.

Kasia was more than old enough to choose for herself, and her parents had sent her to Tillek Hold so that she would have more choice—and fewer memories of the man she had lost.

"Am I at all like him?" Robinton asked, a question that had run circles in his head for a long time.

She regarded him with a little smile on her lips, tracing the line of his mouth with her finger. "Yes, and no. Not in looks. Merdine hadn't your inches: as well for a seaman who'd be clouting his head all the time on beams. He was good-looking, but your face has far more character. You'll grow handsomer as you age . . . and I'll be there to keep the roving women away." She drew his head down to kiss him. "You've lovely bones!"

"Bones, the girl says!" Robinton burst out laughing in surprise.

"Lots of long bones," she repeated with a newly established proprietary delight. "Merdine was much more assertive. Well, he'd have to be as a sea captain, whereas a harper has to be more tactful and persuasive."

"He does?" Robinton mocked her.

"Well, you are both. I've heard you, Journeyman—"

He interrupted her. "Your parents will not object to you espousing a harper? I intend to get my Mastery, but it does mean we'll do a lot of traveling. Will they mind?"

"And a sea captain doesn't travel? A harper doesn't encounter the same sort of hazards—" She stopped there, her eyes darkening with the sorrow Robinton had hoped he had lifted forever.

"I don't know about that," he said into the pause, speaking lightly and trying to restore the happy mood they had been enjoying.

"Sorry, Rob."

"No need to be . . . love," he said, experimenting with using the word in her presence.

"That's what I especially love about you, Rob. Your perceptions and understanding. Merdine . . . was not an understanding man. Not the way you are. And I think—on balance—that's very important in creating a good harmony for a long life together."

They would have explored that topic much further except that they both heard voices along the hallway outside the wood shop. They had straightened themselves and their clothing, and Robinton pretended to tighten a string on the harp. The voices talked on, their owners continuing past the workshop. But that interlude was over.

"I'll carry it for you," Robinton said.

"Then we will both explain its significance to my sister," she said firmly. "Not that she'll need much explanation when we walk in with this beautiful instrument."

Nor did they. Juvana was delighted, saying this was the best birthing day gift her little sister could possibly have. There wasn't another harper in the family so it was about time there was one.

"Melongel's been wondering when you would declare yourself, Robinton," she added, giving him a sly sideways glance.

"And what gave him the need to wonder?" Robinton asked. He had prided himself on keeping his feelings under control.

"Oh, I thought he should consider the matter," Juvana said airily, "especially since my baby sister has been sighing over you for some time. He won't object."

Melongel didn't. He already knew of the Telgar Blood connection of Petiron, and the fact that Merelan was a MasterSinger of Pern-wide prestige made no bar to an espousal.

"But the summer's ahead of us, the busiest season for journeymen harpers," he said more severely, since he did not permit pleasure to interfere with duty. "Autumn Equinox would be a better time for espousal than summer. We will, however, announce the pact tonight and spare Robinton competition for dances."

Melongel could not spare Robinton either the teasing or the envy of those who had also hoped to espouse Kasia. But the public announcement of their intention made their lives far more comfortable.

Rob had sent a formal announcement to his parents—at Juvana's suggestion.

"Mothers need to know such things, Robinton," she said, smiling with just a touch of maternal condescension. "You're old enough to choose your own partner, but even if your relations with your father are poor, you should include him."

Robinton stared at her, shocked. He'd never mentioned anything about his father.

"That's just it, Rob," Kasia put in gently, touching his arm and peering into his face. "You *don't* mention Petiron, ever. But you mention your mother at least forty times a day."

"I don't . . . that's exaggeration," he said, but he relaxed and smiled at her teasing. "I don't want you to think that I don't admire Petiron's music . . ."

"That's what I meant," Juvana said. "He's never your father. Always Petiron." She paused, watching the shock on his face. "It gives a clue to those who have your good interests at heart. Not something a casual person would look for." She wrinkled her nose. "Then, too, I've met your father and I agree: he's a remarkable composer. It's *your* songs, however, that everyone sings."

Robinton didn't know what to say, since he'd had no idea

that he had given himself away simply by not mentioning a subject.

"You've heard me go on and on about my father," Kasia said, now earnestly trying to ease the shock of their casual disclosure. "Mind you, I can see why he'd be hard to emulate."

"Nonsense, I'd far rather have music I can hum or whistle than those intricate and—yes, I'll say it—tortured musical forms."

Robinton couldn't stifle the nervous chuckle at Juvana's remark.

"There, that's better," Kasia said. "If I ever meet him, I'll be oh so punctilious and formal. Now your mother . . . she's a dear and loving person."

Robinton gawked at her. "How do you figure that? Have you met her?"

"Not really, but I've heard her sing. And her face is so expressive that she must be loving. And if she brought you up the way you are now, she's a dear." Then she gave him a warm hug and loving kiss before she relaxed against his arm. He covered her hand with his.

"Should I ask the MasterHarper's permission?" he asked.

"You're a journeyman," Juvana said, lifting one shoulder. "You've the permission of your contract Holder and have officially announced your intent. But I think it would do no harm to tell Master Gennell."

"I'd like to tell the whole world," Robinton said, beaming down at Kasia, still marveling that she would love him. That was when the music poured into his head and he knew exactly how he could publish his happiness. Sonata to Sea-Green Eyes, he would call it, and he hung on to the lyrical line as he often did when there was no opportunity to write music down.

"As Kasia's sister and as your Lady Holder, I will expect you to come to me with any problems you might encounter as you start your lives together," Juvana said, coming to the real purpose of her interview with the pair. "I have already discussed this with Kasia, and she will protect herself, which is her duty, until such time as you are settled enough to contemplate children."

Robinton blushed. He and Kasia had not discussed the natural outcome of their lovemaking, and he realized that he had been remiss in this regard.

Juvana went on. "I offer the suggestion that you should spend several years enjoying each other's company, consolidating your new relationship, especially since neither of you need children to help in your professions." She was quite matter-of-fact, and Robinton knew that she spoke common sense. "You're both young. You have time. I have told Kasia that I would gladly foster any child of yours should your work make it impossible to give that child the advantages of a permanent home."

Robinton managed to stammer out his astonishment at such a magnificent offer: an honor that he had never imagined being offered him. Usually it was the grandparents who offered fostering, or a very close friend. To have his child fostered at Tillek Hold would be a privilege.

"That's an incredible offer, Juvana," he said, getting his wits together. "I'd like to think I'd be a good enough father that a child would not need more than his parents to reassure him, wherever we went."

Juvana regarded him solemnly for a moment. "Yes, you would want to be a good father. And I think you would be. I've watched you with the slow ones, and you're kind and patient, though some of their antics would be enough to drive me to sea in a leaky boat."

Kasia laughed. "Juvana gets seasick just *looking* at a rocking boat."

"This is all—" He gestured with the hand Kasia was not holding to indicate being overwhelmed. "—rather more than I thought espousing entailed."

"That's why there are such wise women as myself," Juvana said portentously, grinning to take any sting out of her tone. "So we'll plan the formal vow-taking for the Autumn Equinox. I doubt our parents can come . . ."

"If they wouldn't mind riding a dragon, I think I can arrange conveyance," Robinton said, wondering at himself for speaking out since he had been delighted her parents lived as far away as Nerat and he'd be unlikely to meet them. But that was just faintheartedness on his part, and silly of him, since he'd been reassured by Melongel, as well as Juvana, that Kasia's parents had no objection at all to a harper in the family.

"Can you arrange such a ride?" Juvana was surprised.

"Yes, sister dear," Kasia said, beaming on her intended. "He's been friends with F'lon, bronze rider of Simanith, ever since he and his mother spent a winter at Benden Hold."

"Really? How useful."

"You wouldn't mind a dragonrider?"

"Who could possibly be so dense as to ignore that sort of a connection?" Juvana asked parenthetically.

Robinton thought of Fax. And he had occasionally encountered the notion—from men who knew little beyond their cotholds—that the Weyr and the dragonriders were an encumbrance, maintained long past their usefulness.

"I'll see if F'lon is willing. I think he might like to come to the espousal."

"I think my parents would very much enjoy coming a-dragonback," Juvana said wistfully. "Is it as exciting as I've heard?"

Robinton was quite happy to give her a full accounting of his various trips a dragonback.

He and Kasia enjoyed the next two sevendays, until they were separated by his duties as the Turn moved into summer, fair weather, and long days, when the journeymen had to travel to the outlying holds to make sure the Teaching Ballads were being correctly taught and sung. Mumolon and Ifor envied Robinton his smooth-paced Ruathan runner, so he volunteered to take the farthest assigned sweep.

"If I can travel faster and more smoothly than you can, it's only right for me to go farther," he said, grinning. It also meant longer distances, which he could use to work on his Sonata. He had done no more than the opening measures so far, and the music was plaguing him.

"You won't get a protest from me," Mumolon said.

"You'll learn, you'll learn," Ifor teased him. "Days more away from the lovely Kasia, though."

Robinton controlled the spurt of rage he felt, reminding himself that, with his intentions announced, his claim to her affections would no longer be challenged. So he made his lips smile and sloughed off the irritation. And retired to his room to write a few more measures of the music that wouldn't leave his head.

Before he left, he had an ecstatic and very long letter from his mother, delighted by his news, asking for a sketch of Kasia and so many details that, laughingly, he suggested that Kasia had better answer. Which Kasia immediately did, including a sketched portrait that Marlifin was able to do for her. Master Gennell sent felicitations and thought he would accompany Merelan, to be sure she made it safely to Tillek Hold. Petiron, not surprisingly, neglected to respond. Kasia's parents, Bourdon and Brashia, expressed delight in her upcoming espousal and readily accepted the possibility—though Robinton was still waiting for an answer from F'lon—of a quick and safe transfer to the west coast. At last F'lon sent a drummed message that he would be there—with whoever needed conveyance.

After a loving and reluctant farewell to Kasia, he set his runner on the northeastern route, up to the Piro River, which separated Tillek from High Reaches Hold. From there he headed across the plateau into the highlands and down the Greeney River to the sea in the corner of Tillek and Fort. There was a rapidly expanding series of holds along the Greeney River, some so new that the hardset was still drying—or so the longer-established holders said with grins. That tour took him most of the summer and into the cooler nights and shorter days of the fall. Occasional runner notes from Kasia sustained him. And each evening he faithfully recorded his doings to be returned, often by the same runner.

He was very grateful when he reached the apex of his journey, a hill holding right below the High Reaches border. He stayed four days, teaching the children, who were at first very shy with him but warmed as he taught them the Ballads and sang them the humorous songs with which he had relaxed many a nervous

student. On his final night Chochol, the holder, had taken him—
and a skin of the rough white Tillek wine—to see the two moons
rise, and then unburdened his mind to the harper.

"Once, twice, maybe, Harper," Chochol said in his rough
voice, pitched low so that not even the herdbeasts grazing
nearby could hear what he said, "I would not worry. Anyone
can come to a disagreement with his Holder. But there
have been eight lots and they arrive scared of their shadows.
Wounded, and the pretty ones have been badly handled." He
paused, indicating with a nod what he wouldn't say about
their condition. "Badly handled." He emphasized the repeti-
tion with a second sharp nod. Then he pointed down the
hillside, which was grassland with a few stunted trees.
"Twice"—he held up two thick, work-callused fingers—"the
women were sure that Lord Faroguy must be dead for such
things to happen in High Reaches. Scared my spouse, that did.
But we see anything coming up here and I tell her we're in
Tillek, holding with Lord Melongel, who's a fair Holder if ever
there was one, and the time hasn't come when one Lord'll run
over what another has owned since his Blood took Hold."

The phrase "run over what another has owned" sent a shudder
of fear through Robinton right down to his guts.

"So'o to reassure her, we've another cot," he said, waving his
hand vaguely over his shoulder, "where we could go did we
see someone coming who ought not. I don't like it, Harper, I
don't like it one bit."

"Nor I, Chochol, and you may be sure I will tell Lord Melongel of your worries."

Robinton did no composing that night for music had gone
out of his head. He had asked Chochol if the women had mentioned names, or where they were going in Tillek, but Chochol
replied that he didn't know because he hadn't asked. He had
seen them safe to the river track to the sea and given them
what they could spare of provisions.

Most nights, though, Robinton would drain glowbaskets of
their last glimmer, penning his Sonata. He also wrote other
music for his Kasia, composing love songs on the long stretches
between holds—though sometimes the notes on the hide

showed the roughness of his travel and had to be corrected. These were only for Kasia, written for her to play for herself on her harp.

He finished the Sonata before he got back to Tillek Hold for the autumn Gather and their espousal.

Kasia welcomed him so warmly that their reunion lasted all night long, which delighted a travel-weary young man who had desperately missed the object of his affections.

They spent almost as much time talking as making love. They discussed their future at length. Now and then, he related the amusing incidents that he hadn't written to her—since most of his letters had been intensely loverly, as she described them. She would treasure them forever. Of course, the Wall Incident had been meat for runners all across Tillek Hold.

"I'll probably never live it down," he told her, stroking her thick hair, rolling a tress on his finger.

"Why would you want to, Rob?" She giggled. "I think it's a marvelous comment on your abilities."

"I had to live up to expectations," he said.

"Which, to judge by Melongel's remarks, you certainly did."

"I'm not so sure of that," he said, worried.

"I *know* you did," she said loyally, poking his nose gently.

He groaned. "I hope I did. Every hold seemed to have some sort of long-term dispute that only I"—he thumbed his chest—"could settle."

"Which I'm sure you did."

"How can you be so sure?"

"Because I know my Rob. Who sees with clear eyes," she said, touching them one by one, which interrupted him when he was about to tell her about the Sonata, "great perception—" She touched his temples. "—and the clever tongue to speak truth and to the point." She kissed him and that ended their conversation for some while.

If he went about his duties at the Hold yawning and only half-there, knowing and kindly smiles absolved him.

During his verbal report to Melongel, he mentioned what Chochol had told him. "Hill holding, well kept. The holder's named Chochol," he said, leading up to the distressing news.

Melongel glanced up at the map and nodded as he identified the place.

"He's given hospitality to holdless fleeing from the High Reaches."

"Oh?"

Robinton shifted uneasily, trying not to alarm unnecessarily and yet to state his fears and reservations candidly. "I was three Turns at High Reaches, you know, and I have great respect for Lord Faroguy, but the last time I saw him, at Benden Hold, for Lord Raid's confirmation, he looked very ill."

Melongel nodded, confirming that opinion. "Hmm. I noticed."

"Well, it seems that Lord Faroguy may be dead and we simply haven't been told."

Melongel regarded him with shock. "How could that be?"

"I don't know, but Chochol thought it possible because he has sheltered several holdless folk—women and children mostly, returning to the relatives' holdings here in Tillek."

Melongel frowned. "I know of several holders who have asked for dispensation on their tithes because of increases in dependents." He shuffled through some hides. "I didn't know the women had been made homeless. Or that they'd come from High Reaches."

Robinton cleared his throat, coming to the most dubious part of what Chochol had told him. "The women said that they had been driven out of holds. Chochol said that some of the younger ones had been badly handled. That they thought Lord Faroguy must be dead for such things to happen."

Melongel scowled, fixing Robinton with a glance that many would have been unable to meet.

"You believe Chochol?"

"I do, because I know there is a very ambitious man in High Reaches who will try to claim succession for himself . . . when Lord Faroguy dies."

"Does this ambitious man have a name?"

Something in Melongel's eyes suggested to Robinton that the Lord Holder knew to whom he was referring.

"Fax."

"That nephew of Faroguy's?" Melongel looked away from Robinton for a long moment. "I think I shall ask Faroguy to join us for the Gather. He might, as you have served him, wish to come."

That suggestion was more than Robinton had hoped for. But Chochol's tale had revived suspicions he had once thought groundless.

"Ah, here," Melongel said, tweaking a hide from the pile and glancing down at the text. "I'll just see what I can find out. Two of these enlarged holders live nearby." He folded his hands across his chest, looking down at a point on the floor. Then he looked up again, giving Robinton a little smile. "Good report, Robinton. Well done. I've met that nephew and, quite frankly, I tagged him as ambitious, too. Would you say that Farevene is able for him?"

Robinton cleared his throat, struggling with being honest without being derogatory. "Let me say that I wouldn't back Farevene in a wrestling match with Fax."

"Frankly, nor would I, but I know Farevene has been well trained to succeed his father, and I would certainly not confirm Fax in his place."

Robinton let a relieved breath out through his lips and said nothing more.

Melongel grinned more broadly now. "Go on, lad. I know you're eager to spend time with Kasia after being so long away. One more thing. You'll be on the panel of the Gather Day Court with Minnarden and myself."

Inwardly Robinton groaned—once more the Wall Incident was raising its head, even if he was appreciative of the honor just accorded him. Minnarden had been very pleased with his application to the study of the Charter and his understanding of the principles of mediation and adjudication. This would be his first time to sit on a Hold Court panel. Kasia would be pleased, even if he wasn't.

"I doubt it will be a long session, Rob, and certainly won't cut into your espousal in the afternoon."

With a clap on the shoulder, Melongel finally dismissed him.

"**A**t the Gather Court? Oh, Rob, that is an honor," Kasia exclaimed when he told her, her eyes wide. Then she giggled. "Melongel really likes you."

"He's working my butt-end off," Robinton said in an unrepentant growl. "I'll be all morning listening to troublemakers' excuses and deciding fines for minor infractions."

"Keep you from being nervous about the afternoon," she said, teasingly.

"Ha! The morning'll make me worse. Having to sit through Court will give me indigestion, having to listen to all those half-truths and alibis . . ." He pulled her into his arms, stroking her hair, which had a soothing effect on his disturbed digestion. Kissing her provoked other sensations, and once again he didn't get around to mentioning the Sonata for Sea-Green Eyes.

Of course, the longer he delayed, the harder it was going to be to work in a playing of it before the Gather. And suddenly he wasn't at all sure of its worth. It was definitely the most serious music he had ever written, and he was quite unsure of its merit. He could be fooling himself. It wasn't as if he could play for a critical listener, like Minnarden, who had seen the rest of his travel songs and liked them. They were insignificant compared to the Sonata—if it was any good at all. Yet whenever he heard the music in his head, it thrilled him, and he felt a tremendous lift at the finale of the final movement. Like making love. And that's what he wanted people to hear when they listened to it—the crescendo that was also an orgasm.

Then it was the day before the Gather and his mother arrived with Master Gennell. What with the necessary hospitality accorded them, he had trouble finding a few moments alone with Merelan, when he could chide her for making such a long journey when she was obviously tired.

"Tired of riding, yes," she said, her voice vigorous. "Your father has sent a short piece, which I'm to sing at your espousal."

"He did?" Robinton was flabbergasted as he took the score from his mother's hand.

"It's not in his usual style, either. I do believe your father is mellowing with age."

Robinton snorted, but as he scanned the music, he realized that this was a softer music, almost gentle, and quite simple, considering the usual style in which his father wrote.

"Minnarden said he would accompany me, as you'll be other-wise occupied ..." And then Merelan hugged him fiercely. "She's lovely, your Kasia, and she is besotted with you. You'll be happy, Robie. I know you'll be happy."

"I am already," he said with a silly grin on his face. "And, Mother, I have some music I need you to look over."

"You do? Just like old times," she said, waiting as he rummaged in his drawers to find the Sonata. "I'm almost jealous that others get to see your music now before I do."

"I always send—"

"I know you do, lovey, but it was such fun to be the first to—" She had unrolled the score and blinked at the first measures. She read on, and started to hum the opening melody. Cocking her head, she took to walking as she read, sometimes half-singing, sometimes nodding her head to the tempi, her eyes never leaving the page.

While his stomach churned and his heart seemed to be squeezed tight, he watched. Fortunately he had moved into their new quarters on the uppermost level of the Hold, well down the corridors from the rooms the old aunties and uncles occupied. There were two rooms with a small bathing facility in what Kasia called a walk-into closet. So there was space for her to pace from the bedroom door across the wide living area.

Abruptly Merelan paused, gave him a bemused look, and sat herself down on the stool by his gitar stand and, propping up the music and picking up the gitar, she started to play it.

He had arranged it for first fiddle, or a gitar, harp, and pipes, with occasional emphasis of a flat drum. It wasn't that long a piece, for all its three movements. He had not added a fourth, as his father would have, because he had said, musically, all he needed to in the allegro, adagio, and rondo. A scherzo would have fractured the mood.

When his mother played the final chords, her hands remained motionless on the strings for a long moment. Then she gave a funny little shake as if she'd had a spasm and looked up at him, her eyes filled with tears.

"Oh, Robie, that is the most beautiful thing you've ever written. Does Kasia like it? For I know you wrote it for her."

Robinton gulped. "I haven't shown it to her. I didn't—know—if it was any good or not." The last phrase came out fast.

"Not good! *Not good!*" His mother returned the gitar to its stand and rose in indignation. "Robinton, you have never written a bad piece of music yet, and *that*"—she pointed a stiff forefinger at the roll—"is the best composition to date. How dare you not give it to her? You said she plays harp. Why, it's the most romantic piece of music I have ever heard. Even better . . ." She closed her lips. "No, there *is* no comparison. You have a far more romantic soul, my dearest son." She put her arms around his waist and hugged him. "If you don't show her that before tomorrow . . ."

"When will I have the time? It *is* nearly tomorrow now, Mother!" He hugged her tightly to him, smelling the scent she packed her clothing with and wondering at how the two women he loved felt much the same in his arms.

"You'd better do it soon, then," Merelan said. "She'll never forgive you for not doing it sooner . . . unless, of course, you've just finished the piece."

"No, I wrote it this summer."

"Oh!" she exclaimed in explosive dismay. "If you were so worried about it, why didn't you send it to me? I'd have reassured you."

Why he hadn't sent it was no mystery to either of them, but he felt relieved and more confident than ever, having her positive opinion. And, he knew that she would never have been so enthusiastic if she didn't truly find it good. That courtesy had nothing to do with his being her son.

"Is there a copy of it, Rob? Master Gennell will want to use it for other espousals. It's so ... so lyric. So romantic. Oh, Robinton, you are such a comfort to me." Abruptly she changed moods. "I'm exhausted after that, love. Will you escort me to my room? I don't think I could find my way back down."

When he had returned from escorting his mother, he prepared for bed himself, since it was late and tomorrow would be an exceedingly eventful day. He smiled and then broke into a chuckle as he shucked off his clothes and settled into the wide bed that he and Kasia would be sharing. It was far too warm to require night-wear, and besides, he seldom bothered and now probably never would, it being so comforting to snuggle Kasia into his arms and have her skin next to his all night long. He exhaled deeply, and then realized that he was far too excited to sleep yet.

So he threw off the light fur and found a long-tailed shirt. His new clothes for the Espousal—well, Gather Day, if he wasn't being self-centered—were hanging on the closet door. He ran a hand down the fine, brocaded fabric which Clostan had talked him into having made up. It really was a fine set, and he could see why cut and fit were so important.

"Do harpers really like wearing bags?" Clostan had sarcastically demanded when Robinton would have settled for the first outfit long enough to fit his torso and legs at Tillek's Weavercrafthall. The Master Healer was as tall as Robinton, dark-haired and handsome, with fine, long hands that were clever in sewing up wounds and gently strong in setting broken bones. He had been at Tillek for the past seven Turns, ever since he attained his Mastery, for the Hold required an experienced healer and Clostan had worked hard to adapt treatment to the needs of a fishing community. "By the Egg, man, you do yourself no favors. You've broad shoulders ..." Clostan flicked fingers at them. "You've a trim waist—" He couldn't pinch much there. "—and long shanks . . . Show them off." Clostan's trousers tended to cling to his strong, muscular legs, just missing a tension that could be called lewd. "Especially during your Espousal . . . show all the girls what a fine one they missed out on. And allow Kasia to be proud of you."

"Because I show off?" Robinton had demanded, almost indignant.

"I can't imagine you ever showing off, Rob," Clostan had said, shaking his head in mock despair. He grinned, a smile that showed his excellent white teeth and echoed in his dark eyes. He turned serious then and grabbed up the swatch of materials the tailor had on hand. He held them up to Robinton's face to see how they looked against the weather-tan the Harper had acquired over the summer. "Hmmm, yes. I know what Kasia's wearing, so we must also consider her colors. Can't clash. Hmmm. I think this rich russet shade of the brocade . . ."

"Brocade?" Robinton was aghast. He was prudent with his marks, and he had brought the sum he felt adequate with him. But brocade . . .

"Well, you can hardly appear in something shabby for your Espousal, can you?" Clostan remarked in disgust. "Look at it this way," he said, mastering his impatience, "you'll be able to wear this to Gathers for Turns before it frays." He rubbed the sample roughly between his fingers, and then pulled both ends of the swatch to show its strength. "You'd have to spend far more to match it for quality over the same period of Turns. Good clothing is an investment."

"And you make many," Robinton said, stung to retort.

Clostan gave him a slightly malicious grin. "I may, but they have all been wise choices, and I can change to fit the mood of the day and the weather of the season. Besides, it heartens my patients to see me well-dressed."

Dispassionately, and because it was his espousal to Kasia, Robinton fingered the swatch, then held it against his face, noting that the rich russet shade did enhance his skin color.

"Tailored correctly"—Clostan gestured for the tailor to take measurements—"you'll be glad you took the time and effort. And you might consider a few new shirts, too," he added, waving another set of colors. "You've only three."

Robinton, extending his arms for their measure, was half-tempted to clout Clostan for his manners. Then he started to laugh. At himself.

"And a new pair of pants. The ones you came with are all but threadbare—in embarrassing spots—since you rode out of here," Clostan added, peering down at Robinton's backside.

Since the harper had that very morning realized that Clostan's observation was all too true, he also ordered shirts and pants, including a pair of leather which would take the harder wear. He had, secretly, coveted the leather pants he had seen Ifor and Mumolon wearing.

When he had returned for the fitting, he had been very pleased with the result and admired himself in the tailor's long mirror. Furthermore, they all fit so comfortably that he wondered why he had never thought of having tailor-made clothing before. But it had been as easy to find something in a Gather stall that was reasonably priced and fit—more or less.

He was grateful to Clostan and brought him a skin of good Benden wine.

"Well, you do me proud," Clostan said, gratefully accepting the skin. "The one drawback with this Hold is its wretched wines." With which sentiment Robinton totally agreed.

Smiling over that episode, he opened the glowbasket over the new worktop he and Kasia had had such fun finding and setting up in their room. He snagged the Sonata from where his mother had left it on the music stand, and taking pen and a new square of hide—Kasia had said she was going to make sure he always had good, fresh writing materials—he began to make a copy of the Sonata for his mother to take back to the Harper Hall. Maybe Petiron would even see it and find few faults, since it was written in a classic style. He grinned ruefully even as his fingers flew across the sheet: Robinton could not really see his father approving of anything his son wrote.

He looked back over the score to be sure he had annotated it properly, and mused over Kasia's possible reactions to it when she heard it the first time. If she was even half as pleased as his mother . . .

He paced back and forth, paused to pour himself a glass of wine, and then went back to the table and proceeded to copy out his Kasia songs. His mother would like them, too. She might even want to sing a few as encores to recitals. He finished those, drinking as he worked, and rolled up the music with a neat ribbon tying the packet, ready to give to his mother. He had a final glass of wine and then, realizing that dawn was not far away, took himself back to bed and willed himself to sleep.

Chapter 13

▼▼▼

Despite his late night activities, Robinton was up at dawn: he'd forgotten to close the curtains over the small round windows, and the sun was shining in his eyes. But he felt rested enough and sprang from his bed. The day was so clear that he fancied he could see the High Reaches shore across the wide bay ... which reminded him that he hadn't heard whether Lord Faroguy had accepted Lord Melongel's invitation to come to his Espousal Day. Not that it was his alone, he corrected himself, for others would be taking vows at this Gather, as well. As he dressed, he groaned as he thought of having to waste this morning at the Gather Court, but at least it would keep him too occupied to worry about anything else.

He joined Clostan at the table for breakfast, and the Healer inspected him critically in his new clothing.

"Yes, I did you a favor, old thing," Clostan said, sniffing a little as he turned back to his bread and cheese.

"You're looking splendid yourself," Robinton replied, now able to recognize good tailoring when he saw it.

Clostan glanced down at himself, as if he couldn't remember what he had put on that morning. "Oh, well enough. I may change for the dancing. That is," he added, nudging Robinton in the ribs and rolling his eyes slyly, "if I'm allowed to dance with the fair spouse Kasia."

"Since it's you and I owe you a favor, I'll let you dance with Kasia when I have to play."

"What?" Clostan affected great horror and surprise. "They make you do a set on your *Espousal Day*?"

Robinton hushed him. "I'm a harper. I take my turn. You wouldn't turn away a sick person today, would you?"

"Well, I'd change my clothes first," Clostan replied, flicking an errant crumb off his sleeve. "I'll hold you to that dance," he said, rising. "I do have rounds to make now." And he was off.

Lord Melongel, looking austere in dark brown with just a piping of gold at the neck and sleeves, entered the dining hall. An approving smile appeared on his face as he noted Robinton's new clothes.

"You are looking the part, that's certain," he said. "Oh, a message was drummed in yesterday from High Reaches. Lord Faroguy regrets."

"Well, I didn't think he'd be able. Is he well?"

Melongel frowned slightly, rubbing at his chin. "Now that's the oddity. I've known Faroguy a long time. Had many messages from him, and he always inquires after Juvana. She spent a Turn with Lady Evelene, you know. Odd that he didn't this time."

Robinton felt a surge of concern. "If he is ill, could the message have come from someone else?"

"Farevene would have asked, too." Melongel frowned. "Well, we've enough to do today without adding other problems. I see you've finished your meal so we'd best adjourn to the Court Hall. We've a full morning."

Robinton rose, suppressing a sigh. Unlike some of the larger Holds, Tillek used a stone building closer to the center of the Holding for such proceedings—right in the middle of the Gather, which was already in full swing. Both official crafthall and independent booths were doing a good business. The entire fishing fleet was moored in the harbor or alongside the wharves, and distant sails indicated that the home crowd would swell even more with the passengers coming in from up the coast. Melongel and Robinton had to slow their steps to the crowd's pace, with people either smiling a greeting or nodding courteously as Lord Holder and harper passed.

Robinton felt a tug on his sleeve and was surprised to see Pessia at his side, and beyond her, the gaggle of Sucho, Tortole, Valrol, and Klada, who peered out from behind the protective bulk of her father until Robinton's eyes fell on her and she ducked away.

"Good Gather Day to you, Lord Melongel," Pessia said with a polite jerk of her head, and then she looked right back at Robinton, a proud if shy smile on her face. "You did a great deal for us, and especially Saday. This is for you and your spouse." She threw a cloth-wrapped parcel at him and, before he could prevent her, ran off, the others following like leaves blown from a tree in a high wind.

"Your Wall folk?" Melongel asked.

"Yes." Robinton tried to see in which direction they had run, but there were too many people milling around, and despite his advantage of height, he couldn't find them.

At Melongel's gesture, he unwrapped the parcel, as gatherers politely skirted the two stationary men.

The cloth was new, the smell of the dye acrid, and when he had removed it, he gasped as he held up the wooden bowl.

"Elegant!" Melongel said. "Truly elegant."

They both examined it with their fingers, feeling the thin, smooth wall and then discovering the band of tiny flowers that ringed the top, so perfectly done that they seemed to blossom from the wood, rather than having been carved from it.

"A beautiful gift, Harper. And deserved."

Then Melongel touched Robinton's sleeve and indicated that they should proceed. They were not far from the Court Hall and the knots of anxious men and women looking their way. Carefully rewrapping his gift, Robinton matched strides with the shorter-legged Lord Holder, and they were soon being smiled into the building by those they would shortly be judging.

Good fortune seemed to favor Robinton that day. They were hearing the representations and alibis of a holder who had been delinquent in managing his fields and cot when a messenger slipped in and handed Lord Melongel a message. He read it, gave a sniff, and then with a slight grin on his face, handed it over to the Harper to read.

"You may leave. Other duties take precedence," Melongel murmured.

Reading the note, Robinton wasn't at all sure if he should take the excuse to leave. The note told him that F'lon had arrived with Holder Bourdon and his spouse, Brashia, who were awaiting him in Juvana's apartment. He dreaded meeting Kasia's parents far more than he dreaded being bored by the Court proceedings. When he did not immediately rise, Melongel gave him a stern look. And so he pushed back his chair, nodded to Minnarden and to the faltering holder, and left.

The first thing he saw outside the Court Hall was everyone looking up at the Hold heights and pointing out the bronze dragon settling himself in the sun. Like rider, like dragon, Robinton thought as Simanith made quite a show of extending his gleaming wings, before, with a smart crack of the tips, he folded them to his back and sprawled, his shorter front legs overlapping the edge.

F'lon was lounging against the front entrance to the Hold and grinned as he saw the Harper hurrying toward him.

"I brought them safely here," he said, slapping Robinton on the shoulder and then holding him off to inspect the new clothing. F'lon whistled and his amber eyes gleamed with mischief. "Someone's taught you a thing or two. The lovely Kasia, perhaps?"

"I'm well able to choose my own clothes," Robinton said. Then he asked in a lower voice, as F'lon hurried him into the Hold, "Why did you have to bring them here so early?"

"Early? It's not *early* by my time, lad. Don't worry. I'll see that they don't rough you up."

When Robinton started to cross the Hall to the stairs, F'lon neatly hauled him in another direction.

"This way," he said, and then pushed Robinton toward the side room that served as a private interview chamber. "And here he is," F'lon announced triumphantly, pausing at the threshold to let Robinton enter on his own.

"Ah, Robinton," Juvana said, rising to greet him and bring him toward her mother and father, seated on the high-backed couch.

Swallowing fiercely, Robinton managed a nervous smile at Holder Bourdon, a grizzled man with deeply tanned skin. His green eyes, slightly darker than Kasia's, were tilted just like hers. His spouse, a sweet-faced woman with fading brown hair, gave Robinton a lovely smile and jumped up eagerly.

"Oh, Journeyman, you cannot know how pleased we are!" she exclaimed, coming forward and grabbing Robinton's free hand. Bourdon had been about to speak, but now he closed his mouth, made a gesture of helplessness, and let her go on. "We've been so worried that she would mourn Merdine forever ..." Her face clouded briefly, then her marvelous smile came out again. "And when she wrote to tell us—" She turned to her spouse for confirmation and Bourdon gave a patient nod. "—we were overjoyed, but never did we expect to be able to attend her espousal so far away from Mardela. And at a very busy season." Bourdon nodded again.

"My pleasure, I assure you, to assist my good friend in every way," F'lon said, bowing.

Holder Bourdon cleared his throat. "Kasia says you're comfortable at sea, too?"

"Well, I don't get seasick," Robinton admitted.

"And not too proud to help gut and salt, either, she says."

"Come, sit, Robinton," Juvana said, gesturing for him to take the other double couch. "I can't imagine that you'd mind leaving Court Hall today ..." She gave him a sly sideways glance. "Your mother has already met my parents and is upstairs, keeping Kasia from a case of nerves."

"Kasia's nervous?" Robinton only just managed to keep his voice from betraying his own nervousness.

Juvana chuckled. "It's her privilege. My, but you look every bit as gorgeous as she does. Clostan?"

"Hmmm," Robinton admitted, shooting a glance at F'lon, who blinked and then rolled his eyes over his friend's prevarication.

"And what's this?" Juvana asked, touching the wrapped bowl Robinton still held. "An Espousal gift already?"

Eager for something to discuss, Robinton showed the bowl and explained how pleased he was that Saday had taken him at his word.

"Oh, the Wall people," Brashia said, and Robinton groaned, heartily sick of that story. "Kasia told us how clever you were then."

Bourdon chuckled. "Got a quick head on your shoulders. No harm in that, lad."

A kitchener arrived with a tray of refreshments, klah and wine with little cakes and biscuits. Robinton leaped to his feet to help her settle the tray. Then, as Juvana asked what her parents wished to drink at this hour, he busied himself passing cups and glasses and the plates of food, regaining some poise in that simple act.

"You're busy at this season in Mardela?" he asked Bourdon politely.

"Packtail are running. D'you know them?"

"We've the northern variety, the bordos," Robinton said, as if he discussed fish varieties every day.

Bourdon nodded with approval. "Good eating, the bordos."

"Will your mother be singing today?" Brashia asked shyly. "We all know about MasterSinger Merelan in Mardela, but few of us have had a chance to hear her sing, living where we do."

"She plans to," Robinton replied, once again grateful to have such a mother—if only she were there with him now, to smooth his way.

"Special music?" Brashia asked, tilting her head in the same charming way Kasia had.

"Some of Robinton's own songs," Juvana said, ignoring Robinton's dire look. "He's far too modest. Melongel's of the opinion that our Robinton is as good a composer as his mother is a singer."

"Now, that's taking it a bit far, Juvana," Robinton protested.

"I don't think so," Juvana replied, unmoved. "Nor does Kasia."

"She's partisan," F'lon said, leaning against the door frame and idly twirling his wineglass, his eyes dancing with mischief. "But I'll allow that Rob has spawned some fine tunes."

"So we'll hear some?" Brashia twisted round on the couch to look in Robinton's direction.

"You probably won't hear anything but Rob's songs," F'lon went on. "Most of today's best songs are his."

"Really?"

"Every new one and half the revised Teaching Ballads our Robinton composed."

If F'lon and Juvana thought they were helping him in this initial meeting with Kasia's parents, they were wide of their mark.

"I thought it was your father who composed so much music," Bourdon said, slightly confused.

"They both do," Juvana said, just as F'lon remarked, "You can sing Rob's stuff."

"Haven't you other Gather guests to collect?" Robinton asked as mildly as he could.

"Oh, no, I reserved the day entirely to help you," F'lon said with a flourish.

"You might like to see the Gather then?" Robinton said, an edge to his voice.

Juvana laughed. "We'll stop, Rob. It's not fair to tease you, today of all days."

"I'm glad to hear you say that, Lady Holder."

"Oh, now come, Rob," she said, touching his arm. "I'm nearly your sister, you know."

Robinton's mind froze for a moment.

"Don't tell me that fact has escaped your clever mind?" F'lon asked, delighted by his friend's confusion. "Which makes Lord Melongel your brother. Doesn't it? Well done, Harper."

He felt Juvana's hand press gently around his forearm and, feeling extremely stupid, he turned to look at her.

"It does, you know," she said gently. Then she grinned at the others. "I never thought I should be able to render a harper speechless."

"But that's not why I want Kasia . . ."

"Of course it isn't," Juvana said.

"Such a dear boy," Brashia said, beaming at him.

"Like the cut of his sail," Bourdon put in.

"Close your mouth, Rob," F'lon suggested from the doorway.

"F'lon, stop propping up the door and go get the harp Robinton made for Kasia," Juvana said, flicking her fingers at the dragonrider. "You know where it is. And tell Kasia that it's gone very well indeed." As soon as F'lon left, she smiled placidly at Robinton. "He can be dreadful, can't he? I do believe that dragonriders are far worse than harpers for teasing, aren't they?"

Robinton was still floundering over the idea of being related to the Lord Holder of Tillek. "Honestly, I had no idea."

"Of course you didn't," Juvana said easily. "Now, Clostan would be instantly suspect of such connivery—but not you."

"Kasia said you've been loaned a sloop for your espousal days," Bourdon said. "Sail much?"

"Only from Fort harbor to Ista, and then the seven-day fishing run with Captain Gostol. He's loaning us the ship."

"Is he?"

"Yes, had us out tacking up and down the harbor the other day." Robinton grinned. "To see if Kasia knew what she was about, for he was very sure I don't.'

The admission did him no harm with Bourdon, who leaned forward and began to explain the foibles of small ships. That kept the conversation going amiably until F'lon carried in Kasia's harp, handling it with the reverence he would ordinarily give only to his Simanith. As he passed it to Robinton, he murmured, "Beautiful piece." Then both Bourdon and Brashia came over to examine the carving, the inlay, and the strings; then, of course, they asked him to play so they could hear its tone.

Playing brought Robinton to complete balance. And seeing that, Juvana made her excuses and left for other duties.

Never had there been such a brilliant Gather Day as this one, when Robinton took Kasia's hand in his in front of the Court Hall, where the Lord and Lady Holders stood with Master Minnarden and the other craftmasters available for this happy duty. That they were the first of six other couples didn't impinge on his consciousness then. He had eyes only for his Kasia. Behind them were their witnesses: his mother, radiant in blue, standing between F'lon and Groghe, who had said he was here in his official capacity as a Fort Holder. Kasia's parents stood on her side: her mother flushed and excited, and her father doing very well at looking proud and dignified.

Never had Robinton had to speak his own words in front of such a huge crowd. Singing words was another matter entirely, but speaking his whole heart in words was something else again. He had to clear his throat, but then, taking a deep breath, he announced his intentions to be a loving, kind, considerate spouse, caring for her all his life, nurturing their children, and providing for the family.

Holding hands, he looked into Kasia's eyes, which were no longer shadowed with an old grief but radiant with joy, as she—who also had to clear her throat before she spoke—declared her intentions in a loud voice. She grinned more broadly when she got to the part about children and winked at him.

"We have heard your promises, Robinton and Kasia," Melongel said, stern in his capacity as Lord Holder.

"And have witnessed them," Master Minnarden said while the other craftmasters murmured their traditional response. The observers cried congratulations and shouted, "Good luck!"

Melongel's face relaxed in a smile as he shook their hands before moving to the next expectant couple. "Brother," he murmured slyly to Robinton.

"So kiss her!" F'lon cried. When neither Robinton nor Kasia moved, he took them by the shoulders and pushed them together.

The lightning that passed from lip to lip seemed to encompass Robinton's entire body—and hers, as well, leaning so trustingly against him. He was almost annoyed when F'lon's hands pulled them apart.

"I'm so happy, my dear daughter," Merelan was saying as she embraced a bemused Kasia. There were tears in his mother's eyes, but she had always been able to cry and remain beautiful. She changed places with Brashia, who hugged her daughter tightly, weeping so profusely that she couldn't speak at all. Bourdon was shaking Robinton's hand fit to render it useless for any playing. F'lon was insisting that he definitely had the right to kiss Kasia—just this once, to show her what she'd missed. Then Merelan was hugging Robinton so tightly that he had to seize her arms to be released.

"Be as happy as I have been with your father," Merelan whispered for his ear alone, and when he tensed, she held him slightly away, giving him a hard, long look. "For we have been happy . . . together." And he realized that she spoke the truth: that it had always been he who had been the problem with his father. "*You've* the heart big enough to love an entire world," she added. Then she released him.

Groghe, rather shyly, kissed Kasia on the cheek and told her she'd be very welcome whenever she came to Fort Hold. Which he hoped would be often.

By then, three more couples had had their vows witnessed to choruses of cheers.

"I need a drink," F'lon announced and began herding them all out of the crowd and toward the Gather tables set around the dance square. There were two tables set upon platforms on either side of the players' dais. The right-hand one was for the newly espoused, and it was there that F'lon led his little group.

A beaming wineman met them halfway, his tray of glasses clinking against each other.

"I know I shouldn't, but I'm serving the Benden wine, which the dragonrider said I must give you," he said, leaning forward to murmur this treachery to them. He beamed warmly at Kasia and held the tray out to her. She couldn't seem to stop smiling, even as she sipped the deliciously cold, crisp Benden white.

They were all served and then took their places at the table as kitcheners rushed forward to serve them.

Robinton never remembered the rest of the table filling up. It was all a blur of happiness: Kasia was his and he was hers and his mother was here. Her parents were quite nice folk, and he no longer felt uneasy with them, listening to the snippets of advice Bourdon was giving him about sailing. But, if F'lon didn't stop teasing him, he'd land him one in the jaw very soon, although Kasia laughed as hard at his witticisms as her parents and his mother.

The MasterSinger led off the singing with one of the love songs Robinton had written for Kasia, though his mother kindly did not mention that. She was accompanied by Minnarden, Ifor, Mumolon, and several local instrumentalists. It was received with rapturous applause and determined shouts for more. Brashia looked stunned as the truly lovely voice rose in joyous phrase and shook her head, murmuring, "She's every bit as good as they said, every bit!"

"Proud of your mother, aren't you?" Bourdon said, leaning across the table, his face flushed with pleasure and the good Benden wine. "Every reason to be."

"And she of him," Kasia said proudly, clasping both hands around Robinton's arm and resting her face against it for a moment.

Their legs were twined under the table so tightly that Robinton hoped no one could see under the cloth—and that he wouldn't be asked to stand. Fortunately, he wasn't. Prepared as he was for the necessity of taking a turn, he was pointedly ignored by Minnarden when the musicians changed round.

His leg went to sleep twice under the table, and when Kasia had to leave briefly to use a facility, she limped the first few steps from cramp. Brashia and Merelan went with her, reassuring Robinton, who couldn't bear her out of his sight, that she'd be fine with them.

As soon as the meal had been served to the main guests and the Lord Holders, those who wished to pay for their meal took places at the tables. Many dispersed to wander about the booths and enjoy the fine weather.

The singing continued in a less formal fashion, as background entertainment.

"Restless, love?" Kasia murmured when she caught his fingers drumming the rhythm.

"Oh, no, no, just habit," he said. "Nothing can make me leave your side. Not today or ever."

"We will dance later though, won't we?" she asked, making her eyes wide and innocent.

"Of course. All night . . ."

"Not *all* night," she murmured back, a sensual smile curving her lips. And then she giggled at his expression.

Dance they did, and Robinton was only going to allow Lord Melongel, her father, and Groghe to partner her. He was furious with F'lon's teasing.

"Don't be annoyed with him," Kasia said, serious for a moment. "He is so fond of you, and I suspect all that foolery of his covers a far more serious problem he can't—won't—talk about." She grinned. "The way he sighs, I'd say he might be in love."

"F'lon?" Robinton was surprised. The idea put a different complexion on F'lon's behavior and Robinton regretted that he hadn't been more sympathetic. He had seen F'lon looking very thoughtful and worried in between his bouts of nonsense. Today was not the day for him to inquire what bothered his friend but he'd find time tomorrow. Then he reminded himself that he and Kasia weren't likely to encounter F'lon on the morrow.

So he permitted the bronze rider to dance with Kasia, and while he watched them dance, he spoke to Simanith.

What is troubling my friend F'lon, Simanith?

There was silence for so long that Robinton wondered if the dragon had heard him at all.

I hear. I do not know. Sometimes he doesn't tell me everything. Simanith's tone, so like his rider's, sounded wistful and anxious. *He thinks a lot about Larna and he's not happy.*

Larna? The name sounded vaguely familiar, but it took Robinton most of the dance to remember: Larna had been a nuisancey little child, the old Weyrwoman's daughter. F'lon had got into trouble with Carola, and his Weyr, over the way he treated the little girl. But little girls grow up. Robinton liked to think that this Larna had grown up into so pretty a girl that F'lon had lost his heart to her. But then, lovers always wanted others to be in love, too. Robinton sighed, and went off to claim Kasia for himself for the rest of the evening.

They managed to steal away unnoticed during one of the popular slow dances, and made it unencumbered out of the glow-lit dancing square and to the extraordinarily quiet Hold. For a Gather, even the old aunties and uncles were out enjoying themselves, and all the kitcheners and drudges with them.

"Look!" Kasia pointed to the heights, where twin globes of lightly whirling green showed them that Simanith was on watch. She waved, and was startled when the bronze dragon blinked.

"Make no mistake, the dragon can see everything that's going on," Robinton said. He waved, too, and laughed when Simanith blinked again.

"Does he *know* what's troubling F'lon?"

"He should, if anyone does," he replied. "But he doesn't."

Then they were inside the Hold, most of the glowbaskets thriftily shut, just enough half-open to show them the way to the stairs.

"You must take Clostan with you the next time you buy clothes," she told him as they hurried up the stairs to their level.

"When I've you to help me choose now?" He snorted at the very prospect of having anyone else.

They had to save their breath for the stairs and arrived, panting and gasping, at the top, Kasia giggling as Robinton handed her into their room, then firmly closed and locked the door. Not even F'lon would have the nerve to bother them here.

Dawn saw them sneaking out of the Hold, carrying their sailing gear and running, hand in hand, down to the wharf where the sloop was awaiting them. They could see bundles of sleeping folk, sprawled across chairs or tables, and some under, as well. Banners flapped lightly over the few booths still left in the Gather square. As they were stowing their gear, laughing and giggling at evading any notice, Robinton glanced up at the Hold heights. No dragon was indolently sprawled there.

Robinton couldn't remember if he'd said good-bye to his mother. He thought he must have, for he knew he had remembered to express his gratitude to Kasia's parents.

While Kasia went aft to take her place at the tiller, he untied the painter as Captain Gostol had shown him, jumped lightly to the bow, and pushed the sloop away from the thick piles. Then he went to hoist the sail, which immediately began to fill. Kasia trimmed the sheet until the sail was nicely taut against the wind, and he made his way astern to sit beside her in the cockpit.

A fisherman, coming up from the cabin of one of the larger ships, waved lazily at them as they made their way across the wide harbor and out into Tillek waters. He was the last person they saw for eight days and nights.

Their world became the sloop and the water and the sky which, for the first three days, was brilliantly blue as only autumnal skies could be in that latitude. Not that it mattered to them what the weather was like: they were with each other. Among other things, they both loved freshly caught and instantly fried fish. Sometimes Robinton caught while Kasia cooked; other times she did the fishing and he the frying.

Then the weather deteriorated, and in the teeth of a gale that came up with ferocious speed, Kasia yelled for him to lower the sail and tie it tightly and secure the boom. Finishing with that task despite the lashing rain and the mounting seas, he went below and got out their heavy-weather gear, dressing quickly in his so he could hold the tiller while she put hers on. When he came on deck again, he dropped his load and dove to help her with the tiller. It was some time before she could release it and don her weather gear, her face pinched with the cold of the rain that battered at them as they dipped and rose with the high seas. The waves broke over them time and again, and at Kasia's bawled order, Robinton managed to reach a long arm for the bailing bucket.

More water poured in to take the place of what he had thrown overboard, but he kept bailing with one hand, while with the other he assisted her hold on the tiller. The little sloop rode to the frothy height of immense waves and then slammed down into the troughs, shaking them to the bones. He knew his teeth were chattering with the cold and could see through the driving rain that she had her jaw clamped shut, lips pulled back, giving the appearance of snarling into the storm. She lay half across the tiller, fighting to keep the sloop's bow headed into the waves. He knew without her having to tell him that one broadside would capsize the ship and spill them into the cold, cold sea. They didn't seem to have much chance of surviving this storm; they'd certainly be better off if they could remain in the ship and afloat.

Somehow, sometime, when the lowering skies had lightened, the wind dropped and the pressure on the rudder eased. They flopped limply across each other and the tiller bar, gasping in the air.

"Quickly," she said, pointing at the mast. "We're in the eye of this storm and must take advantage of that. Hoist the sail halfway up the mast. There's the coastline, and we should find somewhere to shelter for the rest of the storm. There's got to be a cove, an inlet, somewhere to anchor."

Her urgency lent him the burst of energy to do as she bid. Then he helped her hold even that little bit of sail against the force of the wind and keep the rudder headed toward the black bulk ahead of them.

They almost missed the entrance to the cove even with the

prow of the ship pointed at it. Then Kasia let out a whoop of triumph, grinning with disbelief as the sloop passed the mouth of the inlet and left the fury of the sea behind them. Sheltered by the stony arm, the sloop rolled less wildly as the waves carried it toward the indistinct mass of cliff.

They both looked about, deafened by their hours in the storm winds, not quite certain that they had reached a safe haven.

"The anchor ... Rob ... drop it. We can't ... run ... aground," she said, gesturing to the bow. "May be rocks anyway ... no matter."

He dropped the anchor, saw the line run out, then the forward motion of the sloop stopped. He could hear her timbers creaking as she answered the motion of the sea and then swung about on her tether.

Kasia was draped, at the end of her strength, across the tiller bar. He had little strength left himself, but the need to get his beloved below, to what warmth they could contrive, was foremost in his mind. And he did, half dragging her the short space from the seat to the cabin, slamming open the hatch, hoping that the waves had not seeped through and flooded their one refuge. He almost tumbled her down the stairs, but they both made it. She pulled herself into the bunk while he struggled to close the hatch.

She was shaking violently when he reached her. Somehow he got the sodden clothes off her coldly mottled body and rolled her into the furs. She groaned and tried to say something but hadn't the strength.

"Hot, must have hot," he mumbled, trying to make his frozen fingers cope with striking a match to the charcoal-filled brazier that did duty as cooker. Sometime in the past he had filled the kettle with water for a meal that he had never had a chance to cook. Now he waited anxiously for the water to warm enough so he could make klah. He'd heat the last of the fish stew they'd made—how long ago? He could hear chattering and realized that they were both doing it. He swung around to the bunk and rubbed her body as vigorously as he could to stimulate circulation. He nearly burned his finger, touching the top of the kettle to see if the water was hot enough to be useful. He had his answer and sucked at the burn while he poured water over the powdered klah, gave it a swirl, and fumbled to open the sweetener jar. Sweetening was good to offset shock and cold.

He took the first sip—to be sure it wouldn't burn her mouth. Then, pulling her up against his body as he leaned wearily against the bulkhead, he held the cup to her lips.

"Sip it, Kasia, you've got to get warm."

She was so cold she could barely swallow, but she did, and he coaxed sip after sip into her. When she craned her head around, making noises in her throat, her bloodshot weary eyes pleading, he drank, too. That cup drained, he made another and then put the soup kettle on to warm. He had all but fallen asleep when the steam hissing from under the lid woke him. He caught the pot before the pressure flipped the cover off.

It couldn't have been a long rest, but it had been enough for his resilient young body, and he poured soup into two cups, put the water kettle back on. He'd towel her down with warm water. That might help.

He took half of his cup of soup, in between struggling out of his wet weather gear and finding clean, dry, warm clothing from the cupboard. He got out the warmest things Kasia had brought with her and the heavy woolen socks. These he put on her feet, after chaffing them until she moaned and tried to draw them away from him. They were pink with his ministrations.

Now he had warm enough water and soaked a towel, passing it from one hand to the other before he pulled back the fur and laid it against her chilled legs for a few moments, coaxing warmth back into them.

The blueness was leaving her skin by the time he got her to drink all her soup, but she lay limply under the fur, drained by even the slight effort required to swallow. Under them the little ship rocked gently, pulling at the anchor chain, then following the sea, pulled back again. He got in the bunk beside her, covering them both with the other fur and, at last, allowed himself the luxury of sleep.

An urgent need to relieve himself was what brought him back to consciousness. He couldn't move easily, partly because of the weight of Kasia across him and partly because of the resistance of tired muscles. It took him a few moments to remember why he had slept so deeply. Startled, he looked out the little round porthole and saw a shadowed shore through the mist that swirled on the surface. Little waves splashed against the side of the ship, and she rode easily on the anchor.

Trying not to groan as he forced abused muscles to work, he slid out from under Kasia and all but fell off the bunk. Kasia didn't move, but her face wasn't quite so white and her lips were no longer blue-tinged. He tucked the fur about her firmly and staggered up the steps, throwing open the hatch. The air was chill and dank with fog, and the deck was littered with sea wrack. He went hand over hand from the cabin housing to the rail to get to the side and relieve himself. And it was indeed a relief.

Curious, he peered through the fog to see where they had fetched up, but he could see little detail on the shore—if there was a shore. Some of the inlets were nothing but shallow pockets eroded from the cliff by the sea. Whatever! This one had saved their lives.

He went below again.

The brazier had gone out; the charcoal was all ashes. He got more and started another fire, warming his hands as the charcoal began to burn. Kasia moaned, stirred, and then coughed. Fearful of fever, he felt her forehead but it was cold. So were her cheeks. Too cold.

He filled the kettle from the cistern and put it to heat on one side of the grill over the charcoal, then set the soup kettle on the other half. Panting from even that little bit of exercise, he sat on the edge of the bunk and took deep, slow breaths. A shiver ran down his back, and he recognized that he was almost as cold as Kasia.

When the klah was made and the soup warm enough to be

helpful, he roused her, stuffing pillows and the carisaks behind her for support. She turned her head restlessly, batting at him, and coughed again, a little, almost apologetic bark.

"Kasia, wake up. You need to eat, love."

She shook her head, her expression petulant even with her eyes firmly shut.

He talked her eyes open and made her drink, and she gave him a weak little smile and then went back to sleep again.

That seemed a very sensible idea, so he finished his soup and climbed back under the furs. Her arms were cold under his hands and he rubbed them, breaking off only when even that effort proved exhausting.

They slept again.

Robinton began to feel real concern when the second long sleep revived him but seemed to have little effect on Kasia's terrible lethargy. And the cold was increasing. The wooden hull offered no protection to the cold's insidious draining of their body warmth. He had dressed her in the warmest clothes and heated the kettle time and time again, wrapping it well and set-tling it securely near her feet which, in spite of the heavy socks, were like ice to the touch. He forced her to drink, and when she complained that her stomach was bursting with all he made her drink, he found a way to hold her over a bucket to relieve herself.

The fog had lifted enough for him to see that sheer cliffs sur-rounded the little cove, with no discernible track up them to find help. But he did not feel confident in himself to sail the ship out into the sea. Also, he had absolutely no idea where they were: on Tillek's coast or the bleak western end of High Reaches, or if they'd been blown farther down the coast of Fort.

He gave them both another day and when that dawn rose frostily clear and even klah gave him no warmth, he roused her to give him what instructions she could from the bunk.

"If I leave the hatch open, can you see enough to tell me if

I'm doing anything wrong?" he pleaded with her when she seemed unable to grasp his concern. They had little food left, almost no charcoal, and without that small heat to warm the cabin, they would surely freeze in the night.

"They'll come. Search," she murmured.

"They won't see us. We've got to stand out to sea where the sail will be visible."

"You're able for that, Rob," she said with the hint of a smile. "You can do more than you think you can."

"Then so can you," he said bluntly, fear driving him.

She shook her head sadly and closed her eyes again.

He watched her, thinking of how valiantly she had fought the storm. But now the storm was over, and she looked to him, her spouse, to keep his promise to care for her. Only he hadn't thought he'd be put to such a test quite this soon.

"All right, if that's the way it's to be, I'll just have to do."

With fear making his feet heavier, he thudded up on deck. The surrounding cliffs had an ominous look about them. What had been a refuge now seemed a prison.

"We'll just have to get out into the open sea," he told himself. "I can do that much." He licked his finger and held it up but felt only the faintest touch of a breeze. Fortunately it was blowing down from the cliffs and out to sea. They had been mightily lucky to have thrown the anchor down when they did, for the ship would have been mashed against the cliff had it sailed much farther.

He couldn't make up his mind whether to hoist the sail first, or the anchor. At last he decided that if the sail was up, the ship might move toward the open sea once the anchor let it.

He managed both, but was panting by the time he reached the cockpit and took the tiller bar in his hands.

"I've hoisted the sail, Kasia, and the anchor, though I could blow and get more use of the sail."

She murmured something that sounded encouraging, and sure enough, the little ship slowly eased forward and passed the sheltering arm of the cove. The sea was almost too calm when he saw its vast expanse. Once the ship was clear of the shelter, though, the breeze picked up and the sail filled.

"Right or left, Kasia? I've no idea where we are."

"Starboard . . . right, Rob. Go right." He had to ask her three times to repeat her instructions more loudly so he could hear her weakened voice clearly.

"I'm shrieking nowwwww," she protested, and her face came into his range of vision as she lifted herself off the bunk.

That was better, he thought, than lying there like a cut of wool.

"Right," he roared back at her. "I'm going right. Starboard."

And almost immediately had to correct the ship as he saw the jagged reef he had been about to sail into. Panic gripped him, and he struggled to keep his bowels from loosening.

"Stupid dimwit," he admonished himself. "Watch where you're going."

When he judged they were well enough past the rocks, he changed his seat and threw the tiller over to port—he remembered that much of Captain Gostol's afternoon lesson on how to tack. And then he grabbed for the sheet to keep the wind in the sail.

The speed of the sloop picked up, and he rather enjoyed the pull of sheet and tiller in his hand. At least he was doing something.

It was midday, to judge by the sun's position, and the high cliffs along which the ship sailed were totally unfamiliar to him.

"We've got nothing but cliffs, Kasia. Where could we be?"

He saw her raise up and shake her head. "Keep on."

So he did, until the pleasure left the occupation and fatigue began to run along both arms as the sun dropped slowly in the awesomely vast western sea. The cliffs continued unbroken. Had they found refuge in the one cove along this entire coast? Would they find another one for tonight? He doubted he could stand a longer watch. And he ought to eat something and be sure that Kasia did.

"What do I do, Kasia? What do I do?"

"Sail on," she cried back at him.

The sea was calm as night fell, and the breeze died also. So, lashing the tiller as he'd once seen Captain Gostol do for a quick moment of relief, he clattered down into the cabin, startling Kasia awake.

"There's nothing but cliff," he protested as he started the last of the charcoal. He'd have to feed her something. It had been hours since the last cup of soup and some hard crackers he'd found in the cupboard. He'd have to have klah to stay awake.

"It will have to give to beach soon then, Rob. I'm so sorry, love. So very sorry." And she wept piteously.

He comforted her while the water heated. "You kept us afloat all during the storm and used up all your strength, my love. Don't cry. Please don't cry. We can't have the furs all wet on you."

His cajolery made her smile and sniff, and brush away her tears. "But I can't do anything to help . . ."

"That's all right. I'm fine. I just don't know what I'm doing." He imbued the complaint with as much humor as he could. Then he left her with more soup and took his and the klah up to the cockpit.

The night was clear and very cold. But the wind picked up, blowing almost steadily from the south and that, he felt, was to their advantage. Surely, if they got close enough to Tillek, there'd be fishing ships out on a night like this. Or maybe even someone looking for them.

"No, you two got yourself *into* this. You can get yourself *out* of this," he told himself firmly and dragged the heavy-weather gear more tightly about his body, trying to keep warm. "Got yourself in, *get* yourself out." He turned the cadence into a chant, rocking from side to side, which eased the numbness in his buttocks. The chant went to his feet, and he stamped them in turn. And he sang and stamped and rocked and thumped the tiller bar with his hands, inventing new rhythms and altogether enjoying the activity when he suddenly realized that something was coming out of the darkness ahead of him, large and white, and someone was yelling.

"Sloop ahoy!"

"Shards, what do I do now? Steer starboard, right, starboard!" he yelled at the white shape bearing down on him. As hard as he could, he pushed the tiller over and nearly clouted himself in the head as the boom swung past.

They were rescued by the schooner *Wave Eater*. Two sturdy fishermen lifted Kasia aboard to other willing hands. Robinton managed to climb the rope ladder, awkward with fatigue and stiff joints. With the little sloop tied on behind, *Wave Eater* swung round and headed back to Tillek Hold, her mission complete. A glowbasket was hung from the top of the mast to let other ships know that the lost had been found.

The second mate, Lissala, who was also Captain Idarolan's wife, tended to Kasia while Idarolan did similar services for Robinton, remarking on how a mere harper had managed so well.

"Kasia told me what to do," he protested in between spoonfuls of a hearty fish stew, bobbing with root vegetables that had never tasted so good, and bread that had been fresh the day before when the search parties had been organized to locate the missing and long overdue sloop.

"Aye, Harper, but it was you doing it."

"She'll be fine now," Lissala said, returning and slipping into a seat opposite Robinton. "Wise of you to be sure she drank so much. No frostbite, but . . ." She looked sharply at his discolored fingers. Startled, because without his hands he was nothing, he held them both out to her and felt the pinch she gave the tips. "No, they're all right, but another coupla hours out in that—" She nodded her head to indicate the cold night. "—and it might've been different. But we've got you safe and snug aboard." She reached around for a cup and poured klah, holding the pot up and looking inquiringly at Robinton, who shook his head.

"Where were we when you found us?" Robinton asked.

Idarolan chuckled, rubbing his chin. "Halfway up the coast from Fort. You'd've done better to go to port. You weren't that far from a fishhold."

Robinton groaned, but then reminded himself that they'd had no idea at all where they had been blown to by the storm.

"Kasia told me right, starboard," he said, gesturing with the appropriate arm.

"Not to worry. We have you now." Then, as Robinton could not suppress an immense yawn—one part relief, one part being warm, and the other total fatigue—Idarolan added, "Come, man, I'll bed you down."

"Where's Kasia?" Robinton asked, looking up and down the passageway.

"In there," the captain said, indicating a door they were passing by. "You're in here." He opened another door across the way and slid the little glowbasket open. "Take the lower bunk. Ellic's on this watch."

Robinton wondered how long "this watch" was before he'd have to leave the bunk, but he lost hold of the question and never heard the answer as soon as he laid himself down.

Chapter 14

C lostan went over both of them thoroughly. Kasia had recovered some of her normal color and strength by the time they docked at Tillek, where relieved folk helped them onto the wharf and up to the Hold. Lissala supported Kasia on one side and Robinton on the other, though Robinton wanted to carry Kasia and spare her the walk.

"You can barely carry yourself yet, man," Idarolan said.

Robinton had to admit that he was shaky on his feet. He was only too glad to follow Clostan, who met them at the Hold door and swooped Kasia up in his arms to carry her down to the infirmary. By then the Lord and Lady Holder had learned of their safe return and hurried to the infirmary. Juvana hovered anxiously over her sister and Melongel frowned, having clearly been very worried.

"You've both had quite an ordeal," Clostan said with a deep sigh. Kasia coughed politely into her hand, and the healer scowled. "I'll fix a soothing draught to ease that right smart. But neither of you is to do anything for the next three days. I'll go over you again then."

Juvana insisted they stay in one of the lower-level guest

apartments. Their own level was cold, being too far from the source of heat with which the Ancients had warmed the Hold, and they needed the warmth of hearth-heated rooms. Indeed, Robinton couldn't seem to heat the cold out of his bones and was drawn to the fire like a forest insect. Following Clostan's orders, they rested a full day in bed, Juvana keeping hot water bottles in a row under the furs, causing Robinton to complain that his feet were fine—it was the rest of him that wasn't warm.

Mostly Kasia slept, not even rousing when she coughed. Rob dozed fitfully, waking briefly every time she coughed. He woke once to find himself beating out the cadence of "Got in, get out . . ." And another time from a nightmare where he couldn't hear her or see her in the mist that blanketed him. He knew she was calling and he kept trying to answer, but his jaws were frozen stuck.

Captain Gostol came in, apologetic that he had left a search almost too long.

"Kasia's knowledgeable about the sea and little ships. And you two finally having a chance to be alone for the first time. That storm only reached us late the other night—which is when we began to get concerned with you being overdue back in the harbor." He kept turning his sea cap in his hands, working round and round on the brim.

"I did what Kasia told me," Robinton murmured, refusing to take much credit. "You should have seen her handling the sloop in that storm, though. You'd've been proud of her. As I am." He patted her leg under the furs and she smiled wanly up at him.

"You got us home," she said, just the hint of a sparkle back in her eyes.

Then she coughed, a funny dry hack that Clostan's potion didn't seem to ease.

If the medic was concerned about the way the cough hung on, he made no mention of it to Robinton. And soon they were well enough to go back to their own quarters. Juvana had put braziers in both rooms, to take the chill off. The black rock burned hotly, but with a smell and an acrid smoke that some-times irritated Kasia's cough. He suggested returning to the warmer lower level, but she said she wanted to be in the place they had fixed for themselves, with all their own things. And anyway, she added, they would both be spending much of their time in the warmer schoolrooms, when they resumed their duties the following sevenday.

Clostan became very busy, as the unnaturally cold weather brought him many coughs and colds, running noses and fevers. He continued to check up on Kasia, but she kept insisting that she felt fine.

"Except for the cough," Robinton added, chiding her for not mentioning it.

"It's only now and then, Rob," she said. Her listlessness still worried him. She seemed so tired by evening that she would fall asleep in his arms. He didn't mind. She felt so good against him, and he felt so protective of his lovely green-eyed spouse.

The cold was further complicated by three blizzards, following one after the other. No one moved about the Hold or attempted to take the ships out for fish. Lord Melongel was a good provider and, while the weather remained so bitter, opened his stores to those who were short on food. It was essential to keep everyone healthy in this awful weather.

A feverish cough developed and spread from the schoolroom to the old aunties and uncles. Clostan asked for assistance in his nursing duties, and both Robinton and Kasia volunteered, since many of the patients were their students.

Then, one night, Robinton was awakened by Kasia's thrashing. Moaning and mumbling, throwing her arms and legs about, she was burning up with fever. Robinton charged down to the infirmary, where the assistant healer on night duty gave him the powdered herb that would reduce the fever, and the salve to rub on her throat, chest, and back. Robinton detoured to the kitchen and got himself klah and a pitcher of the flavored water that was being used for invalids.

Kasia had managed to throw off the furs and was lying uncovered in the cold room. He quickly covered her and then applied the salve, its pungent smell seeping into his nose and lungs. Then he roused her to take a few sips of the herb drink.

He dozed now and then, in between forcing her to drink. By morning she was delirious, and he was becoming more and more worried. The herb had seemed effective with everyone else he nursed, but her coughing fits were getting harder and longer.

He almost cried out with relief when Clostan, red-eyed and weary, came in. Kasia chose that moment to indulge in one of her coughing spasms, and Clostan came swiftly to the bedside.

"That doesn't sound good," he said, feeling her forehead and cheeks. "You've the salve on? Use more and repeat it every three hours. Here, let's give her my special remedy."

He mixed the draught himself and made her drink it.

"She obeys you more than she does me," Robinton remarked peevishly.

"You're her spouse," Clostan said with a weary grin. "Mind you, most of your patients have recovered, so I'm sure she will."

There was, however, a note in Clostan's voice that caught Robinton's ear.

"You are?"

"Of course I am. She's young and . . . well, she's far less vulnerable than those down the hall." His face fell into sad lines.

"More deaths?" Robinton asked, and Clostan nodded.

"The very old have no stamina. And we've got their quarters as warm as an oven."

He left then, but Juvana arrived shortly afterward and together they moved Kasia down to a guest room, where a fire roared on the hearth.

Together Juvana and Robinton nursed Kasia. Clostan came in several times that day, and yet her fever persisted. To Robinton, it seemed that she was hotter every time he felt her forehead. He knew this wasn't the course the illness usually took and remembered what Clostan had said about the elderlies' lack of stamina. Did Kasia have enough, having so recently recovered from the ordeal of the storm? He didn't even dare ask Juvana her opinion. Her presence verified his fears.

He never left the bedside, except for necessary trips. Juvana ordered a pallet for herself to sleep on. Melongel looked in; so did Minnarden, offering to spell Robinton so he could get some sleep.

Robinton refused. He had promised to care for Kasia and he would. She had to get well. She had to.

But she did not. Just before dawn on the fifth day of her burning fever and hacking cough, when Melongel and Clostan had joined the vigil, she opened her eyes, smiled at Robinton leaning over her, and, with a sigh, closed them. And was still.

"No, no. *No! No! Kasia! You can't leave me alone!*"

He was shaking her, trying to rouse her, when he felt Juvana's hands pulling him away. He clutched Kasia to him, stroking her hair, her cheeks, trying to coax life back into her body.

It took Melongel and Clostan to pull him away from her, while Juvana arranged her on the bed. And Clostan forced a potion down his throat.

"We did all we could, Rob, all we could. It's just sometimes not enough." And Robinton heard the pain of the healer as plain as he felt his own.

Captain Gostol sailed the *Northern Maid* with just Vesna and two others to man her—his crew was also decimated by the fever.

It was Merelan who sang the final farewell, for Robinton couldn't speak. He did play the harp he had so lovingly made his spouse. And when Merelan held the last note until it died away—as his hope had—he flung the harp to join the body of his beloved as it slipped into the sea. The harp gave one last dissonant chord as the wind of its descent strummed the strings. Then all was silent. Even the wind died down in respect for his loss.

He moved his things back into his bachelor room. Ifor and Mumolon did all they could to bear him company, see that he ate, make him lie down in his bed—for he could seem to do nothing at all. "Got in, get out . . ." The refrain haunted him, but he had not the energy to make notations. He felt he could never sing, or compose, again. He tried to rouse himself from this immolation in grief, his terrible loss, but all he seemed to do was sink deeper.

He was sprawled in front of the fire, Ifor and Mumolon having gone elsewhere, either because they had duties or because they could no longer stand to be with him and his grief. The door swung open and F'lon stood there, staring at him.

Robinton looked up incuriously, noted that the dragonrider was there, and then stared back in the fire.

"I only just heard," F'lon said, striding into the room and slamming the door behind him. He picked up what was left of the bottle of wine and poured it into a glass, tossing it back. "I'd've come earlier if I'd known."

Robinton nodded. F'lon peered more closely into his face.

"Say, you really are in a terrible state, aren't you?"

Robinton didn't dignify the question with an answer, waving a hand to send F'lon on his way. He appreciated the dragonrider coming, but F'lon only reminded him of the last time he had seen him: on his Espousal Day.

"That bad, huh?" F'lon looked around him for more wine. "Drunk it all up?"

"Drinking doesn't help."

"No. It doesn't."

Something in F'lon's tone roused Robinton briefly. "What do you mean?"

"Isn't there any more wine up here? Do I have to go back downstairs to get some?"

F'lon was angry, which annoyed Robinton, so he pointed to the cupboard. "There should be one more there," he said.

"You've been counting?"

Robinton shrugged and sighed. He watched indifferently as F'lon found the bottle, made a disgusted noise as he read the label, but pulled the bung and poured a glass for himself. Then he splashed more into Robinton's cup.

"You're not the only one grieving, but at least you're entire," he said after taking half the glass.

"Oh?"

"L'tol—or should I now call him Lytol—lost Larth. Just about the time Kasia . . ." And even brash F'lon could not continue. He downed the rest of that glass and poured another, right to the brim.

"L'tol? Lost Larth?" That much penetrated.

"Yes, and he shouldn't have." F'lon slammed the glass down on the table so hard that it broke at the stem. He cursed as the glass cut into the web of finger and thumb. He sucked it.

"How?" Robinton asked. Dragons seldom died in an Interval.

"C'vrel decided we should straighten up and get some fire-stone practice in during the Spring Games," F'lon said in a sarcastic tone. "We'd fly wing against wing. S'lel's Tuenth came out of *between* flaming and caught Larth all along his side. There were enough of us in the air to cushion Larth back to earth, screaming his head off." F'lon gave himself a sudden shake as if the memory of that agony was etched in his mind. "L'tol fell off and the weyrfolk grabbed him, but Larth was too badly burned. He went *between* right there on the ground."

Robinton saw the tears coursing down the dragonrider's cheeks. He reached out to lay his hand on F'lon's arm, unable to bear his friend's pain.

F'lon brushed the tears aside. "You aren't the only one bearing a terrible loss right now."

"No, I'm not. But I don't seem to be able to bear it either."

"No, you don't. If you want, you can go, too."

"Go, too?" Robinton looked up at F'lon. "What do you mean?"

"Couldn't be simpler," the dragonrider said drolly. "We go out to Simanith, he takes you in his arms, we go *between* and Simanith opens his arms"—which F'lon demonstrated with an upward flourish—"and only the two of us go on to Benden. Simple."

"Yes, simple," Robinton said, thinking almost wistfully of the cold black nothingness of *between* where one felt nothing, heard nothing, was shortly nothing.

Tears filled his eyes and his heart seemed to burst. He'd been cold so long now. It would be simple ... but ... it wasn't simple.

"No, it isn't simple," F'lon said gently, and Robinton realized he had spoken aloud. "There's something in us humans that clings to life even when the most beloved one we have leaves us. Lytol couldn't go when we gave him the option. He was badly burned and too full of fellis and numbweed to be able to decide. And when he could, he decided to go back to High Reaches with his family."

Robinton gave a start. "That's not a wise place for anyone to be right now, I think. Much less a ... former dragonrider."

F'lon shrugged. "His choice. He needs his family right now. I saw your mother is still here."

"Yes, she's been wonderful. Everyone has."

"So, let's get on with life, shall we?" The kindness in that soft gentle suggestion reached and thawed the cold "nothingness" Robinton had been enduring.

"Thank you, F'lon," he said and rose. "I think I'd better eat something, and you look as if you could stand a good meal, too."

Indeed, F'lon looked haggard as well as weary, but at Robinton's suggestion, his smile flickered. Stretching an arm across the harper's shoulder, he wheeled him to face the door and then accompanied him out of the room and down to the warm kitchen to ask for a meal.

It was ironic that the grip of terrible weather broke shortly afterward and milder weather not only improved those who had been stricken by the feverish cough but also allowed everyone's normal duties to be resumed.

Living in Tillek Hold was hard on Robinton, for it was filled with memories: one moment he would think he saw Kasia, just turning that corridor; the next, he would hear the echo of her voice in the room. He was still numb with his grief and tried very hard to overcome it with work and just living.

He briefly roused when Minnarden and Melongel told him that they had proof now of Lord Faroguy's death.

"We asked for confirmation of Faroguy's well-being," Melongel said. "Gave the inaccuracy of the last message as our excuse."

"The one that came back was nearly as badly drummed as the first, and all the towers asked for several repeats to be sure they had heard it correctly before passing it along," Minnarden said. Then he shook his head. "Lobirn never sent so badly formed a message. And Mallan was always good at drumming."

"So we sent . . . a friend." Melongel paused to nod significantly at Robinton. "A runner who keeps his eyes and ears open in the course of his duties. His report has disturbed us all." By "all," Robinton knew Melongel meant the Lord Holders.

"Then is Farevene Lord Holder?'

"No." Melongel's tone was sharp. "Farevene's dead. In a duel."

"With Fax? Then where's Bargen?"

Melongel shrugged. "The runner heard nothing about him, and Lady Evelene is evidently grieving in her apartments. I hope that much is true."

"Then will there be a Council to confirm the new Lord Holder?"

"A Council is convened at the request of the heir. The heir has not been heard from," Melongel said, his face shadowed by anger and doubt.

"Then Fax is in control." Robinton stated that as a fact. An anger and a fear took off a corner of his sorrow. He got to his feet to pace. "That man's dangerous, Melongel. And he's not going to be satisfied with just High Reaches."

"Oh, come now, Rob," Melongel said. "He has the Hold

he coveted, yes. But that's large enough to satisfy anyone's ambitions."

"Not Fax's. And where are Lobirn and Mallan? And Bargen?"

"Yes." Minnarden's voice was anxious. "I worry about them."

"We should," Robinton said, still pacing, and smoothing the hair back from his face. He needed to have it trimmed again . . . Kasia had done it the last time . . . Quickly he seized on Fax's aggression as distraction. "First he takes over the holding from an uncle. He refuses to allow harpers to teach what every holder has the right to know. Then he 'acquires' other holds, dueling the legitimate holders to death and ousting their families from their homes. You can't let him continue unopposed, Melongel."

"Lord Holders are autonomous within their property," Melongel said wearily, as if trying to convince himself.

"Not if they have taken illegal possession."

"That's not specified," Melongel said.

"It will seem," Minnarden began carefully, "as if silence confirms him in the position of Lord Holder of High Reaches."

"I know. I know. And you've sent my messages to the other Lord Holders," Melongel said testily. "You know their response."

"They'll let Fax get away with this?" Robinton was indignant. Couldn't they realize that they were taking an awful risk? "I'd guard my borders, brother."

Melongel shot him a hard look, then relaxed and gave a little smile. "I have. So far all they've done is succor those fleeing Fax's new management. He's a hard man."

"And will the Lord Holders act?" Robinton demanded.

Melongel twisted his head slightly to indicate uncertainty, lifting his hands in helplessness. "I cannot act on my own."

Robinton sighed, knowing that that would be foolish. "Lord Grogellan would support you—especially since Groghe can support your word."

"Grogellan would, but I doubt I could get much support from old Lord Ashmichel at Ruatha Hold. His son, Kale, though . . ." Melongel thoughtfully fingered his chin. "Telgar's another matter, but his Hold borders High Reaches."

"Lord Tarathel's protective, and his foresters are very well trained," Minnarden ventured.

"Lord Raid is too far away to feel anxiety," Robinton said with a touch of asperity.

"I know that Master Gennell wants to know about Lobirn and Mallan," Minnarden said, exchanging another glance with Melongel. "If he isn't satisfied with the answers, he'll withdraw all harpers from the Hold."

Robinton snorted, still pacing. "That would suit Fax perfectly. No one to tell anyone in his Hold what their rights are." Then he paused. "I know High Reaches Hold well. How to get in and how to get out."

"Yes, and Fax knows your face," Minarden said.

"He can't be everywhere," Robinton replied.

"You are far too valuable to be sent on that sort of a task," Minnarden said, his face set in denial.

"I've nothing to lose . . ." Robinton began.

"I have . . . brother," Melongel said.

"You've all to lose if you cross Fax," Minnarden said at the same time. "Master Gennell has men who are versed in quiet investigations. He has arranged all." His expression said clearly that that was that.

After Robinton left that meeting, he realized how he had shut himself away from what was happening around him. He fretted about Master Lobirn, Lotricia, and Mallan. And, considering what the fleeing women had told Chochol, he worried about pretty Sitta, Triana, and Marcine. He was still worrying about their fates when he sought his bed and it was a long time before he could get his mind to stop and let him sleep.

He completed his summer tour of the upper holds, although sometimes the folk, in expressing their sympathy for his loss, caused him more pain than they knew. Chochol's hold was enlarged by several tents, sheltering a contingent of armed men who patrolled the high ground.

"More coming in all the time," Chochol told Robinton in a

lugubrious voice, shaking his head at the terror that drove them from their holds. "Someone ought to do something about that man. They say he's got six, seven spouses, all of 'em pregnant." Then he chuckled and his droll face lit up. "Can't seem to get himself a son."

Robinton laughed, too. "We don't need more of his ilk."

So he was there when Lobirn and Lotricia managed to make good their escape, escorted by a small thin man whom Robinton thought he recognized from his Hall days. But he couldn't be sure. The man had no distinguishing features, being quiet and capable but self-effacing.

"Don't I recognize you from the Hall?" Robinton asked him much later when he found the man by himself, stuffing food into his carisak. By then, Robinton had heard Lobirn's account of the last Turn and a half.

"You may, and again you may not, Robinton. Just forget you've ever seen me. That's the safest thing. I'm going back, as you see."

"Why? You've brought Lobirn and Lotricia safely out."

"I'm going to try for Mallan next. I think I know where I might find him."

"Why? What happened to him?"

Lobirn and Lotricia had had enough warning to manage to escape the Hold before Fax could arrest them. Mallan had not been so lucky.

"Fax doesn't waste anything. Even a loathsome harper can work for his living. If you call that work. Or living."

"What?" Robinton was insistent.

"The mines. The mines always need live bodies."

Robinton felt a shiver of fear shoot up his spine. Mallan's hands would be ruined, digging in rock.

"I'll find him, never fear, Robinton," the man said, pressing the harper's hand firmly, and then he was off, down the hills on the High Reaches side, disappearing into the falling dusk.

Robinton and two men escorted the thin, weary Master and his spouse to the next hold, where he stayed to teach while they went forward as fast as they could travel comfortably. Robinton thought of Lotricia, a shadow of her once plump and generous self, and the plates of food she had brought him and Mallan, and hated Fax more than ever—if that was possible.

Returning to Tillek Hold was almost more than he could bear. He hadn't minded the long journeys between holds, the teaching, even the focus of his thoughts—Kasia's beautiful sea-green eyes, her laugh, her body, the peace she had given him. But seeing the Hold again in the bright afternoon light, remembering with what hopes he had come back the previous Turn, he almost turned his runner aside.

When he came to give Melongel his formal report, the Lord Holder put it to one side.

"I saw your face when you came back . . . brother," he said, "and it decided me. Just being here in Tillek is making it worse, not helping. I'm releasing you from our contract. Master Gennell agrees that you should return to the Harper Hall where you won't always be reminded . . . of Kasia."

Numbed by the suddenness of that decision and yet grateful that it had been made for him, Robinton nodded. Melongel rose. So did Robinton.

"There is always room for . . . our brother . . . here at Tillek Hold, any time you care to claim it," the Lord Holder said formally and held out his hand. "I think Master Gennell wants you to bring that good Ruathan runner back with you." He gave a little smile. "Young Groghe's to go home, too. You can keep each other company. He'll make a good Lord Holder when he inherits."

"He'll be wary of Fax, too."

Melongel's eyebrows rose and his eyes caught Robinton's. "Yes, he will and that's all to the good."

Two mornings later, having allowed his runner a good rest, Robinton rode south and then east with Groghe, retracing their original route and spending two days with Sucho, Tortole, and their family. He had Saday's bowl with him and showed her how much he treasured it.

The wall was up, and many of the capping slabs were athwart its expanse, rather than on one side or the other. To Robinton that meant that at least the two holders had resolved their differences. A small satisfaction to take back with him.

Chapter 15

▼▼▼

I t was easier to be in the Harper Hall again, surrounded by the hopes of the new young apprentices, immersed in his studies for his Mastery, which was what Master Gennell suggested he apply himself to for the rest of the summer.

But it was still a shock when Robinton heard the unmistakable music of his Sonata pouring out the open windows of the rehearsal hall.

How dared they? How had they got the music? He had kept his copy, but he had never . . . Then he remembered that he had given his mother a copy when she'd come for their espousal. But surely she wouldn't . . .

He tore out of his room, pounding down the stairs to the rehearsal hall, trying with the noise of his boots to drown out the music he had so lovingly created for his Kasia. He flung open the door, startling the instrumentalists, his mother, and Petiron.

"How dare you play that?" And he advanced on his mother as if he would rip the harp from her lap.

"How dare *you*?" Petiron demanded, infuriated by the interruption.

"It's *my* music. No one plays it without my permission."

"Robie . . ." his mother began, rising to her feet and starting to come toward him. She stopped abruptly when he recoiled, holding his hands out in protest, as much against the sympathy and pity in her face as against any contact. He almost hated her. How could she have let Petiron see *his* music, the Sonata he had composed for Kasia, only for her? "I loved Kasia, too, Robinton. I'm playing it for *her*. Every time the Kasia Sonata is played, her memory will be invoked. She lives on in this beautiful music. She will be remembered with it. You must allow her that! You need to allow yourself that."

He just looked at her, feeling the anger drain away under her stern gaze. The other players remained so motionless that he scarcely noted their presence.

Then his father cleared his throat. "The Sonata is the best music you've ever written," Petiron said, without a trace of condescension in his voice.

Robinton turned slowly to look at the MasterComposer.

"It is," he said, and turning on his heel, he left the room.

He put wadding in his ears when he went back to his room so he wouldn't have to hear the music. But some of it penetrated, and toward the end of the rehearsal, which was almost a straight run-through, given the quality of the musicians performing, he took the wadding out. Listening to the rondo, and the finale, he let the tears run unheeded down his face.

Yes, it was the best piece of music he had written. And listening to it, somehow he found he could think of Kasia without the terrible sense of loss and the constriction around his heart. As the final chords died away, he sighed and went back to his studying.

He did not go to the performance. Instead he saddled his Ruathan runner and took a long ride, camping out overnight. But his dreams were laden with memories of Kasia and he woke sweating, to lie until dawn, still remembering what he had loved about her: her laugh, the crinkling of her eyes, the lilt in her voice, the way she would swing her hips, deliberately enticing him.

Winter was just settling over Fort Hold with an early snowshower when Master Gennell came looking for him.

"Ah, Rob," he said, coming toward him. Placing a fatherly arm across Robinton's shoulders, he guided the younger harper into his office. "We've an emergency. Recall Karenchok, thin, dark-skinned Journeyman, in the same group as Shonagar?"

"Oh, yes, I do."

"Well, he's broken his leg badly and will be unable to complete his rounds. Would you be willing to take over for him down in South Boll? Until he's able to travel again?"

Robinton was delighted to do so and hastily organized his packs for a noontime departure. He paused only long enough to tell his mother where he was going and why. She listened, nodding her head and giving him an encouraging little smile. As she walked him to the door, she reached up to caress his cheek.

"The Sonata received a tremendous ovation, Rob," she said softly.

He nodded, took her hand, kissed it, and left.

Karenchok's home base was a cluster of seaside holds on the eastern shore of South Boll. It was hot and steamy when Robinton arrived, and the Seaholder greeted him enthusiastically.

"We've all been worried about him, Journeyman. He's very popular here, and so we've kept someone with him, to help."

"You're very kind, Holder Matsen. Master Gennell asked me to thank you for your care."

"We've a very good healer, local woman, but trained properly in the Hall. She's been overseeing his care, but she's busy, too."

The Holder was a short man, stockily built in the barrel, with thin legs that didn't look strong enough to hold up the weight he carried. But he moved quickly as he led the way to the cot set back from the little harbor. There was a long chair out in front, made by attaching a flat-topped stool to a padded chair. Vines had been trained over a lattice to shield the front from the morning sun.

"Ho, Karenchok, brought you a guest," Matsen bellowed, giving advance warning.

A woman appeared in the door, giving the loose long skirt she wore a final twitch. Her smile was guileless as she greeted Harper and Holder.

"Ah. Laela, that's where you got to," Matsen said in a slightly strained voice.

Laela's smile turned on Robinton, and her eyes widened slightly. Then her manner became subtly seductive and her smile warmer.

"This is Journeyman Harper Robinton," Matsen said stiffly. "Laela helps Healer Saretta with hold-bound patients."

"I do my part," she said in a sultry voice, and Robinton felt his lips twitching. He could not deny her sensuality—or that it was affecting him. It was the first time in the nearly nine months since Kasia's death that he had felt this way. He didn't know if this was a good thing or not, but there was no missing the invitation in Laela's voice and eyes as she slid past him. "Karenchok is in good spirits," she said, her laughter trailing her departure.

In spite of himself, Robinton turned to see where she went.

"Karenchok is here," Matsen said, prompting his attention.

"Sorry."

Matsen cleared his throat and led the way into the cot.

Karenchok was sitting by the table, his splinted leg straight out in front of him and a pair of wooden crutches handily slanted against another chair. Robinton did recognize him: one of Shonagar's wrestling partners. Seeing Robinton, Karenchok waved a friendly hand.

"I remember you, Robinton," he said in greeting. "Very good of Gennell to send me help so quickly. Come, sit. Matsen, can you find the wineskin for me?"

Matsen did, and a curious peek at the label on the skin told Robinton that this was a Tillek red, which was likely to be harsh. Well, it was wine and would go down as well as the best.

By late evening he had learned all about Karenchok's accident and admired the man for the grit it must have taken to crawl, with a leg broken in three places, to a path where someone would find him. He'd been riding back to his cot when his runner—"one of the stupidest ever bred"—had been frightened by a tunnel snake and thrown him down into the gully. Once over its scare, the runner had been in no hurry to return to its home, so it had been late night before a search party went out to find him. When Robinton remarked on his fortitude, Karenchok shrugged.

"Well, the misbegotten runner got me into the ditch; it was up to me to get out."

The phrases caught Robinton's attention: "Got into, get out!" Notes began once more to spin in his head.

He didn't get the rest of the tune until much later, but it was a start, and he was grateful to be able to think music again. Although he had spent some time with his mother's family on the west coast, this part of eastern South Boll was quite different, with land sloping down into fine beaches and piers thrust far out to where the water was deep enough to accommodate the fishing boats. He even forced himself to go out to sea in Matsen's sloop, though it was five times the size of the sloop he and Kasia had sailed. But he made another step forward out of grief by doing so.

Tactful questioning of Karenchok elicited the information that Laela was her own person, beholding to none. She gave her favors where she would, and Karenchok was grateful for her generosity. So was Robinton, although he winced when she boldly claimed that she would lift the sadness from his eyes. It annoyed her that she couldn't. Though she tried often enough during his winter stay at the Seahold.

Just after Turn's End at the Seahold, a dragon was spotted in the skies. The children Robinton was teaching at the moment could not contain their excitement. It wasn't often that dragons came this far south. As Robinton shielded his eyes from the brightness of the morning sun on the water, he tentatively spoke the name.

Simanith? Is that you?

It is, and there was such a note of joyfulness in the dragon's voice—so like F'lon's—that Robinton grinned.

What is it? What brings you so far away from Benden? Robinton asked.

You. We've been to the Hall. They told us you were here.

F'lon was half-off Simanith's neck before the big bronze had touched the sand of the beach.

"I'm a father, Rob, I'm a father!" F'lon shouted, waving one arm and charging up the strand to thump the Harper soundly on the back. He had a wineskin thrown over the other shoulder. "A son! Larna gave me a son!"

"Larna? So you *did* get her!" Robinton had to dismiss the pang in his heart. Kasia had been alive when he'd first learned about F'lon's interest in the grown-up Larna, who had been such a plaguey nuisance to Falloner, the boy.

"Dismiss your class, Rob," F'lon ordered. "Off you go, children. Class again tomorrow."

Robinton had to laugh at the dragonrider's high-handed way, but F'lon's exultation brought smiles to the fishermen mending nets on the strand. Robinton hurriedly introduced F'lon to Matsen and the others, and then led his old friend to the cot he shared with Karenchok.

"A fine strong lad, just like his sire," F'lon boasted, splashing wine into the cups Karenchok hastily set out.

"Don't waste this," Robinton said, having had a taste of the white wine that was being so liberally poured. "It's Benden, isn't it?"

"What else would I provide to toast the health of my first son?" F'lon demanded and quaffed his glass dry.

It was a merry time, though all too short, because F'lon was anxious to return to Benden and his child.

"I gather Larna did forgive you for pushing her into the midden, then?" Robinton remarked after listening to F'lon's ravings.

The dragonrider gave him a startled look. "I never pushed her into the midden. That was Rangul. R'gul, I should say. That isn't where he'd've liked to push her, but I"—and he slapped his chest proudly—"got her as weyrmate, not R'gul."

"I'm sure she'll be happier with you," Robinton said, remembering what a stuffy child Rangul had been.

"Of course she will," F'lon replied. Finishing his third, or maybe fourth, glass of wine, he decided he had best return to the Weyr, Larna, and his son. "I've named him Fallarnon."

"A fine choice for a dragonrider-to-be."

"Bronze, of course," F'lon added as he waved a cheerful good-bye to Karenchok.

"He came all the way from Benden Weyr to tell you that?" Karenchok asked, hobbling to the doorway to watch the dragon-rider depart.

"We're old friends."

"*Good* friends." Karenchok lifted his wineglass apprecia-tively. "You don't get good Benden often in South Boll."

Nine days later a runner brought Robinton a short message from F'lon: Larna had died two days after Fallarnon's birth. Robinton sent back a message by the same messenger, ex-pressing his condolences. In his heart, though, Robinton envied F'lon, who had a son to remember his love by.

When Karenchok was finally walking soundly and able to ride again, Robinton reluctantly bequeathed him the Ruathan runner—a much sounder and smarter animal than the weedy elderly runt that had thrown him. He rode Karenchok's back to the Hall, having no other, and it was indeed the most uncom-fortable of riding beasts.

The first thing he did when he got back to the Harper Hall was to tell the beastholder to get rid of this bag of bones and find him a new riding animal. His second action was to find his mother. He didn't like what he saw and taxed her with ques-tions about her health.

"I'm fine, I'm fine, love, really. Just a little tired. It's been a busy winter, you know."

Robinton was not so easily put off and cornered the Master-Healer the next morning.

"She does seem fine, Rob," Ginia replied slowly, "but I know, as you do, that she's not. She's losing weight, yet I see her eating well at table. I've my eye on her, never fear. And Betrice."

"Betrice?" Robinton realized that he hadn't seen the Master-Harper's spouse, who was usually busy about the Hall someplace. "What's wrong with Betrice?" Was his whole world crumbling about him? Were all the people he loved and admired suddenly showing their mortality?

Ginia laid a hand on his arm, her expressive eyes sad. "There is so much we don't know and can't help." She paused and then sighed. "Sometimes people just wear out. But I promise you I'm watching your mother carefully."

"And Betrice?"

"And Betrice," Ginia said with a nod.

At dinner that evening, Robinton sat next to Betrice, noting the slight wobble in her hand as she ate, and trying not to see it. So he regaled her with the funniest incidents he could remember and her laughter was as ready as ever. Once their eyes met and locked and she gave him a funny little smile and patted his hand.

"Don't *worry*, Rob," she said in a low voice, turning her head away from her spouse, who was involved in a lengthy explanation of some legal point with a journeyman whom Robinton remembered as another of Shonagar's voice students.

"Just you take good care of yourself, too, Betrice," Robinton said with as much love as he could put in his low tone.

"Oh, I do. I do."

Robinton had to be content with such reassurance and the next morning accepted the assignment Master Gennell had for him: this time in Keroon.

"You haven't been to the plains yet, have you? Good experience, Rob, good experience. Again it's a short contract." Gennell passed Robinton a piece of hide. "These are the holds you do not go to."

"Do not . . . ?" Robinton was surprised and scanned the nine names listed.

"Yes," the MasterHarper said. "I'm sorry to say, harpers are not always regarded with the respect they formerly were, as I think you've discovered a time or two."

Robinton grimaced. "But why? We're only trying to help. We don't tell people lies . . ."

Gennell cocked his head, a sad smile turning down the corner of his expressive mouth. "There are many who feel that the Duty Song is lies."

"Honoring the dragonriders?"

Gennell nodded. "That's one so-called lie. You have realized that, even in the larger holds, some feel that the Weyr and its riders are relics of a past danger we no longer need to consider."

"But, Master Gennell . . ."

The MasterHarper held up his hand and gave a brief smile. "You have had a long association with the one remaining Weyr. Many nowadays have never even seen a dragon in the sky, much less met a dragonrider. Sometimes Search is misinterpreted, too, although there have been few enough of them lately." He sighed and gestured to the list. "Just save yourself grief and avoid those holds. We can't force people to learn when they've no wish to listen."

As Robinton was on his way out of the courtyard on the new young Ruathan runnerbeast he had used his savings to purchase, a runner came trotting in. A runner who was very familiar to him.

Robinton had formally met Gennell's invisible minion in the MasterHarper's office on two occasions.

"Call me Nip, if my lack of name offends you," the man had said with an amused grin. "I nip in and out, you see."

Master Gennell had smiled. "And you're never to see him, Rob."

"I know," Robinton had replied. But this time he needed information the runner might be able to provide.

"Ah, you, runner, wait a minute . . ." As Robinton reined his mount about, the runner dutifully halted and turned to face him. Robinton smiled. "I thought it was you."

Nip smiled briefly. "I've fooled many."

"Ah, but I'm a harper and as trained to notice details as you are. *Did* you find Mallan?" he asked.

Hope died as the man's face drained of any expression. He shook his head. "He died in the mines. That much I discovered." Then his expression altered to a fierce hatred. "I'll get Fax yet."

"If you don't, I will." And with that promise, Robinton rode out of the courtyard.

Though he was welcomed wherever he went on the Keroon plains, Robinton occasionally felt the resistance to some of the traditional Teaching Ballads and did his best to discuss the concepts with the adults in the hold, reminding them of the Charter's provisions. Often his evenings were spent in copying out that document so that it would be available to counteract the question of "lying." He did feel that he got his message across to the doubters.

Several times he was warned by his host that "yon feller's not so friendly" and, if asked to play in the evening, Robinton carefully restricted his selections to unremarkable love songs or dance tunes. Even so, he sometimes had to ignore sullen looks and manners.

One evening, at Red Cliff Hold, he was astonished to see Nip arrive, dressed as a runner, and bearing a Crafthall reply for the Holder. Robinton waited for a chance to speak to Nip and, by asking him to take a letter directed to his mother at the Harper Hall, managed a few private words with him.

"Didn't expect to see you here," Robinton said, flourishing the letter as if that was what was under discussion.

"How do you think Master Gennell knows where not to send harpers?" Nip said. "Station Masters are the best ones to ask, by the way, should you be in doubt." Taking the letter from

Robinton, he altered his tone and spoke more loudly. "Wal, now, Harper, I'll be sure to take good care a' this 'un fer ye."

When Robinton had done his round in Keroon, Master Gennell sent him on to Nerat, to a settlement that was, happily, devoted to the old ways. Robinton was able to relax his vigilance and do a proper job of instructing the young in their Traditional Songs and Ballads. He was relieved to see that dragonriders often visited this area, collecting fresh fish for the Weyr. He always sent back greetings to F'lon and tried to speak to the dragons. They would look at him, surprised, but they never responded.

Remembering how freely Simanath had spoken to him as a boy and a man, he was baffled by their reticence. But then, he didn't know their riders as well as he had known F'lon and his bronze.

When he returned in the spring to the Harper Hall, one look at his mother had him in a panic. She was nothing but skin and bones, all the beauty leeched out of her face, with dry hair and a hard cough constantly racking her. She leaned on Petiron to walk even the shortest distance.

"You're not all right, Mother, not at all," Robinton said, glaring at Petiron, who nodded, his expression doleful and worried.

"That's why you're home, Rob," Ginia said when he stormed into the Healer Hall in search of her.

He stood stock-still. "Why I'm home?" He could not seem to comprehend what her words implied.

She pressed his arm, her face full of regret and pity. "Yes, I know she's wanted you here. She doesn't have much time left."

"But . . ." Robinton clenched his fists at his sides . . . "I've only just lost Kasia!"

"I know, Rob dear, I know." He could see the tears in her eyes. "She's my dearest friend. All I can do is be sure she feels no pain."

He nodded acceptance of that, feeling the coldness of grief yet to come spreading throughout his body.

"You must help her. And Petiron."

"Her, yes. Petiron . . ."

"He has lived for her, Robinton."

And I never had the chance to live for my Kasia, Robinton thought bitterly.

If he had thought the days after his spouse's death were bad, those he endured while his mother slowly lost all strength, and finally, the breath in her body, were worse. Without discussing it, either he or Petiron was with her, Robinton playing her songs, even the humorous setting of "Got into, get out of," which made her smile and even chuckle. Petiron played for her, too; music seemed to soothe her.

It was Ginia who roused Robinton from an uneasy sleep before dawn three days later. "The end is near."

He threw on pants and shirt and followed her, filled with dread.

The end was unexpectedly peaceful. He held one of Merelan's hands and Petiron the other, and she managed a feeble smile and a press of her gaunt fingers. Then she sighed, as Kasia had done, and was still. Neither man could move. Neither wished to relinquish the lifeless hand he held.

It was Ginia who gently unwrapped their fingers and laid first one hand, then the other across her frail chest.

Petiron broke first, sobbing bitterly. "How could you leave me, Merelan? How could you leave me?"

Robinton looked up at the man who was his father and thought that Petiron was taking Merelan's death as a personal affront. But Petiron had been possessive of her all her life. Why should he change at her death? And yet, Robinton felt immense pity for the man.

"Father . . ." he said, rising slowly to his feet.

Petiron blinked and looked at his son as if he shouldn't be there. "You must leave. She was all I ever had. I must be alone with her in my grief."

"I grieve, too. She was my mother."

"How can you possibly know *my* pain?" The older man clutched at his chest, fingers digging into fabric and flesh.

Robinton almost laughed. He heard an inarticulate sound come from Ginia and held up his hand to answer for himself.

"How could I possibly know, Petiron? How can you say *that* to *me*? I know far too well how you must feel right now."

Petiron's eyes widened and he stared at his son, remembering. Then his sobbing renewed, his spirit so devastated by Merelan's death that Robinton, moving without thought, came around the bed and took his father in his arms to comfort him.

Petiron never wrote another note of music. Merelan had been his inspiration. Her death altered him as she could have wished he had altered during her lifetime. He and Robinton never became friends, but Petiron became easier in his son's company. Master Gennell remarked on how much grief had mellowed the man. The apprentices and journeymen studying composition might not have agreed, for he was as difficult as ever to satisfy, but none of them could fault the depth and knowledge he was able to drill into their heads.

Robinton was resident in the Hall when Betrice died of a sudden failure of her heart. So he was able to help Master Gennell deal with that loss. The entire Hall felt it, from the youngest apprentice to Petiron; and Halanna, now a sedate and plumply happy spouse and mother, put in an unexpected appearance.

"I owe that woman a great deal," she said. "Almost as much as I owed your mother, Journeyman Robinton." She gave him an odd glance out of the corner of her eye. "In spite of what a nasty child I was then, it was those two who finally stuffed some sense in my conceited head. May I sing for her, with you? And for Merelan? I've always kept my voice going, you know."

"I didn't know, but I'm glad you have. My mother would be pleased," Robinton replied and he meant it.

So Halanna sang the music Petiron chose for the occasion,

and her voice was warmer and more expressive than it had ever been while she had trained at the Harper Hall. In fact, it was such a fine voice that Master Gennell, once he had dried his eyes, wistfully commented that it was a shame there were so few women training at the Harper Hall these days.

"Can't you find us some, Robinton, in your travels?" Master Gennell asked. "To be sure, your mother was unusually dedicated, but here's Halanna, still singing, and I understand that Maizella does, too. Find me some new females, will you?"

"You may be sure I'll look," Robinton replied fervently. Anything to bring back the twinkle in his Master's eyes.

And he did look, listening to many hopeful girls as well as boys and trying to interest the better voices in coming to the Harper Hall to be trained.

Robinton attained his Mastery the following Turn and continued to be sent by Master Gennell to handle difficult holders or substitute for ailing harpers or to attend Gathers in distant holds. He was also requested as an arbiter in Hold and Hall. When he could, he drummed to Benden Weyr and asked for F'lon's assistance—and listened to the dragonrider talking about his son, Fallarnon, who was being fostered by Manora, the dignified weyrgirl Robinton had noticed when S'loner and Maidir had died. It was no surprise to Robinton to learn that, three Turns after Fallarnon's birth, she gave F'lon a second son: Famanoran.

F'lon had two worries. The first, and more important, was that the lazy Nemorth would never get off her couch in the queen's weyr for another mating flight, so he could become Weyrleader in place of the four-man leadership of C'vrel, C'rob, M'ridin, and M'odon. The second was that no one would take him seriously about the threat posed by the "upstart Lord Holder Fax."

Jora seemed to favor C'vrel, which further infuriated F'lon.

"Ever since S'loner took Lord Maidir *between*, C'vrel's

been afraid to 'annoy' the Lord Holders. I can understand him treading quietly around Raid—and there's another hide-bound idiot . . ." He glared at Robinton when the Harper made a mild protest. "Well, he is. Does everything the way his father did— only Maidir was not only far more tolerant but also fairer-minded. He does send a scrupulous tithe to the Weyr for which we are all grateful." F'lon grimaced. "I hate being beholden to the man!"

"It is his duty," Robinton said mildly.

F'lon scowled. "Well, we'll teach him his duty when I've flown Nemorth." Now his grimace was darker. "I dread it, I do, Rob. Jora's a fat slug. We oversee what Nemorth eats so she'll be able to climb to a decent height for her flight . . . but she has to be bullied into the air. Jora!" He raised his hands skyward in disgust and frustration. "Imagine having a Weyr-woman who's afraid of heights!"

"I've often wondered how that happened," Robinton murmured.

F'lon snorted. "My father fancied her of the other candidates. There were only four, so low has the Weyr sunk in the estimation of the people of Pern it is pledged to protect."

That made Robinton sit up. "The Red Star's returning . . ."

"No." F'lon pushed that notion away with one hand. "Not yet. For which I am grateful. Not for another three decades, by my reckoning."

"You'll be an old rider by then."

"I'll have two sons to take over for me, should I happen to fail . . ." F'lon showed his white teeth in a challenging grin. Then his expression turned grim again. "They'll know what the Weyr stands for. They'll know—from me—" he declared, prodding his chest, "what dragonriders are meant to do."

"What's the latest on Fax?" Robinton would never dignify the man with his assumed title. As it was, there never had been a Council of Lord Holders, Craftmasters, and the Weyr to con-firm his Holding at High Reaches, usurping Bargen, the old Lord Holder's oldest surviving son—if he still lived.

"Oh, he's busy." F'lon's grin turned wickedly malicious. "Still can't get any male issue, and he's plowing any pretty girl he can find. Isn't safe to be female in High Reaches any longer. And his dueling? Ha!" He raised both hands again. "He's got a grand way to rid himself of any who'd oppose him. He insults a man to the point of a fight. And he always wins. Then he puts in those oafs and dimwits of his in any prosperous hold . . . and continues to encroach whenever he can."

"I'd heard." Reports of Nip's forays kept Robinton as up to date as possible.

"What had you heard, Rob?" F'lon asked.

"I know he's nibbling away on the borders of Crom and Nabol. He daren't try his tricks in Tillek or Telgar. Both Melongel and Tarathel have mounted border guards with hill beacons to spread an alarm."

"Good, good," F'lon said, nodding approval. "But tell me when the rest of our languid Lords are going to take action *against* him. They're going to have to, you know."

Robinton had had arguments with both Lord Grogellan of Fort and Lord Ashmichel of Ruatha. Groghe, fortunately, was more concerned than his father was. The Ruathan heir, Kale, had not been present when Robinton had sounded Ashmichel out. That Lord Holder had discounted Robinton's apprehensions, which worried Robinton still more, since Ruatha not only bordered Nabol but also was one of the most prosperous Holds, due to the fine runnerbeasts it bred. They would be a fine prize for Fax—when he turned his covetous eyes to the grasslands of Telgar and Keroon. "It's foreign to the nature of Lord Holders to distrust one of their number," Robinton said flatly.

"But not to ignore what they don't wish to admit."

"True. I'm doing my best to worry them."

"Did you know that he's espoused a Ruathan Blood?"

"No, I didn't." Robinton leaned forward intently. "Who?"

"Gemma." And when Robinton frowned, unable to place her, F'lon identified her: "She may be only a third cousin, but she's got Ruathan blood if Fax wanted to use that as a pretext to Hold there. A comedown from being nephew or espousing a daughter."

"How many *has* he espoused now?" Robinton demanded.

"As many as he now has holdings, I suspect," F'lon said, and added, with a lascivious leer, "the man's insatiable, and not just for land."

"Surely there's a limit . . ."

"Let us hope so," F'lon said.

The Turn after the birth of Famanoran, Nemorth rose in a mating flight and it was Simanith who flew her. F'lon became Weyrleader at last. M'odon, the oldest of his riders, died quietly in his sleep. This, too, was a bitter winter. Twenty-four dragonriders fell ill of a fever, and the Weyr echoed with the sounds of keening dragons. Nemorth produced nineteen dragons in her second clutch—not enough to make up the losses.

The dissatisfaction with the Harper Hall was insidiously spreading. There had been several cases of harpers being waylaid on their routes and beaten. The worst incident occurred in Crom. The young tenor, Evenek, had been specifically employed by the Lord Holder, Lesselden, to entertain. Evenek had had to audition for Lesselden and his Lady, Relna, who wished to have someone who could instruct instrumentalists to accompany her and to help put on the little evening plays she was fond of writing. Evenek sent a runner message back that he had accepted the position since Lady Relna had a good voice and was pleasant enough, and Evenek felt confident he could satisfy her requirement to train players. He added that he felt that he would stick to the music and the musical training, since Lord Lesselden had made it quite clear that the contract did not require him to teach the "usual harper nonsense." Master Gennell had mentioned some concern for Evenek, but he and the other Masters agreed that the tenor would be clever enough to manage—especially since the terms of the contract had been so specific.

Then a runner—not Nip this time—came directly to Master Gennell, not even stopping at the Fort Runner Station as the messengers usually did. Immediately Master Gennell called Robinton.

"Evenek's been severely beaten and thrown out of the Hold. In fact, if a runner hadn't found him, he'd probably be dead by now. Go get a healer and pick five of the biggest, strongest apprentices to go with you. The runners got him over the Crom border into Nabol to Station 193. D'you know its location?"

Robinton did, since he had often studied the disposition of Runner Stations. He gathered up the group, including the sturdiest healer of the journeymen presently in the Healer Hall, and mounted them on the best of the runnerbeasts available. They made it to the Station quickly, riding hard and changing mounts at Ruatha.

Evenek had been very kindly attended by the Station Master, who had brought in the nearest healer he could reach.

"I've done what I can." Germathen, the healer, shook his head, clearly distressed by the incident. "They broke every bone in his hands. They also mangled his throat so badly I'd be surprised if he ever sings again."

"Does he know who did it?" Robinton demanded, once he had calmed down the vengeful mutterings of his companions: hard to do with rage consuming him, but he knew that retaliation—however satisfying that would be—would achieve nothing helpful to the Harper Hall.

Germathen shrugged. "I think he does, but he won't say—and talking is painful enough for him. I've set all the bones I could, but I'd wish for someone more adept than I to check my settings."

"Can he travel?"

Robinton noticed the Station Master's interest in the answer.

"If you take it by slow stages," Germathen replied. "In fact, I think Evenek will not feel safe until he is back in the Harper Hall."

"If any of us are safe there . . ." one of the apprentices muttered.

"Fort and Ruatha would protect the Harper Hall to the last man," Robinton said firmly. "May I see Ev now?"

The wounded man had been installed in the last, and safest, of the connecting dormitory rooms in the Station. Three older runners were seated outside his door, while the Station Master's spouse sat inside, mending quietly. She rose, one hand reaching for a stout cudgel, when the harpers entered.

Evenek was asleep, his hands swathed in bulky bandages and cushioned by pillows. His face was a mass of bruises, and his neck was covered in bandages as far down as his chest. Robinton was sick to his stomach, and one of the other harpers abruptly retreated from the room. As Robinton stood there, a bitterness welled up in him, of a strength he had not imagined himself capable of feeling—far deeper and more primitive even than that which had assailed him after Kasia's death. He thought, briefly, of asking for F'lon's help to transport Evenek, but with such injuries the cold of *between* was inadvisable.

The joy and relief in Evenek's eyes, his broken attempts to thank them, had an even more profound effect on those who had come to his aid. He managed to indicate that he would endure any discomfort that traveling might cause him.

"Home . . . the Hall . . ." he kept repeating.

Germathen and the Journeyman Healer had a quiet professional discussion and told Robinton that they could start back the next morning. If those in the Runner Station looked relieved, they had succored Evenek when he had most needed their help and Robinton assured them that the Harper Hall stood in their debt.

"To do that to a harper, Robinton, is something I never thought to see," the Station Master said, shaking his head. "I don't know what the world is coming to, I don't."

After dinner, the harpers—quietly—entertained those at the Station.

They brought Evenek safely back to the Harper Hall, where his condition reduced Master Gennell to tears. Later Master-Healer Ginia and her assistant, Oldive, having had a chance to assess his injuries, announced that while they thought they could give him back the use of his hands, he might not be as adept on some instruments as before. About his voice, they could not yet give any reassurance: the trachea had been badly damaged.

It was some time before the shock of Evenek's injuries was absorbed by the Hall. But Lord Grogellan, with his sons, made a formal visit to Master Gennell, assuring the Harper Hall of its firm and unequivocal support, and protection, of the Hall and any harpers wherever they might need assistance.

While such brutality seemed to be an isolated incident, harpers everywhere were warned to be on their guard and to travel with traders or other known-to-be-friendly groups.

Master Gennell, who suffered badly now from joint-ail, began to send Robinton as his representative—and as another set of "eyes and ears." This morning, when Gennell sent an apprentice to ask Robinton to join him in his office, Robinton registered a mild and humorous complaint.

"So where can you send me this time, Master? I do believe that I've met every Lord Holder and most of the minor ones, and been in every Crafthold on the continent. What place can I have missed on my travels for you?"

"I've had a purpose in sending you here and there, to every major Hold and Hall on Pern."

"Really!" With great difficulty, Robinton kept curiosity out of his response. But it was hard.

"Yes, I'm growing old, Rob, and I've to look for a replacement. Of course all the Master Harpers vote as their conscience dictates, but I've made my wish clear. You!"

Robinton stared at his old friend. He hadn't expected that. "You'll be around a long time yet, Gennell," he said with a laugh that died when he saw the expression on Gennell's face.

"No, I think not," the MasterHarper said. "What with this joint-ail and no Betrice to fuss"—Gennell smiled fondly at the thought of his spouse—"the heart's gone out of me. I may call for the election and spend my remaining time on a warm beach in Ista."

"Now, wait a minute, Gennell, I'm much too young . . ."

"The Hall *must* have someone young and vigorous as Master-Harper, Rob." Gennell's manner turned resolute, as well as anxious. "Now more than ever before. I can't leave the Crafthall without someone who appreciates the threat Fax poses the entire world. I must know that other holds will not suffer the same future that High Reaches and now Crom are facing: illiteracy and oppression." He heaved himself to his feet in his restlessness and began to pace the floor. Watching intently, Robinton could see clearly how age and infirmity were hampering the once brisk and energetic MasterHarper. "And someone," Gennell continued, pointing a gnarled forefinger at the seated harper, "who believes, as I do, that Thread will return to menace the land." He wearily brushed back thinning hair. "I don't know what the Weyr is going to do, but it is our beholden duty as harpers to support Benden in any way we can. Your going there as a child, and as a journeyman, has given you an admirable contact in F'lon. He's making himself a shade unpopular with some of the Lord Holders. If you could give him some advice . . ."

"Which F'lon's not likely to take from anyone. Including me," Robinton said sourly.

"I think you underestimate your influence on him, Rob," Gennell said and sank heavily again into his chair, grimacing at the pain. "And I think you've more influence throughout the land now than you may realize. Are you still able to talk to dragons?"

Robinton nodded. "Simanith, at any rate. I suspect that's only because of F'lon. Not that our conversations are anything to write ballads about."

Gennell waggled a finger at him. "It's more than most non-weyrfolk ever have."

"That's true enough."

Gennell smiled briefly. "Nip reports that of all the harpers, you're one that even the Hall's worst critics will accept."

"Except in the High Reaches."

"Fax will overstep himself. That sort of man always does. There've been others like him before. There will be more like him in the future. When we live by the Charter, everyone prospers. When it is abrogated, the whole continent suffers."

Robinton nodded in complete agreement, though the prospect of trying to ensure that the Charter was obeyed was daunting. Especially in the face of Fax's active aggression.

"So, Master Robinton, I have named you my choice of successor."

Robinton demurred, muttering about his youth and the fact that there were plenty of men who would be more logical choices.

"None of them want the job," Gennell said with grim humor. "Minnarden strongly urged me to consider you, as did Evarel, and certainly I've had support from all the resident Masters."

"Including . . . Petiron?" Robinton asked, grinning.

"Oddly enough, yes. Oh, I doubt he would have suggested you, but he did not oppose the selection."

That did surprise Robinton.

"I admit that I got the position more by default than ambition," Gennell said with a hearty chuckle. "I have served the Hall to the best of my ability . . ." Robinton concurred: Gennell was exceedingly popular as MasterHarper. The old Master went on. "I shouldn't care to take on the responsibilities of dealing with Fax, much less Thread."

"You're too kind," Robinton murmured sarcastically.

"I've had you marked as my successor from the moment I saw you talking to the dragons. Do you remember that day?"

Robinton nodded. That had been one of the high points of his childhood. Once F'lon had mentioned that dragons were whimsical about talking to non-weyrfolk. Sometimes they would. More often they would not. F'lon had added with one of his mischievous smiles, "The dragons do like you, Rob." But Robinton had thought that was a secret between himself, the dragons, and their riders. "I didn't realize that anyone was watching."

Gennell grinned. "I've watched you from the moment your mother told me you were piping variations on a theme."

"Have I ever thanked you, Gennell, for all you've done for me?" There was no sarcasm in Robinton's voice now.

"Pssst." Gennell dismissed the matter with a flick of his fingers. "I was your MasterHarper then, as I am now. Be a good Master to all within this Hall and I am doubly repaid. Do not let a tyrant like Fax still the voices of any more harpers."

To that Robinton swore purpose and loyalty.

"Did you hear the drum message this morning?" Gennell asked in a complete change of subject.

"Yes." Robinton smiled. "A new baby at Ruatha Hold. A girl, small but healthy."

Two days later both Robinton and Gennell were called to Fort Hold. Lord Grogellan had refused the advice of MasterHealer Ginia, her very capable young Journeyman Oldive, and the Hold's Healer. He would not allow them to attempt surgery.

"Talk some sense into him, can you, Gennell?" Ginia said, her face red with frustration. "I've done this operation—so has Oldive—and it takes but minutes. If we can't remove the inflamed appendix, he will die from a poisoning of his system."

"You can't cut into him," Lady Winalla said, weeping. "You can't. That's barbaric."

Ginia shook her head. "It is not. It's as simple as removing infected tonsils from a throat, and you permitted me to do that for your children."

"Lord Grogellan will not have his body violated, mutilated . . ." Lady Winalla shuddered with repugnance, her expression stubborn. "His person cannot be carved like an animal!"

"Mother, if it's a question of his life . . ." Groghe said, trying to reason with his parent. "I saw it done at Tillek, didn't I, Rob?"

Robinton nodded. "Clostan performed it on a seaman taken with terrible belly pain. He was back on his ship the next week."

Lady Winalla kept shaking her head, her lips pressed together.

"We will not permit it," she repeated, pressing her handkerchief to her lips as she opened the door to her spouse's room. Grogellan's moans could be heard. "Oh, he must be in such pain, Ginia. More fellis, please. How can you let him suffer so?"

"He wouldn't if he would permit me to—"

"No, no, never. How can you even suggest such a thing?"

"He didn't object when I sewed up that shin wound . . . it's much the same thing," Ginia said urgently.

"But that was a natural wound," Lady Winalla protested. "Oh, listen to him. Surely you can give him more fellis."

"Yes, I can give him more fellis," Ginia said through gritted teeth. "I can fellis him right into death!"

"Oh, no, don't say that, Ginia. Please don't say he'll die."

"I can't say anything else and be honest, Winalla. If I do not operate . . ."

Winalla clamped her hands to her ears and, with a little shriek of protest, half-ran to her spouse, where he twisted and writhed in bed.

He died later that day, in a terrible agony that not even the massive doses of fellis or the application of numbweed on his abdomen could dull.

"No violation, no mutilation, just death," Ginia murmured as she wearily stumbled away from the tragedy. "Once we knew so much more . . ." She shook a bit and leaned on Oldive.

So the Telgar Gather was cancelled and, instead, the Lord Holders came to Fort Hold to confirm Groghe as the new Lord Holder. Fax was conspicuous by his absence.

"But then, he wasn't invited," Gennell said grimly, "because he has not followed the established procedure of taking formal Hold."

"I doubt that bothers him," Robinton remarked. "I wish I knew what he had planned at Telgar."

That question was answered, in part or in whole, when the

Lady Relna of Crom and her two youngest children begged sanctuary from Lord Ashmichel and Lady Adessa at Ruatha Hold. Neither her spouse nor their two oldest boys had survived Fax's forcible entry into their Hold.

Groghe began to drill every man in Fort between the ages of sixteen and fifty. Tarathel and Melongel grimly followed his example and doubled their border patrols.

The following winter, another bitterly cold one, Master-Harper Gennell died of a failing heart. Ogolly, Washell, and Gorazde, frail though he was, drummed messages about the country. They had known that Master Robinton was the named successor, but it would be spring before the requisite number of masters could return to the Hall for a formal election. No one wished the Harper Hall to be leaderless at such a time. Robinton could hear the messages coming in and going out. He found that their import was muffled down in the kitchen of the Harper Hall. There Silvina, Lorra's capable daughter, kept him company and poured out the numerous cups of klah he drank during the long wait.

Her mother had retired to her family home in South Boll three Turns before and Silvina, as dark-haired and energetic as her mother had been, was headwoman in the Hall. Robinton liked her matter-of-fact attitude toward the duties and the disasters of the Hall—and the fact that she had been quite willing to bed him whenever he stopped long enough at the Hall to renew their friendship. She had more sense than to mention any sadness in his eyes, though he knew the memory of Kasia had not dimmed in the ten Turns since her death. Vina accepted him as he was and made no demands, and gave him considerable relief and kindness. He was grateful, and that seemed to be enough for her. She was as bighearted as her mother had been.

"The drums have stopped," she said suddenly, about to pour him yet another cup of klah.

"So they have," he said, realizing that he could no longer feel the vibrations through the stone walls of the Hall. He swallowed and she grinned at his discomfort.

"You could have stayed above and kept count."

"What if—" He stopped at the sound of footsteps on the stairs. Two people, at least, were approaching.

Silvina reached a hand out and gripped his.

A grinning Ogolly and Jerint appeared, a sheaf of small square hides in hand.

"Master Robinton, would you be willing to assume the responsibilities of the Master of the Hall and Craft?" Ogolly asked formally, his tone belied by his wide grin and happy eyes.

"I would be willing," Robinton said though his throat had gone dry.

"It is the *unanimous*—" Jerint paused to be sure Robinton appreciated that. "—decision of all the Masters of this Craft that you accept this position and all its honors, privileges, prerogatives and . . . all that hard work!" He stepped forward, gripping Robinton's hand in his and shaking it hard. "I bless the Egg that it's you, Rob!"

"Who else?" Ogolly demanded, taking his turn to pump the hand of the newly appointed MasterHarper of the Craft. "Who else, dear boy? Who else? Merelan would be so—" Ogolly's eyes teared up and his voice cracked, but he went on. "—so very, very proud of you right now."

Robinton, gripping Ogolly's hand, felt his throat close in response to the mention of his beloved mother. "She would, she would."

"She always said you would be Master," Silvina said. She threw her arms about Robinton's neck to kiss him soundly. "Mother'll be so happy, Rob. So happy. The day you were born she said she knew you were destined for great things."

"Petiron helped take the count, Rob," Jerint put in, and there was a wicked sparkle in his eyes.

"He's proud of you, too, Robinton . . ." Ogolly said quite solemnly. "Really, he is."

Robinton only nodded. Silvina, busy at one of the cupboards, produced glasses and a wineskin, which she held out to Robinton so he could see the label.

"Benden?" he exclaimed.

"Gennell ordered in a supply just for today!" she said. "I've kept it safe," she added, casting a reproving glare at Jerint, "so open this skin. There'll be enough to get every last one of you legless tonight."

Robinton was still hungover the next morning when he entered the office of the MasterHarper. He stopped when he saw there was someone waiting: Petiron. His father had not been backward in toasting and drinking the health of the new Master-Harper the previous night, a fact of which Robinton had taken wary note.

"As one of your first duties as MasterHarper, Robinton, I wish you will assign me to a post," his father said in a stiff and formal tone. "I think you will do well in this office. I wish you the best, but I feel that my presence here in the Hall might cause you embarrassment . . ."

"Really . . . Father . . ." Robinton mentally berated himself that the unused title came out so awkwardly.

Petiron gave a little smile, as if that hesitation was proof enough of his contention. "I think it would be easier for you to assume your responsibilities without . . . feeling . . . well, that I might not agree."

Robinton caught his father's eyes and slowly nodded. "That is considerate, most considerate, but hardly necessary . . ."

"I insist," Petiron said, raising his chin in a stubborn pose his son knew all too well.

"There aren't any major Holds . . ."

"I would prefer a minor one—"

"You are a master and as such deserve—"

"What I ask for."

"But you have that fine new apprentice—Domick? I thought you were very pleased with his progress."

Petiron gave a snort and dismissed the matter with a wave of his hand. "That young man thinks he knows everything. You can have the pleasure of dealing with him."

Robinton managed not to grin. He had heard about the fine rows his father had with Domick, arguing chromatic variations, and he rather thought Petiron might have met his match.

"I just thought that—" he tried again.

"Well, you thought wrong. What contracts are available?" And Petiron held out his hand, all but snapping his fingers at his son to speed him up.

Robinton stepped around to the front of the desk where messages were piled in order and by subject. For the last few weeks of his life, Gennell had kept Robinton up-to-date on all Hall matters, so he knew which pile contained the requests for harpers. He picked it up and handed it to Petiron.

"See if one of these suits," he said, acquiescing to the inevitable. In a way, he was relieved. He *would* indeed feel a slight inhibition that his father might question some of the decisions he would have to make. Especially as Petiron had widely opposite notions about the imminence of Threadfall and what fourth-year composition apprentices *had* to learn even if they were unlikely ever to have to teach theory and composition. It would be easier if Petiron were not here.

"I have made it quite clear to my peers that this is my choice, Robinton, and none of your doing," Petiron said, picking out one message and handing it to his son. "This one will suit me."

Robinton looked at it and blinked. "Half-Circle Seahold? Father, you can't. It's the back end of nowhere. I've been there. The only ways in are by sea or dragonback."

"Still, it is right on Nerat Bay, and any halfway decent captain can get me there. They haven't had a harper in six Turns. There'll be a lot of work to remedy *that* sort of neglect. You are so determined that everyone shall know the Teaching Ballads: here's a challenge for me."

"But there are holds in Keroon, and that one on the Telgar river . . ."

"I have chosen Half-Circle Seahold. Do not deny me, Robinton."

"Please consider another," Robinton insisted, worried about the degree of isolation afforded by Half-Circle Seahold.

"I have chosen, MasterHarper." With that, Petiron made a formal bow and left the office.

"By the Egg!" Robinton flopped down into the comfortable chair that Gennell had occupied and wondered if he would ever fit in it as well as the dear old man had hoped. He had already made—or had made for him—his first official decision. He devoutly hoped it was the right one.

Chapter 16

M any of Robinton's duties that Turn were simply to keep the ordinary daily doings of the Harper Hall going smoothly, accepting new apprentices, conferring journeyman status on those qualifying, and confirming one Master: Jerint, who took over from the frail Gorazde.

F'lon was ecstatic with his friend's rise to the MasterHarpership and would come at the roll of a drum message to take him to any Hold or Hall that required the presence of the Master-Harper. Robinton often availed himself of that courtesy since, in his role as mediator, he did a great deal of traveling. Too, there was always the hope that he'd find a new candidate for the Harper Hall, recommended by the youngster's harper. But only one girl singer was brought to his attention and her parents felt she was too young, yet, to be away from home. She was sixteen, with a sweet voice he felt could be trained up, but she also had a young lad from the next hold whom she was keen to espouse. Singing was second best.

Then there were his necessary appearances at Gathers and the once-a-Turn conclave to which Fax was never invited and where his name was never mentioned, even when Robinton,

Melongel, or Tarathel tried to initiate a discussion about the man's totally illegal usurption of power.

"Why do you fuss so?" the grumpy aged Lord Holder of Igen demanded. His face was a sea of lines, engraved by squinting all his life at the hot sun over his Hold. "Fax is, I do believe, a nephew of old Faroguy and if his sons—"

"Farovene was killed."

"Yes, yes, so everyone says, but Fax is of the Hold's Bloodline, and if the other one, whatever his name was . . ."

"Is," Robinton said firmly, "Bargen . . ."

"Bargen, then, can't stomach a challenge duel, eh? Then he isn't the sort of Lord his holders will follow, is he?" And when Melongel started to protest, Tesner of Igen interrupted him. "Ever think that Faroguy *wanted* a stronger man in his Hold? Huh? Ever think Fax might have been *told* by Faroguy to take Hold?"

No one had an answer for that, even Robinton, though he tried desperately to think of a diplomatic way of expressing his deep and instinctive distrust and anxiety over Fax's aggressiveness. There had been that time, close to Robinton's espousal to Kasia, when Melongel had wondered if the drum messages, purported to be sent by Faroguy, had really originated with the old Lord. Robinton did keep F'lon from speaking in his blunt way lest the Weyrleader antagonize the Lord Holders further.

"Why'd you do that?" F'lon growled at Robinton. "At least we had them *on* the subject."

"There's an old maxim: 'A man convinced against his will, is of his own opinion still.'" Robinton sighed, shaking his head. "We'll have to wait until Fax moves again."

"Or the next Pass starts!" F'lon said bitterly. "Then it'll be too late!"

"Or just right," Robinton added, as he imagined the chaos and backtracking that the return of Thread would cause among those indolent and incredulous Holders and Masters.

T oward the end of the next spring, Nip brought new reports on Fax' activities.

"Man's taken over another hold," he said, slipping into Robinton's room late one night, wearing runner's shorts. He was barefooted, carrying spiked running shoes in one hand. "It's late, I know, but your glows guided my steps to your door again," he added with a grin as he stopped by the chest where Robinton stored wineskins and glasses. The running shoes clattered to the floor.

"Which one?" Robinton asked, gesturing to indicate that he'd need a drink, too, to help swallow the news.

"Not a big one," Nip said. "Not greedy is our self-styled Lord of Three Holds. Just a prosperous one. And he plays no favorites . . ."

Robinton said nothing, letting Nip vent his fury.

"Just ventures a *little* ways into Tillek to nobble Radharc."

"It's not like Melongel to allow him to get away with that."

"Ah . . ." Nip held up a forefinger. "You hadn't heard that Melongel's ill?"

Robinton sat up. "No, I hadn't."

"Had a fall off a runner-beast."

"Melongel's a good rider . . ."

Nip's smile was grim. "So he is, but not when the animal is fed something that sends it into convulsions and pins the rider under him in its death throes."

"How could Fax . . ."

"Who knows, but Melongel is lucky to be still alive."

"Clostan's a very good healer."

Nip nodded. "He is, but he's worried. Almost every bone in Melongel's body was broken. He may never walk again."

Robinton's fist hit the table. "How could—"

Nip was rubbing his finger and thumb together, a very cynical expression on his face. "Fax buys loyalty and service—with the added incentive of fear. Who knows how he managed it. But I'd say he did. Which means there'll be no opposition from that quarter. Oterel's a good lad, but who would expect him to have to deal with this sort of crisis so early in his Holding?"

"How is Juvana?" Robinton owed her for her support when Kasia had died.

"Working as hard as Clostan to save her spouse. They may bring it off yet."

"Is it just your suspicion that Fax was behind the . . . accident?"

Nip laughed. "Who else? It is so timely. Fax espouses the recently"—and he gave another false smile—"orphaned eldest daughter of the deceased holder on Tillek lands—no mention, of course, of any male siblings or relatives."

Robinton thumped the table again in frustration. "Can't something be done?"

"Off-hand, since no one will give us a hand, no," Nip said pragmatically. "That man's determined to own the entire west coast. Slowly, by inches, he moves into an area, eliminating"—Nip drew a finger across his throat—"any opposition. He's got many spouses now, more than a sane man would wish. Doesn't the Charter restrict how many a man can have?"

"No," Robinton replied thoughtfully, pinching at his upper lip. "Actually it doesn't deal with personal relationships at all—at least the usual variety, though it is specific in the *violations*—" Robinton paused. "—such as rape or other unwanted acts."

"Damned Charter was written by idealists."

"Quite likely, but the Charter does work for the majority."

Nip grimaced. "It's the minority, the damaged and oppressed minority in Fax's general area, we're talking about."

Robinton shook his head. "I've done all I can with the Lord Holders."

Nip leaned across the table, the expression in his eyes anxious and intent. "You're the one good with words, Harper. Find some stronger ones before it's too late?"

Robinton nodded though both he and Nip understood the reluctance of any of the Lord Holders to act—singly or together. What would it take to *force* them out of their comfortable—and, they hoped, impregnable—Holds to act? He shuddered. Fax had already committed many offences against the peace of Pern. He shook his head, unable to contemplate the kind of disaster needed. F'lon? . . . no, Fax would enjoy taking him on but Pern needed the Weyrleader's strength and belief as much as Gennell had needed Robinton's in the position of Master-Harper.

"I'll keep my eyes peeled and my ears open," Nip told Robinton, draining the last of his wine and setting it down. "I'll borrow your spare room . . . since you're all alone tonight?"

Robinton chose to ignore the cocky grin and knowing eyes of his roving harper, but he wasn't at all surprised that Nip knew that he and Silvina often spent nights together.

"Are you officially running, Nip?" he called out, sitting down. He would write Juvana a letter. The MasterHarper was at her disposal, if his presence would help.

"Aye, I'll see the letter into Juvana's hands," Nip said, leaning back into the room, one hand on the door jamb. "She'll like to hear from you."

Not much escaped Nip at all.

Not much seemed to be escaping Fax's greed either, Robinton thought. And, though he heard that Tarathel had sent protests to Fax over the minor holdings that had come so fortuitously under Fax's control, that was the end of the matter.

Except that it wasn't. Before Turn's End, Melongel succumbed to one of the fevers so prevalent in the winters at Tillek Hold.

Robinton immediately sent for F'lon and the two went to Tillek Hold to comfort Juvana. The visit was hard for Robinton, since Kasia's spirit was still vivid in his mind in this place, but he tried not to remember, concentrating his attention on Juvana and her grieving children.

"Did you hear that Melongel's . . . fall . . . might not have been accidental?" Groghe murmured to Robinton as they followed those carrying Melongel's body to the *Northern Maid*.

"I had. Do you concur?"

"It's all a bit too convenient, isn't it? A previously sound, sure-footed animal going into convulsions and rolling on its rider?" Groghe snorted. "Runner-beasts don't eat lur-weed, and farmers clean it out of their fields whenever it sprouts. So someone would have had to put it in the animal's manger on purpose."

Robinton nodded agreement, and then had to take his place with Minnarden on the prow of the ship to harp Melongel to his last resting place. When the last harp note was whipped by the breeze, as Melongel's body slid into the sea, he must have only *thought* he heard another harp's last dissonant strum.

He bowed his head and others respected his solitude.

During the next Turn, Robinton kept wondering what would happen next. Fax made no further obvious moves to extend his holdings. Not that Nip, or Robinton, trusted him. Oterel, confirmed at the Conclave following his father's funeral, enlarged the guard posts along his borders. That had been Nip's advice, filtered through Robinton. The MasterHarper also recommended that Oterel make as many tours of his border with the High Reaches as he could to reinforce the determination of his folk. Since most of the border holders, like Chochol, had succored refugees from Fax's initial expansion, they were only too eager to comply.

In the spring of that Turn, Silvina informed him that she was pregnant with his child.

"I will espouse you," he began.

"Oh no, you won't because I do not care to be the spouse of the MasterHarper of Pern."

"What?" Robinton tried to pull her into his arms, but she stepped back, her expression severe.

"I am . . . very fond of you, Rob. We suit each other . . . in an informal arrangement. But I will not espouse you." She shook her head for emphasis. Then, taking pity on him, she approached, putting a gentle hand on his arm. "Kasia . . . is the name you call at night . . . and she is still your spouse. I will not compete with a . . . dead woman." Then she shook herself and smiled kindly at him. "You will be a good father, Rob, and the child will lack for nothing between us."

He argued, off and on, especially when he caught her being sick in the mornings, but she was adamant. She supported her argument with instances from Betrice's life with Gennell.

"You love the Harper Hall more than you could possibly love . . . another woman. It might have been different if Kasia had lived, but I think not," Silvina said in her down-to-earth manner. "My mother loved harpers, all harpers. I think I have inherited this fatal tendency. I do care for you, Rob . . ."

"As you've often shown." He grinned affectionately at her, finally beginning to see what she meant by her insistence on independence.

"As you know, but I'd rather not be tied. I don't really think I'm cut out for sexual loyalty." She gave him a very wicked grin. "There are so many of you to love."

That he knew of no others with whom she had formed any sort of relationship was immaterial.

So he made sure everyone in the Hall and Hold knew that he acknowledged the unborn child and that Silvina had his affection and support. And, as often as he could in his myriad duties, he spent time with her.

When he told F'lon, the Weyrleader was delighted—and asked how many lullabies he had composed. Kasia was not mentioned and, for once tactful, F'lon asked if there would be an espousal, too?

"No." Robinton made a rueful face. "I asked and she refused."

F'lon regarded him for a long thoughtful moment. "I give her full marks for her wisdom. You'll make a loving father but a terrible spouse. Think of all the . . . ah . . . friendships you'd have to forgo!"

Robinton managed a creditable laugh. There was no sense in denying the fact to F'lon that Robinton was enthusiastically welcomed by many holder girls for the pleasure he gave above and beyond the music he played.

Robinton tried to stay in the Hall as much as he could toward the end of Silvina's pregnancy. The winter was a stormy one, and so there were few calls on him to mediate. He taught more classes than he had for many months and was pleased with the way the boys would work for him. The elaborate music of his father had to be put aside since there were no coloraturas available, though he managed to get Halanna to come and sing at Turn's End, reworking a ballad so he could sing with her. Once again he tried to entice her back to the Hall, even offering her a Mastery, but she turned him down.

"What? Live in this cold all the time? I think not, Rob, though it's kind of you to offer me the post and the honors."

"The Harper Hall will get the reputation that girls, and women, are not wanted here," he said, continuing his argument.

She only smiled. "If my daughter is at all musically inclined, I'll send her to you, I promise."

"Even if she isn't?" Robinton asked, pleading.

"You!" And Halanna left him with that ambiguous remark.

Silvina was delivered of a fine big boy in due course and Robinton was besotted with the infant at first sight of him. If Silvina seemed unusually subdued, he at first put it down to the rigors of the final month of pregnancy and the delivery. Then he began to realize that this infant was unusually quiet, sleeping and eating fitfully, and only occasionally wailing in a thin petulant way.

"All right, Silvina, what's wrong with him?" Robinton asked, as the baby briefly waved its fat arms and then sank into unwinking silence.

She gave a long, sad sigh. "The cord was around his neck when he was born. Ginia said he didn't get enough air to breathe normally."

Robinton stared at her, disbelief foremost even as he admitted to himself the hideous fact that this child of his was obviously not normal.

"And?" he asked quietly, slowly sinking to the nearest chair, seeing once again his pleasant dreams turning to ashes.

"He will be . . . slow," she said. "I've seen the same sort of thing before. There've been two cot babes the same way. But they are sweet. And docile."

"Sweet? And docile?"

Robinton tried hard to absorb what that would mean in terms of *his* child. He buried his head in his hands and tried not to think of what could have been. How ironic! That his first— and only—child would be sweet and docile instead of the curious, interested, clever, tall, fine straight child he had yearned for.

"Oh, Robie, you cannot know how sorry I am." Silvina's fingers twined in his hair. "Please, don't hate me. I so wanted to give you a . . . fine child."

"How can I hate you, Vina?" He glanced sideways at the baby. "Or him. I'll care for you both . . ."

"I know you will, Rob."

There was little more he could say, just then. Over the months of Camo's first Turn, he kept looking for signs that his condition might have been exaggerated and the bright intelligence that should have been his legacy might somehow blossom. He was even somewhat encouraged when Camo first smiled at him.

"He knows your voice, Rob," Silvina said sadly. "He knows you bring him something good to eat . . ." She ignored the little drum that Robinton had made with his own hands to amuse his son. The child had regarded it with the vacant eyes he turned on anything that was offered him.

"He has a very sweet smile," Robinton remarked, and then he had to leave the room.

Chapter 17

▼▼

A very weary Nip appeared late one night in the second
month of the new Turn.

"He's at it again," he said, dropping a tattered hide coat to the
floor and pouring himself a drink, he swallowed it down.

"I can get you soup," Robinton suggested when he saw how
blue Nip was about the lips. He rose from his comfortable
chair. Nip shook his head, poured himself a second glass and
came over to the fire. "What's he at?"

"His tricks," Nip said, sinking gratefully into the chair
Robinton had vacated. "How he plans his invasion of holds,
large and small."

"Really?" Robinton poured wine for himself and, hooking
his foot around a stool, slid it to the hearth and made himself
comfortable to listen. "Do tell."

"Oh, you'll get chapter and verse from me."

"If you don't fall asleep first."

"I won't. My subject matter will keep me wide awake," Nip
said bitterly. He downed the second glass of wine. "Pity to
waste it like that, Rob, I know, when it's good Benden, but it
goes to a good purpose."

"I'm listening," Robinton said patiently. He filled Nip's glass a third time. Nip sipped this one slowly.

"He visits his intended victim, all smiles and reassurances, compliments the man on his fine holding. Buys whatever the hold produces, pays over the mark for what he calls the best quality. He asks how such yields are achieved on such poor, good, medium, excellent soil . . . under such trying, hot, cold, dry conditions . . . In short."

"He makes himself a friend of the hold," Robinton said, nodding ruefully.

"Then he sends down a man to learn from the holder. Or he starts buying the produce, at higher prices, and brings others to see how well this holder is doing with his land. I mean, how can they be taken in so easily?"

"Some of those upland holds are isolated. Often they don't get to but one Gather a Turn."

"True," Nip sighed. "Now, he's very canny about how he insults the Harper Hall, especially if the hold in question has one, or is on a well-traveled route. But he is careful with his slanders." Nip pantomimed a dagger being inserted gently in and then slowly twisted. "He gives examples of Harper lies and exaggerations. So he plants the seeds of doubt. *Then* he invites the man and his family to come to *his* next Gather, and sometimes, if the gullible fool believes him, he offers to send men to tend the herdbeasts or the fields, or whatever, while the holder and his family are away."

"So that his men become familiar with the place."

"Exactly." Nip took a sip. "One man and his family never did get back from that Gather, and so Fax has acquired Keogh Hold recently."

"That makes . . ."

"Four."

"I see."

Then Robinton had caught sight of the way Nip was shivering despite the wine and the heat. "Let me take those boots off for you, Nip. They look soaked."

"You're the only man I'd allow such a privilege," the irrepressible Nip replied as he lifted his left leg and then placed his right boot on Robinton's butt. "I know many people who'd love to have the MasterHarper of Pern on the end of their boot!" he added, chuckling. He gave Rob a hefty push—all to help remove his boot, of course.

In spite of Nip's pessimistic report, Fax was quiescent again, seemingly content to ride his extended borders, *encouraging*, as Nip put it drolly, his dependents to increase their production.

Robinton could not spend all his time worrying about where Fax would go next. He had the Hall to run, with all its problems and scheduling, especially when the bias against harpers was increasing. However, when he heard that Nemorth had actually risen in a good mating flight with Simanith, Robinton sent congratulations and had a special visit from F'lon, who looked excessively pleased with himself.

"How did you manage?" Robinton asked, pouring two glasses from the Benden wineskin F'lon had brought to celebrate.

"First we starved the pair of them. I never thought a queen dragon could be so difficult. All the bronzes were needed to snatch anything she killed. She'd sneak out of the weyr at night to get something to eat."

"Who? Jora or Nemorth?"

F'lon blinked and then howled with laughter. "Actually, I meant Nemorth, but I think Jora probably had edibles secreted about the place, because we never did manage to get her down to a decent size. But Nemorth was our prime worry. Like rider like dragon can be all too true. But we succeeded in keeping her from doing more than blood the next time she turned bright gold. My, she was a nasty one in flight." F'lon shook his head from side to side, with an odd grin on his face. "Simanith proved his worth. Caught her high and did her well." Then he exhaled noisily.

Robinton was hard pressed not to laugh out loud, wondering how F'lon had managed his unwieldy mate on that occasion, but there were certain matters one did not discuss, even with such a good friend as F'lon.

ANNE MCCAFFREY

"So, she'll clutch in the winter?"

"So long as she does clutch!"

"Here's to triple her last one!"

"We'll need every one," F'lon said and downed the wine, breaking the glass in the hearth. Robinton, though he regretted losing two such fine goblets, followed suit. "I'll come for you myself when the Hatching's due. Both my sons'll stand."

Before Robinton figured that the youngest would be only ten, F'lon was out the door.

"Well, he is the Weyrleader," Robinton murmured. "And the dragons will make the right choices." He hoped.

He had another, totally unexpected visit that same sevenday, which turned out to have almost as fortuitous a result.

Silvina tapped on the door of his rooms. "You've two visitors, Rob," she said, smiling broadly as she pushed the door open wider to admit the guests.

Robinton instantly rose to his feet to greet the arrivals: a grizzled man and a very gawky shy lad whose eyes were round and so fearful that Robinton increased the warmth in his own smile. The older man pushed the lad forward with a hand that was missing two fingers. He nodded with great dignity to the MasterHarper.

"You wouldn't remember me, likely," he said, "but I've never forgotten my cousin, Merelan."

The injured hand, the deep voice, the tanned, weathered, and faintly familiar face of the man combined with the heavy boots he wore gave Robinton a clue.

"Rantou?" he exclaimed.

"Aye." A huge grin split the man's face. "Rantou from the woods. Fancy you remembering my name after all this time."

Robinton shook the offered hand vigorously and urged the two to take seats, gesturing to Silvina to bring refreshment.

"Why, it's been ... Turns!" Robinton said. "I do remember that summer, and swimming in the sea and all the cousins I didn't know I had ..."

"Heard Merelan had died a while back," Rantou said, his expression sober. "Heard her sing at South Boll Gathers now and then."

"You had a fine voice, or so she often said."

"Did she?" The old man's face lit up. The boy wriggled in his chair, uncomfortable and not certain what to do or how to act.

"She did," Robinton said warmly, turning kindly to include the boy in the conversation.

Rantou cleared his throat and sat forward on the chair. "Well, that's what I'm here for."

"Oh?"

"Yes." Rantou gripped the boy by the shoulder. "This is my grandson, Sebell. He can sing. I want him to be a harper, if he's good enough."

"Why, that's wonderful, Rantou."

"He's better off here, much better than in the woods. I never forgot your father, you know." Rantou grinned slyly. "He didn't think much of us."

"Oh, now . . ."

"Don't mix the truth up, lad—I mean, MasterHarper." Rantou suddenly realized that he had no right to reprimand such an important person.

Robinton laughed. "He hated to lose any promising musical talent."

"I want Sebell to have the chance," Rantou said. "He's smart, he already plays pipes he's made, and our old gitar. Knows all his Teaching Songs and Ballads. We don't have a regular harper down there, too small, but I've seen that Sebell learned as much as we could teach him."

Robinton turned to the very nervous boy, who jerked his chin up almost defensively at such scrutiny. He was as tanned as his grandfather, with a shock of sun-bleached hair and wide-set dark eyes that had been surreptitiously noting everything in the room, from the instruments on the walls to the musical notations on the sandtable. He was ten or eleven Turns, Robinton thought, more bone than flesh, but with the suggestion of height and strength in his frame . . . and bony wrists and ankles that protruded from pants legs that were too short.

"I started on pipes, too, you know," he said gently and pointed to them on the wall.

The boy looked surprised.

"Did you bring yours with you?" Robinton asked.

"He's never without them," his grandfather said proudly and nodded to Sebell.

The boy reached behind him and produced multiple pipes that he had tucked into his waistband, hidden from view under his shirt.

Robinton rose and got his own boyhood pipes. He grinned at Sebell as he tried to make his adult fingers fit the stops that had been made for much smaller hands. Then he did a quick scale and glanced at Sebell. The boy's grin was slightly amused as he repeated the scale, quickly and well.

"How about this one?" And Robinton essayed a more complex arpeggio.

The boy's grin broadened as he set his lips to the pipes and immediately brought forth the same run.

"Which is your favorite Teaching Ballad?" Robinton asked.

The boy began the Duty Song, which was not the simplest of the Ballads, and Robinton joined by piping a descant around the melody. Sebell's eyes twinkled at the challenge, and the two pipers ended the song with quite a flourish, for Sebell had variations of his own.

Robinton chuckled. "Can you sing it for me, too, while I accompany you?"

The boy's treble voice was not the least bit breathy, so someone had taught him a few vocal tricks. It was a good voice, too, and he had a good sense of rhythm and pitch and imbued the words with appropriate feeling. Shonagar would be overjoyed to have a new student.

"He's your kin, Rantou."

"And kin of yourself, as well, Master Robinton."

"Why so he is!" Robinton quickly suppressed a wish that this had been his son, rather than poor retarded Camo. "Why so he is," he repeated more firmly and held out his hand to the boy. "The Harper Hall will be pleased to have you join us. Very pleased."

"He won't expect any favors, kin or not."

"I do him none by giving any," Robinton said and then smiled encouragingly at Sebell.

A tap on the door and Silvina entered with a tray of refreshments, including newly baked cookies that brought an eager expression to the boy's face.

"Silvina, meet Sebell, grandson of Rantou, from my mother's hold and by way of being a relative of mine," Robinton said.

Having settled the tray on the long table, Silvina held out her hand to Sebell, who jumped to his feet and gave her a shy bow before accepting her clasp.

"A new apprentice?" she asked, smiling kindly.

"And a new treble for Shonagar to train. Pipes well, too," Robinton said with pride. He couldn't resist ruffling the lad's hair in his pleasure at his coming. "I met Rantou when I was much younger than Sebell . . ."

"You are related to MasterSinger Merelan?" Silvina asked as she poured klah and passed around the sweetener.

"We were very proud of her, we were, Silvina," Rantou replied proudly.

"We all were," Silvina said and her warm smile included the newest recruit to the Harper Hall, who grinned shyly back at her as she passed him the plate of cookies.

Sebell settled in, a quiet lad but endlessly curious about things musical. He kept appearing to ask if Robinton needed anything until everyone took for granted that he was Robinton's shadow. Sebell also began to play with Camo, trying to get him to hold a drumstick and use it properly on the little drum Robinton had made for him. Seeing the two together caused Robinton some heartache, but he could no more ask Sebell to leave his son alone than he could ignore Sebell's deft and discreet services.

"The lad's so kind to Camo," Silvina remarked one evening to him. "He's not like the other apprentices, helter-skelter and rough, and he seems so genuinely fond of Camo—" She broke off and regarded Robinton closely. "You know, you've a true son of your heart in Sebell, Rob. In fact," she added, cocking her head, "Sebell's not the only apprentice who adores you, Rob. Don't hesitate to give them the love that Camo cannot return. They deserve it, each in their own way, so you're taking nothing from Camo."

"I would I could give the child something," Robinton said wistfully.

"Oh, you do. He always smiles when he hears your voice."

On reflection he realized that Silvina's remark about concentrating on his many "sons" was sound advice. So he stopped yearning for what Camo could never do and, as his mother did, accepted the boy's cheerful smile and praised him for what progress he made: learning to walk, learning to feed himself, learning to do simple tasks for his mother—Sebell, as often as not, helping him.

Robinton had occasional visits from F'lon, especially after Nemorth deposited a very good clutch on the Hatching Ground sands. Not triple her last clutch, but a respectable twenty-four. Sometimes when he asked for conveyance a-dragonback, F'lon would send the blue rider, C'gan but Robinton was just as glad to see the young-faced Weyrsinger. C'gan's infallible good nature was a tonic in itself. In fact it was C'gan who came to collect the MasterHarper for his first official attendance at a Benden Weyr Hatching. Such an event happened all too infrequently. Harper Records spoke of many more in former times. Before the five Weyrs disappeared.

"The older lad's well-grown but, frankly, I think Manora's son's a bit young," C'gan informed the MasterHarper as they hurried to blue Tagath, waiting impatiently in the Courtyard. The blue rider had given the MasterHarper only moments to change into appropriate finery, and now he half-boosted him to Tagath's back. "But F'lon was not going to risk not having both sons dragonriders. No, he wasn't. And it's true we don't have as many clutches. Nor as many eggs in 'em as we should do. That Nemorth's too fat to fly. Up you go!"

"Good day, Tagath," Robinton said, stroking the blue shoulder as he settled himself between neck ridges. He tried to find the best place for his gitar and ended up cradling it in his arms behind C'gan.

Tagath turned his head around to look at Robinton. *Hatching is always a good day, Harper.*

"He answered me!" Robinton said, delighted. He grinned at C'gan.

"Ah, he's not much of a talker, is Tagath. Even to me. I think you surprised him, Harper. Does him good."

Robinton felt his neck snap, and on the rebound his nose connected with the tuning knobs of the gitar as Tagath made a mighty leap skyward. The power in those blue haunches was formidable. Robinton had time to finger his nose and establish that it wasn't bleeding before he heard C'gan give the command to go *between*.

Then they were hanging above Benden Weyr and Robinton caught his breath. The Bowl was alive with people streaming into the Hatching Ground and dragons weaving up to and disappearing down the upper tunnel to where they could watch Impression. Dragon eyes gleamed with the brightest of blues and greens, flashed with the yellows of excitement.

Tagath landed neatly quite close to the entrance to the Hatching Ground, deftly avoiding two groups of holders running in. A hum warned both Harper and dragonrider that the event was almost upon them.

Robinton slid down the blue's side, thanking him and C'gan, then joined those streaming in.

"Over here, Rob!" F'lon roared, vigorously beckoning the Harper to join him on the raised section of the Ground where Nemorth was hunched. "I've been waiting for you!"

Robinton could not fail to notice Jora on the other side of her queen, a large bulk in a vivid green gown that did nothing to hide her obesity or enhance what had once been a pretty face. He bowed ceremoniously to her and then to Nemorth, whose attention was on the small clutch of eggs in the center of the hot Hatching Ground. Jora gave him a nervous grin, her fat fingers making wet creases in the stuff of her gown. He always tried to be nice to her, knowing that F'lon led her a difficult time.

"I was beginning to think you might not be at the Hall," F'lon said, grabbing Robinton by the hand and shaking it so hard that Robinton exclaimed.

"I'll need it to play for you, F'lon," he said, pulling back his hand and making a show of examining it for injury.

"Yes, yes, of course, and you'll make a song for my sons' Impression?"

Robinton did not laugh at the proud and eager father. F'lon's emotions were so obvious: he was torn between the certainty that both his sons must Impress and the fear that neither would.

"Point them out to me, will you?" Rob asked. "Lads grow so fast at this time of their lives . . ."

"The two there to the left . . . See? In white of course, but Fallarnon has my hair. And Famanoran resembles his mother. You remember Manora? The one who kept her head the night S'loner died?"

"They also resemble each other," Robinton remarked, having identified the two by that, more than by F'lon's excited description. "Well-grown lads."

"Fallarnon's the taller," F'lon added nervously.

"Relax, F'lon," Robinton said. "They'll Impress."

"Are you sure?" F'lon's query was anxious.

"You're asking me?"

"Yes, I'm asking you."

He really is asking you, Simanith's voice echoed in Robinton's ears.

"Of course they will. How could they not, F'lon? Relax. Enjoy this moment."

F'lon rubbed hands nearly as nervous as Jora's. She kept peeking around her dragon's neck and *she* certainly looked agitated. Robinton felt more sympathy for the poor woman.

"Simanith says they will," Robinton added mendaciously, glancing up at the bronze who was crouched on the ledge above his queen. Simanith blinked.

"He would know, wouldn't he?" F'lon said and, at the first sharp cracking sound, took hold of Robinton's arm in a vise-like grip.

Robinton tried not to wince, highly amused by the spectacle of the usual supremely confident, proud, and aggressive Weyrleader in such a state.

"It's a bronze!" F'lon cried, his hands tightening perceptibly on Robinton's forearm.

"I'll need this to play," Robinton said again, peeling the dragonrider's fingers free.

"A bronze first is a good sign," F'lon told him urgently. "Easy!"

The little bronze shattered its shell with a second decisive blow of its nose.

"Oh, well done," F'lon cried. "Do you see that, Robinton?"

Robinton nodded, but he'd also seen the expression on Jora's flushed and frantic face. The outcome of this Impression was possibly even more important to her.

The little bronze creeled his hunger, nodding his head in a semicircle, then without another moment's hesitation he lurched directly at F'lon's two sons. Imperiously he butted the taller lad as the younger brother stepped out of the way.

"His name is Mnementh!" the boy cried exultantly, clasping the wet head to his chest.

F'lon let out a gasp that was as much a sob as a cheer. "He's done it. He's done it. He's done it!"

Robinton was now grabbed by the arms, lifted and shaken, and dropped back onto his own feet in the next instant as F'lon ran across the hot sands to assist the newly Impressed pair.

Jora gave a mewling sound and tears streamed down her face. She gave Robinton a glance both piteous and triumphant.

Three other eggs cracked and bronze dragons emerged. Robinton wondered just how good an omen for the Weyr that was. Then he paid more attention to the pairing of the lads. In their white it was difficult to know if all the candidates were weyrbred or not. Loud cheers and shrieks of delight from one group informed him that at least one new rider was hold-bred. And so were the newly Impressed blue and the three greens. A brown dragon broke his shell, and suddenly he was the only dragonet left.

He cried out, craning his neck as high as he could to see around the others. Then, with a sort of a hiccuping *yip*, he veered and stumbled toward the youngest boy on the sands: Famanoran, F'lon's second son. Famanoran had been just standing there quietly, watching, his expression blank, but once he realized that the little brown dragon was heading toward him, and him alone, he raced across the sands to meet him.

"F'lon!" Robinton shouted over the din made by new dragons and riders and pointed toward this final pairing.

F'lon swiveled about, his mouth dropping open, and he caught the moment of Impression.

"His name is Canth!" Famanoran cried, tears of joy marking his face as he patted and stroked his new friend.

"I told you so," Robinton remarked frequently to the exultant Weyrleader father that evening at the feasting. He also had a chance to speak to F'lar and F'nor, for that was how they decided to shorten their names in the dragonrider tradition.

"I don't think F'lon would have forgiven us if we hadn't Impressed," F'lar admitted to the Harper with a rueful grin.

"You had to Fall—" F'nor began, and then added loudly, "F'lar . . . It didn't matter that much about me . . ."

"Of course it did," Robinton contradicted him immediately. "Canth is rather large for a brown, isn't he?"

"Yes, he is," F'nor said with soft pride, grinning foolishly.

Robinton located Manora, already busy making sure that food was reaching the various tables and that everyone had a seat. He congratulated her and she smiled almost absently, her eyes darting from one corner of the Lower Caverns to the other, checking on servers and the served.

"Such a good day," she said with quiet satisfaction.

"You must be proud of them."

"I am," she said. With her usual understated dignity she moved off to take a seat by Jora, who had been left more or less to herself at the high table. The Weyrwoman was paying absolutely no attention to anything but clearing the food from the overflowing plate in front of her. Manora ate slowly and with relish, as dignified as she had been as a young girl.

Robinton took advantage of the fine Benden white that was being served. Lord Raid was present, as he should be for a Benden Hatching, and he was quite relaxed and pleasant to Robinton when they exchanged greetings and remarked on F'lon's double joy.

When he got back to the Hall, Nip had been there and left him a message.

"And what do you bet me that Nabol will fall to him next?"

That was one bet that Robinton would never have taken. Even a Bitran would have passed it up.

Perhaps that acquisition was another reason why Tarathel scheduled an ambitious Gather, inviting everyone, including Fax. Vendross, Tarathel's invaluable guard captain, had flushed a large group of Fax's men in the foothills of Telgar where such a party should not have been. Since he was commanding a much larger patrol, he had the advantage. Their excuse that they had had to detour from winter-damaged tracks to get back to the High Reaches was not well received by Vendross, who escorted them as fast as possible back to the main Crom road. Tarathel was determined to have a few private words with this self-styled Lord of Five Holds to ensure Fax did not try to encroach on Telgar lands. Nip was as suprised as Robinton that Fax accepted.

"As you can see, I maintain several fully trained companies of guards, Master Robinton," Tarathel told Robinton and F'lon, who had arrived early in the Gather morning. Indeed the Hold and its grounds seemed to be swarming with men in Telgar liveries.

F'lon nodded approvingly. "The man has got to be stopped, Tarathel."

The Telgar Holder scowled, unused to such familiarity from a much younger man, even if a Weyrleader was equal in rank to a Lord Holder. Robinton nudged the bronze rider in the ribs, hoping to jar him into more discretion. F'lon ignored the hint.

"And it's up to you Lord Holders to set him right. When Thread comes, he'll be unable to provide adequate help to the holds he's taken over."

Tarathel raised the black and busy eyebrows that gave him such a formidable appearance. "Really, Weyrleader? I had no idea the return was so imminent. May I ask what Benden Weyr will be able to do to provide adequate help to us?"

F'lon stiffened and Robinton kept his expression bland with an effort. As far as the MasterHarper knew, this was the first time a Lord Holder had openly challenged the Weyr. Clearly F'lon didn't like it one bit.

"Benden Weyr will be ready to meet Thread when it comes, Lord Tarathel. On that you can rely," he said with such dignity and purpose that Tarathel nodded approval.

"When it comes," he murmured as he moved off to greet the next wave of guests arriving by dragon.

"Look, F'lon, I've been your friend since we were boys," Robinton said, drawing the dragonrider to one side for privacy, "but you've as much tact as a tunnel snake. It doesn't do the Weyr, or you, any good to antagonize all the Lord Holders."

"I don't mean to, but Tarathel's as hide-bound as Raid, and that's saying a lot."

"Tarathel will be long dead before Thread comes. Were I you, I'd start right now getting young Larad on your side. Unless, of course, Fax decides to duel with him and remove competition."

"Humph!"

Robinton was relieved to note that F'lon did not dismiss that suggestion out of hand. In fact, the bronze rider made a point to seek out the lad who, like any male his age, was gratified to be in a Weyrleader's company.

What happened later that afternoon was so grotesque that afterward Robinton cursed himself, plagued with a sense of guilt that his idle remark could have such devastating consequences.

He saw the beginning: a lad wearing Fax's colors knocking into Larad, at F'lon's side, and then irritably demanding an apology.

Larad was surprised and started to comply but F'lon stopped him.

"You knocked into Larad, boy," F'lon told the lad. "*You* will apologize to young Lord Larad. He ranks you."

"I'm with Lord Fax, dragonrider." The boy's tone and sneer were contemptuous.

Robinton had not yet reached the little group when F'lon backhanded the boy, cutting his lip.

"You will keep a civil tongue in your head and you *will* apologize to Lord Larad, who is of Telgar Blood. I doubt you can claim even half-Blood rights."

"Kepiru? Who gave you a bloody lip?" And a heavyset man, also wearing Fax's colors and the shoulder knot of a captain—though generally those were reserved for ships' captains—pushed through those watching the encounter.

Robinton felt the tension in the air as he reached F'lon.

"Now, what appears to be the problem?" he said in his best conciliatory manner.

Larad gratefully turned to the MasterHarper. He was confused and highly embarrassed.

"That . . . dragonrider—" The captain's tone was as contemptuous as Kepiru's had been. "—has struck my young brother, insulting our Blood. The matter requires redress."

"Redress from your brother to Lord Larad most certainly," F'lon said, bristling.

Robinton caught F'lon by the arm, pressing it hard to cool him down. He was beginning to fear that this trivial incident had been contrived. The underfed lad looked no more like a brother to the captain than Larad did.

"That's right. I observed the whole thing as I came," the Harper said, smiling pleasantly. "An *accident*." He leaned heavily on that word, pulling at F'lon even as he felt the tension and anger building in the dragonrider's body. "This is a Gather, a meeting of folk in good faith and for pleasant purposes." He smiled winningly at the two in Fax's colors, but they were having no more of his mediation than F'lon was.

Then, to emphasize F'lon's indignation, Simanith rose from his perch on the heights and spread his wings, bugling.

"Larad requires an apology," F'lon insisted. "That lout deliberately knocked into him.'

"This *is* a Gather, F'lon," Robinton said urgently, scanning the growing crowd for anyone he could call upon for assistance. He looked beyond to see if he could spot Lord Tarathel nearby. He was relieved to catch a glimpse of Nip and jerked his head. He saw Nip raise a hand in reply and dash off. "Accidents can occur when folk are sometimes less careful in this relaxed atmosphere."

"Enough," F'lon said, shaking off Robinton's restraining hand. "It was as deliberate as the slurs on dragonriders."

"Ha! Dragon*women!*" the captain said in a scathing tone.

That insult inflamed F'lon. "I'll show you dragon*women,*" he said and drew the knife from his belt.

The captain's knife seemed to appear with uncanny speed in his hand and Robinton's fears increased. He made another attempt to gain control of the situation.

"This *is* a Gather," he repeated, stepping between the two men who had eyes for no one but each other.

"Out of the way, Harper," the captain snarled. "Your color doesn't protect you *or* him."

The crowd had backed away the moment the flash of steel was seen and formed a circle around the five. The next moment Kepiru barged out of the way and disappeared from sight.

"Move off, Robinton. This is not your fight," F'lon said, crouching as he shoved Robinton out of the way.

"Wait! The Lord Holder has been summoned!"

"Then let him watch the Weyrleader die!" the captain cried, a wild smile on his face. Crouching, he stepped sideways, not toward the dragonrider but close enough to Robinton so that when he moved, it was the MasterHarper his blade scored. Robinton clutched at his arm, blood oozing out of the long gash.

F'lon let out an inarticulate cry of rage and rushed the captain. "I'll see he regrets that, Rob!"

"Harpers, dragonwomen, much the same cowardly clutch."

"Keep your head!" Robinton called to F'lon. He was too alarmed to feel pain and was grateful when someone wrapped a kerchief around the bleeding wound.

Simanith continued to bugle, and the other dragons picked up the challenge at the top of their lungs. If this didn't bring the other riders to help, surely the calls would alert the Lord Holder and he would be able to stop the fight before more blood was shed.

Perhaps that was why the captain surged forward, determined to finish before he could be interrupted. He was fast, he was clever with the blade, and he was determined. F'lon was equally quick on his feet, but he was livid with anger at the attack on the MasterHarper.

The captain drew first blood, slicing F'lon across the midriff, through the loose shirt, causing a hiss of surprise and pain to escape F'lon's lips. At that, F'lon lost all caution, rushing in to grapple his opponent's knife hand, trying to sink his blade in wherever he could. The captain was stronger and far cooler.

F'lon was accustomed to fair fighting and opponents who would not risk the life of a dragonrider. The captain had no such inhibitions and displayed a knowledge of tricks that had probably brought him victory in other brawls. He was also heavier and, letting fly a kick that had the crowd gasping out "foul play," he unbalanced the dragonrider and flung him breathless to the dirt. Diving on the prone dragonrider, he brought his knife up under the dragonrider's guard and into his ribs.

F'lon gave one massive jerk and died.

Simanith let out a hideous shriek of anguish and pain, launching *between* before the last breath of life left his rider. Robinton was rocked to his soul by that sound and the death of his friend.

An awful silence fell over the Gather. Even those far from the scene and ignorant of what had just happened were stunned by the dragon's cry and his disappearance. Then the keening of the other dragons informed the entire Gather that a dragonrider had died.

"Seize him," Robinton said, pointing to the captain before he, too, could slip away as Kepiru had.

He knelt by F'lon, whose amber eyes were wide open in surprise, their light already fading. Robinton closed them and bowed his head, reeling emotionally and physically from the hideous end to a stupid, senseless encounter.

"I would have apologized," a small, scared voice said beside him.

Robinton lifted his head and put his hand on Larad's shoulder. "No, Larad, you were not at fault."

"But he's dead," Larad said, his voice breaking. "A dragonrider's dead!"

"What's this? What . . . Shards!" Lord Tarathel broke through the crowd and stumbled into the dusty circle. Larad ran to his father, burying his head against him and weeping.

"It was no accident, Lord Tarathel," Robinton said quietly and for the Holder's ears only. "No accident."

The captain was struggling with those who were quite glad to hold him, and less than gently. If no one had wanted to interfere in a dagger duel, no one had wanted the death of a dragonrider—nor the ear-splitting sounds of the grieving dragons.

R'gul and S'lel, with C'gan right behind them, arrived, their faces anguished. Seeing F'lon's lifeless body, R'gul's face became a study in conflicting emotions, none of which did the dragonrider any credit in Robinton's eyes. S'lel was at least honestly distressed, while unashamed tears streaked down C'gan's boyish face as he knelt, hands hovering hopelessly over his Weyrleader's body.

"I've warned him often enough," R'gul murmured, shaking his head. "He would never listen."

Disgusted, Robinton turned away, and it was then that Tarathel noticed his bloody arm.

"For that alone, that man goes to the islands," Tarathel said, his voice taut with anger. "Surely he saw your Master's knots."

"And disregarded them as easily as he ignored F'lon's rank," Robinton said, scanning the faces in the crowd. Fax should be arriving to view the result of his scheme. And that could be a second disaster. The law stated unequivocally that any man who deliberately killed a dragonrider was to be transported to one of the islands in the Eastern Sea. No trial was required if there were witnesses. Which there were. "R'gul, convey this man to the islands. Is that not correct, Lord Tarathel?"

"Yes, it most certainly is," Tarathel said. He had just listened to his son's account of what had happened. "Bronze rider, do your duty."

"But there's been no trial," R'gul protested.

"By the First Egg, R'gul," C'gan said, horrified at the hesitation. "I'll take him myself." He stepped forward to grab the captain by the arm.

"Release my captain!" cried Fax, shoving a rough path through the crowd. He caught the captain by the arm and started to pull him away from C'gan, glaring menacingly at the shorter blue

rider. C'gan had his knife drawn and, though he was much lighter than his would-be captive, his outrage provided him greater strength: he did not relinquish his grip on the murderer.

"Your captain has just killed the Weyrleader," Tarathel said, every bit as resolute as C'gan.

"Who no doubt deserved what he got," Fax said, grinning and showing his teeth, and glancing about the crowd to gauge reactions.

"You know the law regarding murder, Fax," Tarathel replied. "There is no recourse if a dragonrider has been slain. C'gan, since you have—"

"There's been no trial," Fax said.

"Since when did you reinstate trials?" Tarathel said ominously, his hand going to his knife hilt. "I am Lord Holder here. The death occurred on my lands and at my Gather. I judge *your* man guilty of unprovoked attack: first against my son, second against the MasterHarper, and finally and most outrageously against the Benden Weyrleader—an attack that ended in murder. For either of the two second counts, he merits banishment."

"I think not," Fax said. "Release him!"

Suddenly there were other men ruthlessly penetrating the crowd and stepping up to Fax, their aggression obvious in their eyes and manner. They all wore Fax's colors. Tarathel's eyes widened with fury.

"*No!*" Robinton cried, gesturing to the crowd. Fax's crew might be armed and dangerous, but there were only eight of them, while the crowd must number close to a hundred. "*Telgar! Defend your Holder!*"

With a roar of protest, Fax and his men were overwhelmed as those around them grabbed at their arms and bodies, preventing them from drawing their weapons. Even R'gul and S'lel assisted while C'gan tried to keep a firm grip on the murderer. Suddenly the blue rider cried for assistance as the man sagged and collapsed, a dagger through one eye.

And the dragons bellowed with triumph.

One look at the hilt of that slender throwing knife and

Robinton knew who had cast it. He marveled that Nip had been able to fling it so accurately through the milling crowd.

Fax and his men were hurried away to their camp, where they were made to pack up. A force of fifty willing holders and crafters assembled to escort the unwelcome guests all the way back to their borders. Lord Tarathel supplied food and runnerbeasts to those who had none.

R'gul, S'lel, and the other dragonriders took the body of their dead Weyrleader back to Benden. With a fresh wound, Robinton was prevented by the Hold Healer from accompanying his friend, but he drummed the awful message to every Hold and Hall. Only when he had completed that task could he rest.

Nip slipped into Robinton's guest room late that night, rousing the MasterHarper from a restless sleep.

"Bad wound?" Nip asked solicitously.

"Annoying," Robinton replied, pulling himself carefully up in the bed as Nip kindly stuck pillows behind him. He grimaced at the pain of resettling the arm. The Hold Healer had given him quite a lecture on the stupidity of drumming messages with an arm in that condition. It shouldn't have required stitching if it had been attended to immediately, he was told in a sour voice. So he had endured the process, well-fortified by a hefty fellis draft. "Good throw."

"You saved my knife? I'm fond of that blade. Superb balance," Nip said.

"Over there in the first drawer," Robinton said, nodding to the chest opposite the bed. "You'd no idea what Fax had planned?"

"None." Nip shook his head sadly as he retrieved his knife. "You may be sure I would have warned you had I had any idea. I've been lurking"—he grinned—"where I might overhear something of value. But going after the Weyrleader . . ." Nip paused, again shaking his head. "That was something else. I do know that Fax intended to take F'lon out as soon as he could. Tarathel just gave him the perfect opportunity, with his invitation to show off *his* guard companies. And they were taking no chances. I saw several other unlikely pairs—a lad and a bruising fighter—circulating the Gather. Wondered at such a pairing for Fax's men. My wits are slowing down, I think. And then it was too late."

"My feeling, too. Shards, they may have been planning such an assault since the last Telgar Gather was canceled when Grogellan died." Robinton sighed heavily and reached for the numbweed salve.

As he fumbled with the sling around his arm, Nip took over and, with unusually gentle fingers, daubed the sewn wound with the salve. The relief was intense.

"Didn't realize Gifflen got you."

"Gifflen?"

"That was the man's name. I'd marked him as a troublemaker. He's been thrown out of several holds and his apprentice hall for provoking fights and bullying. He's killed often. I preferred that he didn't walk away from this one."

Robinton nodded in agreement. "More would thank you if they knew. I thank you."

"Clever of you to shout like that. Stirred them all to their senses."

Robinton exhaled, remembering. "We've all become soft, you know. Letting someone else take the blame or do the disagreeable."

"That's why Fax controls as many holds as he does." Nip's tone was harsh. "Rob, you've got to shake the Lord Holders awake before he takes another one."

"I've done what I can. Groghe's training men, so is Oterel, and, after this, Tarathel will be wary."

"What about Kale at Ruatha?"

"I plan to see him on my way back."

"How soon before you could travel a-dragonback?"

"I think I've lost that privilege."

"No." Nip shook his head. "Drum C'gan. He'll come anytime. Too bad F'lon's sons aren't a little older."

Robinton frowned. "I haven't had a chance to get to know them, not as I did their father. I should go . . ."

"You should not. You should get to Ruatha Hold as fast as you can." Then Nip was on his feet and at the door. "See you. I'll be in touch."

"Nip, where . . ." But the door was already closing silently behind the man.

Despite the fellis and the numbweed, it took Robinton a long while to sleep again.

Tarathel reluctantly let him start the journey back to the Harper Hall two days later when an equally reluctant healer permitted it. The Lord Holder sent six men as escort.

"Don't be a fool, Master Robinton," Tarathel said, scowling. "The Hall may have played down the attacks made on harpers over the last few Turns, but that doesn't mean they aren't *known*. And Gifflen's attack on you was inexcusable. I've even heard that Evenek was lured to Crom, at Fax's instigation, so he could make him an example." He paused, his voice becoming more gentle. "Did Evenek ever play again?"

"He can play. He'll never sing again."

"Well, then," Tarathel said, stern again, "you'll travel back from here without incident and as I deem you should go—with an escort." He scowled. "It is bad enough that you were attacked at all. I fear a man so lost to honor as Fax has proved himself would not hesitate to attempt your life again if you were not close-guarded."

"He has scarcely had time to return to—" Robinton paused.

"I will believe anything of that man, now," Tarathel said. "You'd do well to limit your wanderings, MasterHarper, or ride with an escort."

"Limit my wanderings? That I cannot in conscience do—not now."

"Be careful then, Robinton." Tarathel pressed his hand warningly against Robinton's uninjured shoulder. "I've put one of my best runnerbeasts at your disposal."

Robinton thanked the Lord Holder . . . though he wasn't so sure how thankful he should be when he tried to mount it. Three men had to hold the black's head. Once he was in the saddle, the runner became obedient . . . at least to Robinton. No one on foot could get near enough to hand the harper his saddlebags. After that, his gear was attached to the saddle when the runner was tacked—and even that took several men.

The runnerbeast was, however, a very smooth-gaited, powerful creature with a habit of charging on ahead, so that Robinton's escort were hard put to keep up with him. Gradually, he got the trick of dealing with Big Black and they came to an understanding—largely encouraged by the sweetener which Robinton would offer the animal when he had reached the saddle unscathed. But reining him in was another story: the trip went faster than perhaps the Healer could have wished. Robinton was almost faint with relief when he saw the children playing on the front court of Ruatha Hold.

The journey was seven days of hard travel. If Robinton regretted the absence of dragon wings, he knew more now about this area than he previously had—information that might prove valuable. The way into Ruatha Hold was appallingly open. He would have to incite Lord Kale to post guards, raise beacons, and alert the outlying cots and holds, in case Fax had his eye on this prosperous Hold.

"Surely there must have been some good reason behind the captain's attack on F'lon," Lord Kale remarked to Robinton as he offered hospitality to the MasterHarper.

He was a tall, slender man with dark hair and gray eyes, but his manner was gentle and it was obvious from the affection in which his stewards held him that he was a good Holder, considerate of his people and painstaking in his dealings with them. That made for contented holders, but it was a frail weapon against a man of Fax's proven character. Robinton was more fearful than ever.

"If you'd been there, Lord Holder," said Macester, the leader of the escort, with an earnest scowl of anxiety, "you'd've known it was no accident, and we're lucky the MasterHarpcr wasn't killed, too. Gifflen was out to do as much damage as he could. And then try to snake his way out of banishment."

"Heat of the moment." Kale smiled patronizingly.

Just then a small girl, her wide gray eyes immediately establishing her as Kale's daughter, toddled up to him, holding her arms out.

"Ah, Lessa, not now, pet." But he picked her up and carried her to the door, where the attendant she had escaped appeared to take her away.

She kicked and screamed, straining backward so that Robinton saw the thin face and the immense eyes, framed by a tangle of dark curly hair.

"Spirited at just four Turns," Kale said with an indulgent smile.

"Lord Kale, as MasterHarper of Pern I implore you to follow the examples of the other Lord Holders in the west, to train men to defend this Hold. To set up a border guard with beacons to alert—"

Kale held up his hand, smiling in condescension. "My people are very busy with ordinary tasks, Master Robinton. It is spring, you know, and we've herds to manage and young animals to train to saddle."

"Did it never occur to you that your fine runnerbeasts would be invaluable to Fax when he needs to cover the plains to Telgar?" Robinton said insistently.

"Oh, come now, Master Robinton, he *buys* our runnerbeasts, and that's good for Ruatha," Kale replied with a laugh. "More klah? Surely you have time to stay the night. Ruatha Hold would be honored."

Suddenly Robinton wanted to put distance between himself and this trusting fool. He got purposefully to his feet, about to refuse, when he saw the weary look on Macester's face and the man's obvious inclination to spend a night in the comfortable surroundings of one of the major Holds.

"And we are extremely grateful for the courtesy," he said as graciously as he could.

The door to Kale's private office was still open after his daughter's entrance and the sounds of a struggle, man against a furious animal, could be heard.

"He's at it again," Macester said under his breath as both he and Robinton moved to the door. Kale, curious, followed them out to the broad outer court, where Big Black was attempting to take chunks out of the Ruathan who had hold of his reins. Robinton noted wryly that none of the escort had taken charge of the beast.

"That's a splendid animal," Kale said, pausing on the top step to take in the scene. "Circle him, Jez," he called to the handler. "One of Tarathel's mountain breeds, isn't he?"

"Yes," Robinton agreed, dispassionately watching the beast's antics. He felt for a sweetener lump in his pocket and, finding one, stepped forward, speaking in soothing tones and reaching for the reins as a very wary Jez circled.

"Easy now, there's a fine lad." His voice got through to Big Black and the animal extended his nose toward the Master-Harper, seeking the treat he expected.

"Quite a handful," Kale remarked.

"Until you're in the saddle," Robinton said, rather pleased he could say that honestly in front of a noted rider like Lord Kale.

Kale chuckled. "Now, Macester, if you'll have your men lead your mounts up to the beasthold"—he pointed up the lane to the left—"we'll see to your comfort."

"And if your healer would check Master Robinton's arm," Macester said, ignoring Robinton's protest, "I would be easier."

"Your arm?" Kale was all concern. "Surely it was only a glancing blow . . ."

"Which required seven stitches," Macester said in a growl.

So Kale hurried the Harper back into the Hold and shouted for the healer.

"I had so hoped to hear some new music this evening . . ." the Lord Holder began wistfully.

"Oh, you will, you will," Robinton said, dismissing his injury. "You've Struan here—" He grinned at the prospect of seeing his old dorm mate, now a very competent journeyman.

"And I understand Lady Adessa plays harp as well as any harper."

"But your wound . . ."

"Didn't touch my throat, Lord Kale." And mentally Robinton reviewed the sort of songs that might alter Kale's indolence. He could but try. In ordinary times—and these were definitely not—Kale would be the ideal Lord Holder, tolerant, easygoing, affable, immersed in his Hold's business and sure of its continuing prosperity.

After Robinton's wound was tended to, he climbed to the drum tower, greeted the young holder on duty there, and asked for and received permission to signal the Harper Hall of his imminent return.

The child, Lessa, appeared briefly at the beginning of the evening entertainment but fell asleep in her father's lap: Robinton was amused, since he'd been singing a rousing song that had occasioned much stamping of heavy boots and rhythmic clapping. One of the nearby holders who had been invited to the evening meal was clever with spoons and joined the other players.

Ruatha's main Hall, with its excellent acoustics, was marvelous to sing in, though Robinton rather thought the wall hangings helped. He sat opposite the largest one, a stunning spectacle of dragonriders hovering above what was obviously Ruatha Hold, though the design of the facade had been improved since the tapestry was hung. There were queens, too, their riders carrying long wands from which flame spewed, matching the ones used by the crews on the ground. He could even make out the Fort Weyr device on the ground crews' shoulders, so detailed was the scene.

Lady Adessa had certainly taken Hold here. He recalled the Hall from a previous visit with Lord Ashmichel, and at that time the chamber had been dark and dingy, the hanging dulled by dust. What was the old saying about new spouses and brooms?

The next morning, after a good sleep in a wide and comfortable bed, Robinton felt well-rested for the remainder of his journey. He only wished, as Jez gave him an experienced leg up to Big Black's back, that he had been able to get more cooperation from Lord Kale. At least the Holder had agreed to setting up border patrols along the Nabolese border and erecting fire beacons on the heights.

"I doubt they will ever be used," Kale had said in parting, leaving Robinton sighing as he turned the black's head south and east to the main ford of the Red River.

On the way back, spouses and brooms did a stately dance in the MasterHarper's mind as he took the incident and tried to make it musical. Melodies seemed to plague him at the most inauspicious moments, but he was grateful for the return of such spontaneity. He used it as a gauge to check his grasp on the essence of his responsibilities.

Nip returned to the Hall several weeks later, looking gaunt and weary.

"You're staying until Master Oldive says you're fit for it," Robinton said, escorting Nip to the healer premises beyond the Harper Hall.

"It?" Nip said, grinning up at his MasterHarper with mischief as he tried to keep up with Robinton's long stride.

"Whatever it is you'll be up to next." Robinton shortened his steps in deference to Nip's condition.

"Let me report first, Rob," Nip said.

"I won't listen to a word until you are gone over, washed, and fed," Robinton said firmly.

Nip knew when to give in to a superior.

Master Oldive commented on the number of bruises and scrapes, and the two swollen and enpurpled toes on one foot.

"He must bounce," the Master said with a sly grin after he had completed his examination. The spinal deformation that marred the Healer's back and brought him to the Hall in the first place seemed to fascinate Nip, who kept trying not to look at it. Long since, Oldive had become impervious to such scrutiny. "Sound, if contused, but no lasting harm that a good hot bath, a double portion of whatever Silvina has in the hearth pot, and several days in bed will not cure."

"Several days?" Nip would have jumped from the examining table but for the restraining hands of both Healer and Harper. "I wouldn't mind a bath, I can tell you," he said more meekly, rubbing dirt-encrusted fingers together. "And some decent food."

So he was given both, and he probably did not notice that Oldive, who joined him and Robinton in Silvina's little office, slipped something in his klah. He had finished his meal before the drug took effect: he was just pushing back the final dish of sweet pudding when he abruptly sagged down to the tabletop, his face just missing a splash of the pudding sauce that had spilled there.

"Good timing, there, Oldive," Robinton commented.

"Yes, rather good, if I say so myself."

Silvina gave them each a jaundiced glance. "The pair of you! You're wretches, dyed-in-the-bone wretches."

"Ever at your service, my pet," Robinton said, giving her a flourish that ended as he took one side of the unconscious Nip while Oldive took the other, lifting the limp form off his bench. With Silvina opening doors ahead of them, they carried the runner up to the Harper's quarters where he was carefully laid down on the bed in the spare room and covered to sleep himself out.

"That was a rotten trick, Robinton," Nip complained when he woke a day and a half later. Then his face dissolved into a grin that was singular enough to give him a totally different appearance. "I needed that." He stretched and took the cup of klah that the Harper had readied as soon as he heard noises from that room.

Robinton was privately glad that Nip's timing was good. He had begun to worry about the man's whereabouts.

"So I'm ready to listen," Robinton said, as he started to pull the chair forward, "unless you wish to eat first."

"No, I'd rather not turn my stomach *while* I'm eating." And with that dour statement, Nip warned Robinton that his report was bad.

"It's as well Tarathel sent so many. Vendross, who captained them, is a good man and a canny leader. He took no chances. There were more of Fax's louts camped at the Crom border. Vendross spread his men out across the border and turned back those that tried to sneak into Telgar lands. There were a good number of Tarathel's regular guards, and those Vendross set to watch at the river holds and report any sightings. The others he sent back home."

Robinton nodded. At least Tarathel would take no chances that Fax might be coveting the broad Telgar valley, not to mention the Smithcrafthall at the junction of the Great Dunto River.

"I sort of went forward three steps and back a few, trying to keep track of how many were splitting off. But the main group of fourteen continued on back to Crom. When I was sure that Vendross . . ."

"Does he know you?"

Nip made a face, tilted one hand back and forth, and then grinned again. "Sort of. He never asks. I never tell. But he trusts my reports."

"As well he should."

"Thank 'ee kindly, MasterHarper sor," Nip retorted cheekily. "So I kept on, ahead a bit, to see which way they might go." He shook his head, his expression sad. "I wouldn't want to be under that man's Hold for any reason. What he does to those unfortunates there . . ." He shook his head, sighed, and then seemed to shake himself out of such reflections. "I'll tell you this, now, Harper, in case you ever need to know." The tone made Robinton regard Nip fearfully. "Oh, I'm not saying you ever do need to know, but times being as they are, a little precaution is not untoward. Lytol who was L'tol"—and Robinton nodded to show that he knew who was meant—"is trying to keep his family's Crafthall going. Managing in spite of Fax, and I have a safe haven in the storage loft. It could well be that a dragonrider and a harper will bring that man down when the time's ripe.

"On the good side, I've found Bargen!"

"Have you now?" Robinton sat up straight with real pleasure at such tidings. "Where?"

Nip gave one of his little chuckles. "Not dumb, our young Lord Holder. He's up at High Reaches Weyr, with one or two others that made it safely out of Fax's clutches. Last place that one'd go."

"What's Bargen doing? Is he well?"

"Well, and doing a few exercises that may annoy Fax."

"Nothing that would endanger any of the innocent . . ." Robinton raised an anxious hand.

Nip cocked his head, grinning. "Little that can be traced back to anyone in particular. I think Bargen's grown up—a bit roughly, but it'll work to his advantage."

"Do remind him that the Harper Hall will assist him any way it can."

Nip smiled ruefully. "When and if the Harper Hall is able, my friend, considering harpers are in nearly as bad odor as dragonriders these days. At that, he could do little with the few men he has except wait." And that ruined Robinton's fleeting dream of seeing Bargen Holding High Reaches in the near future. "Any luck with Lord Kale?"

Robinton shook his head. "The man's too good, too trusting. He's already had Fax as a guest, selling him runnerbeasts, so why would I suggest that Lord unconfirmed Holder Fax would not continue such blameless behavior?"

"Spare us!" Nip waved a hand over his head in despair at such innocence.

"He has agreed to mount a border patrol and build beacons."

"That's quite a concession," Nip said with a degree of sarcasm and a grim smile. Then he rolled his eyes thoughtfully. "You know, as a proper harper, I could drop a word in his ear now and then, keep him on his toes?"

"Have you . . . ever . . . been a proper harper, Nip?" Robinton asked, grinning.

"Oh, now and then," Nip said, wiggling the fingers of his right hand. "Not that I'd dare flaunt the blue in Fax's vicinity." He finished the last of the klah and stood. "I need another bath.

That one only got off five layers of dirt and two of ache. Then I'm for another of Silvina's meals. She's quite a woman, isn't she?"

"One of a kind, as her mother was," the MasterHarper said blandly.

Nip chuckled and, whipping the towel off its peg on the door, whistled as he made his way to the bathing room. The MasterHarper's quarters had its own facility.

Chapter 18

▼▼

N ip departed several mornings later, riding the most
nondescript runner in the Hall's beasthold.

"Out of deference to my toes," he explained. He also had a
fresh set of clothing—which Silvina had taken out of storage,
no doubt outgrown by some apprentice. "Not too good, but at
least in one piece," had been his request.

Between them, Silvina and Robinton forced him to take a
fine fur rug for use until such time as circumstances made him
abandon it.

"There are more holdless than holded up north," Nip said,
fingering the rug. "Ah, a few nights on the ground and it'll
look no better than the old one I . . . lost." And he grinned.

Although Nip reported at intervals, in a message forwarded
with others to the Fort Runner Station, the urgency to defend
against Fax gradually dissipated as nothing much happened
that was reported outside those six holds.

Nothing much, Robinton thought, that Fax would wish
bruited about the continent.

How Nip managed to get his information, Robinton never
knew, but the self-styled Lord of Six Holds had internal

management problems of mysterious natures. A mine collapsed, a very productive one. Several of the larger ships of the High Reaches fishing fleet disappeared in stormy weather. Timber, stacked to season, either burned dramatically or ended up in splinters on its way down the rivers. A blight was discovered infecting grain fields and reducing the yield. Fax's men were forced to attend to all these minor disasters, for which no one could be seen to be at fault, by omission or commission. There were rumors of minor rebellions among the overworked holders, but the revolts were viciously suppressed by Fax's brutal guards, the "culprits" sent to the mines, their families turfed out to fend for themselves as best they might. There were fights among his guards, fights that usually produced several corpses, often those of his more brutal captains and stewards.

So, gradually over the following Turns, even Groghe slackened his vigilance, though he kept his border guards. Tarathel died—of natural causes, Robinton discovered by asking the Telgar Hold Healer outright.

"Oh, quite natural causes, my dear MasterHarper," the man said. "I attended him myself. Bad heart, you know. Never quite forgave himself that the Weyrleader was killed in Telgar Hold while guesting. Though it was trying to keep pace with younger men, like Vendross and young Larad . . . I should say, Lord Larad, now, shouldn't I? Well, old bones can't do what young ones can."

Larad was confirmed by the Conclave after an hour's deliberation. Larad was young, at 15, though a well-grown lad so most of the time was spent picking his mentors, Vendross and Harper Falawny, a former dormmate of Robinton's and an excellent teacher. There was a brief flurry when Larad's elder half-sister, Thella, insisted that the Conclave had to hear her right to the Holding. Lord Tesner of Igen, the most senior of the Holders, was outraged at her impudence and refused her admittance. The other Lord Holders and Masters were only too happy to second his motion. Robinton looked for her during the following reception, wanting to see a woman who was brave enough to speak up as eldest in the Bloodline but there was no sign of her. He often wondered what happened to her because she disappeared from Telgar Hold shortly afterwards.

The Turns were punctuated by the usual Solstice and Equinox celebrations, Gathers, the round of duties that was the MasterHarper's. C'gan was a frequent visitor, always welcomed by Robinton. The blue rider usually brought something for Camo—a toy or a confection from the Weyr's kitchens. He even tried to get Camo to put his fingers right on a pipe and breathe properly through it.

"It's such a relief to talk to you," C'gan would often say. "You're the only one else who cares a tunnel snake's droppings about the Weyr," he often said during his frequent reminiscences about the "better" days when F'lon had been Weyrleader and the Weyr had still been popular and active. R'gul followed a policy of keeping the Weyr to itself, rarely permitting dragonriders to attend any but Benden's or Nerat's Gathers.

"He's afraid—" C'gan paused to be sure that Robinton was aware of his total disgust "—to annoy the Lord Holders. Especially Nerat and Benden, who tithe as they should—and so does Bitra, when Lord Sifer happens to remember to send any. Raid is charmed by his attitude." He rolled his eyes.

"How are the sons progressing?" Robinton wished he had more contact with F'lar and F'nor, and not only because they were F'lon's lads. He could have wished for one of them as his. He had once wished that Camo wouldn't survive his first Turn, as so often happened to babies. It was hard sometimes, Robinton knew—he forced himself to the task—to ask others of the welfare of their children. Like prodding a sore spot to be sure if it was still tender. So, resolutely, he promised himself that he would go to the next Nerat Gather. He would hope to entice his father to leave Half-Circle and meet him there. If C'gan were to drop a hint to the two lads, he could meet them, too.

"Grand boys, and F'lar's got his head screwed on better than F'lon ever did," C'gan said proudly. "And they believe! They believe! I see that they do. Not that they'd dishonor their father's memory by forgetting," he added. Then he sighed.

"We've had more losses. I've never seen so many empty Weyrs and that lazy—" He closed his lips over whatever he might have called Weyrwoman Jora. "I cannot understand why S'loner thought she'd do. Do nothing, of course. Thread's coming and even the Weyr is unprepared." He shook his head sadly.

Robinton, too, wondered. Over three thousand strong the six Weyrs had been at the end of the last Pass. Now, unless he miscounted, there were barely three hundred. And not all of them able to fly Thread. Even C'gan was fast approaching an age when he and his Tagath would be considered liabilities to a fighting wing. The refrain of the Question Song briefly hovered in his mind.

"Gone away, gone ahead . . ." How?

Robinton had more urgent worries than puzzling answers to an old song. His greatest pleasure was in watching Sebell's development as apprentice. In another Turn, he'd probably walk the tables.

With distressing regularity, he heard the ways Fax treated his folk and how few now made their escape. He kept up pressure with the Lord Holders as often and as adroitly as he could. One can pipe a tune only so long before no one hears it as more than noise.

Nip made reports. Robinton even received a brief note smuggled in from Bargen, repeating the promise to reclaim High Reaches as the legal Bloodline heir.

Then Nip appeared late one night, exhausted from having run most of the last day from Nabol.

"He's doing . . . something . . ." he gasped as he hung on the door into Robinton's quarters.

The Harper got the man into the nearest chair and poured him some wine.

"Clever as sin, he is," Nip said, after a long pull of the wine. "I didn't notice they'd disappeared, and then I didn't know where they could have gone. But half the barracks at Nabol are empty. He didn't even let the other half know where their mates had gone."

"Which way?"

Nip shook his head. "I must have been watching the wrong places, that's for certain, and I'm sorry. I'm truly sorry. I thought I was on to his little ways."

"What ways?"

"Strike and grab." Then he sat bolt upright, his face stricken. "Ruatha. I should have gone there! Warned them!"

"Ruatha!" Robinton cried in the same moment.

"Get me a runnerbeast, the fastest you've got," Nip said.

"I'll go with you."

"No, Rob. I can hide in the shadows, but there's too much of you . . ."

"I'm going!" The Harper was changing into old clothes, dark ones, warm ones, and he tossed a spare fur vest toward Nip, who was shivering with the midnight chill now that he was no longer moving.

Robinton paused long enough in the kitchen to dump travel rations into a saddlepack and leave a brief note for Silvina, and then they were out the door, startling the watch-wher, who whined at their appearance and followed them the length of his chain.

They roused the beastman and had him saddle Big Black for Robinton, and a fast Ruathan runner for Nip. They walked their mounts circumspectly so as not to rouse Hall and Hold, and then Nip pointed to the runnertrack which branched off from the main road, a track straighter and faster than the road. Robinton would apologize to the Station Master, and hoped they'd encounter no runners on their way. Once on the straight track, they put heels to their mounts. They ran at a pace that Robinton would have considered dangerous at any other time, but Black and Nip's mount were surefooted and the road was a pale thin ribbon they could follow through the night.

Riding and periodically walking their mounts to rest them, they made the Red River by early morning. Urging the tired animals, they kept them moving at whatever pace they could manage until they turned a bend in the road and saw Ruatha Hold ahead of them.

Despairing, Robinton surveyed the hideous dawn-lit scene. Ropes still dangled from the fire heights of Ruatha Hold— ropes that had allowed Fax's men to approach without arousing the watch-wher. Where had the watchman been? Robinton wondered. Or had he been bribed not to hear? Why had the watch-wher not given an alarm? A row of bodies lay crumpled on the stone of the courtyard. Long bloody lines showed that the dead had been dragged out of the Hold, down the steps, and to this resting place. Men were coming out of the Hold laden with clothing and the fine furniture that Lady Adessa had brought with her. He saw a knot of frightened people being driven from their cots into the beasthold. He saw men riding off in other directions on runners that had been taken out of the beasthold. Ruathan runners! The animals that Fax had coveted . . . and now had possession of. Worse still, as Robinton's eyes returned constantly to the bodies in the courtyard, he noticed smaller ones among the adults and thought of the bright, pert Lessa. She'd've been no more than—what? Nine, ten, Turns at the most. He reeled in the saddle with nausea and fatigue and allowed Nip to urge him and Black farther into the shadows of their shelter.

Distant shouts and a thunder made Robinton look back at the dreadful carnage. The fields were being emptied of their runners and these were being herded back to Fax's beastholds. Groghe must be warned. So must Larad and Oterel. There was nothing Robinton and Nip could do here.

They got the best speed possible out of their exhausted mounts on their way to the nearest of Groghe's border checks, where they roused the startled guards and told them to light the beacons to spread the alarm. They changed to fresh mounts and sped back toward Fort Hold. There, while Nip charged up the stairs to the drum tower, Robinton banged on Groghe's door, rousing not only the Lord Holder but the entire corridor.

"Fax has invaded Ruatha Hold," Robinton said, leaning against the door post to get breath enough to speak. The drums began to roll out their dreadful message. Nip hadn't lost his touch with a drumstick.

"What?" Groghe stared unbelieving at the MasterHarper. "He can't have."

"He has and killed them all, even the children. I saw their bodies. I've warned your border men. The beacons are lit."

"Oh, Master Robinton, you do look awful," Groghe's wife said, guiding the Harper to the nearest chair and sensibly getting him a cup of wine. "You don't mean to tell me dear Lady Adessa's dead, as well. Surely—" She broke off, seeing the answer in the bleakness of his expression. "Oh, how awful! How simply awful! You're right to fear that man, Groghe."

"I don't *fear* him, Benoria, I despise him!" Groghe unbuckled his belt and threaded a hefty dagger onto it before he girded himself again.

"Oh, don't, don't, Groghe!" she cried.

"I've got my eyes well and truly open about Fax, m'dear, and hiding from him is not an option!"

"There's nothing you can do, Groghe," Robinton said, shaking his head. "By the time you can get there, he'll have completed his looting and be on his way back to Nabol."

"Well, then, the guards he'll have left at Ruatha shall see me and my men lining the border, MasterHarper, and know that they may not encroach on *my* lands."

"I'll rouse the Hall. You'll need as many men as you can muster," Robinton said.

"Not you, though," Groghe said.

Down the hall came Grodon, the current Fort Hold Harper, already armed.

"Good lad," Robinton said, catching him by the arm. "Go to the Hall. I want every journeyman and apprentice, anyone who can ride and carry a sword to mount and go with Groghe. If anyone challenges this order . . ." He could not continue.

Grodon gripped his shoulder. "No one will unless they're too deaf to have heard the drums."

"Good man." And Robinton watched him clattering down the hallway.

Groghe was banging on doors to speed the mustering, and the

place was alive with armed men and anxious women. Robinton laid his head against the back of the chair, his eyelids drooping.

"Here." Lady Benoria held up the limp hand in which he still held the cup. She filled it again, tears of distress marking her face. "Are you sure . . . about the . . . children?"

He nodded. He would never forget those lifeless little bodies. How could Fax possibly claim Ruatha, too? Ah, and his heart sank. Lady Gemma.

"Are you hurt?" Lady Benoria exclaimed, touching his arm in anxiety.

He laid one hand on his heart, a dramatic gesture perhaps, but it certainly expressed the coldness that had seized him at the core of his being.

"You should rest," she said.

"I am," he had the strength to say and she went away and let him close his eyes.

Silvina shook him awake. She and Oldive saw him down the stairs of Fort Hold and across what seemed an awfully wide court to the Harper Hall, and his bed. Sebell appeared, holding up a glowbasket to light their way up the stairs.

"Nip?" he asked as Silvina and the lad pulled off his boots.

"Took another mount and was gone. Looked like death warmed over," Oldive said.

"I made up some food for him," Sebell said.

"Good lad!" Robinton said, grateful once more for Sebell's adroit assistance. He wondered where Nip would have gone and why, but it was too much to think about, and as he laid his head down, he realized that his cheeks were wet. The last thing he knew, Silvina was covering him with the fur. As if anything would ever cover over the memory of that early morning scene in Ruatha Hold!

Fax had the country thoroughly stirred up. The major western Lord Holders, resolute Oterel, young Larad with Vendross at his side, Groghe, and Lord Sangel of South Boll, made an orderly march to Nabol to meet the grinning and unrepentant

Fax and protest his usurpation of Ruatha Hold and the murder of the entire Bloodline. Robinton joined them with his senior Masters, who were now all too aware of the full tragedy at Ruatha. Nip's report stated that not only the Lord, his Lady, and the children had been killed, but also anyone in the Holding who was known to have claimed any Ruathan Blood.

In the cramped main Hall of Nabol, Fax, surrounded by contemptuous soldiery, listened to what they said and then told them that if they were not out of *his Hold* by nightfall, he would order them all slaughtered for trespass.

No one doubted that he would implement that threat.

"You are not Lord Holder of Nabol or Crom or Ruatha by any right, other than that of conquest," Lord Sangel said, stiff with outrage but impressive with dignity. "You will usurp no more lands without full contest at arms."

Fax smirked, glancing at the grinning faces of his guards. "Anytime you like," he said, obviously delighted at the prospect. "Is that all you came to say? Well, out with you then."

At a signal, his men began to advance on the group of Lord Holders and Harpers.

"Careful, you at the door," Fax said, raising his voice. "Don't want you trampled in the rush!"

Sangel looked about to burst, Groghe was livid with rage, Oterel dead white; Vendross scowled and, beside him, young Larad managed to look resolute. With stately dignity they turned smartly about and walked in a measured tread out of the Hall, down the steps, and across the narrow courtyard to their waiting mounts. If the runnerbeasts tossed their heads, sidled, and shied, it was because their riders communicated their fury and humiliation to them. Big Black twice tried to rear and kicked out when another animal came close enough. Robinton was sure he would burst a blood vessel before they got halfway to the Nabol border.

They crossed Ruatha without incident. Aware that they were being followed—and that they were to know they were being followed—they stopped only to rest and water their mounts, and eat travel rations from their saddles.

What Robinton noticed, to keep his sanity, was the difference in the very atmosphere as soon as they had forded the Red River. Even the horses, weary though they were, seemed to pick up. Just at the last, as a final insult, their followers made a charge, which startled the last few runners crossing the river. Fax's men lined the river, laughing and calling insults across the water. With those final reminders of their opprobrious rout ringing in their ears, the Lord Holders continued down the Fort road to the nearest border post.

There, at last, they could give vent to their repressed feelings and argue that they should have come in force, with enough men to show Fax that they meant business about meeting any further aggression with equal force and its defeat.

Robinton, food and drink in his hands, could no longer listen to such useless ranting and wandered off far enough so he did not have to hear a recapitulation of what ought to have been said, or done, or implied, or threatened. He felt that, considering the large contingent of armed men that Fax had around him, they had been lucky indeed not to have been harmed—except in pride and dignity. Such a delegation had been futile from the outset and only let them in for ridicule, but some show of protest had to be made! That much he knew. If only R'gul had been willing to let them ride dragons to Nabol, their retreat would not have been such a blow to their esteem. But R'gul had denied them the convenience of dragons, saying he knew too well what Fax's opinion of dragonriders was and had no intention of jeopardizing another dragon and rider. Robinton had argued against confronting Fax at all. Not from a lack of courage, but from a desire to avoid what had happened: Fax's contemptuous disregard of their condemnation. As if Fax cared a straw in the wind.

"Bad idea all told," a voice said at his elbow, almost causing him to drop the klah and his food. They were taken out of his hand by filthy fingers. "You can get more and I'm starving of the hunger. Haven't had a drink in three days. Should have tried to persuade them out of such a meeting, Rob. Fax is still laughing."

"Where were you, Nip?" Robinton asked, regaining his composure. He should have known Nip would have witnessed the whole sorry episode.

"Where I could see." The spy shook his head as he gobbled food almost without chewing. He took a sip of the wine and swallowed his mouthful.

"I'll filch some more for your trip back," Robinton told him. "That is, if you're going back."

"Oh, I'm needed where I will be by morning more than ever, I assure you." Nip crammed the rest of the roll into his mouth, rolling his eyes at his own greedy hunger and chewing vigorously. He took the last sip and handed the cup back to Robinton, almost regretfully. "There's more where you got that, isn't there?"

"I'll get more for you—and me,—more," Robinton said. He slipped back into the camp and helped himself to a skin, as well as a saddlebag full of travel meatroll. Everyone was so busy trying to air their own hindsight wisdom that no one noticed him sneaking in and out.

"Here—" And he stopped, seeing Nip propped against a tree, fast asleep.

He sat down, hoping the courageous little man would rouse to tell him what he had in mind. The gleam of Nip's eyes had suggested that his devious mind had already thought of several interesting ways to harass Fax.

Robinton was almost half asleep himself when he heard his name called. So he left the wineskin and the full bag of food and retraced his steps.

Chapter 19

▼▼

Some good did come out of that disastrous confrontation with Fax. MasterSmith Fandarel withdrew all Masters from the "seven holds." Other Craftmasters followed that example. Fax had been too busy congratulating himself over the acquisition of Ruatha Hold to realize what was happening. He complained bitterly, offering inducements to the Masters to return. Nor did he dare retaliate against those journeymen who remained: as many as could had slipped away before he knew they had left. Even the MasterMiner at Crom had removed himself and set up a new headquarters for his Craft in one of the Smithcrafthalls at Telgar. Despite substantial rewards, Master Idarolan, who had succeeded Gostol as MasterFisher, refused to lay any keels for Fax to replace the ships that had so mysteriously disappeared from the High Reaches fishing villages. All that were left were small sloops or ketches, which were restricted in cargo space or range.

The only Hall that did not withdraw skilled assistance was the Healer Hall. Masterhealer Oldive quietly stated that such a measure went against the purpose and grain of his Craft. He was respected for it, as were those of his Hall who remained to succor the ill and injured. And there were many who needed such help.

"Fax hadn't counted on the loss of Masters," Robinton said, thoroughly pleased. Of course, harpers had long since been driven away or hunted down by Fax. Indeed, it had become almost a crime, Nip said, to admit to owning an instrument, much less playing or singing.

"The man is determined to make life as miserable as possible. He's succeeding rather well. A fact which will eventually go against him."

"We hope," Robinton remarked drily.

"Oh, wait and see," Nip said with unusual optimism.

"I'm waiting."

W hile the MasterHarper waited over the next five Turns, he busied himself improving all within his Hall. He asked Groghe for the best fighter of his guard and had the man teach classes, from apprentice-level on up, in self-defense and, though this did not sit well with the more self-confident young students, when to run and hide and how to do that, leaving the least evidence of escape. To Robinton's surprise, Sebell turned out to be almost ferocious in the drills: only Saltor, the head guard, or his burly assistant, Emfor, would partner him.

"Sebell's amazing," Robinton remarked to Saltor when Sebell had pinned Emfor to the mat in three moves.

Saltor regarded him with amusement. "It's you he's determined to defend, Master Robinton. Keep him at your side and you'll never need to fear."

"Not that I can keep him from my side," Robinton replied, wondering how he had managed to generate such devotion in the lad, kin though he was.

"That goes for every one of 'em, you know," Saltor continued, and Robinton felt decidedly uncomfortable. "Just as well, you ask me," the guard added, then walked off to correct a wrestling hold.

Sebell's prowess was by no means limited to such physical

skills. He soaked up sufficient expertise and abilities to gain his journeyman's rank almost as quickly as his adored mentor had. Robinton reluctantly sent him for a Turn's teaching in Igen Hold, and found out just how much he had come to rely on the lad and brought him back. As if Sebell could sense where Robinton needed help, the young Journeyman assumed many duties so adroitly that both masters and the older journeymen could not deny the MasterHarper his invaluable assistant.

It was Sebell who suggested a new role for young Traller, an exceedingly mischievous apprentice who sorely tried the patience of every master in the Hall with his pranks and strategies to get out of any task he did not like. Traller never seemed to be to blame for boyish tricks . . . it was always someone else in the dorm. He was never *there* when work was assigned and always had a plausible excuse for such an absence. He could ride any runnerbeast in the beasthold, pin a fly to the wall with his dagger at a hundred paces, survive the best tricks of heavier lads on the wrestling mats, and he was totally without conscience. He possessed a lively wit, however, as well as an inventive mind for excuses. He was the personification of contrariness, and yet Robinton liked him, however often the boy was up before him for disciplinary action. He had had a good treble, lost when he hit puberty, and now his best musical skill was drumming. Either in the tower, where he excelled, or on any surface that had any resonance. He drummed with his fingers—one of his dorm mates said he drummed with his toes at night against the bedstead—with sticks, and even upon occasion in the dining hall, with the thigh bones of a fowl.

"It's about Traller," Sebell said one evening as Robinton was relaxing after dinner.

"Ooooh," Robinton groaned, "what's he done this time?" He had run out of any useful disciplines to curb the lad.

"I was thinking, Master, that he might do better training with Nip," Sebell said, a sly smile on his face as he watched Robinton's reaction to the suggestion. "It seems to me that every time Nip reports in he looks more gaunt and tired. He needs someone else—if only to run back here with messages for you." When he saw that Robinton was considering the notion he added, "It's not as if any one will ever control Traller, but all that energy could be useful to Nip."

"I think you've hit on a marvelous future for that young man, Sebell. I can't imagine why I didn't think of it myself."

Sebell chuckled. "You do have one or two other matters to worry about."

Robinton agreed vehemently and went back to solving those that were of the most immediate concern—such as reassigning harpers for the next Turn's teaching duties.

But he was ready with Sebell's suggestion the next time Nip eased himself into the Harper's study, followed closely enough by Sebell with food and drink for the man.

"I've someone you might like to train, Nip," Robinton said.

"Huh?" Nip scowled. "I travel faster alone. And safer. Ah, thanks, Sebell, you're remarkable in anticipation of my needs." He bit into a meatroll and chewed while Robinton went on.

"I think you must at least assess young Traller as a possible apprentice," Robinton said firmly.

"Oh, well, if you put it like that, I'll give him a going over then."

"It's you or back to Keroon for him, because the Harper Hall can't seem to put his . . . special . . . talents to good use. Weren't you saying that you can only be in one place at a time? If I need an assistant, so do you."

Nip gave him complete attention. "Sebell's no lad . . ." He shook his head. "I'd hate to put someone in danger, and it's dangerous up there in Fax's."

"More reason than ever for you to have an . . . assistant," Sebell remarked pointedly.

Nip made a noise in his throat. "You mean 'shadow,' don't you?" he asked, jerking his thumb toward Sebell, who grinned back, quite willing to take the jibe as a compliment.

Robinton blinked and grinned, then laughed out loud, for there was a faint resemblance—the color and set of their eyes, the same dark hair almost to the whirls at the crown, and strong features, chin and nose—that spoke of their distant blood relationship. Sebell was now as tall as the MasterHarper and, over the Turns, had picked up some of Robinton's mannerisms, as well. Their eyes met and they grinned with perfect understanding and mutual respect.

"Come along," Robinton said, although it was late and the apprentices should have been asleep. "He's probably drumming somewhere . . ."

"He's outside," Sebell said, indicating the hallway. "I found him in the drum tower stairwell, trying to see who was making such a late night entrance."

"Well, now, that sounds promising," Nip said and himself went to invite Traller into the room. The two stood regarding each other as warily as strange canines. "If you'll pardon us, Robinton, Sebell," Nip said after a long pause, and taking Traller by the shoulder, pushed ahead of him out the door.

The next morning Nip told Robinton to rename the boy "Tuck" and to designate him as an apprentice on special assignment.

"I told you he was a natural," Robinton said a bit smugly.

Nip snorted. "He will be when I get through with him." Then he grinned in his irrepressible fashion. "He'll be good, too. Thanks, Rob. Oh, and he's coming with me. I've got two runnerbeasts ready and willing. Like any well brought up"— Nip smiled at that description being applied to Tuck— "Keroonian, he rides like a leech." He paused again at the door. "And runs like the wind."

Nip took turns with Tuck to deliver reports over the next two Turns. Then Tuck appeared unexpectedly late one night, grinning with delight when he had startled Robinton from reading Term reports on the current apprentices.

"Nip says that there's something odd going on at Ruatha Hold."

"Oh?" And Robinton was glad to find some distraction from the reports. He didn't agree with some of them, and it always annoyed him when some of his favorite "sons" did not measure up to the high standards he wanted them to achieve.

"Well, it seems that it's not prospering. There've been four stewards, and each one has failed to extract any profit from the Hold." Tuck grinned. "It's as if every attempt fails, some way or another. And Fax's not known to be pleased with any sort of failure."

"Hmmm. That's interesting. A kind of subtle rebellion?"

Tuck gave the sort of snort that Nip affected. "With that bunch of drudges? They're the most useless bunch of incompetents I've seen. And since I've been north—" He gestured with a thumb. "—I've seen every sort of way to avoid hard work that's been invented. And then some. The only jobs that get done in a halfway decent fashion are helped along by an overseer with a whip standing over the workers. Fax has only so many men and too many holdings." He grinned broadly. "Though his supply of metal-knotted whips seems inexhaustible."

" 'One hold, one holder' is a good adage to remember," Robinton said sententiously.

"To be sure." Tuck glided past that. "Nip specially said to tell you about Ruatha."

"What could be happening there?" Robinton asked, more or less rhetorically. "If there is no one *able* to foment trouble, is it trouble, or pure carelessness on the stewards' parts?"

Tuck shrugged his shoulders. He had grown into a wiry man, not much taller than his companion. He might practice being nondescript, but he hadn't quite the knack Nip had and could never disguise the bright, interested gaze of his dark eyes.

"But there's something there. Sort of—" He tilted his hand sideways in a gesture he had obviously learned from close association with Nip. "—a general uneasiness. Like something watching all the time. Only who'd watch? And what are they watching?"

"I should take a—"

"No, you shouldn't." Tuck held up a hand. "Harper blue is a target for any of Fax's soldiery. I don't say the best is at Ruatha, but you're not to risk your neck . . . Master Robinton." He added the title as a respectful afterthought. "Bargen's increased his activities in High Reaches, by the way, now that he has more folk in the Weyr."

"He's being careful, isn't he?"

"Bargen's so careful he's womanish," Tuck said with disgust. Then he sighed. "Of course, he wants to stay alive long enough to take High Reaches Hold back. So no one really minds when he sends *them* out to do what *he* plans. And he's pretty good at making trouble."

"Without embroiling others?"

"They'd rather do something, Master Robinton, than nothing," Tuck said. "They've got some pride left, you know."

Robinton nodded.

"Isn't the Benden clutch about to hatch?" Tuck asked.

"Soon. Jora's dead." Robinton had had the details from a letter sent to Master Oldive by Lord Raid's Journeyman Healer, who had been brought by R'gul to try to keep the Weyrwoman alive. Remembering how Jora had gorged herself at the Impression Feast—and that had been Turns ago now—he had no trouble believing that the woman had died of overeating. The healer had been appalled at the state she was in and had agreed that she should be interred *between*.

"I heard the drums, but did I hear correctly that the queen did produce a gold egg?" Tuck cocked his head hopefully and Robinton nodded. "That's pulling up pretty close, isn't it?" Robinton nodded again, and Tuck asked, "You'll be going to the Impression?"

"I hope to." Robinton wasn't sure that any invitations were going out from the Weyr, but that didn't mean that a Craftmaster could be excluded. There had been few enough clutches and Impressions since S'loner had died.

"Nemorth'll last?" Tuck's expression was anxious.

"Probably. At least that's my reading of queen dragon behavior. Even without her rider, Nemorth will try to last until her clutch hatches."

"D'you think the next Weyrwoman will be an improvement on Jora?"

Robinton gave a snort. "I don't see how any woman could be worse."

"Then the riders'll be on Search, won't they?"

"I would presume so."

Tuck was the one to nod now. "I'd best go."

"Where to?"

"I'm to meet him"—which always meant Nip—"at High Reaches. Fax is there, preparing"—he grimaced—"to go on one of his 'tours.' "

"Tours?"

"Inspections, to find out why he isn't getting what he expects out of his holdings."

"I wish him luck," Robinton said drolly.

"Not him, the poor unfortunates he'll be beating up." Then Tuck was out the door.

Over the next few days, Robinton had a feeling of imminence, of something impending. He was not surprised then to have Sebell escort a runner, mud-spattered and exhausted, into his office. He was stunned by the message.

"Tuck says you'd better come, Master Robinton."

"Come where?" Robinton had been on his feet the instant he saw Sebell's companion. Master and Journeyman helped the man to a chair, and then Sebell poured him wine.

"Fax has left . . . for Ruatha Hold. Dragonriders . . . with him."

"At Ruatha? Dragonriders? With him?"

The runner nodded, sipping the wine. "On Search." And he grimaced. "Takes guts . . . to go to the . . . High Reaches."

Robinton was amazed. "Who?"

The runner shook his head. "You're to do a Nip and Tuck, he said."

"How much time do I have?" Robinton asked, waving aside the objections he could see Sebell about to utter.

"Fax is forcing his march. You'd best be in place."

"Hmmm, yes, I had, hadn't I?" Robinton felt a surge of wild

excitement and sighed with relief. He ignored the pointed anxiety on Sebell's face. "Take care of him, will you, Sebell?"

And Robinton bolted down the steps to Silvina's rooms.

"I'll need rough clothing, suitable for a drudge," he told her.

"And what are you up to?" she demanded, hands on her hips as she glared up at him.

"Now, don't you start on me, too," he warned, far more sharply than he intended, and pointed to the keys on her belt. "I have to look the part."

"If you think you can do a Nip, you're gone in the head, Rob. Send Sebell for you."

"No, not Sebell," Robinton said angrily. "I won't risk him."

"But you will yourself?" she complained as she reluctantly led the way down to the storage rooms. "How can you possibly disguise your height?" she demanded, trying another tack to dissuade him.

He immediately pulled in his shoulders, scrunched down, and with one hand bouncing loosely, affected a hobbly gait.

"A limp might even be better," she said after a moment's observation. "Hmmm. As if you'd been kicked by a boot in the wrong place." Then she sighed in surrender.

By the time Sebell joined them—a look at his Master's face and Sebell kept his objections to himself—the two had found appropriately ragged clothing for Robinton to wear. Even Sebell had to agree that, once Robinton assumed his odd stance and gait, he no longer resembled the tall, dignified Master-Harper of Pern.

"If you've time, I can cure them in the midden," Silvina suggested helpfully, but her eyes gleamed with mischief.

Sebell began to chuckle at Robinton's expressive shudder and was caught off balance when Robinton thrust the clothing into his hands and told him to see to it.

"The smell will undoubtedly keep others from examining me at too close range," he said with a long-suffering sigh. "Now, while I'm away, Sebell, you'll tell everyone that I've caught a fever and keep them out of my rooms."

Sebell nodded, though he was clearly unhappy with his

Master involved in such a subterfuge. Still, he knew when to keep his comments to himself.

Robinton waited until he got to the Red River before he put on his disguise. Black had sidled away from the saddle pack holding the reeking clothes. He left the runnerbeast with the border guards and warned them to be extra vigilant.

From there Robinton made his discreet way to the beasthold at Ruatha to discover that there weren't but two sorry-looking milch animals to be cared for. He was looking around the beasthold in dismay when a wing of dragons appeared midair and a frightened man came running so fast he was in danger of tripping over himself as he shrieked his message at the top of his lungs:

"*Dragonriders*, and *Fax* comes. *Dragonriders* . . ." Still yelling, he disappeared into the Hold.

In his guise of a witless drudge, Robinton could come out to stare up at the amazing sight of a full wing of dragons, some of whom had the remnants of flame still trickling beyond their muzzles, appearing in Ruathan skies. One after another, they bugled. They sounded surprised, he thought. As the dragons wheeled to come in for a landing, he spotted a blue who had to be Tagath. That confirmed his suspicion that this was F'lar's wing, after all. Searching at the High Reaches would take the nerve of F'lon's son. Maybe he could get a word with C'gan somehow. Maybe even get a chance to meet the adult F'lar at long last. He wondered if R'gul had authorized the Search in this area. Somehow he doubted it. Then he put his mind to the pressures of this moment.

A witless drudge would be terrified and rush to find shelter from such a frightening sight, he thought, and he shambled as fast as his assumed limp would allow him to join the other drudges milling about the courtyard.

The Warder, his face ghastly, appeared on the steps to verify the message and then started yelling conflicting orders at those nearby, grabbing the nearest drudge and propelling him toward the Hold.

"We must prepare. We must do something! There has to be food! There has to be order in this Hold . . . and you are . . . going . . . to . . . work your nuts off!" Each pause was to allow him to kick or shove some ragged body into the Hold.

Robinton managed to evade the full force of the kick aimed at him, but he went willingly into the Hold. There he paused briefly in dismay at the sight of the once beautiful entrance hall and the main Hall seen past the broken-hinged double doors that led to it. Then someone bumped into him, and that restored him to his character.

An old woman struggled to hand out brooms and mops; another shaggy-haired drudge distributed other cleaning equipment. They were herded up the steps to sweep and ready rooms that had not been used, to judge by the appalling condition of them, since the massacre. He was pushed into a room that had obviously had its window left open for Turns: leaves, branches, and dirt were piled like snowdrifts in the corners. The hearth held ashes that had hardened into rock. The bedding was soiled and damp and would have to be discarded. Though what would be available to take its place, Robinton didn't know. Nor was a single cleaning going to do much more than loosen the surface layer of dirt thickly caking the bare floor. The steward raced from one room to another, yelling for haste, for more clean water, for more effort from each and every drudge, bestowing kicks where he felt the cleaners faltered. How any steward worth his mark could have allowed the once graceful Hold to fall into such desuetude, Robinton could not understand. Even a monthly sweeping would have kept this room habitable.

He did manage to clean the floor before Fax and his entourage arrived. Then he was hauled by the scruff of his neck out into the hall and sent down to help stable Fax's runnerbeasts.

The main Hall had survived the concerted attack by the drudges, and looked slightly better. There were damp spots here and there, and no one had been able to reach the crawlers or their filmy webs, which hung in tatters from the ceiling. There was huge confusion, yells, shrieks, and the excited barking of the spit canines coming from the kitchen, and Robinton was just as happy to be sent to care for the runnerbeasts. He just hoped that someone had cleaned up the beasthold.

He saw Fax scowling fiercely, beating his boot with a heavy baton-whip. He saw Lady Gemma, great with child, being lifted off her mount by two of Fax's strongest men. He could see her wincing, although the men were handling her with great care. Several of the ladies in this very mixed group rushed to her assistance once she was on the ground, supporting her as she waddled up the steps and into the Hold. He felt immense pity for her, hoped that the quarters she was to inhabit had been in better condition than the one he had tried to clean. Was Fax trying to kill the woman? Probably, if some of Nip's earlier reports bore any truth—and they undoubtedly did.

Robinton was prodded to take several beasts at once, which was awkward, given the infirmities he was affecting. Two of Fax's bullies came along to oversee him and the other hastily organized drudges who were to tend to the mounts. Ruathan bred, Robinton thought drolly, come back full circle. The two milch beasts that had inhabited the Hold were gone. Probably they were what was being offered the Lord Holder tonight and would be tough as old boots.

He did no more than the others, despite being cuffed and kicked to "do a proper job of it." Although he knew very well that the drudges in the Harper Hall and Fort Hold were well cared for, he discovered a heretofore unexpected sympathy for those whom life had deprived of the wit or energy to achieve more than such lowly positions. He felt sorry for the tired runnerbeasts, though he was almost as tired as they before he and the others were given sickles and sent to cut fresh fodder. His limp and his groans were heartfelt by now. With nothing to eat so far this long day . . . and if what he suspected were true, there was unlikely to be enough food in the Hold to feed the visitors, much less the residents. He wondered if the dragonriders had brought their own provisions. And how was he to reach C'gan if he spent the entire livelong day drudging? It was too bad that he had never established as much of a contact with Tagath as he had had with Simanith.

When the armsmen finally allowed that the beasts had been properly cared for, Robinton followed the other five men back to the Hold. They were muttering about their expectations of food. Darkness had set in, and as an additional mark of the poverty of the Hold, the glowbaskets gave glum illumination.

"Bread, if we're lucky," one said, trudging along.

"When's luck got anythin' to do wiv us?" another demanded. "I'd be anywheres but here."

"Yes, always the gripe, never the go," the first one said. "Who're you?" he suddenly asked Robinton, peering up at him.

"Came wiv dem," the MasterHarper said, jerking a thumb at the soldiers striding along in front of them. He wanted to straighten up, to relieve the ache in his back, but doubted it would help and besides, he daren't unbend. He was still a good head taller than his erstwhile companions.

The first man made an inarticulate sound in his throat that was half snarl. "Goin' on wiv 'em then?"

"Not goin' nowhere but here," Robinton said in a dour voice.

They made for the kitchen entrance and the first man recoiled, startled at the chaos within, the slamming and clanging of pots, and the screams as a drudge was hit. One male voice rose above the others, giving orders, yelling if the response wasn't immediate.

"*Shards, it's burned on the one side and raw on the others!*" That sentence was bellowed in a tone of fury and frustration. A canine yipped piteously. Robinton could hear slapping and more screams and groans as the cook evidently vented his feelings on his helpless drudges.

"Us'ns'd have it, if it's meat," the first drudge muttered to himself, wistfully licking lips. He took a deep breath.

"Smell's all we's likely to have," the other said.

Not that the smell was at all appetizing. But Robinton used their interest in the kitchen activities to cover his movements as

ANNE McCAFFREY

he stealthily backed off into the shadows. He had noticed as
they passed the main Hold door that there were no guards
either at the door or in the Hall. He couldn't enter in his guise
of a drudge, but surely he could sneak into the guard barracks
and change into something . . . more appropriate.

He slipped in just in time to hear one of the underleaders
assigning posts for the evening, and he ducked into an alcove
as they tramped past him, the dim glowbaskets neatly shad-
owing him.

Fortunately many of Fax's soldiers were of a generous size
and they had brought several changes of clothes with them. He
found the cleanest and, happily shedding his filthy, sweaty
rags, put them on. A bit loose at the waist and a bit short in the
leg, but he used his own belt and secured the trousers. He took
the sleeve of his shirt and scrubbed at his boots, getting the
worst of the stable muck off them.

"Where the shards were you?" a harsh voice called.

Robinton whirled around to see a guard underleader in
the doorway. "Relieved me'sel," he muttered, wondering if the
sudden pounding of his heart would give him away.

"Up to the Hall, then. Want every one of you up there 'case
those sharding dragonriders doan know they's manners." The
grin suggested that the man was aching to teach dragonriders
manners.

"Yuss," Robinton said. He squared his shoulders, which was
not easy after a day's crouching, and passed the underleader
cautiously, as if expecting a kick on his way. But no kick came.
A quick look back told him that the man was bending over his
saddlebags, extracting his sword belt.

Reaching the Hall, Robinton slowed before he stepped on the
heels of Fax's two underleaders, who were escorting their Lord
into the Hall with one of his ladies. The Warder was effusively
bowing them in. Robinton slipped along the wall as if he had
been in the wake of the latest arrivals and took a position
halfway between the guards already in place. Neither took
note of him, their attention focused on the dragonriders seated
at one of the trestle tables set up perpendicular to the raised
dais that held the head table. With relief, Robinton spotted

C'gan's silvery head and then looked up the table to spot the young rider, F'nor. There was no mistaking his lineage as F'lon's son: it was there in the cocked head and the slight smile. F'nor was watching his half brother at the head table, talking to one of Fax's ladies seated beside him. Lady Gemma occupied the seat on the other side. F'lar didn't seem all that happy in such company. Just then a crawler dropped from the ceiling onto the table, and Lady Gemma noticeably winced.

Fax went stamping up the steps to the head table. He pulled back his chair roughly, slamming it into the Lady Gemma's before he seated himself. He pulled the chair to the table with a force that threatened to rock the none-too-stable trestle-top from its supporting legs. Scowling, he inspected his goblet and plate.

The Warder approached the head table, clearly apprehensive.

"A roast, my Lord Fax, and fresh bread, Lord Fax, and such fruits and roots as are left."

"Left? Left? You said there was nothing harvested here."

The Warder's eyes bulged and he gulped. "Nothing to be sent on," he stammered. "Nothing *good* enough to be sent on. Nothing. Had I but known of your arrival, I could have sent to Crom—"

"Sent to Crom?" roared Fax, slamming the plate he was inspecting onto the table so forcefully that the rim bent under his hands. The Warder winced again.

"For decent foodstuffs, my Lord," he quavered.

Robinton felt a sudden ripple, like an odd push at his mind.

"The day one of my Holds cannot support itself *or* the visit of its rightful overlord, I shall renounce it."

The Lady Gemma gasped, and Robinton wondered if she had felt the same remarkable ripple he did. As if confirming that, the dragons roared. And Robinton felt the surge of . . . something.

F'lar felt it, too, the MasterHarper thought, for he sought his half brother's eyes and saw F'nor's almost imperceptible nod. And those of the other wingriders.

"What's wrong, dragonman?" snapped Fax.

Robinton admired the way in which F'lar affected no concern, stretching his long legs and assuming an indolent posture in the heavy chair.

"Wrong?" He had a voice like F'lon's, a good baritone with flexible intonations. Robinton wondered if the man could sing.

"The dragons!" Fax said.

"Oh, nothing. They often roar . . . at the sunset, at a flock of passing wherries, at mealtimes." F'lar smiled amiably at Fax. His tablemate, however, was not so sanguine and gave a squeak.

"Mealtimes? Have they not been fed?"

"Oh, yes. Five days ago."

"Oh. Five . . . days ago? And are they hungry . . . now?" Her voice trailed into a whisper of fear, and her eyes grew round.

"In a few days," F'lar assured her. Robinton watched him scan the hall with a good appearance of detached amusement. "You mount a guard?" he asked Fax casually.

"Double at Ruatha Hold," Fax replied in a tight, hard voice.

"Here?" F'lar all but laughed, gesturing around the sadly unkempt chamber.

"Here!" Fax changed the subject with a roar. "Food!"

Five drudges staggered in under the weight of the roast herdbeast. The aroma that reached Robinton's nostrils had not improved in the short while since he had left the kitchen court-yard. The odor of singed bone was most prevalent. And there was the Warder, sharpening his tools for carving.

Robinton was not the only one to see Lady Gemma catch her breath, her hands curling tightly around the armrests.

The drudges returned with wooden trays of bread. Burnt crusts had been scraped and cut from the loaves. As other trays were borne in by the drudges and passed before Lady Gemma, Robinton could see her expression turning to unmistakable nausea. Then he saw her convulsive clutch at the armrest and realized that the food was not the principal problem. He saw F'lar lean toward her to say something, but she stopped him with an almost imperceptible shake of her head, closing her eyes and trying to mask the shudder that ran down her body.

The poor woman looked to be going into labor, Robinton thought.

The Warder, with shaking hands, was now presenting Fax with a plate of the sliced meats . . . the more edible-looking portions.

"You call this food? *You call this food?*" Fax bellowed. More crawlers were shaken from their webs as the sound of his voice shattered fragile strands. *"Slop! Slop!"* And he threw the plate at the Warder.

"It's all we had on such short notice," the Warder squealed, bloody juices streaking down his cheeks. Fax threw his goblet at him, and the wine went streaming down the man's chest. The steaming dish of roots followed; the Warder yelped in pain as the hot liquid splashed over him.

"My Lord, my Lord, had I but known!"

Robinton felt a repeat of the powerful ripple, and thought it was triumphant.

"Obviously, Ruatha can*not* support the visit of its Lord." F'lar's voice rang out. "You must renounce it."

Robinton stared at the dragonrider. Everyone else did, too. The MasterHarper also caught the sudden blinking of F'lar's eyes, as if the bronze rider had astonished himself, as well. But F'lar straightened his shoulders and regarded Fax in the silence that fell over the Hall, broken only by the splat of crawlers and the drip of the root liquid from the Warder's shoulders to the rushes on the floor. The grating of Fax's boot heel was clearly audible as he swung slowly around to face the bronze rider. From his vantage point, Robinton could see F'nor rise, hand on dagger hilt. It was all he could do not to gesture for F'nor to stay seated, to take his hand off the knife.

"I did not hear you correctly?" Fax asked. His voice was expressionless, and Robinton was glad that the man's back was to him.

"You did mention, my Lord," F'lar drawled with a good command of himself, Robinton noted with almost paternal pride, "that if any of your Holds could not support itself and the visit of its rightful overlord, you would renounce it."

Then, with admirable self-possession, the dragonrider, his eyes still on Fax, speared some vegetables from a serving dish and began to eat. F'nor, still on his feet, was glancing around the Hall as if he thought someone else had spoken, not F'lar. That was when Robinton realized that those odd ripples of power had not emanated from the dragonriders, or the dragons. But where had they come from?

Fax and F'lar were silent, their gazes locked. Suddenly a groan escaped Lady Gemma. Fax glanced at her in irritation, his fist clenched and half-raised to strike her. But the contraction that rippled across her swollen belly was as obvious as her pain.

Fax began to laugh. He threw back his head, showing big, stained teeth, and roared.

"Aye, renounce it, in favor of her issue, if it is male . . . and lives!" he crowed.

"Heard and witnessed!" F'lar snapped, jumping to his feet and pointing to his riders. They were on their feet in an instant.

"Heard and witnessed!" they responded in the traditional manner.

Robinton had seen the guards slip hands to their belts and did the same with his hand when the dragonriders rose. But as there was no sign from Fax, who continued to howl with contemptuous laughter, they all relaxed and some even had half-grins of snide amusement.

The lady beside F'lar, Lady Tela, was obviously concerned about Lady Gemma, but clearly didn't know what to do. Someone had better help her, Robinton thought. She was in obvious pain and distress.

It was F'lar who acted, bending to assist her out of her chair. She grabbed his arm and murmured something, her lips turned away from Fax's eyes. F'lar's eyebrows rose, and Robinton saw him press her hands reassuringly. He wondered what they were saying.

F'lar beckoned to two of the Warder's men and pushed Lady Tela to Gemma's side.

"What do you need?" the bronze rider asked her, his voice carrying. Fax snorted.

"Oh, oh . . ." Her face was twisted with panic. "Water, hot, clean. Cloths. And a birthing-woman. Oh, yes, we must have a birthing-woman."

F'lar looked about the Hall, then signaled to the Warder. "Have you one in this Hold?"

"Of course." The Warder sounded affronted.

"Then send for her."

The Warder caught Fax's nod and then kicked the drudge on the floor. "You . . . you! Whatever your name is, go get her from the crafthold. You must know who she is."

With a nimbleness probably developed from years of avoiding kicks, the drudge moved with astonishing speed and scurried across the Hall and out the door to the kitchen.

Fax came down to the platter of roast and began slicing meat, which he speared on the point of his knife and ate from the blade. Occasionally he would glance up in the direction the women had taken and bark out a laugh. F'lar sauntered down to the carcass and, without waiting for a direct invitation, began to carve neat slices, beckoning his men over. Those of Fax's men who were seated at the table waited, however, until Fax had eaten his fill.

The men standing on guard were not relieved, and the proximity to food became almost unendurable. Bad as the roast was, it was food, and Robinton's belly rumbled. He was also very thirsty and his feet hurt. His whole body hurt, for that matter. He vowed not to get so unfit ever again. A Master-Harper ought to be ready for anything. Clearly he was not.

The drudge returned rather more quickly than he had thought possible. She strode right through the main door, leading a woman at least slightly cleaner than herself, though almost as ancient. The birthing-woman stopped in the doorway, frozen by the sight of those in the Hall.

F'lar strode up to her and took her by the arm, leading her toward the steps.

"Go quickly, woman, Lady Gemma is before her time." He was frowning with concern. The drudge caught the other arm and pulled the old woman past the guards and to the stairway.

F'lar stood watching until they disappeared into the upper level. Then he made his way to the riders' table, where he spoke quietly to F'nor and the rider Robinton recognized as bronze Piyanth's rider, K'net.

Robinton would have given anything to sit, or to have a piece of the trimmed bread that lay in a bowl two strides from him on the guards' table. He noticed that the other two guards were surreptitiously shifting their feet and easing their shoulders.

The waiting continued. Nothing could be heard from the upper level, but there were sounds of weeping and scufflings rising from the kitchen: no doubt the Warder rewarding the drudges for their efforts.

Then suddenly there was a screeching, and one of the women came running out of the upper hall and paused briefly at the top.

"She's dead . . . dead . . . dead . . ." Her cry reverberated down the staircase and through the Hall, causing yet more crawlers to be loosened from their strands.

"Dead?" Fax whirled, watching the woman's hysterical progress down the stairs.

"Oh, dead, dead, poor Gemma. Oh, Lord Fax, we did all we could, but the journey . . ." She ran to where Fax was sitting.

Casually Fax slapped her and she fell sobbing in a heap at his feet.

Robinton saw F'lar reach for his dagger hilt. Women in the Weyr were rarely treated in such a harsh manner. It would definitely go against a dragonrider's grain. Robinton tightened his hands into fists, willing the bronze rider to relax.

The men were muttering, not all of them happy to hear that their Lady had died. Fax, however, seemed decidedly pleased.

"The child lives," cried a voice from the top of the stairs. Robinton looked up to see the drudge who had gone for the birthing-woman. "It is male." Her voice was rough with anger and . . . hatred? Robinton was astonished.

Rising, Fax shoved the weeping woman out of the way with a heartless kick and scowled at the drudge. "What are you saying, woman?"

"The child lives. It is male," she repeated in a firm voice that belied her apparent age.

Incredulity and rage suffused Fax's face. The Warder's men, on the verge of cheering, stifled themselves.

"Ruatha has a new Lord," the drudge continued.

The dragons roared.

The drudge's eyes appeared to be focused on Fax as she made her way down the stairs. Robinton was altogether astonished at her sudden assertive behavior, as well as the robust quality of her voice. She even seemed oblivious to the roar of the dragons outside.

She didn't see her danger, as Robinton certainly did, when Fax erupted into action, leaping across the intervening space, bellowing denials of her news. Before the drudge could realize his intent, his fist crashed across her face. She was swept off her feet and off the steps, and fell heavily to the stone floor where she lay motionless, a bundle of dirty rags.

"Hold, Fax!" F'lar cried as the Lord of the High Reaches lifted his foot to kick the unconscious body.

Robinton had started forward, too, but caught himself before he inadvertently dropped out of disguise.

Fax whirled, his hand closing on his knife hilt.

"It was heard and witnessed, Fax," F'lar cautioned him, one hand outstretched, "by dragonmen. Stand by your sworn and witnessed oath!"

In spite of himself, Robinton shook his head at such a challenge, made to Fax of all people.

"Witnessed? By dragonmen?" cried Fax. He gave a derisive laugh, his eyes blazing with contempt, one sweeping gesture of scorn dismissing them all—just as he had dismissed the Lord Holders and Masters in the hall at Nabol. "Dragonwomen, you mean."

But he took a backward step as the dragonrider moved forward, knife in hand.

"Dragonwomen?" F'lar queried, his voice dangerously soft. Glowlight flickered off his circling blade as he advanced on Fax.

That's right, F'lar, Robinton thought, remembering another scene all too vividly. But this young man had his temper well in hand, unlike his father, and he had the same lean powerful build the younger F'lon had possessed.

"Women! Parasites on Pern. The Weyr power is over! Over

for good," roared Fax, leaping forward to land in a combat crouch.

Robinton spared a look at the others in the Hall. Fax's men were obviously looking forward to a good fight and the death of this unwary adversary. The dragonriders had spread out, circling, as if to keep the guards from interfering. Their expressions reflected confidence in the abilities of their wingleader, especially C'gan, whose grinning face reassured Robinton.

Fax feinted, and F'lar neatly swayed away. They crouched again, facing each other across six feet of space, knife hands weaving, their free hands spread-fingered, ready to grab.

Again Fax pressed the attack. F'lar allowed him to close, just near enough to dodge away with a backhanded swipe. Fabric tore and Fax snarled. He lunged immediately, faster on his feet than Robinton would have expected for such a bulky man. F'lar was forced again to dodge; this time Fax's knife scored across the dragonrider's wher-hide jerkin.

Fax plowed in again, trying to corner F'lar between the raised platform and the wall. Robinton caught his breath, hoping that neither would stumble over the unconscious drudge.

F'lar countered, ducking low under Fax's flailing arm and slashing obliquely across his side. Fax caught at him, yanking savagely, and F'lar was trapped against the other man's side, straining desperately with his left hand to keep the knife arm up. F'lar brought up his knee, at the same time making himself collapse. As Fax gasped from the blow to the groin, F'lar danced away; but Robinton could see blood welling up on his left shoulder.

Red with fury and wheezing from pain and shock, Fax straightened up and charged. F'lar was forced to sidestep quickly, putting the meat table between them and circling warily, flexing his shoulder to assess the damage.

Suddenly Fax seized up a handful of fatty scraps from the meat tray and hurled them at F'lar. The dragonrider ducked, and Fax closed the distance around the table with a rush. Robinton nearly cheered when F'lar instinctively swerved out of the way just as Fax's flashing blade came within inches of his abdomen. At the same moment, the bronze rider's knife sliced down the outside of Fax's arm. Instantly the two pivoted to face each other again, but Fax's left arm hung limply at his side.

F'lar darted in, pressing his luck as Fax staggered. But the older man must not have been hurt as badly as F'lar assumed: the dragonrider suffered a terrific kick in the side as he tried to dodge under the feinting knife. Robinton's throat closed. Doubled with pain, F'lar rolled frantically away from his charging adversary. Fax lurched forward, trying to fall on him for a final thrust. F'lar somehow got to his feet, attempting to straighten up to meet Fax's stumbling charge. His movement took Fax by surprise. Fax overreached his mark and staggered off balance. F'lar brought his right hand over in a powerful thrust, his knife blade plunging deep into Fax's unprotected back.

Fax fell flat to the flagstones, the force of his descent dislodging the dagger so that an inch of the bloody blade reemerged from the point of entry.

A thin wailing penetrated the silence. Robinton looked up to the top of the stairs, where a woman stood, cradling a swathed bundle in her arms.

"The new Lord Holder," Robinton murmured. The guards on either side of him regarded him with surprise.

Do I come forward as MasterHarper now? he wondered, looking about to see who would take charge. F'nor, C'gan, and K'net strode forward, ready to ring F'lar in case any of the guards wished to retaliate.

F'lar, wiping his forehead on his sleeve, half-stumbled to the still-unconscious drudge. He gently turned her over, and even from where Robinton stood, he could see the terrible bruise from Fax's fist spreading across her filthy cheek.

"Do any of you care to contest the outcome of this duel?" F'nor challenged. His hand carefully remained at his side, but he stood as if ready to grab his dagger at the first sign of attack.

Something about the drudge—her thin face, the set of her eyes—caught Robinton's attention. F'lar gathered the limp body up in his arms, the clump of dirty hair dropping downward. As the bronze rider swung her around, Robinton got a second good look at her face, and something stirred in his memory.

He blinked. No, he had to be mistaken. They'd all died. Everyone with any trace of Ruathan Blood had been killed that day. The girl couldn't possibly . . . incredibly . . . be Lessa?

And yet . . . Ruathan Blood had produced many dragonriders and a few Weyrwomen, too. They had strong minds, strong . . . powers? And Robinton blinked again. That was what he had felt pulsing through the Hall, what had caused the dragons to roar and F'lar to act so outrageously in challenging Fax. And it made sense to the MasterHarper. Very good sense. *She* was why Nip thought Ruatha was subtly rebelling against Fax. *She* was a full Ruathan, and they had always had strong women in the Bloodline. Strong enough to be Weyrwomen, especially now, at this crucial time for Pern.

It was all Robinton could do to restrain the shout of triumph that swelled within him. C'gan! He'd have to tell C'gan so the blue rider could watch out for her at the Weyr, keep her from being manipulated by that other do-nothing, R'gul. They had to be sure that it was F'lar's dragon Mnementh who flew the new queen, so that F'lar would be Weyrleader. Thread would be falling any time now. Of course, they'd know when the Red Star was framed by the Eye rock in the Star Stones on Benden's rim, when the rising sun balanced on the Finger Rock at Solstice. Maybe not this Turn, but in the next few, that warning sign would be obvious to all who witnessed it. As today's event had been witnessed. And, as MasterHarper, he should add his voice to those of the dragonriders. His was the more important, even though he was not supposed to be here.

"You got here, I see." The voice was a soft whisper at his side.

"Nip, you'll frighten the heart out of me one of these days, appearing like that." Robinton leaned back against the wall, sighing with relief. "Where've you been?"

Nip pointed to the kitchen, and indeed, now that Robinton

got a good whiff of the man, he recognized the odors of singed bone and stale food.

"Well, I don't know about you, but I'm hungry and there's—well, some bread . . ." Robinton strode to the table and grabbed a slice in each hand, chewing vigorously.

"Where'd he take her?" Nip asked.

"Lessa?"

"*Lessa?*"

Fortunately Nip was so astonished that he had gasped the name out in a startled whisper.

"Ssshhh. Only person I know of who could do what she did today . . ." And Robinton grinned.

"What about F'lar? That was a grand fight he fought. Got hurt, too, I think."

"Didn't seem to hinder him." Robinton kept looking up the stairs, waiting for F'lar to reappear. "And I think it's about time one of us started taking charge here, don't you?"

"Indeed, though I think the dragonriders have it well in hand. Fax bought loyalty. His death has lost the marks they need. They'll scatter at your command."

The MasterHarper was glad enough to shed the helmet, which had worn a sore ridge around his brows.

"You'll be wanting to make your way back to Nabol or Crom or High Reaches," he said, addressing Fax's soldiers. "I don't think the dragonriders will detain you."

"Who the shard are you?" demanded the underleader whom Robinton had encountered in the barracks.

"MasterHarper Robinton, and this is my colleague, Journeyman Harper Kinsale," Robinton said in a firm commanding voice.

"The MasterHarper?" the armsman repeated, dumbfounded, looking from one ragged man to the other. "Now, wait just a minute," he began, suddenly with a new lease on his authority.

Just then the drums in the tower started.

So Tuck had been here, too, Robinton thought, delighted. This sort of thing could be rather a lot of fun—if it didn't involve quite so much hard physical work.

"By the Egg!" the underleader snarled. "It'll be all over if we can't silence those drums . . ."

Two dragonriders immediately took positions at the stairs, hands on their knives.

"I'd advise you all to make a sudden departure," Nip-Kinsale said, nodding at C'gan, who was quick enough to pick up the message.

"Lord Groghe's men will be arriving soon enough from his border posts," Robinton added. "I spoke with them on my way here. Were I you, I'd be well gone by the time they get here."

His advice caused the soldiery to reconsider their positions. They could scarcely fail to understand that Fax's protection had died with him. Most of them looked worried and glanced anxiously about the Hall.

"B'rant, B'refli," Robinton said, picking out riders whose names he knew, "accompany them to the barracks so they can pack. I suppose the runners have had enough of a rest to go through the night. At least as far as the Nabol border." Then he turned to K'net. "How long do you think it will take Lord Groghe's men to make it here?"

"Not long," K'net said amiably. "Of course we riders could go get a few if we needed them." He made to signal F'nor, who was walking toward the door.

"We'll go," the underleader said.

"I'd like you to send someone to collect Bargen from the High Reaches Weyr," Robinton said to F'nor, who was staring at him. "He's the legitimate heir to that Hold, and we'll have to see if there's any of the Bloodlines left alive in the other ones Fax took over."

"I didn't know he survived," F'nor said, surprised.

"I've a list of where the other survivors got to," Nip said. "Oterel at Tillek Hold has given refuge to several, you know."

"No, I didn't, but it's like him. We've a lot of work to do, then, haven't we?" Robinton smiled happily at the thought. One hold, one holder. That point had been well proven over the past Turns. He hoped it could be a moral lesson for a long time. "And we must do something about—" He stopped, realizing that Fax's dead body had already been removed from the Hall.

"First thing I had my fellow drudges do," Nip said. "They

took an uncommon pleasure in dumping him into the midden. In the old days, he could have been left out for Thread to dissolve. Neater that way." Then he added, as the MasterHarper shuddered, "Well, that was a deterrent, you know."

A hungry wail alerted them to another problem that required an immediate solution.

"And a wet nurse for the new young Lord of Ruatha Hold," Robinton said, trying to remember if there were any nursing women back at Harper Hall.

The others regarded him blankly.

"I doubt any female here has succor for him, and I intend to keep the babe alive, since he had such trouble getting here," Robinton said.

"We'll find one, somewhere," F'nor said firmly.

"Get Tuck to send another message," Nip suggested.

Before they could start that search, F'lar appeared on the steps, racing down them.

"Has that creature come this way?" he demanded, catching F'nor by the arm.

F'nor seemed to know that F'lar was referring to the drudge.

"No. Is she the source of power, after all?" F'nor was astonished.

"Yes, she is." F'lar looked angrily about him. "And of Ruathan Blood, at that!"

Robinton grinned with intense satisfaction.

"Oh-ho! Does she depose the babe, then?" F'nor asked, gesturing to the birthing-woman who occupied a seat close to the blazing hearth.

F'lar looked blank, his body half-turned to go about his search for the missing Lessa. "Babe? What babe?"

"The male child Lady Gemma bore," F'nor replied, surprised by F'lar's uncomprehending look.

"It lives?"

"Yes. A strong babe, the woman says, for all that he was premature and taken forcibly from the dead dame's belly."

F'lar threw back his head with a shout of laughter. Then they all heard Mnementh's roar, followed by the curious warble of the other dragons.

"Mnemcnth has caught her," the bronze rider cried, grinning with jubilation. He strode down the steps and into the darkness of the main Court.

Robinton could just see the huge bulk of the bronze dragon, settling awkwardly onto his hind legs, his wings working to keep him balanced. Carefully Mnementh set the girl on her feet and formed a cage around her with his huge talons. Robinton could see that she was facing the wedge-shaped head that swayed above her.

Not afraid of a thing, that one, the MasterHarper thought, and wisely he decided to let F'lar handle the interview with the recaptured Lady of Ruatha.

The two fragments of bread that he'd managed to eat were insufficient to calm his growling stomach, and for once, hunger got the better of his harperly curiosity. There had to be something edible on that roast carcass and he meant to have it before he expired of starvation. Besides, F'lar had better learn to handle the girl now, before she Impressed a queen. Then he grinned to himself. He rather thought the young bronze rider up to the task.

He did find some edible if tough bits off the roast, quite a few, and he shared them with Nip and Tuck, who had descended from the drum tower.

"Good lad," Robinton mumbled, his mouth full of the hard-to-chew meat.

"Where were you hiding, Master Robinton?" Tuck asked, accepting slices from the Harper's knife.

"I was a drudge during the day, before I changed into soldier," Robinton said with a sigh. "I never understood the word 'drudge' properly before now. I shan't be one again, I assure you."

Nip and Tuck smothered their chuckles at his vehemence.

"All well and good for you two. You're used to it," the Master-Harper went on, finding yet another not-too-scorched bit.

A sudden bestial scream startled them and brought them to the Hold door. Then Lessa's cry: "Don't kill! Don't kill!" They raced to the front door. F'lar was on the stones, where evidently the watch-wher had pushed him. They saw the beast, launching a second attack on the fallen dragonrider. But Mnementh's great head swung around to knock the watch-weyr out of the air. Motivated by Lessa's shriek, the watch-weyr, trying to avoid F'lar, performed an incredible twist midair and fell heavily to the ground. They all heard the dull crack as the force of its landing broke its back. Before F'lar could get to his feet, Lessa was cradling the hideous head in her arms, her face stricken.

"It was truly only defending me," Lessa said, her voice breaking. She cleared her throat. "It was the only one I could trust. My only friend."

Robinton watched F'lar pat the girl's shoulder awkwardly. The bronze rider would have to do better than that and yet the awkwardness was appealing.

"In truth a loyal friend," F'lar said. The light in the watch-wher's green-gold eyes dimmed and died.

All the dragons gave voice to the eerie, hair-raising, barely audible high keening note that signified the passing of one of their kind.

"He was only a watch-wher," Lessa murmured, obviously stunned by the tribute.

"The dragons confer honor where *they* will," F'lar said drily.

Lessa looked down for one more long moment at the repulsive head. She laid it down on the stones, caressed the clipped wings. Then, with quick fingers, she undid the heavy buckle that fastened the metal collar around its neck. She threw the collar violently away.

She rose in a fluid movement and walked resolutely to Mnementh without a backward glance at Ruatha Hold.

So, thought Robinton, F'lar did manage to persuade her to abandon Ruatha Hold and become Weyrwoman. He was not surprised, though he did wonder just what F'lar had said—or done—to convince her to leave her beloved Ruatha Hold.

F'nor, C'gan, and four others remained on the steps as the other riders strode into the Court to wait for their dragons.

"We need to get Lytol from High Reaches," F'nor said as one by one the riders mounted their dragons. "To take charge here."

"Good idea," Robinton said.

"And who might you be?" F'nor spoke without rancor, but he had clearly not missed the fact that Robinton was wearing Fax's colors.

C'gan chuckled. "The MasterHarper of Pern, F'nor." He turned to Robinton. "I thought I recognized you standing on guard at the wall, but the light was poor and I couldn't imagine how you'd been able to sneak yourself into Ruatha."

While F'nor regarded Robinton with growing respect and interest, Mnementh launched himself up and out of the courtyard, the other dragons following in quick succession.

"Do you think I would have missed tonight for anything?" Robinton asked. Then he looked past the others, to the dining tables in the Hall, and asked wistfully: "There wouldn't be any decent wine, would there?"

WHO'S WHO

NAME	DRAGON	COLOR	ID	LOCATION
Adessa			Lady Holder, Lessa's mother	Ruatha Hold
Agust			Master Harper, Voice	Harper Hall
Anta			child	Benden Hold
Ashmichel			Lord Holder	Ruatha Hold
B'rant	Fanth	brown	dragonrider	Benden Weyr
B'refli	Joruth	brown	dragonrider	Benden Weyr
Barba			bossy child	Fort Hold
Bargen			Lord Holder	H'Reaches Hold
Benoria			Lady Holder	Fort Hold
Betrice			midwife	Harper Hall
Boslor			Master Harper	Harper Hall
Bourdon			Seahold captain	Greystones Hold
Brahil			brother	Istan Hold
Brashia			Bourdon's spouse	Greystones Hold
Bravonner			F'lon's half brother	Benden Weyr
Bristol			Harper	Telgar Hold
Brodo			cotholder son	Benden Hold
Brosil			3rd brother	Istan Hold
C'gan	Tagath	blue	dragonrider	Benden Weyr
C'rob	Spakinth	bronze	bronze rider	Benden Weyr
C'vrel	Falarth	brown	dragonrider	Benden Weyr
	Calanuth	bronze		Benden Weyr
Carola	Feyrith	gold	Weyrwoman	Benden Weyr
Carral			Rantou's spouse	Pierie Hold

NAME	DRAGON	COLOR	ID	LOCATION
Chochol			hill holder	Tillek Hold
Clostan			healer	Tillek Hold
Cording			Maizella's spouse	Eastern Sea Hold
Creline (d.)			MasterHarper	Harper Hall, Fall's End
Curtos			child	Fort Hold
Dalma			trader	Sev Ritecamp train
Domick			Jrym Harper	Harper Hall
Donkin			treble singer	Harper Hall
Drevalla			child	Benden Hold
Dugall			Segoina's spouse	Pierie Hold
Ellic			seaman	*Wave Eater*
Emfor			guard	Fort Hold
Emry			suitor	Tillek Hold
Erkin			cotholder son	Benden Hold
Evarel			Master Harper	Benden Hold
Evelene			Lady Holder	H'Reaches Hold
Evenek			tenor singer	Harper Hall
Falawny			apprentice	Harper Hall
Falloner/				
F'lon	Simanith	bronze	Weyrleader	Benden Weyr
Fallornan/				
F'lar	Mnementh	bronze	bronze rider	Benden Weyr
Famanoran/				
F'nor	Canth	brown	dragonrider	Benden Weyr
Fandarel			MasterSmith	Smithcrafthall
Farevene			1st son	H'Reaches Hold
Faroguy			Lord Holder	H'Reaches Hold
Fax			Lord Holder	H'Reaches Hold
Forist			Merelan's kin	Pierie Hold
Furlo			Masterminer	H'Reaches Hold
G'ranad (d.)		bronze	Weyrleader	Benden Weyr
Gennell			MasterHarper	Harper Hall
Germathen			Healer	Nabol Hold
Gifflen			assassin	(at Telgar)
Ginia			MasterHealer	Healer Hall
Gorazde			Master Harper	Harper Hall
Gostol			MasterFisherman	Tillek Hold
Grodon			1st year app.	Harper Hall
Grogellan			Lord Holder	Fort Hold
Groghe			Lord Holder	Fort Hold
Halanna			contralto student	Istan Hold

NAME	DRAGON	COLOR	ID	LOCATION
Halibran			Halanna's father	Istan Hold
Hayara			Lady Holder	Benden Hold
Hayon			Hayara's eldest son	Benden Hold
Idarolan			captain	*Wave Eater*
Ifor			Jrym Harper	Tillek Hold
Isla			cot keeper	Harper Hall
Jerint			Master Harper	Harper Hall
Jesken			weyr lad	Benden Weyr
Jez			beastholder	Ruatha Hold
Jonno			child	Benden Hold
Juvana			Lady Holder	Tillek Hold
K'net	Piyanth	bronze	bronze rider	Benden Weyr
Kailey			Jrym Harper	Wide Bay Hold
Kale			Lord Holder	Ruatha Hold
Kalem			Jrym Shipbuilder	Tillek Hold
Karenchok			Jrym Harper	South Boll hold
Kasia			Juvana's sister	Tillek Hold
Kepiru			lad with Fax	(at Telgar)
Kinsale aka Nip			Harper/spy	Harper Hall
Klada			shy cotholder	Tillek Hold
Kubisa			primary teacher	Harper Hall
Kulla			hospitable	Nerat border
Laela			woman	South Boll hold
Landon			2nd son	Ista Hold
Larad			1st son	Telgar Hold
Larna			F'lar's mother	Benden Weyr
Lear			1st year app.	Harper Hall
Lessa			daughter	Ruatha Hold
Lesselden			Lord Holder	Crom Hold
Lexey			slow child	Harper Hall
Libby			Kubisa's girl	Harper Hall
Lissala			seawoman	*Wave Eater*
Lobirn			Master Harper	H'Reaches Hold
Londik			treble app.	Harper Hall
Lorra			Headwoman	Harper Hall
Lotricia			Lobirn's spouse	H'Reaches Hold
Lytol/L'tol	Lartha	brown	dragonrider	Benden Weyr
M'odon	Nigarth	brown	oldest rider	Benden Weyr
M'ridin	Cortath	bronze	bronze rider	Benden Weyr
Macester			guard	Telgar Hold
Maidir			Lord Holder	Benden Hold
Maizella			daughter	Benden Hold

NAME	DRAGON	COLOR	ID	LOCATION
Mallan			Jrym Harper	H'Reaches Hold
Manora			woman	Benden Weyr
Marcine			dancer	H'Reaches Hold
Mardy			woman	Harper Hall
Marlifin			Masterwoodsmith	Tillek Hold
Matsen			Seaholder	South Boll Hold
Maxilant			Harper	Ista Weyr
Melongel			Lord Holder	Tillek Hold
Merdine (d.)			Kasia's 1st spouse	Greystones Hold
Merelan			MasterSinger	Harper Hall
Meren			Station Master	South Boll
Miata			teacher	Benden Hold
Milla			kitchener	Benden Weyr
Minnarden			Master Harper	Tillek Hold
Morif			weyr lad	Benden Weyr
Morjell			Jrym Harper	Fort Hold
Mosser			cotholder son	Nerat border
Mumolon			Jrym Harper	Tillek Hold
Murphytwen			holder	H'Reaches Hold
Murphytwenone			holder son	High Reaches Hold
Naprila			child	Benden Hold
Naylor			holder	Pierie Hold
Neilla			woman	Harper Hall
Nip (*see Kinsale*)				
Ogolly			Master Archivist	Harper Hall
Oldive			MasterHealer	Healer Hall
Oterel			Lord Holder	Tillek Hold
Patry			Merelan's uncle	Pierie Hold
Pessia			cotholder daughter	Tillek Hold
Petiron			MasterComposer	Harper Hall
Pragal			weyr lad	Benden Weyr
Raid			Lord Holder	Benden Hold
Rantou			forester	Pierie Hold
Rangul/R'gul Hath	bronze		Weyrleader	Benden Weyr
Rasa			child	Benden Hold
Relna			Lady Holder	Crom Hold
Ricardy			Master Harper	Fort Hold
Ritecamp, Sev			trader	o.a.a.
Robinton			MasterHarper	Harper Hall
Roblyn			Merelan's father	Pierie Hold
Rochers			woodsman	South Boll

NAME	DRAGON	COLOR	ID	LOCATION
Rulyar/R'yar	Garanath	brown	dragonrider	Benden Weyr, ex Harper Hall
S'bran	Kilminth	bronze	bronze rider	Benden Weyr
S'loner	Chendith	bronze	Weyrleader	Benden Weyr
Saday			cotholder, woodcarver	Tillek Hold
Saltor			Head guard	Fort Hold
Saretta			Healer	South Boll Hold
Sebell			Jrym Harper	Harper Hall
Segoina			Merelan's aunt	Pierie Hold
Sellel/S'lel	Tuenth	bronze	bronze rider	Benden Weyr
Severeid			Master Harper	Harper Hall
Shelline			1st year app.	Harper Hall
Shonagar			Jrym Harper	Harper Hall
Shreve			cotholder son	Nerat border
Sifer			Lord Holder	Bitra Hold
Silvina			woman	Harper Hall
Sirrie			healer	Harper Hall
Sitta			pert girl	H'Reaches Hold
Sortie			cotholder son	Nerat border
Stolla			Headwoman	Benden Weyr
Struan			Jrym Harper	Ruatha Hold
Sucho			herder	Fort Hold
T'rell			Weyrlingmaster	Benden Weyr
Tarathel			Lord Holder	Telgar Hold
Targus			cotholder	Nerat border
Tesner			Lord Holder	Igen Hold
Tinamon			Healer	Benden Weyr
Torlin			cotholder son	Tillek Hold
Tortole			cotholder/forester	Tillek Hold
Traller aka Tuck			Jrym Harper	o.a.a.
Triana			dancer	H'Reaches Hold
Valrol			holder	Tillek Hold
Valden			forest holder	Tillek Hold
Vendross			guard captain	Telgar Hold
Vesna			2nd mate	*Northern Maid*
Warder (no name)			steward	Ruatha Hold
Washell			Appr. master	Harper Hall
Winalla			Lady Holder	Fort Hold
Wonegal			MasterVintner	Benden Hold
Yorag			Master Healer	Benden Hold

ABOUT THE AUTHOR

ANNE MCCAFFREY is one of the world's most popular authors. Her first novel was published in 1967. Since then, she has written dozens of books, of which there are more than twenty-three million copies in print. Before her success as a writer, she was involved in theater. She directed the American premiere of Carl Orff's "Ludus de Nato Infante Mirificus," in which she also played a witch.

McCaffrey lives in Wicklow County, Ireland, in a house of her own design, Dragonhold-Underhill, so named because she had to dig out a hill to build it. There she runs a private stable, raising and training her beloved horses for horse trials and show jumping.